Praise for *The Cactus Creek Challenge*

"Two couples + too many chuckles and chortles to count = a doubly delightful read. Those who pick up Erica Vetsch's fun-filled story will be roped in from the start and will flip pages faster than a chuck wagon cook does flapjacks, as they race to find out how her captivating characters deal with the many challenges that come their way. Another winner from a talented storyteller!"
—Keli Gwyn, author of *Family of Her Dreams*

"The characters stole my heart as they stepped up to the challenge of walking a mile in another's shoes, so to speak. By trading professions for a month, the characters creatively carried out tasks outside their own comfort and talent. Ms. Vetsch skillfully weaves multiple sub-plots together to create a novel true to the historical West sprinkled with humor and wit and a good dose of sigh-worthy love."
—Audra Harders, author of *Rough Road Home*

"Vetsch brings Cactus Creek—and romance!—to life in Ben and Cassie's beautifully executed love story. Her warm words made me smell bread baking and romance brewing. . .two heady effects that worked perfectly together. Kudos, Erica!"
—Ruth Logan Herne, bestselling, multi-published author

"A story full of adventure and laughter with not one, but *two*, romances. The characters are sharply drawn. Ms. Vetsch has the delightful ability to turn a phrase in a way that brought a smile of pleasure to my lips."
—Linda Ford, author

". . .I love how Erica Vetsch sprinkles fresh language (biscuits as hard as doorknobs) and characters (every single one is unique) into an ageless story of change, love, and restoration. You'll find yourself challenged in Cactus Creek, too. I loved this book!"
—Jane Kirkpatrick, bestselling author of *A Light in the Wilderness*

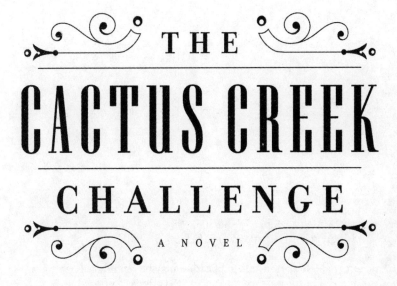

THE CACTUS CREEK CHALLENGE

A NOVEL

ERICA VETSCH

SHILOH RUN PRESS

An Imprint of Barbour Publishing, Inc.

© 2015 by Erica Vetsch

Print ISBN 978-1-63058-927-1

eBook Editions:
Adobe Digital Edition (.epub) 978-1-63058-931-8
Kindle and MobiPocket Edition (.prc) 978-1-63058-930-1

All scripture quotations are taken from the King James Version of the Bible.

Cover design: Faceout Studio, www.faceoutstudio.com

Published in association with Books & Such Literary Agency, 52 Mission Circle, Suite 122, PMB 170, Santa Rosa, CA, 95409-5370, www.booksandsuch.biz

Published by Shiloh Run Press, an imprint of Barbour Publishing, Inc., P.O. Box 719, Uhrichsville, Ohio 44683, www.shilohrunpress.com.

Our mission is to publish and distribute inspirational products offering exceptional value and biblical encouragement to the masses.

ecpa Member of the
Evangelical Christian
Publishers Association

Printed in the United States of America.

DEDICATION

As always, to my husband, Peter, the hero of my story.

CHAPTER 1

Cactus Creek, Texas
Saturday, March 31, 1888

Y*ou'd think, after all this time, I'd be over him.*

Cassie Bucknell's chest constricted as it always did when she encountered Sheriff Ben Wilder. She didn't need to examine him. She knew him by heart—from his scuffed, high-topped boots to the leather-banded black hat on his dark brown hair—but she looked him over just the same. A longing ache made her drop her gaze, and she regained control of herself lest someone guess her thoughts.

Around her, voices buzzed, men laughed, women gossiped, and people jostled to find their seats before the town meeting commenced, but Cassie heard and felt little beyond the beating of her heart against her ribs.

"I declare, we're cheek by jowl in here. Are we all going to fit?" Jenny Hart took the seat next to her, gathering in her skirts. "I am beginning to have sympathy for sardines." The new town baker righted her straw bonnet after an elbow knocked it askew. "I didn't even know there were this many people in town, much less that would come to a council meeting. I fear the schoolhouse will burst." Her Southern accent, so different from the Texas twang Cassie was used to, was as rich and beautiful as her clothing.

"Normally, you can hardly get a quorum to attend." Cassie dragged her attention back to her surroundings. "But today they're announcing the Challenge contestants. Everybody wants to see who they are."

"I never heard of such a thing being done by a town before, and I can't believe you talked me into entering."

I can't believe I entered myself. Cassie surveyed her little kingdom, this schoolhouse-turned-temporary-council-chambers where she'd taught for the past seven months. Women occupied the desks where her pupils normally sat, and around the edges of the room and crowding the entryway, men lounged and waited for things to get under way. "This is the first time they've opened the Challenge to women."

Dr. Bucknell—mayor, head of the town council, and Cassie's father—rose and placed his fingertips on the teacher's desk. "Ladies and gentlemen, thank y'all for attending today. I know you're anxious to get to the Challenge part of the meeting, but there are a few other matters to clear up before we do."

Cassie kept her eyes focused forward on her father, but she knew where Ben was as easily as a compass needle knew north. Across the room to her right, he stood next to Carl Gustafson, the livery stable owner. Not as tall as Carl—nobody in town matched Carl's height—he still stood nearly a head taller than Cassie herself. He would have his thumbs hooked into his gun belt, and the star on his placket-front shirt would be shined to a gleam.

When the three councilmen—her father, also the town's doctor; Ben's father, the newly retired sheriff; and Hobny Jones, Cactus Creek's only attorney—finished dealing with preliminary business, a ripple went through the crowd. Who would be chosen this year?

"Because interest in the Cactus Creek Challenge has grown so much, the council has decided to increase the number of contestants from two to four. We've extended the Challenge this year to include women, and we will choose two women and two men to compete." Cassie's father adjusted his necktie. "We took the names of all those who signed up and put them in these punch bowls. Men's in this one, and women's in this one."

Mrs. Pym, across the aisle from Cassie, sighed and dabbed

her upper lip with a lace hankie. "I do hope they're careful. Those were my grandmother's, the only matched set of punch bowls in this part of the state."

Cassie hid a smile. The punch bowls made an appearance at nearly every town function, and each time, Mrs. Pym said the same thing. Everybody in town knew the history of those crystal bowls. They'd traveled all the way across the country and had survived a stagecoach robbery. Mrs. Pym had dined out on that story for two decades.

"Who do you think it will be?" Jenny removed her lace shawl, laid it across her lap, and straightened her cuffs. She wore a pale blue satin dress and, as always, was one of the most stylish women in town. Perfect golden curls piled high on the back of her head, and her summer-sky-blue eyes studied everything carefully. She had a guarded tenseness about her mouth that rarely relented, as if she feared something but was determined not to give in to the fear.

Cassie quit biting her lower lip. "We'll know soon." Her glance flicked to Ben's face, then away. He was smiling, and even though it wasn't directed toward her, his grin had a way of making her stomach feel swoopy and her chest hollow.

Jenny adjusted the strings on her bag. "I can't believe I'm doing this."

"I thought you agreed that it would be a good way to feel part of the community and make a place for yourself in the town."

Her mouth twisted in a rueful smile. "In a moment of weakness, I might've said something like that. But at *this* moment, I'm wishing I could snatch my name out of that bowl and go hide in my kitchen."

Cassie knew how she felt. And yet, just as this was a chance for Jenny to meet new people and become known in the town, so it was for Cassie, too. She'd grown up in Cactus Creek, but so many people—she glanced once more at Ben Wilder—still thought of her as a child, the youngest of the Bucknell girls, the mayor's daughter.

But she wasn't just the mayor's daughter, or the kid sister of Louise and Millie, or even the little hoyden she had been. She was a grown woman, properly educated and trained at one of the finest normal schools in the country. She had a teaching certificate, charge of a dozen children each day, and the trust of the superintendent of schools. She was a grown-up, and it was high time people realized it. Her hands fisted and she raised her chin.

"Our first contestant is. . ." Her father paused for dramatic effect, riffling his fingers through the slips in the bowl labeled MEN. "Carl Gustafson."

Carl grinned, and Ben slapped him on the shoulder. So the livery stable would be one of the locations. Ben's father, Obadiah Wilder, wrote Carl's name on the blackboard.

"Our other male contestant will be"—once more fingers dug into the bowl and removed a name—"our new sheriff, Ben Wilder."

Applause broke out, and Carl elbowed Ben, pointing to his badge and making a "hand it over" gesture. Several folks cheered when Ben waved.

His dimples made Cassie's heart start bumping again.

"And now for the ladies' names."

There weren't nearly as many ladies who had signed up. After all, most women worked in their homes, and the Challenge winner would be difficult to choose under those circumstances.

"Mrs. Jenny Hart."

Cassie reached out and clasped Jenny's hands in her lap. "Congratulations."

A polite round of applause swept through the room, not nearly as raucous as that given to the men.

Jenny's face froze in a tight smile, and her face paled until Cassie worried her friend might faint.

"Well, look here, my own daughter, Miss Cassie Bucknell." Her father beamed. "Our schoolteacher."

Cassie's mind spun, and her hands went clammy. For a moment, she knew just how Jenny must be feeling. She'd been chosen. Relief and anxiety clashed inside her. She forced her muscles to relax and her lungs to exhale. More applause, then the room quieted.

"I maintain it isn't proper for women to be included in the Challenge." Mrs. Pym's whisper pierced the brief silence. Several glares turned her way, and she harrumphed. "Still, I suppose it's for a good cause."

Cassie's cheeks heated, but she tried to ignore Mrs. Pym and not let anything dampen her pleasure. Attorney Jones wrote her name up on the board. Right next to Ben's. Silly that seeing them up there together should give her a thrill.

"Now, I believe we should let folks know the causes we'll be trying to raise money for and remind folks how the Challenge works." Her father rested his hands on the back of the chair. "Each of our contestants will be swapping jobs for one month with a fellow contestant. They will be responsible for the running of the business or holding of office of the other, and we, as the town, will be the judges of who does the best job."

Hobny Jones set two glass candy jars from the mercantile on the desk. One bore a white label that said BOOKS in black letters, and the other had a green label that said PUMP.

"Cassie and Mrs. Hart will be raising money for new textbooks for the school and new hymnals for the church." Hobny's voice squeaked, as if his vocal chords needed oiled.

She wished he wouldn't call her Cassie in front of the town. It should be Miss Bucknell, as befitted her station as schoolteacher. The scant shelf of schoolbooks beside her teacher's desk drew her attention. They were mostly tattered, old, and in some cases written in German or French or Norwegian. Most of her students were using books passed down to them from their parents. If the school could provide at least a couple of sets of McGuffey Readers, some history, spelling, and arithmetic books, how much easier would it be for her to teach and for the children to learn? With more families moving into the area each term, the problem of not enough schoolbooks would only worsen. She resolved to do her best to run Jenny's bakery well and win the Challenge, not just for herself, but for her students.

"If one of the ladies wins the competition"—her father lifted the jar—"all the money raised will be split between new textbooks for the school and the purchase of hymnals for the church. I, for one, will be rooting for the ladies, not just because one of them is my daughter. Hymnbooks on Sunday would go a long way toward smoothing out the bumps in our congregational singing."

Laughter rippled through the room.

"Now, if one of the men wins"—he picked up the other jar—"all the money raised will go toward the installation of a new town pump and horse trough on Main Street. I'm sure you can all agree that hauling water from the creek is adequate, but a town pump would be a big improvement. Let's have the contestants come forward."

Cassie found herself standing between Jenny and Ben on the platform. She was used to standing in front with many pairs of eyes looking at her, but this time was very different. She wasn't in charge, and the people watching her now would vote on how well she completed the Challenge.

Her mind clicked and hummed, formulating plans for how she would run the bakery for the month. Though she was adequate in the kitchen, thanks to her mother's training, she hadn't done much baking beyond bread and cookies, nothing like the fancy cakes and pastries Jenny turned out that had been such a hit with her customers.

Jenny would be as good a teacher as she was a mother. Sweet Amanda Hart, Cassie's youngest pupil, was the spitting image of her mama, shy and withdrawn. She touched a tender place in Cassie's heart. Cassie could rest assured her students were in capable hands. Things couldn't have worked out better.

April is going to be a wonderful month. This Challenge will be long remembered as the best one the town ever had.

Her father turned the glass jars so the labels faced the assembly. "Now, these jars will be placed in Mr. Svenson's mercantile, right on the front counter opposite the post office boxes. It's up to you, the townspeople, to observe how our contestants are faring, how well they're doing another person's job, and vote by donating money to the cause and the contestants you want to support. Each Saturday afternoon, the contestants will be available at the mercantile to answer questions and campaign for their cause." He circled round to the front of the desk and perched his hip on the corner.

"As an added bonus, my son-in-law, Donald Penn, will be putting up the grand prize of one hundred dollars to the winning cause." He motioned to where Donald stood in the back.

Donald raised his hand, though Cassie imagined everyone in the room knew him. As the only son of the wealthiest rancher in the Texas Panhandle, Donald could well afford the one hundred dollars. His wife, Cassie's oldest sister, Louise, threaded her arm through his and squeezed, laying her auburn head against his shoulder briefly. He patted her hand, and jealousy shot through Cassie. Not that she begrudged her sister her happiness with Donald or wanted Donald for herself. It was just that she longed for that closeness, to matter to and belong to someone.

But not just any someone.

For her, it had always been and always would be Ben Wilder.

Not that he saw her that way. No, he still treated her like a child to be humored, patted on the head, and sent on her way. The big lunkhead.

Still, once she'd successfully run the bakery for a month and campaigned for her cause, surely then he would finally notice she was all grown up. Winning the Cactus Creek Challenge would be a feather in her cap.

Competing in the Challenge alongside Ben had to be some kind of a sign, right? An indication that Ben was God's will for her life? She'd been sure of it for so long. If only it wasn't taking Ben such a long time to realize they belonged together.

"Before you all leave..." Her father raised his voice above the folks who had begun talking and making motions to leave. "I have one more announcement."

Everyone stilled.

"In order to keep the Challenge from growing stale, the council has decided to add one more twist this year."

Cassie's senses sharpened. She knew that tone. It flowed straight from the fun-loving reservoir deep in her father's personality, the one that few people suspected until the joke was played on them.

"In order to liven things up and keep everyone on their toes, Ben and Carl, you will be trading jobs with the women. Mr. Gustafson, you'll be trading places with Mrs. Hart and will run the bakery for the month, and Ben, you'll be teaching school in Cassie's place."

A hundred words crammed into her throat and lodged there, and she knew her jaw had dropped open, leaving her gaping like a bullhead. Finally, something squeaked out. "We're doing what?"

She couldn't miss the mischievous glint in her father's eye or the suspicious twitch to his white moustache. "That's right. Carl, you'll be baking dainty treats. Ben, you'll be instilling knowledge in our youngest citizens. Mrs. Hart, you'll be in charge of the livery animals and equipment, and you, Cassie, are tasked with the safety of the community."

Folks broke into conversation, but all she could see was the shocked expression on Ben's face and the way his hand went to the star on his chest. His eyes locked with hers, something that normally sent her senses spinning. This time, though, the shocked and stubborn gleam she saw there got her hackles up. Didn't he think she could do his job?

Then again, could he do hers?

She took it back.

April was going to be the longest month of her life.

⌘

Though he'd tried to hide it, Ben hadn't been thrilled when his name was chosen. After all, he'd been waiting what seemed his entire life to land the job of sheriff. Now he was expected to give it up for four weeks? His father had needled him into throwing his name into the hat—*punch bowl*—saying it was his civic duty, people needed to see him taking part in community activities, and a half a dozen other reasons, all of which seemed plumb puny now.

Swapping places with Carl wouldn't have been too bad. The big livery stable owner was more than capable of keeping order in the town for a month.

But swapping with a girl? And not just any girl, but Cassie Bucknell, the fire-headed tomboy who had always been more trouble than a wagonload of barbed wire?

The minute this crowd cleared out, he was going to state his protests and withdraw his name.

Carl crossed his arms over his burly chest, his lips a thin line that disappeared between his bushy moustache and beard. "This is ridiculous. What are they thinking?" he muttered.

They had to wait quite awhile for the crowd to thin, what with all the talking and teasing and laughing they had to endure.

"Never thought I'd see you in an apron with flour on your hands, Carl," one man joshed.

"Sheriff, you might want to bring your handcuffs and leg irons to the school. I've heard some of those little boys can be a might rowdy," another joked.

Ben smiled and nodded, looking over their heads. Cassie Bucknell stood beside the Widow Hart, fidgeting as she listened to Mrs. Pym, who was probably talking about either those punch bowls or her various aches and pains.

What possessed Cassie to enter this silly challenge in the first place? She was a nice kid, but he still thought she looked like a little girl playing dress-up in that long skirt and with her hair piled up on her head. Shouldn't she be in a pinafore and braids instead of pretending to be grown up? He still remembered her barefooted in the creek with a frog gigger, stalking bullfrogs. Skinny, freckled, with eyes too big for her face. Always leaping before she looked.

How on earth would she manage the jail and the sheriff's duties for a whole month?

She couldn't. That was all there was to it. He'd have to back out of the Challenge, and the sooner the mayor and the council knew it, the sooner they could find someone else to take his place.

Cassie glanced up, and even from several feet away, he could see how green her eyes were. Funny how all the Bucknell girls had red hair, but they all had different colored eyes. Louise's were pale blue, Millie's were brown, and Cassie's were green as spring grass. Louise had been in his class in school, with Millie a year behind. Cassie had been several grades younger, always running and yelling and haring around, trying to keep up with the boys at recess, but once the bell rang, she'd sit at her desk, prop her chin in her hand, and look out the window, staring into her daydreams.

Just a kid. A kid who had no business wearing his badge for a day, much less a month.

He edged through the crowd to her side and touched her elbow. Jerking his head to the corner, he drew her away from folks.

"What are we going to do?"

She shrugged, tilting her head in that saucy way she had. "I'm going to be a sheriff for a month, and you're going to teach school."

"That's ridiculous. You can't be sheriff. You're a girl."

Her pointed little chin came up. "What's that got to do with it?"

"It's got everything to do with it if trouble comes calling."

"This town hasn't seen trouble in a month of Sundays."

He tipped his hat back and put his hands on his hips. "Well, missy, if you think that, then I must be doing my job right."

"Don't call me missy. It's Miss Bucknell to you." Her green eyes snapped.

"Ha. It's Cassie or missy or little girl, just like it's always been." He caught himself reaching out to tug her braid like he had for years. Only she wasn't wearing braids. Funny how he missed the feel of it in his hand.

"You're impossible, Ben Wilder."

"So you're always telling me."

She turned away from him, greeting someone across the room and heading that way.

He followed her with his eyes. Sassy today. Come to think of it, she'd kind of been that way with him ever since she got back from that fancy eastern school last fall. He touched his badge and then rested his hand on the butt of his sidearm, turning to listen to more good-natured razzing from townsfolk.

When only the Challenge contestants and the council members remained, Ben stepped forward.

"You know I'm all for going along with things, and the last thing I want to do is put a damper on the festivities, but the notion of us trading places with girls"—he glanced at the widow—"er, ladies. . .is ridiculous." He turned to his father, the man he admired above all others and hoped to emulate. "Dad, you can't be serious about us swapping with girls?"

The legendary former lawman leaned back in his chair. "I don't see a problem. Are you afraid to teach school, Son?"

How could he say this in a polite way? He thumbed through a few responses and came up with nothing that wouldn't earn him a tongue-lashing from Cassie, but he had to tell the truth.

"What I am afraid of is that little Cassie Bucknell isn't up to protecting this town."

She snorted and opened her mouth to answer, but her dad held up his hand. With a mutinous scowl, she crossed her arms and tapped her foot. Ben almost smiled. Not that he was a gambling man, but it sure would be fun to play poker with Cassie. Everything she thought or felt played out on her face, and he never had any problems reading it. She was as transparent as glass.

"Why don't you think she'd make a good temporary sheriff?" Dr. Bucknell asked.

"She's a. . .a. . .girl." The truth was so obvious he didn't know how else to express it. "She's a kid. The rowdies down at the Royal or at Barney's Bar will take one look at her and trample this town worse'n a stampede of longhorns. You wouldn't want to see your daughter facing down some puncher on a bender, would you, sir?"

The doc smoothed his neatly trimmed moustache, regarding Ben. "My Cassie's smart and resourceful. I fully expect she's up to the job. And it isn't as if she'll be doing it alone. An experienced deputy like Jigger won't have any trouble providing her with backup."

She nodded with every statement her father made, chapping Ben's hide like sandpaper.

"But, sir, the safety of the town is at issue, not to mention the fact that I've never taught school a day in my life. It was one thing when I thought I'd be switching places with Carl, here. One look at him, and the carousers would hightail it. You can't tell me the town will be better for having a little girl in the sheriff's office and a widow woman in the livery."

"And I've never baked anything more complicated than biscuits, and I tend to burn those." Carl found his voice. "A stable is no place for a lady like Mrs. Hart. I don't know which is rougher, some of the stock or some of the customers. She'll ruin her clothes, even if she doesn't get hurt. I think this is a bad idea."

Mrs. Hart looked as if she might agree with him, but she said nothing.

Hobny Jones shrugged, his jagged eyebrows plunging toward one another. "Maybe we should reconsider. If you remember, I raised just these concerns when the idea of men and women switching jobs first arose."

"No, we've thought this through, voted upon it, and announced it to the town." Doc tapped together his papers and slid the chair into the kneehole of the desk. "The contestants just need to sign the contracts, and we'll be all set."

Ben settled his hands on his hips. "This isn't going to work.

If I had known you were going to make us swap with helpless gals, I never would've put my name into the mix. We're all going to regret this."

"Helpless?" Cassie sliced a glare his way. "We're far from helpless, and it's about time you realized it. Where's my contract?" She stepped forward, reached across the desk, and plucked an ink pen from the stand.

"What good does it do you to sign yours if I don't sign mine?"

"Nonsense, Son." His father stood. "The purpose of the Challenge isn't to make things easy on the contestants. After all, if we did that, where's the challenge? It's to stretch you, to make you see things from a different perspective. To walk a mile or two in someone else's shoes. You might be surprised by what you learn about the person you trade places with and, more importantly, what you learn about yourself."

His tone said he'd had enough of this discussion, and, as a dutiful son, Ben clamped his mouth shut on all he wanted to say. The only thing that would surprise him about trading places with Cassie Bucknell was if some disaster *didn't* befall her sometime this month. This month? More like in the first twenty-four hours.

Hobny sorted through the papers and set one in front of each of the contestants. "It's a basic contract with the town that outlines the requirements of the Challenge. Once you sign, you're legally bound to fulfill the contract for the full thirty days. If you back out, you agree to pay the town the sum of twenty-five dollars, which will be used for the eventual winner's project."

Cassie signed first and handed the pen to Ben. He dipped it into the inkwell, still scrambling to find some way to get out of this. One glance at his father's determined stare and the mayor's challenging smirk, and he scrawled his name and thrust the pen at Carl. Carl signed, slowly, as if he could barely force his fingers to move, before passing the pen to Mrs. Hart. She daintily extended her wrist from her lace cuff and wrote her name in neat, small letters.

Hobny collected the papers, waving each one to help dry the ink. Ben's father and Dr. Bucknell shared a grin and a wink.

It was on their heads when things went wrong. Ben would do his best.

Heading back toward his office, he matched strides with Carl, his boots kicking up dust. This month was going to be like wrestling a sack full of wildcats.

"This is going to be a mess, isn't it?" Carl broke into his thoughts. "Can you imagine a little hothouse flower like Mrs. Hart cleaning stalls and forking hay out of the mow? She doesn't belong out here on the prairie at all, much less in a stable. All those ruffles and lace and flounces won't last long in a stable. I bet she'll take one look at Misery and the muck heap and scoot right back to whatever big city she came from."

"Yeah, and what do you think Cassie Bucknell is going to do with my job? The spring trail drives will be heading through here any day now. One of those outfits hits town and busts loose, you think Cassie's going to be able to stop them? They'll snap her like a twig."

"At least you have a deputy to help her out. I work alone."

"So why'd you sign the contract?"

Carl shrugged. "Folks were so excited, I hated to let them down. Why'd you?"

"I guess for the same reason. That and when I saw the competition I was up against, I figured it'd be an easy win." He grinned. "You can't bake, Mrs. Hart looks like she wouldn't know one end of a horse from the other, and Cassie will probably accidentally lock herself into a jail cell before the first day is over. All I have to do is babysit some kids for a few hours every day. I'm a shoo-in for the win."

They passed the mercantile, the milliner's shop, and the feed store in silence before arriving at the jail. Jigger sat out front, his chair tipped back and leaning against the adobe wall. Wood chips littered the boardwalk as he reduced a stick to sawdust with his jackknife. "I heard you two were going to play schoolmarm and pastry chef." He brushed a few shavings off his vest.

"Word travels fast in this town." Ben shook his head, surveying the peaceful street.

"Nothing better to do than gossip on a quiet day like this. Can't say I'm looking forward to taking orders from a slip of a girl with no notion of how to run a jail, but this year's Challenge is shaping up to be fun to watch."

"Wish I was watching this one from a safe distance. I'm not exactly looking forward to teaching school any more than Carl is to selling pies and cookies."

"It's not the selling I mind so much as the baking. I can just about boil water, and I make good oat bran mash—no complaints from my horses, but I cannot sell mash in the bakery. I'll be lucky if I don't poison someone."

"Don't you think it's about time you got married again? You need someone to take care of you," Ben said.

"You should talk." Carl ran his hand down his beard.

"Me? What do I need with a wife? You forget I have a ma and pa who live in town. If I want a home-cooked meal, all I have to do is head over there. You've been alone for what, three years now? That's more than long enough."

"Not for me. I won't marry again."

"Why not? You like being alone?"

"This land is hard on people, especially women. I would not want to lose another one. Anyway, why are we talking about marriage? I thought we were talking about the Cactus Creek Challenge."

Ben dug a toothpick out of his shirt pocket and tucked it into the corner of his mouth, savoring the flavor of the peppermint oil he'd soaked it in. "You don't mind running the bakery, but you can't bake. I don't mind teaching school, except for the kids. We've got a dainty widow who's supposed to run a stable and a redheaded kid who's supposed to protect the town. What could possibly go wrong?" He pushed his hat back and studied the buildings across the street, including the cute little bakery just opposite, with its lace curtains, window boxes, and pretty blue-painted door. He couldn't imagine a bruiser like Carl inside such a feminine establishment. Up the street at the livery, a wagon sat up on blocks, its wheels removed for new rims. Misery, Carl's unpredictable and moody stallion trotted around his turnout pen, stomping and bucking and looking every inch the temperamental stud he was. A wheelbarrow of dirty straw stood in the open doorway, a pitchfork sticking out of the mound. Miss Jenny would never survive.

He wasn't sure which pairing was more wrong, Carl and Jenny or him and Cassie.

A couple of cowboys all but fell through the swinging doors of the Royal Saloon and staggered up the boardwalk before disappearing into Barney's Bar and Pool Hall. He recognized the Shoop brothers, the town's resident rabble-rousers. Nope, he knew which one was worse.

"How come we seem to be the only two who realize what a mistake this is?"

CHAPTER 2

Monday morning, the first of the month, Ben was jumpier than a flea at a dog show. Walking from the boardinghouse to the school on the edge of town, he reminded himself that he'd given Jigger thorough instructions and consoled himself that if real trouble broke out, he'd just be at the school. From the front steps of the schoolhouse he would have a clear view down Main Street and could come running. He rubbed his gritty eyes, regretting his insomnia the night before.

Kids ran and squealed and laughed, looking like a crowd of a hundred rather than the dozen or so he knew they were. The white-frame building might as well've been the Texas Penitentiary with the dread he felt at each footstep. One of the few board-and-batten buildings in town, the school was brand-new, having been built the summer before.

Most of the older structures in Cactus Creek were adobe, wood being at a premium out here on the treeless prairie. There were even some stick-and-daub and sod houses, though nobody lived in them anymore. They were used for storage or stables. Since the arrival of the Fort Worth & Denver Railway to town just last year, it was easier to get building materials and supplies out here to the Panhandle. Cactus Creek even boasted a lumberyard now, and as a result, several houses were under construction. The doc had the nicest house in town, a two-story affair with a big porch and tall windows. The only building taller was the new church, if you counted the steeple.

The kids stopped and stared as he drew up to the steps. The door stood open, and he felt their eyes on him as he went inside, a condemned man being led to the gallows. In the foyer he took a deep breath and gathered himself. This was no way for a grown man and a sworn officer of the law to act. If the citizens of Cutler County, Texas, knew how skittish he was, they'd take back his badge.

"Good morning."

He whirled on his boot heel. Cassie replaced the stoneware lid on the water cooler in the corner of the entryway and tucked a stray curl behind her ear.

"G'mornin'." He tucked his fingertips into the pockets of his jeans. "Nine o'clock, you said."

"That's right." She crossed her arms at her waist, looking about twelve years old. "Do you want me to show you around?"

"I suppose." He followed her into the schoolroom. Long shafts of sunlight flowed through the east windows and lay in blocks on the floor and desks. The smell of paper and chalk dust and lunch pails took him right back to his own school days. Her skirts brushed the floor, and the fabric whispered and rustled with a sound he'd never associated with her before. She'd pinned her bright hair up high on her head, and the mass looked too heavy for her slender neck. How on earth would she manage the job of sheriff for a whole month?

"The attendance book is here with all the children's names, ages, and grade levels. I've placed a schedule in the back of the book. The students know the routine, and they'll help you. You shouldn't have any trouble as long as you stick to the routine. Though you should know that there are some pranksters in the group."

"We'll do just fine." He grinned, hoping he sounded more confident than he felt. "Teaching can't be that hard. I'm pretty good with my figures and I spell good." After all, if a girl barely out of pinafores could do it, surely he could.

"You spell *well*."

"Yes, ma'am, I do." He grinned.

"So you think teaching is easy? That what I do is so insignificant?" She straightened, and her green eyes pinned him in place. "Do you place no importance on getting a proper education? How do you expect the next generation to take their place in society if they aren't well schooled? Teachers have a great responsibility. You might be educating the next governor of Texas or president of the United States."

He burst out laughing at her passionate eruption, but when her eyes sparked and grew hot, he shifted his weight. "Not that it isn't important, but do you really think one of those scoundrels outside is going to be president? You might be aiming just a bit north of optimistic."

She sighed. "Well, if you're that confident, then there's nothing else I need to tell you. I guess I'll head down to the jail and begin my duties. If you'll hand over your badge and gun, I'll be on my way."

His hand was already reaching for the badge, but he froze. "My gun?"

"Your pistol." She pointed to the Colt holstered at his side. "You surely won't need it in school. It wouldn't be proper to have a weapon in the classroom."

He laughed and plucked the star from his shirt. "Cassie, you can *borrow* the badge, but the gun stays with me. This pistol goes with me everywhere—work, church, even the necessary. I'd feel unclothed without it. And you don't need to worry about the kids. I never leave this"—he patted the gun butt—"unattended."

"How am I supposed to be the sheriff without a firearm?" She put her hands on her hips and stared up at him.

He almost patted her on the head since she looked so cute and disgruntled, but he figured she'd take to that about as well as a rattlesnake to having his teeth brushed. "Well, your dad said you were a smart little thing who would figure out the best way to do my job without my help, so I'll just leave that up to you."

"He said I was smart and resourceful. He did not call me 'a smart little thing.'" She crossed her arms and tapped her lip with her finger.

"Well, there you go. You always were a quick one. One of the sharpest little girls in school, I always thought. When you weren't getting stuck in a tree." He couldn't resist teasing her about that particular incident, and he didn't miss the tightening of her lips. "I imagine you'll figure out how to get the job done. Either that or you can call it quits now and back out of the Challenge."

Sparks snapped in her eyes. "You're impossible, Ben Wilder." She snatched the badge from his hand and stomped out.

Ben chuckled and shook his head. Always haring off in a snit, just like a kid. He'd give her a week at the most. She'd cave and quit, and he could go back to sheriffing, and she could go back to dressing up and sitting behind a desk all day. But for now he was the teacher, and he'd best do some teaching.

"If you're gonna teach 'em, you'd best go round them up." He braced himself with a deep breath and walked outside.

He was met on the steps by a pair of grubby faces. Grubby identical faces.

"You're the new teacher, ain't you?" asked one.

"We heard all about you from our pa. He says if we're bad, you'll lock us up in the jail. Is that true?" asked the other.

"Ma says you can't lock kids up, but we never know when Pa's joshin' us, though I guess we should know, since he joshes *all* the time."

Ben found his head swiveling between them as they took turns peppering him with their words.

"Mama says we're *exactly* like him, but that just makes him laugh."

"Will you lock us up in the jail? We want to know what it's like."

"Can we ring the bell?"

"The bell?" Ben tried to grab hold of the conversation, but it proved to be slippery. The boys finished each other's sentences and budged in on each other's words almost seamlessly.

"To call the kids in."

"Miss Bucknell rings the bell every morning."

"She said we could if you said it was all right."

"We figured you wouldn't mind if we rang it, since we're finally off pr'bation again."

"Miss Bucknell puts us on pr'bation seems like every other day or so, but we ain't been bad in pert near a week, so can we?"

Feeling as if he was the rope in a tug-o-war, he nodded. "Sure, go ahead."

They bolted past him and returned with a handbell, wrastling it between them, four dirty little hands grabbing at the handle, clanging the clapper in discordant little jerks.

"That's enough, boys. Thanks." He took it from them, standing back as kids streamed past him. He counted an even dozen, the smallest a girl with long golden sausage curls and large blue eyes who looked to be about six or seven, and the biggest a girl of about fifteen or sixteen who blushed and ducked her head when he looked at her. In between were an assortment of kids in overalls and pinafores. None of them as individuals looked too threatening, but as a group, they appeared just this side of terrifying.

While they clattered their lunch pails and slapped books onto desktops, he hung his hat on a peg by the door and made his way to the front of the room. Sliding the chair out, he sat and regarded them. Twelve pairs of eyes stared back.

He'd rather face the Sam Bass Gang unarmed and in nothing but his long johns.

Stop being so foolish. It's a roomful of kids, not outlaws. You told Cassie you could handle it, and you can.

What should he do first?

His eyes fell on the attendance book. Aha!

"I'm going to take attendance. I'll call out your name, and you let me know if you're here or not." That way he could match names with faces and kill two birds, as it were.

One of the twins snickered. "How're we gonna tell you if we're not here?"

A titter went through the group, but he gave them his best stern look, and they quieted.

"Amanda Hart."

Silence.

He quickly counted the names in the book. Twelve names, twelve children.

"Amanda?"

Her age was listed as seven. He looked at the youngest girl, closest to him on the front row all by herself—or rather he looked at the top of her head. She stared at her hands.

"That's her," one of the twins said, pointing to the little girl. "She don't talk much, not even hardly to Miss Bucknell. And she never talks to men at all."

Wonderful. What was he supposed to do with a student who wouldn't talk to him? He checked the box next to her name.

"Ulysses Harrison?" *Ulysses? Really?*

"I'm here, and so's my brother." The twins pointed at each other, shoving and tussling.

"Quincy?" He placed two more checkmarks. "Settle down, boys."

He went on down the list until he finally called out Mary Alice Watkins, the oldest girl in the school. When he was done, he looked at the clock. Only a couple of minutes had passed. This might turn out to be the longest day of his life.

"You're supposed to pray. Then we say our psalm," Ulysses— or was it Quincy?—piped up.

He closed the attendance book and remembered that Cassie had mentioned putting a schedule somewhere. Oh yeah, the back of the record book.

1. *Take attendance*
2. *Prayer and psalm*
3. *Primary reading*

And so on. The only things he read on the list that didn't give him the heebie-jeebies were recess, lunch, and dismissal.

Prayer. He prayed all the time, but he wasn't all that comfortable praying in front of others, especially not this little hoard of monsters. An idea struck him.

"Anybody want to volunteer to pray this morning?"

Quicker than a wink, Quincy—or was it Ulysses?—hopped to his feet. "I will." And before he received permission, he clamped his eyes closed, slapped his hands together under his chin, and launched into a dreadful Scottish accent.

> "Some hae meat and cannae eat
> Some would eat that want it
> But we hae meat and we can eat
> Sae let the Lord be thankit."

His eyes snapped open and he plopped into his seat, beaming. Snickers and snorts rippled through the classroom.

"That ain't no school prayer, you mug. That's saying grace before you eat." An older boy seated behind them poked him in the shoulder.

"It's the only prayer I know." Quincy shrugged. "One prayer's pretty much as good as another, ain't it?"

"Naw," his twin piped up. "You gotta say a special prayer for every occasion. Miss Bucknell says a different prayer every morning."

Quincy shrugged again. "Next time *you* pray then, if you know everything."

"Boys, that's enough. Now, what psalm are you working on?"

All the students slid out of their desks and stood up straight. Mary Alice started them off.

"Psalm forty-six. God is our refuge and strength, a very present help in trouble. Therefore will not we fear, though the earth be removed, and though the mountains be carried into the midst of the sea; though the waters thereof roar and be troubled, though the mountains shake with the swelling thereof. Selah. There is a river. . ." And they went on right to the end. "Be still, and know that I am God: I will be exalted among the heathen, I will be exalted in the earth. The Lord of hosts is with us; the God of Jacob is our refuge. Selah."

And like a little well-trained army, they all sat down. Through it all, while Amanda Hart had stood and sat when everyone else did, she never opened her little mouth, staring up at him through her pale lashes as if she thought he might hop over the desk and grab her. Now that he had time to study her face, he saw that she was the spitting image of her mama. A little porcelain doll. Had something happened to make her so man shy? He'd have to go careful with her.

Consulting his list, he saw it was time for the primer reader class. Calling upon his memory of school days past, he searched for a ruler. His teachers had always rapped the desk with their ruler and called for a class to come forward. Cassie must keep hers in a drawer somewhere.

The instant he opened the top drawer, something fluttered and shot upward. He rocked back so hard he tipped his chair over, his feet going skyward and his head colliding with the chalk tray on the blackboard. Stars burst in his skull as laughter and squeals erupted.

He scrambled to his feet, kicking the chair and grinding a stick of chalk to dust under his boot. His first instinct was to grab for his gun, and he had almost cleared leather when he remembered where he was. A panicked bird swooped past his nose and flapped around the room. Kids scattered and hollered, some screaming and some laughing.

Ben gathered his scattered wits, clomped down the aisle, and opened a window, continuing on to the next. One of the older boys on the far side of the room followed suit, opening the three windows on his side. Grabbing his hat off the peg in the cloakroom, Ben shooed the bird, yelling and swatting. He didn't know if he wanted to catch the thing, squash the thing, or just get it to leave. Students fled before him, scrabbling over desks and darting away from the bird. At last, the infernal avian menace gained his freedom, swooping through an open window.

Gasping, he turned and faced his pupils, hands on hips, one fist gripping the brim of his hat. Some of the girls huddled in a corner, and the twins lay in a heap on the floor, howling with laughter. The glee on their awful little faces made his blood boil.

He marched over to them, hauled them up by their overall straps, and glared. "I don't suppose you know how that bird got in that drawer, do you?"

They stopped laughing, though it was obviously at great effort. Gulping, they each donned an angelic expression, wide-eyed as newborn calves.

"You two scared about ten years off my life with that little stunt, and you frightened the girls. What do you have to say for yourselves?" He gave them each a little shake. His heart still thundered in his chest, and he wondered if his hair was turning gray as he spoke.

"That was beaut. Way better than we thought. Miss Bucknell didn't even squeal when we did it to her. You should've heard yourself holler. Worse'n a girl." One of them snickered, and then they both let go with belly laughs.

Heat surged through his veins, up his neck and into his face. The little horrors. "Now I understand about you being on probation." He marched them to the back of the room. "You'll each stand in a corner for one hour. Don't even think about turning around." He stood them, one in each of the rear corners of the room so he could keep an eye on them, and marched to the front.

"The rest of you find your seats." He hadn't meant to bark so harshly, but he was mad clean through. Digging in the drawer, his fingers closed around the wooden ruler, and he rapped it on the desk hard enough to take a chip out of the end of the ruler.

"First Primer Class, come forward."

Amanda Hart slid off her seat, gripping a battered blue and white copy of *McGuffey's First Reader*. All the blood had left her face, and she trembled from head to foot. Without a word, she placed her toes on a crack in the board floor, looking as if she wished she could turn into that bird and fly away. He closed his eyes and prayed for patience.

He hadn't a clue what to do next. Did she even know how to read? How did a person teach someone to read? The minute school was out, he was going to head to his parents' home and share a few choice words with his father for putting him in this mess, plunk twenty-five dollars on the table, and call it quits. If things had gone according to plan, he'd be currying horses and cleaning stalls right now down at the livery, not trying to think of a single blessed thing to say to a little girl so she wouldn't burst into tears.

Movement caught his eye and he glanced up, sure the twins were up to something. But it was Mary Alice. Her hand rose slowly.

"Yes?"

"Sheriff Wilder, sometimes, when Miss Bucknell is real busy, I help out with the younger kids, especially Amanda. If you'd like, I could work with her on her letters this morning."

It probably wouldn't be appropriate, but he wanted to race down the aisle and hug Mary Alice. Her offer of hope was like a lasso landing on a longhorn mired in quicksand.

"Thank you. That would be fine."

He consulted Cassie's list.

"Second Primer Class, come forward."

Nobody moved.

"Second Primer Class, I said, come forward." He planted his knuckles on the desktop and stood. "Enough of this foolishness."

Again, Mary Alice's hand rose, slowly, halting about halfway up.

He dragged his hand down his face. "Yes, Mary Alice?"

With a pitying tone that reduced him to about boot high, she said, "The twins *are* the Second Primer Class, and you told them not to move from their corners for a whole hour."

By afternoon, he felt like he'd crossed the *Llano Estacado* barefoot in the blistering August heat. His head hurt, he was hoarse, and he couldn't make sense of even the simplest lesson. The older kids' grammar exercises had left him feeling like a complete fool as they instructed him on the proper parsing of sentences containing gerund phrases, and as for geography, why on earth would kids need to learn the exports of Brazil by heart?

Just before three o'clock, he closed the record book and dismissed school. Today had been the biggest waste of his time since he didn't know when. This kind of book learning might be all right for kids east of the Mississippi, but how were they going to survive in the West if all they did all day was spell long words and learn poetry?

He glanced at the calendar. Only twenty more school days in April.

This was going to be the longest month of his life.

⁓⊚

Cassie pinned the badge on her lapel and walked away from the school. That man could drive her crazy quicker than she could skip a rock across Cactus Creek. *Teaching was easy, was it? He didn't need her advice, did he? Well, fine then. Sink or swim, Benjamin Wilder.*

She entered the jail, or at least she tried to. The door stuck and ground hard against the floor. She had to throw her shoulder into it to get the rotten thing to even move. Glancing down, she noticed the deep, pale groove worn into the floorboards in a perfect arc. The hinges squealed as if being tormented.

After the bright morning sunshine, she had to let her eyes adjust to the dimness of the interior. A musty fog hung in the air, lingering testament to dust, boot scrapings, and unwashed men.

33

Grime clung to the two front windows, defeating the sun that tried to penetrate the gloom.

She froze when someone in the rear grunted. A squeaking sound, like ropes being pulled taut, came from the cells. She'd thought she was alone.

"Who's there?" Fiddlesticks. Her voice had trembled. What kind of sheriff quaked at the first sign of something amiss?

Another grunt and more squeaking. She ventured toward the dark cells. A shadowy figure turned on the bunk, his hat falling to the floor.

"Is that you, Jigger?"

"My mercy! What time is it?" He hauled his bulky self up off the protesting bunk.

"It's after nine." The musty smell was worse back here. Cold iron bars, dirty blankets, aged straw pallets. When was the last time this place was even swept out?

"Miss Cassie." He grinned, his face pale and his beard jutting. Jigger hauled at his belt and smoothed his wrinkled shirt to little effect. "Sheriff for a month."

"So it seems."

"Don't you fret. I can handle everything for you. Don't worry your pretty little head. You won't have to do a thing." He swiped at his beard and ran his fingers through his wiry, unkempt hair. "Where's my hat?"

"There. And what do you mean you can handle everything?"

Grabbing up his battered headgear, he scratched his armpit. "Just that. I reckon I can take care of the town this month, and you can walk around wearing the badge and raising money for your cause, letting folks pretend you're the sheriff." He nodded as if this made perfect sense. "Ben told me what he expected of me, and it ain't nothing I can't handle."

"Oh, he did, did he?" Her hands went to her hips.

"Well, sure. We figured that's what the town council really wanted, what with having him and you swap jobs. No lady can be a sheriff, not a real one, but if you was just to be a. . .well, a figurehead, so to speak, then it would be all right. The town would be safe, law and order would continue, and you could stay out of trouble."

She took a firm grip on her temper. Men, and lawmen in particular, were the most exasperating creatures upon the face of the earth.

"Jigger, let's get one thing straight. For the month of April, in the year of our Lord eighteen hundred and eighty-eight, I am your boss. I will *be* the sheriff of Cutler County, not just pretend to be, and *I* will be responsible for the safekeeping of this town and its citizens. It is your job as the deputy to follow my orders, assist me in keeping the peace, and otherwise make yourself useful. Is that understood?" She used her best teacher voice, even going so far as to point at him with her index finger, a tool she'd found quite powerful in dealing with children and simple men like Jigger.

He blinked as if a kitten had just turned into a bobcat in front of him. "Yes, miss." Scratching his other armpit, he shifted his weight. "Are you sure?"

"I'm quite sure. Now, I have a few orders for you." Parking her hands back on her hips, she surveyed the nasty little cells. "I want you to haul these filthy straw ticks out back and burn them. They're not fit for dog beds."

"But what'll I. . .I mean, the prisoners sleep on? You can't make 'em sleep on the bare ropes."

"You let me worry about that. For now, just get them out of here. This place is going to get a thorough scrubbing. A hog wouldn't want to live in here, and I'm certainly not going to work in such grimy surroundings for a whole month. Whose responsibility is it to keep this place clean?"

Jigger shrugged. "Mine, I guess, but Ben don't seem to care if I sweep up or not."

"Well, I care. I'm going to get this place clean, and you're going to keep it clean."

"Yes, miss." He began throwing aside blankets and dragging

the straw ticks off the bunks.

She covered a smile. "I'll be back soon. I just need to go down to the mercantile. But first, where is the key to the gun cabinet?"

"Miss?" Jigger straightened, sticking his finger in his ear and popping it out as if he hadn't heard her correctly.

"The gun cabinet. A sheriff can't do her job properly without a firearm. As your previous boss didn't see fit to take care of this issue, I shall do it myself."

"I don't believe Ben meant for you to go around town armed, missy." His brows came down, and his jaw jutted.

"I'm not interested in what Ben meant. And don't call me missy. My name is Cassie or Miss Bucknell, or for the duration of this month, Sheriff Bucknell. Now, where is that key?"

He dug in his pants' pocket. "I got it right here. Do you even know how to shoot?"

"Point and squeeze the trigger, right? I've done my fair share of target shooting." With Ben, as it turned out.

And just like that she was fifteen, sitting on the riverbank, watching Ben reload. Sunshine dappled the creek water and cast reflected light on the undersides of the overhanging trees. Insects buzzed, birds chirped, and her heart overflowed just being with him.

"Can I try it?"

"Girls don't shoot guns." He flipped the cylinder shut, raised the pistol, and fired at the log on the far bank. Cassie barely had time to get her hands over her ears and brace herself. A puff of smoke and chips flew off the log as the sound of gunfire ricocheted off the water and the far bank. She flinched even as she grinned, proud of his ability.

"Girls don't get the chance." She tried not to wrinkle her nose at the tang of gunpowder hanging in the air. "I think men are afraid to let women have guns for fear they would soon rule the world."

He laughed and pushed his hat back, his eyes sparkling. "Okay, Miss Sassy Mouth, let's see how you do. Stand up." He handed her the pistol butt-first.

It was heavier than she'd expected, and she used both hands to hold it level. Closing one eye and squinting with the other, she sighted down the barrel.

Ben shook his head and pushed on her wrists until she was aiming at the dirt. "That's no good. Here, let's try it this way." He led her over to where a branch grew parallel with the ground, about elbow high. "Brace your forearm along here, then rest the other wrist on it holding the gun. Cock the pistol, aim at the log, and squeeze the trigger."

She did as he said, aware of how close he stood behind her.

BANG!

"Did I hit it?"

His smug laughter rang out. "If you hadn't closed your eyes, you might've seen where you shot."

"But did I hit it?"

"Not even close. Try it again, and try to keep your eyes open."

By the time they'd burned through his entire box of ammunition, she was getting pretty good. The target was a mass of splinters and bullet holes, and her arm ached from the kick of the gun, but she was ridiculously proud of herself for impressing Ben.

Until he reached out and tugged her braid, winking at her like she was a child. "Not bad, sprout. Dunno where you'll ever use this talent, but it was fun. I need to get back to work, and you need to hustle on home. You probably have some schoolwork or chores to do, don't you?"

"Target shooting ain't the same as shooting at a man." Jigger's statement yanked Cassie out of the past.

"Nevertheless, I have a job to do." She took the keys from him.

"You planning on carrying a rifle around town?"

"I'd prefer a handgun."

"Then you don't need those keys. We only keep the rifles and shotguns in the rack. Ben's got another Colt in his desk drawer. Are you sure I can't talk you out of this?"

"No, you can't." She sat and pulled open a drawer. Paper

crammed every inch, jamming into the slide so the drawer stuck. "Them's our wanted posters. The gun's in the belly drawer."

She pulled out the middle drawer and lifted the gun. It was as heavy as she remembered, gleaming blue-black with a dark wood grip, smelling of gunpowder and oil. "Is it loaded?"

Jigger scrubbed his bristly whiskers, then reached over with an enormous paw and removed the pistol as if it were a toy. "Treat every gun like it's loaded."

Snapping open the chamber, he leaned over and plucked a box from the drawer, deftly inserting five bright, shiny bullets into the cylinder. "Only load it with five if you're going to carry it around. You don't want a live round under the hammer. You'll wind up shooting your foot off." He snapped the chamber closed. "This is plumb foolish. Like giving a gun to a baby."

"I'm not a baby, thank you very much. I'm your boss."

Jigger's expression changed from slightly befuddled and tolerant to focused and stern in a flash. "When it comes to being safe around guns, little missy, I'm not just your elder, I'm your better. I'm the one who could end up getting killed while you play Miss Sheriff in Petticoats. I'll go along with your games, but only so far, for the sake of this ridiculous Challenge and because Ben told me to look out for you. If you're determined to carry a gun, you'll do it safely or not at all."

She blinked, fighting the embarrassment swirling in her cheeks, and took a deep breath, knowing he was right. "I'll be careful. I'm not a fool. I realize guns are dangerous, but if I don't carry one, no one will take me seriously. I intend to do this job and do it well. Now, where can I find a holster? I don't want to put the gun in my pocket." It was so heavy, it would rip the cloth in no time, and if she hid it in her pocket, it was just the same to anyone watching as if she wasn't carrying a gun at all.

Jigger found a stiff leather gun belt. "Here."

She wrapped it around her waist, but it was too big. Jigger ended up punching more holes in the leather so she could keep it on. The unfamiliar weight at her side reminded her of his stern warning to be careful and treat every gun as if it was loaded. He'd yank the thing back in a heartbeat if he knew she hadn't fired a pistol since that one time with Ben.

"I'm going down to Svenson's Mercantile. When I get back, I expect those straw ticks to be gone." There, she'd reestablished her authority. "Start as you mean to go on" was her motto.

By midafternoon her arms ached and her fingers stung from the lye soap she'd used to scrub every inch of the inside of the jail, but the place was finally clean. Not that she'd anticipated wearing out a scrub brush on her first day as sheriff. Jigger had abandoned the jail after the first hour, saying he needed to patrol the town, though she suspected he was just tired of following her orders and toting buckets. It was just as well he'd left, because if she had to hear one more time that "Ben's not going to like this," she might hurl a bucketful of sudsy water over him.

Might be the first bath he'd had in a month.

Anyway, Ben would either be pleased with her efforts or he wouldn't even notice. No man could object to someone cleaning his office, especially when it was in such dire need of cleaning.

And she'd come up with a splendid idea sure to garner her plenty of votes in the Challenge.

At the mercantile, she'd purchased several yards of pillow ticking as well as some serviceable calico, charging them to the county since the supplies were for the jail. Tonight she'd borrow her mother's sewing machine and create new straw ticks, pillows, and a set of curtains for the windows. After that, she'd tackle the disorganized paperwork and institute some sort of filing system.

While sweeping the boardwalk in front of the jail, her attention was drawn to a commotion up the street. Several men emerged from Barney's, and a pair of them circled one another, fists up.

She dropped the broom and trotted toward the fracas.

As she drew near, she identified the combatants. The Shoop

brothers, Melvin and Alvin. She'd gone to school with both of them, though they were older than she, about Ben's age, and they were a shiftless, lazy pair who drank and fought and eked out a living on a spit of land north of town. Rumor had it they rustled just enough calves every spring to keep them in beer and cigars for the year and otherwise left work strictly alone. There was another brother, older, but he hadn't been seen in these parts in a while.

"You take it back, you flea-bitten son of a motherless goat."

"I won't. And who're you calling a son of a motherless goat, you fool? We're brothers, and we had the same mama."

"I'm going to pound you to perdition, you idjet!"

A ring of spectators had formed as Melvin, the older of the pair, took a mighty swing at Alvin. If he'd connected, he'd probably have fulfilled his own prophecy, but as it was, he missed by a good two feet and wound up staggering and crashing into a hitching post. Alvin laughed so hard he lost his balance and hit the dirt, raising a puff of dust. He scrambled up at the same time Melvin stopped draping himself across the hitching post, and they ran headlong at one another, clashing and grappling, grunting and straining to knock each other over.

Cassie stepped forward to take on her first real test as sheriff. "That's enough. Break it up." She used her best teacher voice, expecting immediate and total obedience.

They appeared not to hear.

As she drew close, they lost their grip on each other, and one of them—she thought it might've been Alvin—flailed to keep his balance, elbowing her in the eye and knocking her onto her backside in front of the entire town. Her skirts flew up over her knees, and she banged her elbows on the hard-packed dirt in an effort to keep her head off the ground. A laugh went up from the spectators, and shame washed over her.

Hands reached for her, and she realized as she was hauled up that her gun had fallen out of her holster and lay in the dusty street. She wrenched away from the helpful hands and snatched up her pistol. The Shoop brothers ignored her, once more wrapped in a muscle-straining clinch.

What was she going to do? She had to stop them, or what good was she as a sheriff?

Jigger reached out and pulled her back when she moved to tuck into the fray once more. "Don't."

"I have to stop them. I'm the sheriff. We can't have brawling in the street."

"Just leave 'em be. They'll run out of steam in a minute or two."

"Leave them be?" Her cheek throbbed, her backside stung, and her elbows protested. She jammed the gun back into the holster. "Is that what Ben would do?"

"Sure it is. He knows better than to get between them boys when they're tusslin'. They ain't armed, and they never hurt anyone but themselves anyway. Anyway, what could a slip of a girl like you hope to do against those two ornery buzzards?"

His patronizing tone irked her. Exhausted from scrubbing that infernal jail, embarrassed by her failure in her first attempt to uphold the law, and tired of being treated like a child, she surveyed her options and then marched into the barber shop next to Barney's.

Jake stood at the window watching the proceedings, his hands stopped in midair where he'd been stropping a razor. His customer stood alongside him staring through the glass, white foam dripping from his chin and a sheet draped about his throat. The barber's eyebrows rose, but he didn't stop her when she lifted a bucket of dirty, whiskery, soapy water and toted it outside. Taking careful aim, she sent the contents of the bucket into a silvery arc that splatted over the Shoop brothers in a bay-rum soap scented cascade.

They broke apart, blinking and sputtering, yelling and wiping soap scum and hairy water from their eyes.

"Hey," yelled Melvin. "What's the idea?"

"The idea is, if you're going to fight like dogs in the street, you're going to be treated like dogs. Now, unless you want to be hauled to the jail for creating a public disturbance, I suggest you quit your brawling and go home." She turned to the onlookers. "You all go about your business. This fight is over."

She stared from one face to the next, letting them know she meant business. Until she realized one of the faces was Ben's.

Chapter 3

The faster she tried to work, the further behind she got. Jenny Hart used the back of her wrist to wipe stray hair off her cheek. The hands on the bakery clock judged her, and she hollered up the stairs, "Amanda Jane, hurry up. You're going to be late for school."

With dough clinging to her fingers and flour dusting her apron, she plopped the last loaf of marble rye into the pan to rise. Hefting the stoneware bowl of muffin batter she'd whipped up earlier onto her hip, she prepared to ladle the apple-cinnamon concoction into the prepared muffin tins.

"Mama, can you button me?" Amanda tripped down the stairs, her schoolbooks under her arm and her golden curls bouncing. The back of her pristine pinafore hung open.

Jenny plunked down the heavy bowl. "Yes, of course. Then you're going to have to hurry. Be a good girl for Sheriff Wilder today. He's bound to be nervous." Wiping her hands on her apron, she glanced at the chaos surrounding her. No time to clean up, no time to sweep, no time for anything but getting Amanda to school and hurrying to the livery. Late her first day. Not a good way to start this Challenge.

With more than misgivings, she closed the back door to the bakery, waved to her daughter, and braced herself for her encounter with Carl Gustafson. A giant of a man with bushy, red-gold hair and a flowing red beard, he was a regular customer at the bakery. Though she'd met him practically her first day in Cactus Creek, she still couldn't claim she really knew him all that well. At first she'd thought he might have been interested in her, since he came to the bakery like clockwork every Friday, but he made his purchases, speaking only when necessary, and tipping his hat brim before leaving.

She'd had plenty of offers from frequent customers since arriving in Texas. Not that she was looking for a husband. No, she had no desire to step into that particular quagmire again. But though other men had approached her, Carl always hung back. Cassie had mentioned that Carl had been widowed a few years ago but gave no details, and Jenny didn't pry. Perhaps he was still mourning the woman, or perhaps he had the same bad taste in his mouth about marriage. He was invariably polite when he came to her shop, and he watched her intently while she packaged up his standing order of six sugar cookies, one loaf of sourdough bread, and one apple turnover.

The earthy odor of animals hit her when she was still twenty paces from the barn. Hay, horse, and harnesses. And standing in the open doorway of the board and adobe barn, Carl stood, pitchfork in hand. He was so. . .big. . .he seemed to fill the whole barn.

"I thought maybe you weren't coming."

"I'm sorry I'm late."

They had spoken at the same time.

"The day starts early here." He leaned on the pitchfork.

She spread her hands. "I'm sorry, Mr. Gustafson. I can't get here any earlier. I have to see Amanda off to school."

He pursed his lips, then jerked his chin. Did that mean he understood, or that he was upset?

"If you'll just tell me what I should do, I'll get to work."

The wide brim of his brown felt hat hid his eyes, but he held his shoulders at a stiff angle, and his jaw was rock solid. "This is ridiculous. You're half the size of my pitchfork. There's no way you can do a man's job around here." He jabbed the handle of the pitchfork into the hard-packed dirt, making the steel tines quiver.

She didn't know what to say. Misgivings had burdened her sleep the night before, but she refused to let them show. Walking small and apologizing for living was part of her old life. She was a new woman, and she could take care of herself and whatever obstructions arose. Hopefully.

"I signed up for the Challenge. I'll see it through."

"Are you going to wear that to work in a barn?" His tone was disapproving.

She glanced down at her plainest skirt and severest linen blouse. Her husband had taken great pride in seeing her well-dressed, a showpiece for him to parade about town. As a result, she had very few utilitarian garments. She'd worn the least ruffled, most practical outfit she had.

"My attire is no concern of yours, Mr. Gustafson." If he could be tart with her, she could be a bit fresh right back. She'd had quite enough of being judged for what she wore.

He rolled his eyes, as if imploring the heavens for patience or common sense. "The council must be out of their minds. The mayor has no idea what it takes to run this place, or he'd never have suggested a woman take it on. Have you ever even been around horses?" He turned and headed into the barn without waiting for an answer.

Assuming he meant for her to follow, she eased in after him. A wheelbarrow stood in the center of the aisle, and several equine rumps faced her. The wheelbarrow was heaped with malodorous stall bedding and buzzed with flies. Huge horsey feet shifted weight, and tails swished. Beyond the large block of light falling through the doorway, the interior of the cavernous barn lay in dimness.

She entwined her fingers and twisted her hands, sure it wasn't in her best interest to mention she'd never spent much time around horses. Her family had employed coachmen and grooms back in the city, and when she'd married, her husband had rented animals when he needed them.

"What would you like me to do?"

He ran his work-roughened hand down his beard, his brow puckering. "You'll need to feed and water all the horses, turn out the ones that need exercise, curry 'em all, clean the rest of the stalls, repair and clean harnesses and saddles, pick out hooves, get horses reshod when they need it, keep the barn in good repair, go over the buggies and wagons every day, rent out horses, maintain all the tools, order feed, stack grain bags, fork hay. The list is about as long as my arm." He shook his head.

She straightened to her full height—all five feet one inch of it. "Surely that list doesn't all need to be accomplished in one day?" She tried to inject a little humor into her voice, but his list of duties had made her want to gulp. "Mr. Gustafson, I appreciate your concern, but I assure you, I'm stronger than I look. I'm sure I can manage."

"And I am just as sure you cannot." He sighed, stirring the dust motes dancing in the sunshine slanting through the doorway. "Still, I don't have much choice. I let myself be talked into signing that contract. I gave my word, and I won't go back on it. But if you decide the work is too much for you, come find me. I'll be playing baker, twiddling my thumbs, and waiting for closing time."

His tone did little to bolster her confidence, and the notion that all she did all day was sit behind a counter chafed. Who did he think filled all those cases and shelves every day?

Carl heaved another sigh, this one hard enough to part her hair. "I will at least get you started." Leaning the pitchfork against a stall partition, he pushed his hat back and eased his suspenders on his shoulders. "I waited on the feeding, thinking you'd show up earlier. One scoop of grain for each horse, and a couple of forkfuls of hay. Hay's in the loft. After they've been fed and watered, you can turn most of them out into the corral. Leave one team and two saddle horses inside in case someone wants to rent a rig or take a ride. Rate sheet is on the wall over there." He motioned to a tattered bit of paper tacked to the rough boards beside the door. "One thing, though. Stay away from Misery." He jabbed his thumb toward the west wall of the barn. "I turned him out this morning, and you shouldn't need to fuss with him."

"Misery?"

"My new stallion. He's wild still, so stay clear of him." Sliding his pocket watch from his jeans, he shook his head. "I'll see you around five, if you last that long." Without another word, he strode away.

Jenny stood there for several long minutes, staring out the door, shocked at his abrupt departure. Not only had he given her the barest of instructions, but he hadn't waited to let her tell him about the ins and outs of running the bakery. As if his job was difficult, but hers was. . .she laughed to herself. . .a piece of cake. She'd show him who would last the day and who wouldn't. She snatched up the pitchfork.

And promptly underestimated the weight, clonking herself on the head with the wooden handle.

"My stars and garters, girl, pull yourself together." She rubbed her crown and tried to remember everything he had said needed to be done. Food, water, clean stalls. . .and a whole bunch of other things.

"Ma'am?"

She jolted out of her thoughts. "Yes?"

A short, thick-set man with a balding pate stood in the doorway. "Carl around?"

Her first customer. "Come right in." She gave her best Southern belle smile and went to greet him. "I'm sorry. Mr. Gustafson isn't in right now. Perhaps I can help you?"

"Naw, just tell Carl the feed he ordered is in, but he has to pick it up today because they piled it on the loading dock, and Ralph over at the depot said it can't be there when the evening train rolls in."

She swallowed, wiping her hands on her skirts. "How much feed is there?"

He tugged at his earlobe. "He ordered an even ton. Forty

bags. He paid for it in advance, but he didn't pay for hauling it and stacking it here. If you want that, it'll cost ya extra."

Forty bags of grain, each weighing fifty pounds.

"Thank you. I'll see that it's taken care of before five." *Though I have no idea how.*

The man slapped his thigh. "By sugar, I plumb forgot. The Challenge started today, didn't it? Interesting little twist they threw in there this year, ain't it?"

"Interesting." That was one word for it.

"Well, I'd best get back to the feed store. Best of luck to you, ma'am."

"Wait. I had a question you might be able to help me with."

"Shore thing."

"Do you have any idea where Mr. Gustafson keeps the horse feed here, or is the stuff at the station what I'm supposed to feed the horses this morning?"

He cackled and hitched his pants up on one hip. "Carl threw you in at the deep end, didn't he? I s'pose it's all part of the competition. He can't help you too much or you might win. I'll show you where the bins are." He led her to the back of the barn. "This room's where the feed is kept and where you can stack the grain you pick up at the depot." He opened the door and a familiar scent rolled out. She was used to the smell of wheat flour and oats in her baking, and under the dust, barnyard odors, and hay, the grain smell hung in the air. "Across the way is the tack room. That's where you'll find the harnesses, saddles, and such. And next to that is the toolroom. Pitchforks, shovels, hand tools for working on the wagons, and the like."

Lifting the lid on one of the bins that lined the walls, he bent over the edge. "The scoop's in the bin. One scoop of grain for each horse, and a couple forkfuls of hay. Hay's upstairs." He showed her the metal scoop. "Just climb the ladder and fork it down into each manger."

"Yes, Mr. Gustafson mentioned that part. Thank you so much Mr...?"

"Lewis. Barton Lewis. And it's no trouble. You need anything else, just holler. I'm a few doors up across the street at Lewis Feed and Seed." He sauntered away, and Jenny put an imaginary halo and wings on his stout little frame.

She scooped up a measure of grain, barely able to reach it in the bottom of the bin but refusing to give up until she'd wrestled it out. She'd had enough of being treated like a china doll. Her husband, a small man in both mind and body, had married her because she was petite, and he thought he could push her around.

Which he had. First with words, then with his fists.

Jenny hadn't stood up to him then, but she refused to be bullied now. She'd show Carl Gustafson that she could do his job as well as he could, and maybe even better.

But first she had to gather her courage and actually approach one of the gigantic equine beasts under her care.

"Hello, pretty horse. Are you hungry?" She edged alongside the brown animal in the first stall. He. . .or she, Jenny hadn't taken the time to check, obligingly sidled over and gave her more room. She dumped the food into the wooden box hanging from the wall and checked the water bucket in the opposite corner. Half full.

"You eat that, and later I'll get you some fresh water."

The horse ignored her—which was just fine—and shoved its nose into the feed box. Jenny sighed. One down, many to go.

By the time she'd gotten them all fed, her arms ached, and she'd learned that some of them were nicer than others. One black-and-white-spotted horse had crowded her, putting his nose between her shoulder blades and shoving her against the manger, and one droopy-eared, loose-lipped old fellow had leaned on her, pressing her into the wall as if she were a pillow for his comfort. She'd kicked and squirmed, finally kneeing him in the belly before he moved over.

In the corner stall by the toolroom, an animal that was more to her size and liking roamed freely behind a half door. Round as a dumpling and sweet as an apple fritter, the copper-colored, pint-sized mare whiffled her soft lips over Jenny's palm, looking at her with doe eyes. Her dainty feet stirred the straw, and she blinked ridiculously long lashes. Of all the horses in the place, this little sweetheart seemed to be glad to see Jenny for reasons other than a bucket of grain.

"My, my, aren't you a little beauty?" Jenny took a more confident breath after she bravely petted the tiny mare's neck. "I can't believe you're hungry. You're built like a puffed pastry." Reluctantly she left the friendly little pudding and resumed what she could remember of the long to-do list Mr. Gustafson had rattled off.

Upon opening the door, she decided the tack room scared her to death. Miles of leather hung in precise loops from pegs. Sheepskin-padded spars stuck out from the wall, cradling saddles. Three pairs of enormous collars had been hung up so high, she'd need a ladder to reach them, much less get them down. The room smelled of leather and soap and oil. And was more organized than a spoon rack.

She closed the door and opened the one labeled TOOLROOM, sucking in a gasp and raising her eyebrows. Fascinated, she stepped inside, trying to take it all in.

The tool bench was spotless, polished to a shine that almost put her kitchen table to shame. On the wall over the work surface, every tool hung in perfect splendor, precisely aligned, none missing, none left lying around. Carl had gone so far as to paint an outline on the pegboard around each tool so he would know where everything was and could see at a glance what was out of place or missing.

Not a shaving of wood or blade of hay lay on the floor, and even the window at the far end gleamed.

None of this matched up with the impression she'd had of Carl Gustafson. His long hair and untrimmed beard, the enormous boots and thick-fingered hands, the gruff manner toward her, none of it had prepared her for such orderliness and care.

Perhaps there was more to the livery stable owner than she gave him credit for.

⁓◎

Carl strode up the street, guilt and frustration writhing in his middle. What kind of a man made a woman slave away in a barn all day? What were the councilmen thinking? Jenny Hart had no more business cleaning out stalls than he had crocheting doilies. He reached the front door of the bakery and stomped his boots to clear them of stable remnants before entering.

He ducked through the doorway and stopped, surveying the little room. Though he'd been in the bakery every week since the first of the year when Mrs. Hart opened the place, he hadn't taken a lot of time to notice the layout or just how feminine it was. Before she'd turned it into a bakery, the place had been a cabinetmaker's shop.

The interior consisted of four little tables (each with four ladder-back chairs), a long counter, and a doorway leading to the back where he assumed the kitchen lay. And lots of shelves.

Each table had a pretty glass vase of flowers and a white lace tablecloth. The windows were hung with cheerful yellow curtains with red ribbons holding them back, and bless him if each chair didn't have a flowered calico cushion. You couldn't get more girly than flowery cushions.

He inhaled, savoring the smells of cinnamon, vanilla, and sugar as he approached the glass cases. On the bottom row, loaves of bread—rye, sourdough, wheat, and white—stood shoulder-to-shoulder like horses in their stalls. On the middle row, pies and pastries, doughnuts and fritters, turnovers and tarts. And on the top row, cookies, muffins, and something called petit fours in all kinds of fussy colors. More cakes and pies sat on shelves behind the counter.

His mouth watered, and he had to remind himself he wasn't there to eat, but to sell this stuff. Which shouldn't tax him too much, considering there wasn't one customer at the moment. He found a stool behind the counter. A little frilly stool with a curved-metal back. One that looked like it would crumble if he so much as parked a hip on it.

A flutter caught his eye. In the corner by the window hung a birdcage. Inside, a couple of parakeets hopped and twittered. He hadn't the foggiest notion of how to care for birds, so he hoped she'd taken care of that chore. They were bright little things with black eyes like rivets and happy little whistles. He stooped to get a better look. Something about them reminded him of Mrs. Hart. Maybe it was their size or bone structure. She was as tiny as a bird, too.

More guilt smote him. What if she didn't heed his warning about Misery and went into his pen? What if she fell climbing the ladder to the haymow? A dozen dangers hovered in any barn, and he was familiar with all of the ones in his own. He'd feel lower than a rattlesnake's belly if something happened to her while she was playing stable master. She'd shown up dressed for church, not for slaving away among thousand-pound animals with minds of their own.

The door opened, and Doc Bucknell came in. He grinned. "Good morning, Carl. How are you settling into your new role as town baker?"

Biting back a snarl, he turned from the birdcage. "I just got here. Mrs. Hart can't get to the livery until after she sees her little girl off to school, so I wasted half the morning waiting for her." Well, not half the morning, since it wasn't even nine yet, but since he usually started work before seven. . .

Doc seemed unconcerned. "Oh, well, that's fine. Family first. I'm honored to be your first customer of the day. The wife sent me over with this when she heard I was checking in on all the Challenge contestants." He patted his pockets, found what he was looking for, and handed over a slip of paper. "She and Millie finally settled on what they wanted for the wedding."

He took the paper, opened it up, and read, "Three-tier white cake with raspberry filling, buttercream frosting with pink sugar roses."

"The wedding?" He looked up, squinting.

"Sure. My middle daughter, Millie, is marrying Ralph Campion at the end of the month. This is the order for the wedding cake." He leaned in and lowered his voice, though there wasn't a blessed soul around to overhear them. "Just between you and me, the wife wasn't too pleased this morning when she realized the Challenge will still be going on when the wedding day arrives. I had to do some tall talking to assure her you were up to the job of providing a wedding cake. I told her I had every confidence in you."

That makes one of us. A wedding cake? He didn't even know what buttercream frosting was, much less how to make it. And pink sugar roses? The paper suddenly outweighed an anvil.

"For now, I'll just take one of those crumb-topped apple pies." The doc pointed to the glass case. "Might smooth over things with my wife if I supply the dessert for supper tonight."

Carl fetched the pie, grateful for the little tag behind the display plate that told him what it was and how much she charged for it. The doc paid him, and he tucked the money into the painted metal box Mrs. Hart used as a till and bid farewell to his first customer.

He'd probably better get the lay of the land in the kitchen. If he was supposed to make a wedding cake by the end of the month, he'd at least need to know where the stove was. Pushing open the door to the back, he stopped cold.

Not a bare inch of table or counter space to be found. Pots, bowls, pans, spoons, tins, bags, and he didn't know what all covered every surface.

How did she work in this chaos?

He stood with his hands on his hips, closed his mouth when he realized it was hanging open, and shook his head. Visions of his own workspace, where he put away a tool before getting another one out, came to his mind. If this was how she left her kitchen, what would his barn look like at the end of the day?

The thought made him a little queasy. Who would've thought that little buttoned-down, every-hair-in-place, butter-wouldn't-melt-in-her-sweet-little-Southern-mouth miss could be hiding such a secret?

Stepping farther into the kitchen and letting the door flop behind him, he examined the dishes piled high in the dishpan. While they were coated with batter and dough and flour and such, it all looked fresh. Nothing was crusted or moldering. That was encouraging.

Had she used every one of these just this morning? He swallowed and ran his fingers through his hair, gripping his scalp.

He'd barked at her about being late this morning, and she'd probably put in a full day's work before the sun was even up. What a clod he was.

Lifting the corner of a tea towel, he found a row of bread pans full of dough. What was he supposed to do with that? Was it ready to bake? How could he tell? Shrugging he let the cloth fall back. Time enough to deal with that later. First, he had to clean up this mess or go mad.

⁓◉

By late afternoon, Jenny wanted nothing more than a cool drink and a hot bath. Her first customers had been easy enough, coming in, taking their horses that Carl boarded for them, and riding away. Friendly enough, not overly talkative, almost ignoring her.

The men who rode in about four were different. A group of eight cowboys swung off their mounts, flipping their reins over the hitching posts. A couple of them sauntered into the barn where she still wrestled with the pitchfork and wheelbarrow. "Where's Gustafson?"

"He's not here today, but I'm sure I can help you." She leaned on the pitchfork and swiped her sleeve across her forehead, leaving a grimy smear on the linen. She'd gained a blister, stepped in the most indescribable excrement, and nearly broken her back with all the lifting and wheelbarrowing. Still, she was almost done.

At that moment, one of the horses cocked his tail and let drop another pile of work for her. She stifled a sigh.

One of the cowhands elbowed the other, his brows going high. They wore leather chaps and wicked-looking spurs, dust-covered from head to toe. "Well, now, we'd like that. First, tell us what a pretty little thing like you is doing in this great big barn all by yourself."

"I'm cleaning stalls." Wilted as a week-old wildflower, she reached for some Southern hospitality. "Did you need boarding for your horses?"

"Yes, ma'am, we were hoping to get them grained, watered, curried, and turned out in a corral so we can pick 'em up later." He shifted his weight. "Don't seem right having a lady do such grubby work. 'Specially a little thing like you."

The other cowhand nodded. He darted a look at her and turned red as a rose, shoving his hands into his back pockets. The rest of the crew stood in a knot behind them.

"It's all part of this year's Cactus Creek Challenge. Mr. Gustafson and I have switched jobs for the month of April. I'll tend his livery, and he'll tend my bakery."

"Big Carl's working in the bakery? Talk about a buffalo in a pansy patch." He grinned, two deep creases denting his darkly stubbled cheeks.

"What's the word, boss? We going to howl at the moon or what? I didn't ride all this way into town to stand here in the sun," one of the men in the back hollered.

"I assure you, gentlemen, I can care for your animals. If you're not pleased with the service, you don't have to pay." Though what Mr. Gustafson would say about that, she didn't know.

The boss of the outfit—a man of about twenty-five maybe—lean and masculine, tugged his gloves off and tucked them under his belt, studying her. "Fair enough, but we'll pay up front. It'll be late when we're ready to leave, and you won't want to wait up for us, I'm sure." He dug a ten-dollar bill from his pocket. "This should cover things. And you keep the change." Turning to his men, he raised his voice. "Unstrap, boys. Hang your gear on the fence and turn your mounts into this corral."

"But, sir, isn't that part of what you are paying me for?" She didn't want to take their money for nothing.

He winked. "It's no trouble, ma'am. Some of those saddles weigh more than you do."

In no time, saddles draped the fence, and their mounts were nose-deep in a pile of hay. The man in charge dismissed his men who took off for the saloon like thirsty cattle to a watering hole, but he hung back.

"Ma'am?" He cocked his head, studying her. No doubt about it, this man was a charmer. "Is there anything else you'd like me to help you with? If you don't mind me saying so, you look a little. . .out of your territory?"

The one item that had been preying on her mind for several hours leapt to her tongue. "That's kind of you, Mr. . . I'm sorry, I don't know your name."

"Name's Hawkins, Brady Hawkins, ma'am, but the boys mostly just call me Hawk. I'm the ramrod out at the Clover Leaf Ranch."

"Hawk. I'm Jenny Hart. You'd have my undying gratitude if you'd show me how to hitch up a wagon. There's some feed down at the depot that I'm supposed to get moved before five, and I fear it will take me the rest of the day."

He raised his fingers to his lips and let out a piercing whistle. Before she could catch her breath, his crew came running back, skidding to a halt.

"What is it, boss? Indians?" one asked.

"Naw, we're just going to do the lady here a favor. Slippy, you harness a team. Breaker, you and the boys head to the depot. There's a shipment of grain we're going to tote down here."

Jenny put her hand on his arm. "Mr. . .I mean, Hawk, I can't ask you to do that."

Swiftly, he covered her hand with his own, smiling down into her eyes. "Why not? You said it would take you all day by yourself. It won't take us more than half an hour."

She eased her hand free, stepping back and lacing her fingers. "Are you sure?"

When a couple of the men grumbled, Hawk quelled them with a glare. "Boys, what would your mamas say if they knew you ran off from a woman who needed your help, just so you could soak in a skinful of rotgut?"

They had the grace to look embarrassed, ducking their heads and tipping their hats before hustling toward the train station. The wagon was hitched with an ease Jenny envied as she tried to observe the procedure so she could duplicate it.

In a short amount of time, the first load, half the bags, were on the wagon and headed back to the livery. Her heart lightened. She hadn't realized how much the task had been weighing on her mind. She rode high on the seat next to Mr. Hawkins. "I can't thank you enough. I think I'd have perished under those grain bags."

He slapped the reins, shrugging. "No trouble, ma'am. Like I said, it goes against how I was raised to leave a lady in the lurch."

On the second and final trip, they passed the bakery, and Carl Gustafson emerged onto the boardwalk, hands on his hips.

Jenny suppressed a smile and averted her gaze until she had herself under control.

His reddish beard seemed to reflect the sunlight, and she couldn't read his expression. Did he think she was cheating on the Challenge by accepting the help of Mr. Hawkins and his friends?

Mr. Hawkins pulled the wagon up. "Afternoon, Carl. Nice day, isn't it?"

"Afternoon, Hawkins. You out for a drive, Mrs. Hart?"

Something flashed in his eyes, and heat pooled in her cheeks, but she decided to brave her way through it.

"Mr. Lewis from the feed store came by this morning to tell me that a shipment of feed had arrived. Mr. Hawkins and his men were kind enough to help me transport it."

He smacked his thigh. "I forgot that was coming today. You should've left it for me to take care of tonight."

"I might've been tempted, but Mr. Lewis said it had to be off the train platform before five. It's no problem. Mr. Hawkins has been very helpful. As a thank you, I'd like to treat him and his men to whatever they'd like from the bakery. When they come by, give them whatever they ask for, no charge."

As they rolled back toward the livery stable, Jenny wondered how long it would take Carl to realize he was wearing one of her frilly aprons.

<hr>

Carl watched his biggest wagon roll down the street, hardly able to believe what he'd just seen. Jenny Hart—she of the touch-me-not demeanor—riding down Main Street with Brady Hawkins, bold as fresh-polished brass. And wasn't Hawk soaking it up?

Something clawed up his gut and took residence in his chest. Something he quickly tried to squash and evict. *He was just being nice, and what do you care? She needed help, and he provided it. You're the idiot for not thinking about that delivery and how she would get it from the station.*

Perhaps he shouldn't have slammed the door so hard. One of the little vases teetered on the table, and he grabbed for it, catching it just before it fell. The parakeets squawked and flapped, chastising him for being so loud.

He entered the now-clean kitchen. One full bowl remained on the center worktable. She'd left it there, so he should probably do something with it. Giving it an experimental stir, he sniffed. It smelled like. . .cinnamon? Maybe it was cookie dough. That must be it. He grabbed a clean baking sheet off the shelf and stoked the fire.

Spooning up a glob of the sticky stuff, he dropped it onto the pan where it promptly spread out and made a run for all four corners.

"What? Stop that." He scraped it into a cookie-sized mound, but no matter how he tried, it continued to lose form and flatten out.

Maybe it wasn't cookie dough after all. Dabbing his finger into it and tasting didn't enlighten him, though whatever the concoction was, it was mighty tasty. He did a mental gallop around the shelves in the front room trying to match the taste and texture to anything in the display cases.

The back screen door squeaked, and two bright blue eyes peeped around the corner. Mrs. Hart's little girl. She eased inside but stood within a step of the door, every muscle stretched taut, her little bow of a mouth slightly open.

She was the spitting image of her mama and reminded him of a skittish filly, ready to bolt at the first sign of trouble.

For once, he wished he wasn't such a big man. If he were a more normal size, she most likely wouldn't be so guarded.

Maybe he should pretend he didn't see her. Go about his business and let her get used to him, just like he would a scared horse.

"Well, it ain't cookies." He kept his voice low, talking to himself. "Maybe it's supposed to be a cake." Scraping the stuff off the pan and back into the bowl, he went to the dishpan and washed the cookie sheet, then dried it and replaced it on the shelf. "If I was a cake pan, where would I be?" He stroked his beard, eyeing the assortment of pans and sheets and molds.

From the corner of his eye, he could tell she hadn't moved a muscle. Careful not to rattle the metalware, he slid down a round pan. "Guess this will work."

When he closed the oven door on the now-full pan, she'd eased onto a little stool in the corner, her lunch pail and books on her lap.

"Now, I suppose I'd best tend to this bread dough." Removing the tea towels, he sucked in a breath. The dough, which had looked like perfectly formed loaves just a few of hours ago, now ballooned and mushroomed over the sides of the pans and flowed onto the counter. "Oh, great. Now what do I do?"

He clearly couldn't bake it like this. Maybe if he wadded it up and stuffed it back in the pans?

The instant he touched it, it deflated and began to subside. Relief trickled through him. If he could just get it back where it belonged, he could bake it up and Jenny Hart would never know he left it too long. Except once it started losing size, it didn't seem to stop. He quit poking at it, puzzled. What had been an enormous amount of dough just moments before was now barely enough to fill even half of each bread pan.

Hoping the little girl wasn't watching, he flipped the pans one onto the other and reduced four loaves to two. That should do it. Maybe Jenny would think he'd sold two others. Quickly, he shoved them into the oven next to the cake.

How long did one bake a cake, anyway? Or bread, for that matter. He had a pretty good idea that it wouldn't help to keep opening the door to check on them, so he busied himself wiping down the counter where the bread dough had sat and sweeping the floor again. It seemed flour sifted out of every crack and crevice of the room and dusted the floor when he wasn't looking.

The bell on the front door jangled, and he went to wait on customers. Hawkins and his crew filled the small room, looking as out of place as Carl felt.

"Thanks for helping Mrs. Hart out. I appreciate it." He decided to take the high road, though it still rankled him that he'd left her in that position—and that she'd chosen Brady Hawkins to help her out of it.

"It was our pleasure." Hawk squatted and all but pressed his nose to the glass, peering at the lower shelves of baked goods. "I believe I'd like that pie right there." He pointed to a cherry pie with fancy lattice on top. "Boys, point out what you want. It's on the house."

They took their sweet time, and every last man wore a smirk, winking and elbowing each other, whispering behind their hands as they checked out every goodie in the place. Carl was ready to toss the bunch of them out on their duffs, but he gritted his teeth and waited.

By the time he'd served all eight men and they'd trooped out with their purchases, the bakery case looked like a horde of locusts had descended. How on earth was he supposed to fill it up again?

As Hawk, the last to leave, opened the door, he turned and grinned. "I gotta say, Carl, you sure look fetching in that apron." He laughed and scooted out the door like his tail was on fire.

Carl looked down and groaned. He'd put the ridiculous garment on while he washed the dishes to keep his pants dry and promptly forgot about it. Smacking his forehead, he sank onto the stool behind the counter.

No wonder Jenny—Mrs. Hart—had been laughing at him, standing like an idiot in ruffled calico right there on Main Street for all the world to see. He whipped off the apron, wadded it up, and as he was winding up to throw it across the room, something tugged at his pant leg.

He looked down at the little girl who pointed toward the kitchen door. He sniffed, his heart dropping.

"My cake." Plunging into the kitchen, he gasped, inhaling a lungful of smoke, his eyes stinging. Wrenching open the oven door, he reached for a towel to shield his hand and yanked out the smoldering cake. The molten pan quickly heated through the tea towel and scorched his fingers. Yelping, he flung the pan at the dishwater where it sent up a gout of steam. Smoke continued to pour from the stove where the cake had overflowed the pan and charred in great dollops on the bottom of the oven.

Sucking on his hand, he backed away, bumping into the shelf where he'd piled the muffin tins. They promptly clattered to the floor, scaring him into leaping away and barking his hip on the corner of the table.

"Oh, my sainted aunt Jemima!" He roared out his pain and frustration. "Lord, give me strength!"

The little girl gave a wide-eyed little squeak and bolted for the door.

CHAPTER 4

Mortified and angry at herself for handling the brawl so poorly, Cassie gathered her pride and her skirts and threaded her way through the crowd now disbursing in front of the saloon. Her cheek and her tailbone stung after being knocked in the dirt, but her pride hurt the worst. Some of the dirty water had splashed her skirts, not that anyone would be able to tell, since the garment was damp and filthy from scrubbing the jail all day. Humiliation trickled through her. She'd been bounced on her behind, and made a complete fool of by a couple of morons. And in front of Ben.

Boots thumped on the boardwalk behind her, and she knew who it was without having to turn around. She braced herself for Ben's censure as she wrestled with the door to the jail. If he was going to laugh at her or chew her out, it was best done where the rest of the town couldn't see.

"Cassie, wait."

"I'm busy." She put her shoulder into the door, but since she'd scrubbed both the floor and the door, the wood had swollen and stuck harder than ever. Humiliation burned her eyes. Couldn't even get into her own jail.

A large hand pressed into the wood just over her head and shoved. Giving way with an ease that disgusted her, it fell open, skidding along the groove in the floor.

"Thank you." She hurried inside before he could notice how wet her eyes were becoming. The strong smells of lye and carbolic greeted her, much better than the musty, hasn't-been-cleaned-since-the-Lincoln-Administration miasma of earlier.

Expecting him to follow her inside, she turned at the desk. Ben remained in the doorway, his hands on his hips. He blinked once, then again. She clasped her fingers at her waist and waited.

"What did you do to my jail?" He eased into the office, doing a slow turn.

"I cleaned it. And not any too soon? A hog would've backed out of this place and run."

He tipped his hat back and scratched his forelock. "Are those curtains?"

"I was going to buy some calico and sew up a set, but then I remembered Mother had these from the old house. They didn't work in the new place, and she didn't mind if I brought them here. Honestly, I don't know how you stood it before. If it wasn't for the grime coating the windows, I'd have felt I was sitting in a fishbowl. Anyone could look in."

"That's what the shutters are for." He motioned to the heavy slabs of wood on either side, each with a gun loop cut through.

"But they're ugly. And it makes the room so dark with them closed."

Ben sent her a half-scornful, half-pitying look. "They weren't built for beauty. The curtains have to go."

"They most certainly do not." She jammed her hands on her hips, all thought of tears banished by his lordly manner. "I'm the sheriff for the month, so this is my office. If I want curtains, I'm going to have them."

"You're being ridiculous." He stepped toward the café rod she'd spent a long time hanging.

She darted between him and the window, spreading her arms to protect the flowered calico. "I said they were staying."

His face was only inches from hers, and her heart hammered in her ears. From this distance, she could see the green flecks in his brown eyes and the dark stubble along his jawline. Not to mention his perfect lips.

Cassie swallowed. *Don't let him know how he affects you. Be mature. Stand strong.*

His lashes fanned his cheeks in a slow blink, and her knees turned to water. He brought his hand up to her chin and tilted her face toward the sunlight. "I don't think you'll have a black eye, but that must've hurt." Worry washed through his expression. "I knew this was a bad idea. What was your father thinking?"

She shook her head, struggling to find her voice. He smelled like the mint toothpicks he liked to chew on, and sunshine, and grown man. "One of them clipped me with an elbow when I tried to get between them. That's how I wound up knocked to the ground."

His lips hardened, and his eyes narrowed as he examined the damage. "I'm going to talk to your father. Where was Jigger during this little dustup? Didn't he tell you to stay back and let them wear each other out first?"

Though his expression was forbidding, his fingers gently brushed the hair away from her temple and grazed her cheekbone. Strangely, the sting under her eye had all but disappeared at his touch. Instead, a thousand sparrow wings flapped along her veins.

Knowing she'd do something stupid like rise up on tiptoe and brush his lips with hers if she didn't put some distance between them, she planted both palms on his chest and shoved him back. The curtain rod clattered to the floor, and he stumbled, ramming his hip into the corner of the desk and letting out a yelp. Cassie scooted away from the window, trying to calm her pulse.

"What'd you do that for?" He rubbed his hip, his brow scrunched.

"I don't like to be crowded." It sounded lame, even to her ears.

Ben shook his head as if she had rocks for brains. Which she very well might, if she couldn't get a better grip on her behavior than this.

"Regardless, the curtains can't stay." He held up his hands. "Now, before you sock me or something, just listen. You can't keep the curtains because they interfere with closing the shutters."

"I don't care. The shutters are ugly. I don't even know why you have them, especially on the inside of the building. If you want shutters, hang them outside like a normal person."

His patronizing laugh grated on her like a squeaky slate pencil. "You really have no idea, do you? The shutters are on the inside for protection. If someone tried to break into the jail, we can close them up. If they were outside, they wouldn't do us any good during an assault. We'd get shot up if we had to run out and close up the shutters. And if you've got frilly curtains and fancy brass rods in the way, we could get shot before we could rip them down and close things up."

Understanding dawned, and she hung her head. Another stupid mistake. She picked up the fallen curtain rod and laid it on the desk.

He walked over to the cells and peered through the bars. "New straw ticks? New blankets? What's next, feather pillows? Cushions for the chairs? You're going to have this place so swanky, folks'll be breaking the law so they can spend a night in here." The teasing lilt had returned to his voice, flicking her oversensitive feelings.

"You're not funny. You do know that, don't you?" Cassie slid the desk chair deeper into the kneehole to hide the cushion she'd sewn.

Seeking to change the subject and put him on the defensive for a change, she asked, "How did it go at school?"

He flipped his hat expertly onto the rack on the wall. "No trouble at all, unless you count a bird hidden in the desk drawer, a primer class that won't say a word, a schedule not even Clara Barton could organize and complete, and two holy terrors that look like little angels and lie like serpents."

"Oh my, a bird?" Her heart lifted. She didn't even try to quell her laughter, remembering well her own shock when the twins had pulled that stunt on her.

"Flew up and scared me rigid. I had to chase that dumb bird

a couple of miles around the room. Kids were screaming, books and pencils flying everywhere. I was a one-man stampede. Finally got it shooed out the window, after which I wanted to take a nap."

"I guess I should've warned you. The twins can be. . .creative. . .when it comes to pranks."

"I gathered that. I only stood them in the corner for a while, but I have to admit, cuffing them to their desks started looking like a good idea, especially after they put a tack on Mary Alice's chair, tied Pierce's shoelaces together, and dropped the water dipper down the privy. I did *not* retrieve it. They're going to bring money from home to get a new one tomorrow."

Her laughter filled the room until she had to wipe tears from her eyes. "All on the first day? They weren't pulling their punches, were they? Maybe teaching school isn't as easy as you thought." She couldn't resist giving him a saucy grin.

"It would be easier if I wasn't bogged down trying to stuff so much useless information into their heads. I can't believe you make them learn such a load of. . .nonsense. No wonder the twins are up to mischief every day. They're bored out of their heads, and they know as well as I do that once they're out of school, they won't use a blessed scrap of all this book learning. As long as they can read and write some and do some ciphering, that should be enough."

"It isn't useless information." She felt as if he'd just slapped down everything she'd studied for and held dear.

"If you can explain to me how the son of a cattle rancher who will grow up to be a cattle rancher will ever use parsing participles or need to know when the Magna Carta was signed, I'll agree with you."

"You assume he would grow up to be a cattle rancher and never aspire to be anything else. And how is more knowledge of the world we live in and the language we speak a bad thing?"

"It's a bad thing if they're spending so much time learning things that don't matter that they miss out on the things that do."

Her mind boiled over with things she wanted to say, but his hubris and illogic made it impossible to clarify her thoughts. She put her chin in the air. "I guess importance is a matter of opinion."

He shrugged. "I guess it is, honey, and I'm too tired to fight with you anymore today." Hands on his hips, he surveyed the room. "I like the improvements you've made around here. You just can't keep the curtains. Everything else looks fine."

Honey. He'd called her honey. Suddenly, she could forgive him anything.

"After all," his cheeks stretched in a broad, annoying grin, "I should've expected it from a girl, all this sprucing up and daintiness. I suppose after I win this Challenge and get my badge back, me'n Jigger will have to start using coasters for our coffee cups and putting doilies and bud vases in the cells."

The man was an imbecile.

<hr />

"Is that all you have?" Jake from the barber shop scowled. "I was hoping for something to satisfy my sweet tooth."

"Put some honey on them. They're fresh. What more do you want?" Carl set the tray of biscuits on the counter.

"Not biscuits."

"Too bad, because that's all I got. The Clover Leaf hands cleaned me out of pretty near everything on Monday, and what they didn't take got snapped up yesterday." He scratched his beard. Ungrateful public. He'd spent all morning making biscuits. He'd even rolled them out and cut circles with a glass instead of just dropping spoonfuls of dough on the pans, and this was the thanks he got. It wasn't his fault the council had stuck him in a bakery when all he knew how to bake was biscuits.

"You want some or not?"

"Naw, I'll go over to the general store and get a stick of candy." Jake shoved away from the counter and slammed the door on the way out.

It had been the same all day. What was he supposed to do? He'd ruined that cake thingy, and the bread he'd punched down and baked on Monday would make a nice doorstop, but it wasn't fit for eating. Jenny had left more batter and dough before she headed to the stable this morning, but he hadn't any notion what it was or how long to cook it.

With a sigh that ruffled the paper doily on the display shelf, he went about transferring biscuits from baking sheet to plate. Fluffy, flaky, sourdough biscuits lined every shelf and filled every corner. His mama's recipe, the only thing she'd ever taught him to cook. He'd even brought his sourdough starter from home yesterday to make the first batch.

How would the doc's wife react to a cake made out of biscuits? The idea of being responsible for that wedding cake still made his gut hurt.

The back door squeaked. Must be time for the little missy to get home. Taking up the baking sheet, he headed for the kitchen.

Her dress was blue today, the same color as her eyes. . .and her mama's eyes. Two wee braids lay on her shoulders, smaller around than his thumb, and each ending in a perfect little bow. He envisioned her mama parting her hair, brushing it, plaiting it while they talked, the way his mother had fixed his sisters' hair when they were little.

The child stood by the door as if prepared to bolt, and he turned away from her, going about his business.

"I think I'll mix me up a batch of biscuits." Dragging open the flour drawer, he measured out the right amount and dumped it on a spoonful of sourdough starter in the bottom of the bowl. "You know, I have me a little problem that I wish someone would help me with." He kept his tone quiet and conversational, careful not to look at her.

"You see, awhile back, I sold some feed to a fellow who was passing through town. He needed some grain for his team and his harness needed some repairs. Trouble was, he was short of cash. So, being the softy that I am, I took a horse in trade." He scraped a spoonful of lard into the mixing bowl.

"You could hardly call her a horse. She's a dumpy little pony, shaggy and round as a pumpkin. Way too small for any of my customers to want to rent her. I suppose she could pull a pony trap if she was broken to harness, but she isn't. And she's due to foal any day now." A little milk went into the bowl.

Just as he'd hoped, Amanda placed her books on the counter and edged closer.

"This baby is going to need a lot of care. It's bound to be small. I just wish I had someone I could count on to look after it while I'm stuck here in the bakery."

Stirring the dough, he dared a glance Amanda's way. She now stood with her fingertips on the worktable and her chin resting atop them.

"Baby horses need a lot of caring for, especially if you want them to grow up liking people and not be afraid of them. There's lots of training that someone can do before you ever put a saddle on a horse. Things like getting them used to wearing a halter and used to having people touch them, pick up their feet, mess with their mane." He sighed. "I just wish I had the time. The sooner you start on something like that, the easier it is. And that baby is going to show up any day."

He plopped the dough onto the floured worktable and rolled it flat with the rolling pin. "And I wish I had someone who could run down there from time to time and check on the little mama. The guy who sold her to me called her Short Stack, but I don't like that name. Maybe someone will come up with a better one."

While he went for a new baking sheet, Amanda edged closer, picked up the biscuit cutter, and began cutting rounds out of the sheet of dough. Carl hid his smile, but he couldn't deny the burst of pleasure that shot through his chest. He'd needed to bake another batch of biscuits like he needed another head, but it had been worth it to build a bit of a bridge between himself and the little missy.

The bell on the front door jangled. "Customers. I'd best go

see what they want, though if it ain't biscuits, they're clean outta luck."

Alvin and Melvin Shoop slouched at one of the tables. Two bigger knuckleheads couldn't be found in the state of Texas. Many's the time Carl wanted to clang their brainpans together. At least Ivan wasn't with them. Of the three, the oldest Shoop brother, Ivan, was the most cunning and dangerous. Lazy as a hound dog on a hot afternoon but sly as a rattler trying to get into a henhouse. He hadn't been seen around these parts for a while, and when and if he did come back, it would be too soon.

"We come to get us some cake." Melvin shoved his shaggy hair out of his eyes.

"Too bad. We're out. Got some biscuits if you want 'em."

"I don't want no sinkers. I want cake. This is a bakery, ain't it? Where's that purty lady who makes the cake?"

The reek of whiskey surrounded them like a fog. The notion that they'd come into this place tighter than ticks raised his ire. What if they'd wandered in when Mrs. Hart was here alone?

"If you don't want biscuits, then I don't have anything for you. And I don't serve drunks. Get on out of here and sober up." He crossed his arms and gave them each a hard stare.

"You got no call to throw us out. We ain't even half drunk." Alvin shot up out of his chair, sending it rocking backward into the wall, setting the birds to flapping and squawking.

"Then that's half too much."

"I ain't leaving till I get some cake." He held up his puny fists.

"You don't want to start a fight you can't finish, Alvin." Carl loaded his voice with warning but had a feeling he was casting pearls before swine.

Melvin bolted up. "It's two against one. I think we can take him, Al." He staggered, blinking.

With a speed that he'd been told was surprising in a man of his size, Carl grabbed them each by the bib of their overalls and hustled them toward the door, knocking into chairs and brushing aside tables as he went. Nudging the blue door open with his foot, he shoved them outside where they tumbled off the board-walk to sprawl in the dirt.

"You two couldn't take my grandma in a fight if you were stone-cold sober. Now git." He dusted off his hands. "Before one of you gets hurt."

Alvin bounced up and came at him, arms swinging. Timing his response, Carl smacked the heel of his hand upward into Alvin's hooked nose. Blood spewed and Alvin screeched, flying backward to land hard on his rump. His hands went up to cover his offended appendage.

"I warned you. Melvin, pick him up and take him to the doc's or down to Jake's. They'll set his nose and pack it with cotton. And don't let me ever hear of you causing trouble in this bakery again, understood?"

When he turned around, Amanda stood in the doorway, her face pale as biscuit dough, and her tiny mouth hanging open. He gave her a feeble smile, chagrinned that she'd had to see that.

He took one step toward her, holding his hand out, and she backed away, eyes wide. Though Carl went still, she didn't, turning quick as a flea and racing through the bakery and kitchen. The back door slammed, and his shoulders slumped.

⁓⊙

Jenny trudged along behind the buildings lining Main Street. Weariness had seeped into her marrow, and all she wanted was a hot bath and some willow bark tea. Her forearm throbbed with every step, but she tried to ignore it. Maybe if she didn't look at the wound, the pain wouldn't be as severe. As she drew near the bakery's back door, Carl stepped outside, tossing a full bucket of water into a wide arc to splat in the scruffy grass. The ease with which he accomplished the task made her jealous.

"Afternoon." She pushed her hair off her forehead with her good wrist. If her mother could see her now, her mortification would know no bounds. Not a shred of the fine Southern manners her mama had worked so hard to instill remained at the moment. Jenny was bedraggled and filthy and smelled of horse. Her dress was ruined, and her shoes were. . .better not to think about her shoes.

"How'd it go today?" The sunlight caught the reddish threads in his hair and beard and lit his hazel eyes.

"Fine, I think. All the horses are accounted for, eating their heads off, and I didn't break or lose anything in your workroom." She sagged onto the bench by the back steps, letting out an unlady-like groan and leaning against the siding with her eyes closed.

He frowned and set the bucket inside the door. "This is crazy. You can't keep up this pace. The livery is no place for a woman."

"I'll adjust to the work. It's just taking me a few days to get into the rhythm of it. I'm used to working hard, and once I get organized, things will come easier." She fervently hoped she was telling the truth. A few more days like this might have her begging the council to be released from the Challenge.

"I think I might change which project I'm raising money for though." Jenny cradled her aching arm in her lap. "After toting water up from the creek for fifteen horses and one fat little pony, I'm all for Ben's watering trough and pump. It would be a sight closer than hauling water from the creek."

"You've been toting it from the creek by the bucketful?"

"Yes." She raised her head and opened her eyes to look up at him.

"Mrs. Hart, there are water barrels behind the barn. I take them down to the creek in a wagon and fill them up about once a week. Anyway, that's just for topping off the buckets. It's a sight easier to lead the horses to the water than the other way around."

Jenny sagged back against the siding and stared at her raw, beat-up hands. "Well, I sure could've used that information sooner." She forced herself up. If she sat much longer, she wouldn't be able to move. "How'd it go in the kitchen?"

He followed her inside where the scent of baking hung in the air, as familiar to her as breathing. Yet not a pan or spoon out on the table, not a mixing bowl or cookie cutter on the counters.

How did he manage it?

He threaded his fingers through his shoulder-length hair, brushing it back. "Today went great if you like biscuits."

"Biscuits?" She pushed open the door into the front room and stopped. Every shelf, every plate, every spare inch of counter space was layered in stacks of biscuits. Laughter started deep in her stomach and bubbled up her throat, cleansing away some of the day's aches, filling some of the cracks in her heart that hadn't known laughter in a long time.

"It's not that funny. That's all I know how to make." He growled the words, his glare hot enough to start a fire.

His gruffness only made it more hilarious, and she couldn't stop laughing. Holding her side, leaning against the counter, she whooped and gasped. For a moment, he stood stiff, tall, and terrible, and she was afraid she'd truly offended him, but then his beard twitched, and he broke into a smile. His laughter joined hers, filling the bakery with the unaccustomed sound.

"Oh my," Jenny wiped her eyes. "That's quite a sight."

"I suppose it is pretty silly, but it's not all my fault. If *somebody* hadn't given away half the inventory to a crew of ranch hands, I wouldn't have run out of stock so quickly."

His gruff, deep voice, so different from the razor-sharp tenor of her husband's, rumbled in his broad chest. The fact that he could laugh with her was different, too, and somehow eased the tension that had arisen between them.

"That was bad of me, I suppose, but I had to reward them somehow. They were so nice to move all that feed. They even stacked it in the feed room and filled the bins for me."

His red-gold eyebrows bunched, and he crossed his arms, his muscles bulging. "I should've remembered the order and taken care of it myself. It's my fault you had to worry about it at all. I feel like a buffalo at a square dance in this girly bakery, and you have to feel like a rose in a patch of prickly pear working in the barn."

She shrugged, trying not to wince. Her right forearm

throbbed with every heartbeat. She'd need to soak it in cold water this evening. "I think we're doing all right. Nothing too disastrous has happened."

"Unless you count getting caught by a crew of rowdies while wearing a frilly apron, or an overabundance of biscuits." He sighed. "This is going to be a long month."

Perhaps she should change the subject. "Whatever did you say to Amanda this afternoon? She raced into the barn today like her hair was on fire."

His complexion grew ruddy, and he shifted his weight, his big boots scraping the floor. "I should apologize. Was she very upset?"

Her heart lurched, and her temper flared. Every protective-mama inclination she had burst to life. "Apologize? What did you do?"

"I think I scared her. I feel terrible about it, but I forgot she was even in the building. I never thought she might peek through the door and see us." He rubbed the back of his neck, still not looking at her.

A thousand thoughts raced through her mind, and forgetting her sore arm, she planted her hands on her hips. "Perhaps you should explain what happened." Her lips felt stiff, and her chest hurt. Though her knees knocked, she held fast to her vow never to cower to a man again. Not even a giant of a man with hands the size of Easter hams.

"Melvin and Alvin Shoop showed up pop-skulled as 'possums, being loud and rude. When they wouldn't settle down, I tossed them out of the place, and in the process, Alvin might've gotten his nose broken." Carl rubbed the heel of one hand with his opposite thumb, his eyes unfocused, as if remembering. "There was some blood and some yelling, and Amanda saw it all. I tried to reassure her, but she lit out quicker than a sprite."

Tension leeched out of her limbs, and she drew a shaky breath. Amanda had run into the livery like someone was chasing her, but she'd climbed right to the haymow, and when Jenny had checked on her, she found her daughter playing with a litter of kittens. Mary Alice had come by and invited her for tea, offering to bring her back before dinnertime, and Amanda had gone off, happily enough.

"The Shoop brothers like to come by from time to time, and they usually reek of drink. Amanda knows she's supposed to go upstairs or out back when they show up."

"So they do cause trouble in here." His frown could start a fire.

"Not really trouble. They're just a nuisance. Most of the time they get their cake or cookies and go. And the sheriff is just across the street, so they tend to mostly behave themselves."

"Well, they won't bother you anymore. They've been warned."

His tone sent a shiver up her spine, and she wasn't sure if she should be comforted or scared.

The back door creaked, and Amanda skipped into the bakery, her braids bouncing with each hop. "Mama, tea was very nice, and Mrs. Watkins says she has a pinafore pattern she can loan you. I think the new pony at the livery should be called Copper, 'cause she's the same color as your copper saucepan after you polish it." She skidded to a halt when she saw Carl. Her lips tucked into each other, and she froze, as if hoping he wouldn't see her.

Jenny's heart broke a little. How many times had she seen Amanda react the same way when she encountered her father, shrinking into herself, waiting for the cutting words, the sneering look, or the quick slap?

How would Carl react? Amanda's timidity had always enraged Robert.

His voice, though still deep and rumbly, softened. "Copper is a great name for that little lady." He kept his eyes on Jenny. "She's due to foal any day now, and I was just remarking this afternoon that it sure would be nice if I had someone to check on her from time to time. And when that foal comes, it's going to need some special care, someone small and quiet who likes baby things. Someone like that sure would come in handy, and I was thinking the little missy would be just the person for the job."

The way her daughter's eyes glowed with hope, but also couched uncertainty, made Jenny bite her lip. She had to be careful to keep Amanda from getting hurt again. The child had already suffered so much. What if the livery man held out the hand of friendship only to withdraw it or turn mean later?

"I don't know if that would be wise." And yet she wanted Amanda to feel a part of the community, to make friends and feel secure. Torn, Jenny leaned against the counter. "Ouch!" She straightened, cupping her injury.

"What's wrong?" He was beside her in an instant, towering over her.

"It's nothing." She whispered the words through tight lips.

"Whatever it is, it ain't nothing. Did you hurt yourself?" Without waiting for an answer, he reached for her arm, fumbling with the tiny cuff buttons before freeing her wrist and pushing up her sleeve.

"What is this?" His roar rattled the glass in the windows and sent the parakeets into high-pitched chirps. "What did you do to yourself?"

Before she could react, Amanda flew toward them, her little arms flailing. "Leave my mama alone!" Her tiny fists pummeled his flat stomach, and he grabbed her hands, holding her away from him. At his touch, she screamed and writhed.

"Hey now, little missy, I'm not hurting your mama." As she continued to struggle, he spanned her waist and lifted her to eye level, arms outstretched as she wriggled and swung at him. "Take it easy."

"Let me go! Let me go!" She beat at his forearms.

Carl set her down and backed away, his face a mask of remorse.

Amanda retreated until her back hit the glass-front display case, her eyes wide and her face pale. She seemed as shocked as the adults at her outburst.

Jenny dropped to her knees before her daughter. "Sweetie,

Mr. Gustafson wasn't hurting me. He wasn't yelling because he was angry. I think he was just surprised. Mama hurt her arm a little today at the stable, but I'm going to be just fine."

Amanda gulped and blinked, relaxing a fraction but still regarding Carl with wary eyes. Jenny touched her shoulder, running her hand down Amanda's arm until she could lace their fingers and give them a squeeze. "Why don't you go get me a cold, wet cloth, and then you can scoot upstairs. I'll be up shortly."

Carl waited until the little girl left after bringing in a dripping cloth. "Will she be all right alone?"

"Amanda needs time by herself when she's upset." She always had.

He took Jenny's arm in his big hands. "I'm sorry. I had no idea I'd set her off like that. What made her think I was hurting you?"

Jenny stiffened and jerked, but he hung on. "Hold still." Bending to examine the wound, his hair fell like a curtain alongside his face. The light from the window fell in a solid block over him, and the golden-red strands glowed, making her think of conquering vikings. Nothing about Carl Gustafson resembled her deceased husband, unless it was his strong will and certainty that he knew what was best, regardless of the situation.

Jenny winced as he probed the edges of the wound. Now that she saw it again, it hurt worse than ever. The individual teeth marks had begun to blend into an overall angry, purple bruise. In a couple of places, the skin had broken, and though she'd dabbed them with cold water when she first got bitten, they now oozed a watery pink that made her feel light-headed.

"This is a bite. What did you do? Which horse did this?" His voice was hard, and his muscles bunched.

"Does it matter?" She tugged her arm from his grasp, and this time he let it go. "Please, I can take care of it myself."

"Of course it matters. It's too big to be that pony. And the draft horses are too lazy to bother biting anyone. I can't imagine one of the saddle horses biting you unless you did something foolish."

"It wasn't a saddle horse or a draft horse or that sweet little pony."

He glanced up, and she felt shot through. "You got too close to Misery, didn't you? Even after I warned you. I told you to stay away from him." He jammed his fingers through his hair as if he would like to rip it out. "He's barely even halterbroke. A month ago, he was running wild."

"He also got his halter twisted and torn off his nose. It was wrapped around his neck, and I was afraid he would catch it on something and strangle himself."

"Then you should've come for me."

"It was *my* job." The fact that he was right just made her more determined to hold her own.

"You should see Doc Bucknell and get him to treat this." He took her arm again, cradling it. He stroked the skin alongside the wound, sending shivers and sparks up her arm.

"Nonsense. It's a silly little wound, and it doesn't need a doctor." She trembled. No man had touched her since her husband died, and she couldn't remember the last time a man had touched with gentleness. Carl's hands were huge and work-worn, nothing like Robert's diminutive, smooth banker hands, and yet the horseman's touch was almost a caress.

Jenny firmly removed her arm from his grasp once more.

"If you won't go to him, I'll bring him to you."

Carl's autocratic, domineering statement snapped her raw emotions. She would not be backed into a corner, told what to do by a man who wouldn't listen to her or treat her like she was a person with her own will and intellect.

"I can take care of myself, Mr. Gustafson. I don't need you or any man to boss me around."

For a moment he stood his ground, his expression dark, but then he turned and stomped out, the back screen door slamming in his wake.

Chapter 5

Ben hitched up his gun belt and mounted the steps to the school, bracing himself. Friday at last. If he could just get through today, then he'd have two whole days of reprieve when he wouldn't have to listen to mind-numbing recitations, referee playground squabbles, or hear one more time, "That's not how Miss Bucknell does it."

I'd rather haul a hundred prisoners to the state pen in Huntsville all by myself than wrangle these kids one more day.

His footsteps echoed in the empty room. At least he was early enough to enjoy a little peace and quiet. Heaven knew he wouldn't get any once the children showed up. Funny how he didn't remember being so noisy as a kid. Maybe he had been. Maybe he'd ask his ma. Then again, maybe he wouldn't. He hadn't enjoyed school very much, preferring to be out of doors playing in the creek or riding his horse, tagging after his older brothers, or best of all, hanging around the jail pretending to be a lawman and watching his father sheriff. He'd known from the time he was a little gupper that he never wanted to be anything but a lawman, and the minute he could put aside the pencils and books, he'd shot through the schoolhouse door and hadn't looked back.

Until now.

He went to the blackboard behind the desk and began scrubbing away his chicken-scratch marks from yesterday. Penmanship had always been his nemesis, and his temporary students took great delight in asking him to "show them" a word or math problem, just so they could laugh at his slanted writing. He felt like a hypocrite making them practice their letters on their slates.

The door creaked, and he waited to see who would be first around the partition. His heart sank, but he tried not to let it show when Mary Alice Watkins pranced in. There wasn't any other word for how she minced her way toward him. Long about Wednesday, she had stopped wearing her hair in thick braids and piled it up on her head instead—with varying results that made him wonder if her mother had given her permission or she was putting it up on the way to school without benefit of a mirror. She'd also started smelling like way too much rosewater, and she'd developed a strange flutter to her eyelids every time he looked at her. He was flattered and bewildered and embarrassed at these signs that she was nursing a crush on him. Such a thing had never happened to him before, and he didn't know what to do about it.

Ben arranged his features in what he hoped was a neutral expression. "Good morning, Mary Alice."

She blushed a painful pink and bobbed her head. One of her hairpins gave up the fight and clattered to the floor, and the pink deepened to red. He turned back to the blackboard to allow her time to compose herself, thankful that little shoes were pounding up the steps so he and Mary Alice wouldn't be alone.

Calling the class to order, he half-listened to the now-familiar psalm and prayer. The schoolroom was stifling, and once everyone was back in their seats, he opened the windows on the leeward side of the building to catch a breeze.

"Amanda, you can go sit with Mary Alice." The little girl scooted out of her chair and edged around him as if afraid he might grab her or smack her. Something more than shyness was causing this, but he hadn't had time to investigate further. His lawman's sense told him someone had abused or frightened the girl, but he couldn't reconcile the little he knew about Jenny Hart with child abuse. She was quiet and kind and well-spoken—by all accounts an excellent mother. Next time he saw Cassie, he'd see what he could find out. If he was doing something that scared the little girl, then he wanted to stop doing it.

"Second Primer Class." He took his chair behind the desk and reached for the second McGuffey Reader, dragging it toward himself and flipping it open to page fifty-five. A picture of a mother rocking her child accompanied a poem. He sighed as the twins jostled and elbowed their way to the front.

"Knock it off, boys. You're supposed to have this poem memorized. Ulysses, you start."

Ulysses scuffed his nose with the heel of his hand and tugged at his overall strap. "Can't."

"You can't? Why not?"

"Didn't learn it." His chin came up, and he tilted his head.

"Quincy? How about you?"

"Nope. Not a word." Quincy had lost a tooth yesterday, courtesy of his brother and another wrestling match. A baby tooth, fortunately. At least the gap in his smile made him easier to identify.

"Why not?" He slapped the book closed. Bad enough he had to assign this stuff, but if they weren't even going to bother to learn it, then what were they all doing here?

They shrugged.

"Well, you're going to learn it now. Go back to your desk and get to it." Little horrors. When he was a kid, if you showed up to school not knowing your lessons, you had a hide tanning coming.

"Third Primer Class, bring your arithmetic books and tablets."

They shuffled to the edge of the platform and put their toes on the crack in the floor. Two boys and a girl, all about nine or so, the biggest class. Bekah handed him her paper, but the other two stood there empty-handed.

"Well? Where's yours?"

Thomas and Isaac slanted looks at each other. "We didn't do it."

A flicker of panic went through his chest. The twins and trouble went hand in hand, but Thomas and Isaac were good kids who hadn't given him a lick of problems.

Perhaps they were testing him. Testing his resolve. Would he be the teacher and make them learn, or was he just babysitting for the month so they could do whatever they wanted?

Though the temptation to let the whole herd run maverick for thirty days appealed, his competitive side reared up. There was the Challenge to consider, his standing in the community, and his desire to win. Win the Challenge, win at whatever battle of wits and wills he now found himself in with these kids. Not to mention Cassie would string him up if he let everything slide at the school and would crow over him forever if she trounced him soundly in the Challenge.

"Go back to your seats. You, too, Bekah."

He rounded the front of the desk and perched his hip on the edge. Crossing his arms, he surveyed twelve youngsters who all looked back at him—except Amanda, who stared at her lap.

"How many of you left your homework unfinished from last night? I want to see your hands."

Seven hands went up, all of them male.

He studied them, trying to appear stern, when in reality, he couldn't think of what to say. More than half his class had kicked over the traces before he'd even taught a full week.

"Why?" The word popped out, though he hadn't meant to ask it.

Ulysses shrugged. "Why bother? You said none of this stuff was going to help us survive out here on the prairie. It wasn't going to help us be better cattle ranchers or to fight off Indians or outlaws. You said that memorizing poems about mothers was sissy stuff, and you couldn't believe we were wasting time on it."

Guilt settled on Ben like a bad smell. He pinched the bridge of his nose. Cassie was going to kill him. He had said those things, hadn't he? In a fit of boredom and frustration at being cooped up in that schoolhouse wondering if his town was going down the river while Cassie made pillows and curtains.

Quincy piped up. "No point in wasting time learning stuff that won't do us no good later, right?"

The boys all nodded, and even a couple of the girls looked like they might be buying what was being sold.

Mary Alice frowned and shook her head. "This isn't right. We are supposed to learn these lessons. What will Miss Bucknell say if she finds out you boys aren't doing your assignments?"

All of them except the twins had the grace to look at least a little bit bothered by the prospect. Quincy and Ulysses slouched, and Quincy jiggled his leg. Ulysses propped his chin in his hand and stared out the window, the perfect picture of boredom.

Ben was lassoed and tied with his own piggin' string. He should've kept his tater trap shut, no matter how tedious or useless he found the book learning these kids were subjected to. His collar felt tight, and he tugged at it, rubbing the back of his neck and feeling the knots growing there. Time to start trying to wriggle out of this mess.

"Mary Alice is right. Miss Bucknell will be upset if she hears you left your work undone. It doesn't matter if you think it's boring or if I think it's the most ridic— Well, a man has to do what he has to do, no matter if he likes it. Your job is to learn this stuff, and my job is to teach it to you, so that's what we're going to do. I'll stop complaining about it, and you'll do your homework, and that's how it's going to be." He rubbed his hands together, trying to drum up a little enthusiasm.

No one appeared enthused.

He glanced at the clock. Relief trickled through him. "It's close enough to time for the morning recess."

The words were barely out of his mouth when every kid but Mary Alice jumped to life and streamed out of the schoolhouse like a freight train on a long downgrade. Mary Alice chose to stand, smooth her skirts, look up at him through her lashes, then sashay toward the door. She wobbled a bit, and he noticed the high heels on her button-up boots. The shoes were clearly too large for her, perhaps borrowed from her mother or an older sister?

Poor kid. Childhood was short enough without rushing it. He had cause to know. One day he was gigging frogs and climbing trees down by the creek, the next he was facing down the Cactus Creek Schoolhouse Gang and losing.

He was halfway to the door when Mary Alice tumbled inside, her hair falling from its pins and her face pale as a linen duster. "Sheriff, you better hurry!" She stumbled out of his way and pointed to the door. "The twins!"

Needing no other explanation, he bolted. Left to their own devices, the twins were most likely either fighting like two badgers in a gunnysack or plotting the overthrow of the known world. Clattering down the steps, he glanced up the street toward town but didn't see them.

Mary Alice clung to the doorjamb behind him. "Around back! Hurry!"

He rounded the building, where nine children stood with their backs to the siding and their eyes all but bugged out. Half a dozen paces from the outhouse, one of the twins held a bottle with a rag hanging out of it while the other lit the rag with a match.

"Stop that!" He took two steps, but the one holding the bottle—Quincy, Ben noted the missing tooth—glanced over his shoulder, then hurled the bottle through the open door of the privy, turning and flattening himself in the grass as it arced toward the outhouse.

It was a perfect shot. The bottle didn't so much as clank off the seat before disappearing down the hole. There was a moment of dead stillness when Ben kissed his temporary teaching assignment and his hopes of keeping his job as sheriff good-bye, then a whoosh, a flash of light, and a concussive blast that hit him hard enough in the chest to spin him to his knees.

Boards flew out and up, the roof tilted off backward, and the ground lurched. Ulysses, who had been hopping up and down clapping his hands now lay on his back staring at the sky.

Ben's ears rang, and a curious, floating feeling occupied the space between his ears. The schoolhouse wavered and wobbled...or was it him that was wobbling? He planted his palms on the ground, trying to clear the dizziness from his brain. After a moment, he forced himself to his shaky knees. Glancing behind him, he noted that the kids against the schoolhouse appeared to be all right, though some still held their hands over their ears, and Amanda had her eyes screwed up tight. Staggering forward, he made it to Ulysses.

To his shock and chagrin, the boy was laughing. A giggle at first, then great gouts of laughter that shook him from his scuffed boots to his curly hair. Quincy crawled over, and they collapsed into the grass, howling and rolling, holding their sides.

Ben wanted to throttle them.

And he would as soon as he stopped trembling like a wet kitten.

Relief that they weren't dead, anger that they'd done something so dangerous and foolish, and a tinge of awe at their audacity made him light-headed. He sagged onto the ground and put his head between his knees.

Shouts and people running helped clear his senses. Half the town raced toward them across the empty lots between the schoolhouse and the dry goods store. His heart sloshed into his gut. Cassie was in the lead.

Right behind her came Jigger, moving faster than Ben had seen the rather tubby old fellow go in quite a spell.

"Ben, what happened? Are you hurt? Are the kids hurt?" Cassie's finger punched the air as she counted her students, and her glare muted the prostrate twins' laughter to stifled snickers. She went to her knees and took Ben's chin in her hand, looking into his eyes and feeling along his shoulders and arms as if to make certain he wasn't injured.

He had to admit, her concern felt kind of nice and the worry in her green eyes was like a salve to his scattered wits. But when she saw for herself that he was in one piece, she smacked his shoulder. Hard.

"What on earth were you thinking?" She stood and glowered down at him. "You blew up the outhouse?"

Indignation propelled him to his feet with an awkward lurch. "Of course I didn't. It was these two limbs of Satan." He reached down and hauled the twins up by their overall bibs. "You could've killed yourselves. Or one of the other kids."

Quincy had the gall to look offended. "We made them stand back first. We ain't stupid."

"All evidence to the contrary," Ben shot back.

Jigger, gasping and panting, picked his way through the debris to where a wisp of smoke and a lot of stench floated up from the hole where the outhouse used to be.

"Must've been a fair amount of gas down there." He stepped back, waving his paw in front of his face.

Doc Bucknell had stopped at the schoolhouse, bending and looking into eyes and talking to each pupil. When each one from Mary Alice down to Amanda had been checked, he started toward Ben.

"A little excitement in an otherwise dull day?" He squatted and examined Quincy first. "I take it you were one of the masterminds behind this little charivari?"

"What's a shiv-a-ree?" He grinned at the doctor with his missing tooth, looking angelic.

Ben cut in. "Don't let his exterior fool you, Doc. This isn't a nine-year-old. This is actually a pint-sized Jesse James in disguise. And this"—he nudged Ulysses in the shoulder—"is his brother, Frank. Get close to them at your own risk."

Cassie put her hands on her hips. "What do you two have to say for yourselves? Look at this mess. When your mother finds out, you'll be lucky to see daylight before you're old enough to vote." Authority and sternness rang in her voice. The terrible light in her eyes—half anger, half disappointment—had the boys squirming and studying their shoes. Even Ben felt guilty, and he hadn't done anything wrong.

"What's going on here, Son?"

Ben looked away from Cassie and into the eyes of his father. Though he'd retired from being a career lawman, the aura of strength and toughness that had made Obadiah Wilder one of the most respected men in the state still clung to him like a second skin. When Ben looked at his father, he saw everything he ever aspired to be.

And feared he would never become.

"Just a little. . .mishap."

Dad quirked a silver eyebrow. Without needing an explanation, Ben knew his father had surveyed the sight and instantly figured out what happened. He had that uncanny ability—something that had made getting away with much of anything as a boy impossible for Ben and his brothers.

The twins looked at Obadiah Wilder, their mouths open and adoration glowing on their faces. Here was a legend in the flesh. A man that men talked about with awe. A fearless lawman who even had a dime novel written about him. When Ben's father bent a stern gaze on them, they froze, hitched up their overalls, and hung their heads.

Ben wondered how was it that everyone in this town could get these boys to toe the line but him. This day could not possibly get any worse.

Jigger sauntered over, put his hands on his hips, and announced to the assembly, "I guess Ben isn't in any danger of winning the Challenge, is he?" Laughter rippled through the crowd.

Ben bit back a growl and didn't look at Cassie, who had to be gloating. Not that he blamed her. He'd want to gloat, too.

Time he took control of things. "All right, folks, the excitement's over. Nobody was hurt, and these two culprits"—he waved toward the twins—"have just volunteered to give up their Saturday morning and build a brand-new privy for the school."

Slowly, they dispersed, still chuckling, leaving Ben, Cassie, and the kids. Ben waved the children over. "School's dismissed early today."

With shouts of approval, they bolted off, no doubt afraid he would change his mind. When the twins tried to escape, Ben clamped down on their shoulders. "Not you two. You're going to clean up this mess and stack the wood. We'll see what can be reused and what we have to buy from the lumberyard in the morning."

Cassie covered her lips, but her eyes sparkled at the dejected tilt of their shoulders.

"Never counted on having to rebuild it. What a waste of a Saturday morning." Quincy stuck the tip of his tongue through the gap in his front teeth.

Ulysses let out a sigh. "It was a beaut explosion though." He followed his brother toward the scene of the crime.

Ben refused to look at Cassie. A man could only take so much.

This was supposed to be his day off from this blessed Challenge, but there was no rest for the weary, it seemed, or the wicked. Ben shifted his grip on his toolbox and rounded the corner of the schoolhouse.

The little renegades were waiting, sitting on the fulcrum of the seesaw, shoulders bowed, scowls evident.

"Morning, boys. Ready to get to work?"

"I 'spose." Ulysses scuffed the dirt with his toe.

"Guess you should've thought of the consequences before you threw that bottle of whiskey into the privy, eh? Speaking of which, where did you two get your hands on a bottle of liquor?"

"We found it." Quincy straightened and tugged his earlobe. He looked away too innocently.

"Found it where?"

They looked at each other for a long minute. "In Daddy's desk."

Ben rolled his eyes. "You just happened to find it there and happened to stumble upon some matches, and I suppose you happened to trip, and the lit bottle just happened to fall in the outhouse hole?" He let the toolbox *thunk* to the ground, rattling the tools. "Where did you even get the idea to blow up an outhouse?"

"Uncle Tyler. He said some kind of gas built up inside outhouses, and sometimes, if you were lucky, if you threw a match in there, it would make a little pop when it exploded. We wanted a big pop, so we threw in a whiskey bomb."

He rubbed his hand down his face. *Thanks a lot, Uncle Tyler.* They were lucky they hadn't blown their fool heads off.

"We'd best get busy if we're going to be done by noon."

A stack of new boards from the lumberyard, delivered last evening, sat in the grass. Ben had picked over the remains of the exploded outhouse and decided there was nothing worth keeping. At least some of the smell had dissipated.

"You boys ever build anything?"

"Nope. You gonna teach us?" Quincy picked through the toolbox, lifting Ben's hammer and testing the weight.

"Yup. Let's get organized. If you have any questions, ask."

From that moment on, Ben didn't have a scrap of peace. The boys talked to each other, over each other, and about each other.

"I bet you wonder about our names. Everyone does. Ma named us after presidents because she wants us to grow up to be famous men. I'm named after a general. But Daddy says he was a drunk and a Yankee, and he can't believe Ma would curse us with Yankee names."

Ben had no doubt the twins would be famous. . .or infamous. . .someday.

"Ma says we should try to be good, and so does Miss Bucknell, but we don't hardly ever feel like being good. Being bad is a lot more fun. And we're pretty good at it."

"You are that." Ben nearly hit his thumb with his hammer, he was trying so hard not to laugh. "Hold this board for me."

By the time they had the new floor and east wall in place, he'd heard a detailed description of each of the kids in the school all the way from "Mary Alice acts like everybody's mother. You can't hardly get away with anything because she blabs to Miss Bucknell before you even do nothing," to "Amanda Hart is such a baby. She's scared of everything. Once I told her I was thinking about chasing her with a mouse, soon as I caught one, and she ran away screaming. I didn't even have to chase her or find a mouse and she was already running. Girls are babies."

And he learned a lot about Miss Bucknell, too.

"We can't never fool Miss Bucknell. She can tell us apart better than Ma can."

"Ever'body can tell us apart now that you knocked my tooth out."

"She lets us read dime novels if we're good. I read one about how your pa helped catch the Dickenson Gang, and it was crack. I think when I grow up I'm going to be a sheriff. Or an outlaw. I haven't decided."

Look out, Texas. If the twin tornadoes hit the outlaw trail, it would rain rattlesnakes and prickly pear for a decade.

"Miss Bucknell is nice most of the time. She let us use our new pocketknives to sharpen her pencils, and she didn't even get mad when we whittled them down to nubs. She said it kept us quiet for a whole hour."

Ben strangled his laughter and sawed the next piece of wood.

"I wish she wouldn't make us memorize so much, especially the gazindas. I'm fine with the timeses, but I can't figure the gazindas."

He paused and glanced up to where Quincy sat on a board across the sawhorses, fingering the nails in a paper sack. "The gazindas?"

"Yeah, like two gazinda four twice, two gazinda six thrice, two gazinda eight four times. After I get past the five gazindas it gets too hard."

"Boys, I think it's time to take a break and get a drink of

water." He took out his bandana and wiped his face. The gazindas. Heaven help them.

Sitting in the shade of the schoolhouse, he stretched out his boots and crossed his ankles. The twins plopped down on either side of him and emulated his pose.

"So, what would you boys study if you could learn anything you wanted in school?"

Quincy picked up a pebble and fired it at a clump of brush. "Nothing. I hate school."

"C'mon now. Anything."

"I want to learn to track and shoot and start fires without matches."

"I want to learn to ride a horse and speak Comanche and hunt and cook over a fire. All the stuff we'll need if we want to be outlaws."

"Or sheriffs?" Ben asked.

"'Zactly. Any of that would be better than memorizing poems and spelling words and the names of the presidents."

A ghost of an idea began to take shape in the back of Ben's mind and continued to grow. By the time he'd cut the half-moon shape into the door and tightened the screws on the new hinges, he had a new plan of attack for school Monday morning.

He let the boys go just before noon and packed up his tools. A quick glance at his watch told him he'd have time to get some lunch at his folks' place before he had to be back in town for campaigning for the Challenge. Leaving his toolbox inside the school, he hotfooted it the quarter mile west along the main road toward the little ranch his folks had retired to.

"You home?" He eased through the back door. His mother turned from the stove, a wooden spoon in her hand and a flowered apron covering her dress.

"Benjamin. You're just in time for lunch." She raised her dewy-soft cheek for his kiss. No matter how big her sons got, no matter that every one of them stood more than six feet tall and upheld law and order, they would forever be her boys, and they would greet her with a kiss on the cheek. "You'll have to eat quickly, though, because I have an appointment in town before the speeches. Cassie has a little something planned down at the jail, and she invited me."

Ben's curiosity stood straight up like a prairie dog and sniffed the wind. "What's she doing?"

Ma shook her head. "It's something for ladies only. You weren't invited."

"Come on, Ma. It's my jailhouse. If she's planning something, shouldn't I know about it?"

"It's not yours at the moment. You don't apprise Cassie of everything you do at the school, do you?"

She had him there. Ben relaxed. He'd find out from Jigger later.

His father limped in. "Hey, Ben."

"What's wrong? You hurt yourself?"

"I had a little disagreement with one of this year's crop of colts."

Ma sniffed. "Disagreement. You got piled up like last week's laundry." She slid a bowl of stew in front of him. "There's fresh bread. Had to bake it myself this week. I've been buying from the bakery, but I'm afraid Carl isn't quite the baker Jenny is. When I went in yesterday morning, there wasn't a blessed thing to choose from in the case but sourdough biscuits."

Ben grinned. "At least I'm not the only one making a hash of his temporary job."

"At least Carl and Jenny and Cassie haven't blown anything up." Dad bent a wry look on him. He bowed his head and said the grace, then sopped some bread into his stew.

Ma took her seat across from Ben, leaned back to pluck an envelope off the sideboard, and handed it to him. "We heard from Marcus yesterday. He's well, finally done with his under-cover work for the moment."

"Made a big arrest. Caught the railroad clerk who was em-bezzling." Dad beamed, his chest puffing out. "Marcus is a born lawman. There isn't a puzzle he can't work out, and he's never been scared of anything. Got a commendation from Pinkerton himself."

Ben scanned the letter, reading the latest exploits of his oldest brother. As the youngest of three, Ben had always looked up to Marcus and Jonah. And all three boys had idolized their father, the bigger-than-life lawman they all aspired to be like.

"Any news from Jonah?"

"Not for a while. Last we heard he was heading into Indian Territory on the trail of a bank robber who knocked over some banks in Missouri. I wish Jonah'd quit the bounty hunting. He could get an appointment as a US Marshal in a blink." A frown crossed Dad's face, a worried look that often touched his expression when his middle son's name came up in conversation.

"You know Jonah. He likes being his own boss. And he's the best tracker I've ever seen next to you, Dad." He shoveled a spoonful of stew into his mouth, savoring Ma's good cooking. Much better than the fare he got at his boardinghouse, and certainly tastier than anything Jigger might pull together on the jailhouse stove.

"I taught him everything he knows. Him and you and Marcus."

"Wish you'd thrown some lessons in on how to wrangle kids. The twins are going to be the death of me."

"I heard you spent the morning putting the outhouse back together. How're you going to convince the town that you're doing the best job in the Challenge when all the evidence is pointing the other way? You're a good carpenter, but as a kid minder, things seem to be going begging."

He shrugged. "Guess I'll have to turn on the charm. I'll be lucky if they let me keep my badge after this thing is over. I still can't believe y'all made us swap with the girls. It's been a mistake from the start, and I have a bad feeling that something terrible's going to happen. You heard about Cassie getting knocked on her bustle by one of the Shoop brothers when they were brawling?"

"I heard she dumped a bucket of shaving water on the pair of them and sent them off with a flea in their ears. Smart girl." Dad shoved the last bite of bread into his mouth.

"The next time she might not be so lucky."

"Will you relax? Nothing's going to happen. Keeping law and order in Cactus Creek isn't exactly the same as being the sheriff in Dodge City. We cleaned out all the outlaws and rabble back in my day. A scuffle from the Shoop brothers is probably going to be the highlight of Cassie's 'lawman' career."

And with those words, Ben's father cut him right down to size. His father, the famous lawman, the fearless leader of posses, the legend in his own time, thought being the sheriff of Cactus Creek, Texas, tame enough that a woman could handle it.

Sometimes it stunk having a legend for a father.

CHAPTER 6

I ain't no waiter. Ben won't like you turning his jail into a teahouse." Jigger scowled and hitched his belt. "This is a turrible idea."

"Relax. After all the work I've put in on this place, getting it spruced up, I'm entitled to show it off a bit." Cassie turned the vase of flowers on the desk, then turned it back again. Excitement fluttered in her chest. "I don't imagine many of the town's women have been to the jail, and I need their votes. What better way to show them how I'm doing than to invite them to tea and let them see for themselves?"

Jigger harrumphed and clunked a chair down hard on her clean floor. Three small round tables, borrowed from the café, filled the office.

"You go get cleaned up, and don't forget to pick up the pastries from the bakery. I sent Carl a note yesterday that I wanted two dozen tea cakes. Then hotfoot it back here. The ladies will arrive in less than half an hour." Cassie polished the gun rack, rattling the chain looped through the trigger guards.

The old deputy grumbled and slammed the door on his way out.

She smiled. The door. Though it had cost her a few splinters and a banged thumb, she'd managed, with Jigger's help, to remove it from its hinges, plane the bottom, and rehang it so it no longer scraped on the floor. This improvement, however, was offset by Jigger's new tendency to slam the door whenever he disapproved of what Cassie was doing. . .which was pretty much every time he left the building.

She fussed around the room, straightening tablecloths and plumping the new pillows on the cots in the cells. Every few seconds she checked the clock, willing it to hurry.

Cassie was straightening the map of the Texas Panhandle when Jigger returned carrying a towel-covered basket on his arm. She turned and gasped.

"Don't you start in on me. I got enough from Carl over at the bakery."

He wore a white shirt so stiff with starch it practically crackled, and he'd parted his hair directly down the center and slicked it down like a schoolboy's. She'd never seen him so clean and presentable.

He dropped the basket on the desk. "And Carl didn't have your pastry thingamabobs. He just had sourdough biscuits."

"I can't serve sourdough biscuits to my guests." Cassie hurried to the desk to peek under the dish towel. Sure enough, two dozen or so perfectly round, perfectly browned biscuits filled the basket.

"No choice, unless you can whip up some cookies or something in the next couple of minutes."

She tried to ignore the satisfied smirk on his face at this hiccup in her plans. "Biscuits it will have to be then. Stoke the fire and get the kettle boiling. Our guests will be here any minute now."

Before she got the last biscuit on a serving plate, Mrs. Pym entered, her mouth pursed in a vinegar vat pucker. She leaned heavily on her cane.

"Good morning, Mrs. Pym. I'm so glad you could come."

"Don't know why you couldn't have tea at your mother's house like a civilized person. I've never been in jail before." Her piercing eyes pinned Jigger. "What are you doing dressed like a parson going courting? You look ridiculous."

Her deputy reddened and gulped, but before he could snap

back, Cassie intervened. "Mrs. Pym, you're not exactly 'in jail.' I just thought it might be nice to show some of the ladies in town the progress I've made this week. Tea is almost ready. Why don't I show you some of the improvements?" She put her hand under the older woman's elbow and led her toward the cells.

Her mother and sisters were the next through the door, and they took over amusing Mrs. Pym, which meant they listened to a laundry list of her aches and pains, as well as her opinion on everything from the spring weather to the price of calico to whether or not the church should invest in an organ.

For his part, Jigger stepped up and handled pouring tea and serving biscuits, though he grumbled and blushed and looked with longing at the door.

All twelve ladies, every one she'd invited, toured the jailhouse and admired how clean and bright it was. Cassie drank in their compliments. Everything was going so well, she released Jigger from his bondage to patrol the town.

Mrs. Wilder patted Cassie's arm. "You've worked wonders here, Cassie. The place was fairly grimy when Obadiah was sheriff, and it just got worse when Benjamin took over. And neither one would let me clean the place. They swore they'd never be able to find anything again if I tidied up, and they didn't want to make the place so nice that lawbreakers would want to stay. Benjamin declared that this was his kingdom, and he didn't want anyone interfering with the way he ran it. He's always been like that, not wanting anyone to touch his belongings. Even when he was a child he didn't want me or his brothers messing about in his room. How did he take it when he saw what you've done?"

Cassie twisted her fingers. She'd had no idea Ben had felt so strongly about anyone touching his possessions. All things considered, he'd handled things rather well. Before she could answer, the door opened, and Jigger came in dragging a reluctant man.

"What's going on?" Cassie skipped out of the way as Jigger dragged the man toward the cells.

"I'm arresting Wally Dunn." He had Wally by the collar and

gave him a little shake.

The ladies all looked on with interest. Cassie felt their eyes on her, and she set her shoulders, taking charge. "Why?"

She wanted to kick herself. She should've said "On what charge?" or something else that sounded official.

"He laughed at me and called me a strutting rooster, just because I combed my hair and put on a clean shirt." Jigger's jaw jutted, and he glared at poor Wally. "He's disrespecting the law, and I ain't gonna put up with it."

Several of the ladies put their hands over their lips, and Mrs. Pym tapped her cane on the floor. "You do look like a strutting rooster, Jigger Donohue, whether you're wearing a boiled shirt or not. If you start arresting everyone who thinks so, there won't be room enough in this jail."

Everyone froze. Then Jigger released Wally, who stumbled into the desk and upset the vase of flowers, spilling the blooms. The water gushed out and soaked the seat cushion on the chair. Jigger growled, loosened the string tie at his neck, and glared at Cassie.

"This is all your fault. The jail ain't no place for women, especially gabbity old crones and uppity little girls. I quit. I'll be back when the month is out and not a second before." This time when he slammed the door, the glass in the windows rattled.

For a moment, no one spoke. Wally picked himself up, bobbed his head to the ladies, and scooted for the door, leaving it open behind him. Cassie's mother sent a sympathetic look her way and began gathering her things. Mrs. Pym seemed oblivious to the effect of her words and popped the last of her biscuit into her mouth. Cassie's guests began scooting back their chairs. Unable to speak for mortification, Cassie could only nod as they filed past.

The clock chimed the half hour, and Ben stuck his head through the doorway, eyebrows raised.

"Jigger just said he was quitting and hustled down the street like he was late to a fire." He scanned the room full of ladies, then scowled right at Cassie. "What on earth have you done to my jail now?"

꧁⊙

A tea party? In his jail? Ben pinched the bridge of his nose against the headache that threatened to pound right out of his skull.

"Woman, don't you know that a man's office is sacred? It was bad enough that you had to sissify everything in here, but did you have to invite the women of the town in to gossip and guzzle tea?"

"They did not *guzzle*. What a vulgar word." Cassie jerked the vase upright and grabbed a tea towel to mop up the water.

He slammed his hat against his thigh. "You've set my jail on its tail, driven off your deputy, and you want to argue about my word choice? Look at this place." Café tables, flowers, teacups. A shudder rippled through him. "I'll never be able to look an outlaw in the face again."

"What are you talking about?" She continued to fuss with the flowers and the water. "Everything in here is temporary. As soon as the month is out, you can go back to working in a hovel."

Ben took hold of her arm and forced her to look at him. "You don't get it, do you? You might waltz out of here at the end of the month, but I'm the one who's trying to earn his reputation as a lawman, and none of this"—he waved toward the remains of her little soiree—"none of this helps me do it."

"Why are you so worried about your reputation? People in this town love you. They've known you practically all your life. You don't have to prove yourself. You've been groomed for this job since you were a kid."

Unable to stand the sight of so many feminine fripperies in his jail, Ben began stacking teacups and clearing the tables. The sooner they were out of here, the sooner he could start erasing this image from his mind. "Of course I have something to prove. Every day I have to prove that I'm not only worthy of wearing that badge, but that I'm a worthy successor to the man who wore it before me." He snatched up a fistful of teaspoons and threw them into the basket on the corner of his desk. "I not only have to prove it to the law-abiding citizens of Cactus Creek and every renegade who'd like to tear up the town, but I have to prove it to my father, too."

Cassie stilled. "Your father?"

"That's right. The legend himself, Obadiah Wilder. And according to him, since he cleared out all the real outlaws and roughnecks, it's quiet as a church supper." It stung just to say it. He'd probably carry the scar of his father's comments all his born days. The fact that he might be right only made it worse. "Even a girl can handle the job. How humiliating is that?"

That was when she hit him in the face with a sopping-wet tea towel and marched out.

✺

"Even a girl can handle the job?" Outrage flowed clear through Cassie's fingertips. She stomped along the sidewalk and headed for the creek to clear her head before she had to stand in front of the town and defend her work of the past week.

Even a girl can handle the job. Except she couldn't...or at least she hadn't handled it very well this week. She'd gotten knocked on her tush in front of the town, embarrassed by Ben, and walked out on by her sole employee. Not the best of weeks.

She ducked under the low-hanging branches of a gnarled cottonwood and sank to the ground, drawing her knees up and wrapping her arms around them. A soul-cleansing cry sounded good about now, but she couldn't give in to the urge. Some girls looked fragile and pretty when they cried, but not Cassie. Her face got red, her nose ran, and her eyes looked like she'd rubbed them with pepper flakes. She couldn't turn up in front of the town all blotchy and bedraggled. A rock poked her behind, and she reached beneath her, plucked it up, and flung it into the muddy water. Righteous anger would sustain her better than tears.

Why did Ben have to be so unreasonable? So blind? So focused on his precious career that he couldn't see what was right in front of his face? It was like he was obsessed.

Well, isn't that a little pot and kettle of you?

Of course it isn't. Ben and I are nothing alike in that respect. I'm not trying to slay any ghosts and prove myself.

Aren't you? Isn't that why you're so eager to win this competition, to prove to Ben and everyone else in town that you're a capable adult? To get Ben to notice that you're not a child anymore?

"Oh, be quiet." She squashed the irritating inner voice. "You have bigger fish to fry. You have to convince Jigger to come back to work." No way could she make her first report to the committee and the town and announce that her deputy refused to work with her any longer. She might as well just hand Ben the Challenge on a platter.

Cassie pushed herself up from the creek bank and dusted her hands. That niggling voice clamored for her attention, but she stuffed it down. "Enough wallowing, girl. Time to do something about your situation."

Saturday trading was in full swing on Main Street, with a group already clustered around Svenson's Mercantile. A glance at the watch pinned to her lapel told her she had just under half an hour before she would have to stand up and give an account of her first week as sheriff. She put her hands on her hips, surveying the buildings. Where was Jigger likely to be? He practically lived at the jail. Did he even keep a room at the hotel or the boardinghouse? Did he hang out at the café or the bakery?

The Amarillo House Hotel was the closest. She'd try there first. Nodding to Mrs. Pym, who shuffled by with a basket on her arm, Cassie entered the hotel lobby. P.J. leaned on his elbow behind the counter.

"Howdy, Miss Cassie." He smoothed down his cowlick. "Fine day, ain't it?"

She resisted the urge to correct his grammar and put on a pleasant smile. "Hello, P.J. It is a fine day. I'm looking for Jigger.

Have you seen him?" Better not to admit she didn't know where her deputy lived.

"Oh, sure. He came in awhile ago. Went straight up to his room. Face like a thundercloud, but wearing his best church meeting clothes."

"Which room?"

"Six, at the end of the hall, but—"

She was halfway up the stairs already, eager to get her groveling done. Her shoes sank into the new hallway runner, muffling her footsteps. The door to number six stood open on the left, overlooking the alley behind the hotel. Men's voices, low and rumbly came from inside the room. She stopped.

"Nope, not if you offered to make me the Prince of Persia in the bargain. I've had it. Bad enough I have to take orders from a girl who has no more notion about being a lawman than I have about knitting petticoat lace, but to be ridiculed by the likes of Wally Dunn and Mrs. Pym? No, sir."

"C'mon, Jigger, she needs you."

Cassie put her fingers over her lips to stifle a gasp.

Ben. . .in the room.

"She don't need me to serve tea. Do you know she made me climb on a chair and sweep down cobwebs? Me. A seasoned lawman. I ain't no chambermaid. And I ain't toting no more buckets or sweeping. She even told me I couldn't sleep on her new straw ticks until I took a bath." Indignation rang in his voice. "I told her you didn't like anyone messing with your stuff, but she didn't listen, just went ahead and scrubbed the place down and emptied the desk and threw out my favorite old serape."

"You know she means well. I'll admit, she shouldn't have made you dress up and serve tea."

"No, she shouldn't have. How do you think the punchers down at the Royal will treat me if they know I was playing butler to a bunch of busybody biddies? It's embarrassing. This whole Challenge has been one disaster after another, and we're not hardly through the first week."

Cassie grimaced.

"C'mon. It hasn't been that bad."

"Before this week, had you ever been knocked down in the street by one of the Shoop brothers? Or served tea in the jail? Or had an outhouse blown up? Or been caught standing on the street in an apron? I don't even know what's happening down at the livery, but I imagine it hasn't been all roses and sunshine."

"That might be true, but doesn't that just prove what I'm saying? Cassie needs you. I need you, Jigger. It's our duty as lawmen to protect our citizens, especially women."

A little warm fuzzy spot opened in Cassie's heart. Ben was a protector by nature, and he was determined to look after her. As much as that infuriated her from time to time, she couldn't help feeling cherished.

Ben went on, "Someone's gotta be there to protect Cassie from her own stubbornness. She's so focused on proving to everyone that she can do my job better than I can that she's apt to leap first and say oops later. She's always been just like a headstrong filly that way."

The warm fuzzy spot died under a cold dousing of reality. She ground her back teeth and raised her hands, rigid with frustration. Why did he always have to go that one little bit further and ruin everything?

"I guess you're right," Jigger said.

"Then you'll come back?"

"For you, but I ain't taking any of her sass no more. You tell her that, will you?"

"You can tell her yourself. She's standing out in the hallway."

Cassie jerked.

"Come on in, Cass. Jigger has something to say."

Feeling like a child called on the carpet, she eased around the door frame. How did she get herself into these predicaments? Best to bluster through it and not give Ben the satisfaction of gloating.

"Jigger, I've come to apologize for today. You were right, I shouldn't have forced you into the role of waiter. I am sincerely sorry, and I am asking you to reconsider and come back to work for me." She laced her fingers and straightened her arms, locking her elbows and holding her hands low.

Jigger, his hair now in its familiar tangle, scratched his armpit. "No more cleaning?"

"Not unless I do it myself."

"No more tea parties?"

"Not in the jail."

"What about my serape?"

She rolled her eyes. "Jigger, that thing smelled like an old horse blanket."

His chin went up, and she noticed several nicks from where he'd cut himself shaving. He had tried for her. The poor man. She had hounded him and bossed him around and turned his world upside down.

"I'm sorry. I didn't throw the serape out. I just took it home to wash it. I'll bring it back as soon as I can." Which would be after a couple more washes. It really was indescribable.

He pursed his lips and squinted at her out of the corner of his eye. He was going to make her work for it.

She nearly choked on the helping of humble pie being served up to her. Ben had his index finger across his lips, but she knew he was laughing. The wretch. He'd get his comeuppance, and she only prayed she'd be there to see it.

"Please, Jigger. I can't win the Challenge without your help."

Cassie held her breath.

"Fine. I'll come back."

Whew.

CHAPTER 7

T he next morning, Cassie felt more herself. She'd left the gun and badge off and dressed in her best gown, a pale yellow-sprigged cotton that brought out the highlights in her red hair. The tiny green flowers scattered across the fabric and the green bow at her throat matched her eyes, and for the first time in a week, she dabbed a little bit of rose-scented perfume on her wrists and behind her ears.

A hint of shadow hung just under her eyes, testament to the wakeful night just past. The jailhouse tea had been a disaster, and the memory left her feeling small. In the dark of night, she just knew for certain Ben would never see her as an adult woman. He would fall in love and marry someone else, and she would live her life in spinsterhood, cherishing her unrequited love.

In the light of day, she told herself to stop being so dramatic.

As she walked to church with her family, Cassie half-listened to her sister's chatter while she tried to come to grips with her roiling emotions.

"The Challenge is distracting everyone from my wedding. You haven't even been into the dress shop for your final fitting, Cass." Millie clasped her Bible to her middle and nudged Cassie. "If you have to walk down the aisle in a dress with the basting stitches showing, it's your own fault."

"I forgot. I'll get there tomorrow, I promise." Perhaps she could go during her lunch hour. Jigger could watch the jail now that he was back on the payroll.

"And if we have to have sourdough biscuits instead of wedding cake, dear Father, I'm never going to let you forget it." She threaded her hand through Father's elbow and gave a happy little skip. "I can't believe the wedding's only a few weeks away."

Cassie had to force down the rush of envy she felt at her sister's happiness. Once Millie married, Cassie would be alone at home, the only single Bucknell girl, and nobody's sweetheart.

They filed into church and sat in their usual place, two rows behind the Wilder family, where Cassie could stare at the back of Ben's head without anyone noticing. Jenny and Amanda slipped into the other end of the pew and sat with Cassie. Amanda smiled up shyly as always and squeezed Cassie's hand.

"Good morning, sweetie. You look so nice," Cassie leaned down to whisper.

"So do you, Teacher," Amanda whispered back.

After the preaching, Cassie felt as small as a worm. The entire sermon had been on the Golden Rule and loving one's neighbor. The more the pastor spoke, the worse she felt. The delight she'd taken at Ben's struggles at the school ate at her like hungry wolves.

As soon as church dismissed, she found her most reliable student and enlisted her aid. "Mary Alice, help me round up the kids. I want to talk to them. But keep it quiet. Have them meet me behind the church."

In a few moments, her students began to assemble. "Quick, now. Gather 'round." She drew them to her like a mother hen, so hungry to see their faces.

"I've missed you all so much." She hugged a couple of the girls. "But"—she looked askance at the boys—"I'm hearing some things I'm not too pleased about."

The twins looked up at her with angelic expressions, as if they had no idea what she was talking about, but Thomas and Isaac and Mike and the others reddened and shifted their weight, not wanting to meet her eyes.

"I have a suspicion that you were having some fun baiting a

THE CACTUS CREEK CHALLENGE

new teacher, but that's got to stop. It isn't nice, nor is it fair to Mr. Wilder."

Thomas raised his hand, just as if they were in school. "But, Miss Bucknell, we just wanted to help you win the Challenge."

Her heart warmed, and she wanted to hug his thin shoulders. What great kids.

"That's very sweet of you, Thomas, but it isn't right. You have to behave for Mr. Wilder just as you would for me. No more birds in the desk drawers and"—she gave the twins her best stern "you'd better behave or else" teacher stare—"no more explosions. Got it?"

They sighed and nodded. "Yes, ma'am."

"I tell you what. If you all do your best, learn your lessons, and do exactly as Mr. Wilder tells you for the rest of this month, I'll take you for a picnic along Cactus Creek on a school day. We'll play games and fish and loaf around for a whole day with no lessons. Agreed?"

Sunbeam smiles all around.

"But you can't tell him I talked to you. It will be our secret."

Hunched shoulders and happy, covert grins.

"All right, you can go. And I want to hear good reports back from all of you." She touched Mary Alice's arm to hold her back, waiting until the rest of the class had scampered off.

"Mary Alice, I have a special task for you. I'd like you to watch out for Mr. Wilder especially and report back to me whenever you can. Just come right down to the jail if you would. Will you do that for me?"

"Of course, Miss Bucknell. I'll help Mr. Wilder all I can."

"I confess, I'm a bit worried, what with your exams coming up so soon. When you come to report to the jail, I'll give you some extra tutoring, just to make sure you don't fall behind, all right?"

"That would be nice. Mr. Wilder is hopeless at grammar." She blushed. "But he's awfully nice. And the boys have been dreadfully naughty since you've been gone."

"Thank you, Mary Alice, and thanks for taking care of Amanda, too. The month will go by quickly, and we can get back to normal, though there won't be much left to the school year by the time the Challenge ends."

Mary Alice left with her mission clear, and Cassie leaned against the side of the church. Had she done the right thing? Would she regret it if she lost the Challenge after stepping in to help Ben manage the class?

"You look as sober as I feel." Jenny Hart drew her attention. She flicked her fan, stirring her golden curls.

"It's been a long week."

"You're telling me. I guess I can cross 'get bitten by a horse' off my life goals list, along with 'get blisters on my blisters.' I've never ached so much in my entire life."

"And I can cross 'scrub out a jail cell' off mine along with 'get knocked on my backside in a street fight.'"

They looked at one another and laughed.

"We are a pair, aren't we? I've just been bribing my class to behave themselves for another three weeks, and I enlisted one of my own students as a spy. If I didn't know better, I'd say I just threw the competition into my opponent's favor."

Jenny raised her eyebrows. "And how is it going with Ben? Is he still treating you like a child?"

"Like his favorite little sister." Cassie pulled a face. "I swear, I could stroll by that man belting out the national anthem and juggling butcher knives in my bathrobe, and he wouldn't notice me other than to pat me on the head and tell me to run along."

"I'd like to see you juggle." Jenny stuck out her tongue. "At least you haven't been yelled at by a viking, made to feel like a slob due to the state of your kitchen, and had your daughter scared half out of her skin by a giant tossing louts out of your store."

"Carl yelled at you? And he scared Amanda?" Cassie's hackles rose. "Where is he?"

"Now, don't rush off to scold the poor man. In his defense, he only yelled when he found out I'd been bitten by a horse he'd told me to stay away from. And he did treat the wound for me, though he grumbled the whole time. But when he hollered, Amanda lit out like a mouse with a hawk on her tail. I actually felt bad for him. He's been trying so hard to break through her shell, and it was working, too. But I fear he undid all his work in one instant."

"Mary Alice says having Ben at the school has set Amanda back some, too. She still hasn't said a word to him." Cassie's heart ached for the little girl and for Jenny. "I can't even imagine what you've gone through that Amanda is still so traumatized."

Jenny's eyes grew bright, but she blinked hard. "It's been a trial, but we're getting better every day. A little at a time the sunshine is coming back into my life. I feel so much freer and happier here in Cactus Creek. It's terrible to say it, but the day Robert died, I drew my first easy breath in eight years."

"I was thinking just yesterday that you and Carl might make an interesting couple." Cassie tested the water.

"Oh, no. I've no desire to travel that road once more. I refuse to ever allow any man to dominate me again, and I would never put Amanda through the agony of having to live with another man." The certainty in her voice, the jaded edge, made Cassie's heart break. And yet might not all her protesting mean she was fighting the notion herself?

"But all men aren't cut from the same cloth. Carl's a good man, and you know he would never hurt Amanda."

"He might not mean to, but what if he did without intending it, like he scared her with his yelling? She's so fragile, if he ever even indicated he was displeased by something she did, it would shatter her."

Cassie had to wonder if Jenny was really talking about Amanda or projecting her own feelings on her daughter in order to keep both of them emotionally safe.

"You'll be at dinner tonight?"

"Yes, we're looking forward to it. It sounds like your mother has invited half the town."

"That's Mother."

She'd invited the Wilders—parents and son—too. Cassie didn't know if she was excited to see Ben again or dreading it.

~~✺~~

Ben took off his hat and brushed the dust from his pants as he followed his folks up the steps of the Bucknell house. The place was still so new he could smell the fresh paint and wallpaper paste. Doc Bucknell had the nicest place in town. Their first house, right on Main Street, had been smaller, darker, and mostly adobe. The new house had porches and gables and enough gingerbread trim to make any woman happy.

"Come around to the back under the trees. The party got too big for the dining room." Doc Bucknell waved them around.

Trestle tables had been set up under the trees that grew along the bank of Cactus Creek. The creek itself was up, fed by spring rains. It didn't exactly bubble and gurgle, but there were a few ripples and eddies in the muddy brown surface that wouldn't exist in a month or so when the water level went down.

Plenty of folks were already gathered. Carl leaned against a tree talking to Doc Bucknell's son-in-law, Donald Penn, and his soon-to-be-son-in-law, Ralph Campion. The oldest Bucknell daughter, Louise, sat in a chair in the late-evening shade, her hand resting on her swollen middle. Donald Penn had swaggered around town like he was the first man ever to announce he had a child on the way. Ben shook his head. Though Donald didn't smoke, he'd handed out cigars to every man he met.

Sauntering over, Ben took note of the other dinner guests. Jenny Hart stood next to Louise, Amanda tucked into the circle of her arm. He winked at the little girl and gave a low, two-fingered wave. She rewarded him with a slight smile and a flutter of her hand.

The screen door slapped, and Cassie emerged holding a

platter. Before he realized what he was doing, he'd mounted the back porch steps and taken the heavy plate from her hands. "Where do you want this?"

Her cheeks were flushed, probably from the heat of the kitchen, and her eyes sparkled green in the lowering sun.

"Anywhere on the table will be fine."

He found himself seated beside her at dinner. She had on the yellow dress she'd worn to church, and her sleeves fell back from her hands, showing her delicate wrists. The bones were so fine, he couldn't help but compare them to his own brawny arms.

Donald leaned toward him across the table. "So, Ben, are you in any danger of winning the prize money, or will Cassie carry it off?"

"Depends on how folks feel about explosions." He grinned. His strategy from the moment he'd scraped himself up off the schoolyard had been to meet every taunt with a smile and a joke, to downplay the incident as much as possible. "At least the school got a new privy out of the deal."

Down at the end of the table, Dick Grabel, the owner and sole reporter for the *Cactus Creek Chronicle*, flipped open his notebook and scribbled a few lines. "I'd love to do an article on each of the Challenge contestants this year. I've done some preliminary interviews with Deputy Donohue and a couple of the students at the school. Tomorrow I'm interviewing Brady Hawkins from out at the Clover Leaf. I understand he and his men had some dealings with Mrs. Hart at the livery. And if they're sober, I'll try to get something from Melvin and Alvin Shoop." His smile was part inquisitive, part predatory, and a ripple of unease traced its way up Ben's neck.

Dick was known for writing some rather sharp-toned articles that left a bit of a sting and caused plenty of discussion over the checkerboard at the mercantile. His take on the happenings of the Challenge would have a strong effect on the voting public, and not just for the Challenge but for the next sheriff's election as well. For the rest of the meal, Ben kept his attention away from the reporter, hoping he'd forget about the interview.

The meal was excellent. . .until it came time for dessert.

Carl, red in the face, rose, went into the kitchen, and returned with a large platter holding a tiered cake. "I've been practicing for this wedding coming up, and I'd like your opinion."

The cake was a bit lopsided, and the frosting sagged a bit, but Carl's smile broadened when he cut into it. "This is my best one yet."

Carl handed the pieces around, and Ben took his, admiring the ruby jelly between the layers. He sank his fork into the sponge, but before he could taste it, Millie gave a squeak and dropped her fork. Jenny's eyes widened as her lips closed around her first bite, and she slowly drew the fork from her mouth.

Cassie raised her cake plate to her nose and sniffed, then set the plate down and pushed it away.

"What?" Carl's knife stilled.

Jenny forced her bite down, then reached for her water glass, gulping the contents. She blinked, coughed, and swallowed hard.

The big liveryman's shoulders drooped. "It's not good, is it? I knew it." He left the knife sticking in the cake and sagged into his chair.

"What. . ." Jenny's voice rasped and she cleared her throat. "What flavoring did you use?"

"Vanilla." His eyebrows bunched.

"How much vanilla?"

"Just the one bottle."

Mrs. Bucknell giggled first, then her laughter rippled down the table until all the women were engulfed.

"A whole bottle?" Cassie chortled.

"Too much?"

"By about a bottle or so." Jenny shrugged. "A cake this size would take about a teaspoon and a half, maybe."

Dick Grable scribbled furiously in his notebook, and Millie cast uncertain and blaming glances at her father.

Jenny removed Amanda's slice of cake before she could taste

it and sent a sympathetic smile Carl's way. "An honest mistake. I'm sure the next cake will be flawless."

Mrs. Bucknell rose and began clearing plates. "Ben, I wonder if you'd do me a favor."

"Yes, ma'am. What can I do?" He pushed his dessert toward the center of the table.

"I was planning on sending Cassie over to Mrs. Pym's," Mrs. Bucknell said, "with some of these leftovers. Her back hasn't been feeling too well, and it might be nice if she didn't have to cook for a couple of days. Ben, if I pack up a basket, would you carry it over and see Cassie home?"

"Sure thing." He stood and pulled Cassie's chair away from the table as she rose. Jenny's eyes sparkled, and she winked at Cassie, leaving Ben puzzled. What had he missed? His mother had a cat-who-ate-the-canary look about her, too, and wasn't meeting Ben's eyes. Those kinds of signals among women usually didn't bode well for a fellow, but for the life of him he couldn't imagine what they were hatching.

He found himself walking up a side street, a basket hooked over his arm and Cassie by his side.

"Louise is looking well." Cassie plucked a long stem of grass from the edge of the path and feathered the seedy top through her fingers as they walked. "Donald wants her to move into town next week so she'll be close to medical help when the baby comes. But she says it will be awkward having her dad as her doctor, and she won't have him in the room unless something goes wrong. Louise says Mama can deliver a baby as well as Daddy can anyway. I imagine in the end, she'll come to town, and Mama will deliver the baby, and Daddy and Donald will pace the hallway until it's all over."

"Donald's about busting his buttons now. I can't imagine what he'll be like when he actually has a baby to hold."

"Between the wedding coming up and the baby, it's hard to get in a word on any other topic in our house right now. But Millie's very serene about all the wedding plans. She says as long as she is married to Ralph at the end of the day, the rest of it doesn't really matter. Daddy says he wishes she'd have mentioned that before he started paying for wedding gowns and flowers and her hope chest and whatnot." She smiled and tossed the grass blade aside, raising her face to the cool evening breeze. She paused and turned to the west where the sun had set, but pink and purple and blue and golden splashes still decorated the horizon, painting her face in the beautiful tones of sunset.

A whiff of roses drifted toward him. "The twins told me they think you smell pretty."

What on earth had made him say that? He wanted to squirm.

She flicked him a glance from under her lashes. "They talk about me?"

"They said you were the only teacher who could tell them apart, and that they like you because you don't stay mad at them even when they're naughty. They said you dress real pretty, too."

She smiled fondly. "At least someone appreciates me. I love those little terrors. Did they ask you about becoming sheriffs? It's their dearest wish. Or at least it was last week."

He laughed. "They told me they hadn't decided yet whether to be sheriffs or outlaws. Since they were so good at being bad, they might just head out on the outlaw trail. Heaven help us if they do. The country will never be the same."

They arrived at the Pym abode, and Ben opened the rickety front gate. Cassie's skirts swished, and the smell of roses wrapped around him again. The twins were right, she did smell good. And dress pretty. And though she had a quick temper, she sure didn't stay mad for long.

"What are you two up to this fine evening?" Mrs. Pym greeted them from a rocker on her front porch. "You sparkin'?"

Cassie gasped, and Ben rolled his eyes at the old lady.

"Now, don't be like that, Mrs. Pym. You'll embarrass Cassie. We brought you some food from Mrs. Bucknell. She thought you could use a little help, what with your back bothering you and all." What a silly notion, him sparkin' Cassie Bucknell. That would be like kissing his sister. Not that he had a sister, but if he did, she'd be just like Cassie Bucknell.

"And well I could use the help. My back's been achin' something awful, and it's a sure sign something terrible is going to happen. Last time it hurt this bad, the weather brewed up a tornado. You remember that?"

Cassie slipped inside with the basket and returned quickly.

Before the old lady could trap them into a discussion of her aches and pains and their prophesying abilities, Ben tipped his hat. "I'd best be getting Cassie home, Mrs. Pym. She's got a big week ahead of her, and so do I." He took Cassie by the elbow and all but propelled her down the walkway. "Good night, ma'am. Hope you enjoy the food." He hustled Cassie through the gate and away from the house.

"Sorry about that," he said as soon as he was out of earshot.

"Don't be. You saved us from a lengthy and tedious discussion." She let out a little laugh that made his chest suddenly feel lighter. She looped the empty basket handle over her arm and raised her hands to her forehead, smoothing her red hair, now a deep auburn in the dusk.

"No, I mean the part about her asking if we were sparkin'. I hope she didn't embarrass you."

"Why would that embarrass me?" She turned a direct gaze upon him. Faint starlight glittered in her eyes, and several of her freckles stood out against her pale skin. Her lips were parted slightly, and bless him if he didn't smell her rose perfume again. He wished the twins had never mentioned it. Surely that was the only reason he was noticing at all.

"I don't know. I guess because we aren't courting. Because it's such a silly idea."

She blinked and a little line formed between her brows. "A silly idea." She swallowed, and the lace collar at her throat bobbed. "You think it is a silly idea for someone to court me?"

He backed up a step. "No, of course not, not in a couple of years when you're old enough. I'm sure your daddy will be guarding the gate then."

Her hands went to her hips. "In a couple of years? Do you even know how old I am?"

He did a mental gallop. "I went to your last birthday party. You turned sixteen." There. Pride that he'd remembered broadened his grin.

"You went to the last birthday party I had here in Cactus Creek. I'll have you know I've had three birthdays since then, all of them in Philadelphia while I was at school, and I'm coming up on another one in a couple of months. I'm almost twenty years old, and that's more than old enough to be courted right now."

Almost twenty? The notion slammed through his brain. Impossible. Why, he was twenty-four, and little Cassie Bucknell had been a full four grades behind him in school. . .uh-oh.

He rubbed his palms against his thighs. "I guess the time got a little away from me. The fellows around here must be slacking then if nobody's come courtin' yet. When they do, you let me know, and I'll check 'em out for you. After all, you're like a little sister to me, and I want to make sure whoever marries you is up to snuff."

The *thwack* of the basket hitting the side of his head stunned him.

"Ben Wilder, you're an idiot." Cassie picked up her skirts and marched away from him toward her house, leaving him standing in the road looking after her, and by sugar if he didn't spy the glisten of tears in her eyes before she turned away.

He rubbed his temple. "Now what did I say?"

Jenny thanked her hosts and turned to find Amanda so they could head home. The dinner had been pleasant—except for the cake—though she was weary of parrying questions from Dick Grabel for his newspaper.

"She's over here." Carl's voice rumbled softly.

Amanda lay curled up in the corner of the porch swing, her head pillowed on her arms, eyes closed.

"Poor thing is tuckered out." He leaned against a post and crossed his arms.

Jenny studied her little girl. "Or playing 'possum." She ran her finger down Amanda's cheek and under her chin, eliciting a giggle and a squirm.

"Time to go, punkin. You have school in the morning."

Amanda pushed herself up, yawning and setting the swing wobbling with her movement.

"How about if I carry you? It's a long way on tired legs." Carl straightened and held out his hands.

Jenny held her breath, pressing her lips together. It had to be Amanda's decision, but she hoped the little girl wouldn't hurt Carl by refusing.

Amanda studied him, so serious, too serious for such a little girl. Finally, she nodded and let her legs swing over the side.

Gently, as if aware of the gift he'd been awarded, Carl lifted Amanda and perched her on one strong forearm. He offered the other to Jenny. "It would be my pleasure to see you both home."

With the same sense of foreboding, Jenny hesitated before taking his arm. Cassie's teasing about them making a nice couple flitted through her mind, but she knew she'd never retrace that path, no matter who the gentleman was. And besides, she was getting well ahead of herself. Carl Gustafson had never given any indication that he had or ever would have any feelings for her.

Still, his muscles under her palm reminded her of the powerful draft horses she curried every day. Strength to burn and practically oblivious to it because they didn't know any different. How often had she wished she were bigger, stronger—strong enough to protect herself from her husband, to protect Amanda? And her husband had been a slight, nasty man, not a giant like Carl.

A cool breeze kicked up, and she shivered. "I forgot my shawl at the stable. It's hanging on a peg in the tack room."

"We can swing by there and get it. I want to check on that mare before I turn in anyway." He glanced down at Amanda. "You remember that pony I told you about?"

A bob of the head.

"She was looking kinda broody when I saw her this afternoon. Might be ready to drop that foal anytime now."

Amanda whispered something Jenny didn't catch.

Carl smiled. "Copper it is, then. That's a fine name for her."

Jenny gaped. Not only was Amanda allowing Carl to carry her home, but she'd actually spoken to him.

He eased Amanda to the ground when they reached the livery, digging in his pocket for his keys and opening the padlock. With a lot less effort than it took Jenny, he rolled aside the huge doors.

The familiar smells of horse and hay and dust wrapped around her. It was startling how much she felt at home here after only a week. Carl lit a lantern, and Jenny took Amanda's hand and bent to speak to her.

"You need to stay by me. No running or jumping or making noise, all right? The horses are all tucked into bed, and we don't want to startle them."

Carl unlocked the tack room and held the lantern high so she could retrieve her shawl; then he helped her settle it around her shoulders.

"Let's check on Copper then." Without waiting for permission, he wrapped his arm around Amanda's waist and lifted her up so she could see over the half door into the pony's stall. "Here, put your toes on this slat." He positioned her so she could perch on the gate, her arms resting along the top spar, and stood at her back so she couldn't slip off.

Jenny joined them. The shaggy pony came to Amanda and nosed her, whiffling her breath along the girl's arm. Amanda giggled and reached out to straighten the flyaway forelock.

"Round as a tick, ain't she?" Carl scratched the mare's ears.

Copper stamped her hind foot and swung her head around toward her side. Her flanks tightened in the lantern light, and she stretched her neck. Then she relaxed and nosed Amanda again.

"Aha. Looks like I was right. She's showing signs of foaling tonight." Carl set Amanda down and opened the stall door. Hanging the lantern high on a hook, he ran his hand along the pony's mane and down her neck and side.

"Perhaps we should go then." Jenny took Amanda's hand, but her daughter shook her head.

"Can't we stay? I want to see the baby."

"Oh, honey, we can see the baby tomorrow. We don't want to be in the way here. Mamas like privacy when they're having babies."

Carl caught Jenny's eye. "Wouldn't hurt none if you stayed. In fact, I think it would be a good thing. Miss Amanda has already said she'll help me with the baby, and if she's going to be in charge of it, she might as well see it born." Carl eyed the mare. "It won't be long, if I'm any judge, before the baby gets here."

He came out of the stall and closed the gate, leaving the lantern behind. "Mares usually make a pretty fair job of foaling without too much interference, so we'll just wait here and watch. I didn't ask the man I got her from if this was her first foal, so we'll stand ready to help, but Copper will take care of most of it on her own." He lifted Amanda back up where she could see, bending to put his head on a level with hers.

To Jenny's surprise, he reached out and put his hand on the small of her back, drawing her alongside Amanda. "It's a beautiful thing, watching the birth of a new life." He stood behind them, close enough she could feel the heat from his skin.

Copper lowered herself to the straw, then got up and paced. Every now and again, she stood spraddle-legged, her neck stretched out, and her sides pumping like bellows.

"Why does she do that?" Amanda looked over her shoulder at Carl.

He slid a glance at Jenny, who nodded that she would explain. "Having a baby is hard work. Her muscles are pushing to get the baby out."

In an hour, it was over. Carl wrapped Amanda in a canvas apron to protect her dress and opened the stall door to lead her inside. On the straw, a dark brown, slick-haired, long-legged foal lay, eyes unfocused and sides rising and falling in jerky little breaths.

"Let me see how Mama reacts before you get too close, all right? Some mamas are very protective of their babies." He stood between Amanda and the foal as Copper scrambled to her feet. The cord joining the baby to its mother broke, separating them.

Jenny's eyes burned with the beauty of it all as Copper nudged the foal, licking it and whickering in a way Jenny would have sworn was pride at her accomplishment. The mare let Carl touch the foal, his big hand cupping the top of the baby's head. With a quick swipe, he made sure the foal's mouth was clear of any mucus; then he squatted and held out his hand to Amanda.

"Come here, darlin'. Sit right here." He patted the straw, and when Amanda sat down and crossed her legs under the canvas apron, he lifted the foal and draped the baby across her lap. "My dad used to do this with all his horses. He said if you knew you were going to raise and train a horse from birth, you should hold it and touch it and kinda put your mark all over it as soon as it's born. He said if you do that, then a special bond forms between you and the horse that can never be broken."

Amanda's eyes glowed, and her cheeks flushed as she cradled the baby in her thin arms. "Am I going to raise and train this baby?"

"You sure are. There's no way I can do it. I'm too busy, and even if I wasn't, I'm too big to ride a pony. I'm thinking you should have Copper and this little one, too, for your very own. You're just the right size, and you've got the time and the gentle ways this pair needs. You two go on and take a little time to get acquainted." He pushed himself up and came out of the stall.

The mare continued to nose and lick the foal in Amanda's lap, including Amanda in her nuzzling and drawing giggles.

Jenny drew Carl farther into the aisle. "Mr. Gustafson, I wish you would've conferred with me before gifting Amanda with two horses." She knotted her fingers at her waist.

"What?"

"We have no place to keep animals, and we cannot afford to rent space or buy food or equipment." She kept her voice low, but his high-handed manner in just announcing that Amanda could have the horses scraped her unhealed wounds. "Now I'm going to have to be the one to tell her she can't have them."

Carl rubbed the back of his neck under his long hair and shrugged. "It won't be a problem. Just keep them here."

"I told you, I can't afford that. The bakery is adequate for our needs at the moment, but I don't have enough left over to cover the expense of livestock."

"You don't have to spend money. I'll keep them here for nothing. They don't eat that much. You're overreacting. Look at her. This is the most relaxed I've seen that little girl since you came to town. Most of the time she's walking on eggshells so thin it's like she's afraid to breathe. She's laughing and talking and enjoying herself now. Don't be so stern with her. You keep such a tight hold, she hardly has room to be a kid. All kids need something little and newborn to love. Don't take that away from her."

Jenny's temper went from warm to white-hot in an instant. How dare he assume that Amanda was withdrawn because she was a harsh mother? The man had no idea how hard she'd worked to help Amanda overcome her fears, to get past the cruel treatment they'd suffered. And how dare he make an offer without consulting her first, as if she had no say in the matter?

"We will not be beholden to you for the care of a horse. And in the future, don't make such sweeping offers without checking with me first." She refused to be under any man's thumb ever again, and if anyone was going to make decisions regarding her daughter, it was her.

"You'd rather disappoint your daughter than take anything from me? Why? What did I do? You've been cagey and defensive around me since the day we met."

"And with good reason. You've bossed and criticized and taken over where you have no business. You don't think I have enough brains to run your livery stable, you've yelled and stormed at me, and now you're trying to buy my daughter's affection." Even as she hurled the awful accusations at him, she knew she was being unreasonable, but it all reeked of Robert. How often had he tried to wheedle his way back into their affections by bringing gifts and promising never again to hit them or yell at them? She couldn't run the risk of letting Carl get close to Amanda and then pull away. She couldn't accept the gift without running the risk that Amanda could get hurt.

Carl backed away, his hands up. "Lady, you've got me all wrong, but I'm not going to try to change your mind. I don't buy people's affection. I was just trying to be nice. Maybe you should examine your own self before you accuse others. My offer to Amanda still stands. She's welcome here anytime."

Jenny thrust aside the guilt her conscience tried to throw on her and turned away from him. "Amanda, we need to go. It is well past your bedtime, and you have school tomorrow. Thank Mr. Gustafson and come with me."

She knew she had come across as hard and unfeeling, but a mother had to do whatever it took to protect her child. The world outside the front door was full of danger. There was absolutely no sense in inviting it inside.

CHAPTER 8

Ben stacked primers and readers and spelling books and history tomes, then rounded the front of the desk and perched his hip on the edge. He crossed his arms and surveyed the classroom. The twins sat with their chins propped in their hands, elbows on their desks, waiting. Mary Alice twirled a stray curl around her finger and studied him from under her lashes. And Amanda gently swung her feet, her slate on her lap.

"I want you to put all your books and slates away. Today we're going to do things different."

This met with straightened backs and curious glances. Papers and books shuffled, and pencils dropped into their trays.

"I had a talk with some of you about what you would like to learn, stuff that would be practical and interesting. Some of you have indicated that you might be interested in learning about being a lawman, so I thought I'd teach you a few things that might come in handy. Even if you don't ever wear a badge, you should know how to take care of yourself out here on the plains."

Mary Alice's hand went up slowly in the back. "Mr. Wilder, is this just for the boys? What about us girls? Other than the Cactus Creek Challenge, I've never heard of a girl sheriff."

"You girls are going to learn right alongside the boys. There's plenty of stuff you should know that you won't learn from books."

"What about Miss Bucknell's lessons?"

"Miss Bucknell can teach Miss Bucknell's lessons, and Mr. Wilder will teach Mr. Wilder's lessons, all right?"

Though she said no more, Mary Alice continued to look doubtful. But the rest of the children, even Amanda, looked interested and eager, something he hadn't seen on their faces at all last week.

"Today's lesson is going to be on observation and surveillance. One of the things a lawman has to understand is how to spot the thing that is out of place or the person who is acting out of the ordinary. I try to observe everyone I meet, to read them, so that if their actions change, I can spot it. I make mental notes about folks so I know if something's wrong. I can stave off a lot of trouble by catching it early."

Isaac raised his hand.

"I know y'all are used to raising your hand and waiting to be called on, and that's all right for regular school, but I want you to feel free here to ask your questions whenever you think of them. Just remember not to be rude and talk when someone else is talking, and things will go fine. Go ahead, Isaac."

"Did you observe us? Did you make mental notes about us?"

"Sure."

"Like what?"

Ben rubbed his chin, pleasantly surprised with how things had gone so far. Every eye was on him, everyone listening.

"Well, I noted right off that you must've shot up over the winter. Your ma has let out your pant legs a couple of times." He grinned when Isaac stuck his leg out to reveal the newly turned down cuffs on his school pants.

"I also noticed that Sarah and Elizabeth trade lunches almost every day and that Thomas can't work on his math problems unless he has a sharp pencil. Bekah chews on the end of her braid when she's thinking really hard, and Pierce is the fastest runner in school."

"We noticed stuff about you, too." Ulysses crossed his legs up on the seat.

"You did? Like what?"

"You write with your left hand, and you always chew on

toothpicks that have been dipped in peppermint oil."

"Very good. What else?"

"You're not very good at grammar, but you're pretty good at Texas history," Chris volunteered.

"I'll give you that. Grammar was my worst subject in school."

"You can hammer real good. You must've built stuff before." Quincy tugged at his earlobe.

"That's true. All those corrals out at my folks' place? Courtesy of yours truly. Let's talk about some of the things a lawman looks for, then I'm going to give you an assignment." He scooted back until he was sitting on the desk. "A lawman is always on the lookout. For people hanging around where they shouldn't or doing something out of the ordinary. For example, if a group of men rode into town, men I didn't know, and they took up positions across from the new bank when they finish building it, watching who came in and who went out, I'd be mighty suspicious and I'd keep an eye on them. Or if a fellow I knew was always hard up for cash suddenly showed up at one of the saloons and bought a round for the house, I'd be wondering where that money came from."

"Or if your ma brought home a package," Pierce said, "and she hid it in the bottom drawer of her bureau, and it was near your birthday, you might surmise she had your present already?" He grinned.

"You might draw that conclusion. So how do you go about surveillance without someone knowing what you're doing?" He moved to the blackboard. "Let's draw—" He almost said the saloon, but changed it to something a little more kid-friendly. "Let's draw the mercantile." He made a few quick lines. "Here's the front door, and here's the counter where the candy is. We'll put in the stove, the back door, the hardware counter, and the dry goods areas. Now, if you were going to set up surveillance, where would you want to be?"

"I'd stay by the candy."

"Why, Ulysses?" Ben took up his seat on the desk again.

"Because I like candy." Laughter all around.

"That's not a bad idea if you didn't have to keep it up too long. Nobody would wonder about a little boy hanging around the candy jars. Mary Alice, where would you watch from?"

"The table in the back where the catalog is. You could stand there for a long time turning pages in the mail-order catalog without making folks suspicious."

"Excellent. I agree. Now if I was going to hang out in the mercantile, I'd try to get a seat at the checker game. Lots of time to look around and study things, but nobody would remark on it if you sat there all afternoon."

"So is that what Mr. Potter and Mr. Jenkes are doing? Watching folks? They sit there every blessed day but Sunday." Chris snickered. "My ma says they're going to grow roots."

"I think they just enjoy each other's company and a good game of checkers, but"—he put up his finger—"a good sheriff also makes use of such people. If I wanted to know who had been in the store on a given day, I'd ask them. If I wanted to know who had gotten a letter or parcel at the mail counter, those old boys would know, and they'd have a pretty good idea where the letter came from or what was in the parcel."

He slid off the desk. "This morning, your assignment is to pair off and head into town. I want one person in each pair to take a tablet and a pencil, and I want you to make observances. I've got six places for you to observe, one for each pair. I want to know who comes in, who goes out, what they purchase, and who they talk to. If you don't know the person's name, describe them. Tall, short, what clothes they have on, how they talk or move. Go ahead and pair yourselves up."

Their partnerships were predictable, and he was glad to see Amanda with Mary Alice. "All right, the depot, the mercantile, the bakery, the feed store, the livery, and the jail. Pick one and find an inconspicuous spot to observe. Bring me back your findings by noon. I'll be around town checking on you, but don't approach me. I'll find you. Don't let folks know what you're up to.

If they ask, tell them it's a school assignment."

They scampered away like puppies let out of a pen, and he shoved his hands into his pockets, strolling after them in the morning sunshine. For the first time in a week, he felt pretty good about teaching school. No more struggling to understand all the exceptions to the rules of grammar. No more stuffing unwanted facts into little minds. They'd responded so well this morning to learning surveillance, he had high hopes for the afternoon when they went over physical traits from wanted posters.

Speaking of which, he should go get a sheaf of them from his office. Of course that would mean facing Cassie. After her outburst last night, he wasn't sure how she'd receive him. Seemed like these days they couldn't be in the same room for long without a fight breaking out. Which was a shame, since they'd always been pretty good friends.

He was stunned that she was almost twenty years old. How had that happened? She still seemed like a kid to him. He cast about his mind for single men in Cactus Creek, because sure as sagebrush grew in Texas, the young men would be lining up to court her soon.

He scratched his chest, frowning. Which one would be worthy of her? She deserved someone special, to be sure, but which one of the ranch hands or shop clerks or railroad men would do?

Striding through the open door of the jail, prepared to either apologize for whatever he'd said the night before to set her off or try to kid her out of her bad temper if she still had a snit on, he stopped short at the sight before him, all thoughts of last evening rocketing out of his head. "What are you doing?" His voice bounced off the sturdy adobe walls.

She jumped, dropping a sheaf of papers that fanned out across the floor. "You scared me. Why aren't you at the school? Is something wrong?"

"Nothing's wrong. The kids are working on a field assignment. What have you done to my desk?" Every drawer stood open and papers littered the desktop and the chair, and several piles stood on the floor.

"I'm cleaning it out. My father donated a filing cabinet from his office when I explained the tortured nature of your paperwork. From what I can tell, you ascribe to the 'shove-it-in-any-old-drawer' school of organization." She stooped to pick up the circulars she'd dropped.

He picked up a stack of papers off the desktop and plopped them into the top left-hand drawer. "Quit messing with things that don't concern you. You're just supposed to babysit the jail for three more weeks, not turn everything on its head. I swear you're more trouble than a wagonload of barbed wire."

She snatched the papers back out. "That's absurd. The jail was a dump, and I'm fixing it up. I promised no more tea parties, but I can't work in here until I get things straightened up. Once I get these wanted posters filed alphabetically and these circulars filed by date, everything will be in apple-pie order. You'll thank me later." She put her fists on her hips and glared up at him.

For some reason, he wanted to laugh. She looked so determined and cute standing up to him that way.

"All right, John L. Sullivan, put your mitts down and go to a neutral corner. I just came to pick up a handful of wanted posters. I need them for a lesson this afternoon."

"What on earth could you need wanted posters for?"

"Now, now," he waved his finger at her. "You told me to butt out of your business, so now I'm going to politely ask you to do the same. It's only fair." He scavenged a dozen or so of the pages from a stack on the desk. "I'll get these back to you in case one of these desperados shows up on the evening train." With a wink, he sauntered out, leaving her pink-cheeked and no doubt biting her tongue. Served her right to be the one left befuddled for once.

He spied Mary Alice and Amanda disappearing into the bakery. That would be the toughest place to observe, since it was so small, but at least Amanda was familiar with every inch of the place and could probably slip in and out like a ghost. Carl might not even notice she was there.

Isaac and Thomas were assigned to the depot at the east end of town. Ben headed over there, figuring to work his way back toward the school, checking in on each pair as he went. When he got to the platform, he mounted the steps and eased into the waiting room. Ralph Campion sat behind the counter, a visor on his forehead. The telegraph at his elbow clicked from time to time. He glanced up from the newspaper he read. "Morning, Sheriff. Oops, I mean Teacher."

"Morning. Anything interesting going on?"

"Nope, quiet as a church supper. No trains due until the noon from Fort Worth rolls in. What are you doing today? Playing hooky?"

"The kids are doing some fieldwork today."

"Think you'll win the Challenge?"

"I don't know. What do you hear around town?"

"That the destruction of the boys' outhouse at the school might've set you back, except nobody else seems to be doing much better. There was nearly a riot at the bakery this morning when there was nothing new in the cases but biscuits—again. I'm surprised you didn't hear the uproar. Folks want their pies and cakes and apple fritters, and Carl's got nothing but sourdough dodgers to give them. Though he does have plenty of those. I didn't tell folks they were lucky not to be eating his cake. You might win the Challenge by default."

Ben rapped on the countertop. "Guess we'll have to see how things shake out. Good to see you, Ralph."

He headed back out into the sunshine. He'd caught a glimpse of the boys hiding in one of the baggage carts near the end of the platform. Not a bad place, as long as nobody wanted any bags moved.

The twins had drawn the livery stable. He'd best go check on them. No telling what trouble they might be up to.

Mrs. Hart met him in the doorway to the stable, pushing a

wheelbarrow of dirty straw toward the muck heap. He hurried to her side.

"Here, let me help you."

"I've got it, thanks." She trundled by him and upended the contents, brushing her forehead with her wrist. "I've learned to make more trips with smaller loads. What can I do for you, Sheriff? Do you need your horse?"

"Thought I'd just check on him. I haven't ridden him in a week, what with the Challenge and all. He must be getting pretty fresh."

She leaned in to whisper, "If you're looking for a couple of truant students, I spied the Harrison twins climbing into the loft about twenty minutes ago."

"It's all right. They're doing a little school project. Just ignore them unless they decide to see if the muck heap will burn." Ben winked, and she smiled.

He tipped his hat, strolling down the aisle to where his horse, Ranger, was stabled. The buckskin whickered, and he petted the soft black nose. "Hey there, big fella. You look good."

"I turned him out in the corral for most of yesterday. He was kicking up his heels pretty good."

"I'll try to get over here after school tonight and take him for a run. Don't want him going soft on me. I never know when I'll need to chase a bad guy." Ben stifled the frustration that rose in his chest. "Not that much of that stuff happens around here."

"We feel better knowing someone like you is around, because trouble has a way of popping up where you least expect it. Perhaps things are so calm in Cactus Creek because the bad guys know we have a capable sheriff who looks out for his town." Jenny tugged off her gloves and tucked them into her apron pocket.

Ben shrugged, feeling better in spite of himself at her praise. "I guess I'll go up yonder and check in on the boys, make sure they're not getting into trouble." He mounted the ladder and swung himself into the hayloft.

The twins were crouched in the open doorway of the loft

where Carl loaded in the hay each summer. One scribbled in a tablet, and the other pointed down the street and whispered something. Ben smiled. Those two were already so observant, it was scary. Properly trained, they'd either be the greatest crime-fighting pair in history or the wiliest desperados Texas had ever seen.

A commotion downstairs drew their attention. Hooves on the hard-packed dirt first, then raised voices.

"Piece of trash horse you lent me. I could've gotten there faster if I'd have been the one carrying him."

"How dare you return an animal in this condition? You should be horsewhipped yourself. Look at these welts, and all this sweat." Mrs. Hart's voice pierced the late morning sunshine.

"I paid in advance, so you're not getting another dime out of me. This is the laziest pile of bones I've ever seen. I want my money back. How dare you rent me a stubborn knot head on the fast path to the glue factory? He could hardly put one foot in front of the other. If I hadn't let him taste my quirt, I'd still be plodding out there on the prairie."

Ben lay down and poked his head through the hole where the ladder stuck up. A small man stood with his hands on his hips, glaring at Mrs. Hart. Something about the man was familiar, but Ben couldn't quite place him, at least not from this angle. The horse, a sorrel, stood with his head down, sides heaving, sweat dripping from his flanks and neck. Ben gripped the edge of the opening, anger flaring.

"Sir, that is a kind and willing horse. Or at least he is in the hands of someone who knows what he's doing. I've never had a single complaint, and if you think you're going to abuse a horse from this stable and then get your money back, you are gravely mistaken. Now, either get out of this barn right now, or I'll have the sheriff after you."

"Ha! The sheriff. I heard the only law around here is a little girl no bigger'n you. If I want my money back, I'll get it." He pushed past her toward the tack room where Ben knew the money box was kept. "And if I want to, I'll help myself to a little more cash."

Ben pushed himself up and put his boot on the top rung, glad he had insisted on going around heeled. His Colt might prove handy.

"Stop right there."

Ben froze. That wasn't Mrs. Hart's voice. He ducked to get a look at the barn aisle.

"I saw you return to town, and figured I'd come over and check things out. I see my concern was warranted. This horse is in pitiful condition. You should be ashamed of yourself, and if you don't vacate these premises, you'll be enjoying the hospitality of the Cactus Creek jail until such time as I decide to release you."

Cassie, playing sheriff. She stalked through the barn, taking the reins of the trembling horse and leading him into a stall and shutting the door.

The strutting rooster sneered. "Well, if it ain't the little girl playing sheriff." He circled around until he stood between Cassie and the door. Jenny edged away from him and went to stand beside Cassie, bringing her pitchfork with her.

"I'm not playing. I *am* the sheriff, and you'll show some respect or you'll find yourself behind bars." Cassie put her hand on her sidearm.

Quiet as he could, Ben leaned farther out of the loft over their heads, slipping his revolver out of the holster and pointing it at the offensive little man. When the fellow chanced a glance up at Ben, Ben flicked the gun barrel toward the door, staring hard and demanding without words that he get out.

The customer stopped midleer and put his hands up. His eyes widened, and he backed up. "Fine, I'm going. I'm going. Dunno what kind of a crazy town this is, women running the livery and the jail. . . What are your menfolk doing? Needlepoint and crochet?" He spun on his boot heel and disappeared though the barn door.

The girls sagged against each other, and Cassie gave a weak

laugh. "Whew. That was close. I'm glad he folded his tent and decamped."

Jenny glanced up and caught Ben's eye, but he put his finger to his lips, winked, and disappeared. The twins sat in the straw staring at him, and he cautioned them to be quiet, too. They nodded, golden curls bobbing in the shaft of sunlight pouring in the hay door. He leaned down to listen.

"Thank you for your help, Cass. What a singularly unpleasant man. I had better tend to this horse. Poor thing. If I had known how he would be treated, I never would've rented him out. I would've let the man have Misery. He'd have torn him to shreds and stomped on the bits that were left."

"If you need any more help, give a shout, and I'll come running."

Ben waited until he spied Cassie out on the street below before descending the ladder. Going to the stall where the winded horse stood, he put his arms on the top of the door.

"Thank you, Ben. That could've gotten ugly." Jenny backed the animal into the aisle.

"What will be ugly is if you ever let on that I was in the loft. Cassie will flay me alive. She already thinks I'm butting in too much on her sheriffing. If she knew I'd backed her up here, she'd blister me raw." He reached for the cinch and unbuckled it, stripping the saddle and blanket from the horse.

"This poor beast. What should I do for him?"

"Give him just a couple of sips of warm water to take the edge off his thirst, then start walking him slowly until he cools all the way down and his breathing is normal. You can sluice him down with a few buckets of water once he's cooled out. Check those welts, and if any are open, there's some salve in the tack room. When he's dry and clean, put him in a loose box with lots of straw in case he wants to lie down. Give him all the hay he wants and about a half bucket of water. And tomorrow he's going to be sore, so walk him around the corral a couple of times a day, and let him rest otherwise." Ben ran his hand over the horse's ribs. "And delay as long as possible telling Carl what happened. If he finds out about this while that joker is still in town, Carl's liable to slam him over his knee and break him like kindling."

"You're right. I won't tell him if I don't have to. And I'll take good care of the horse. I feel responsible, letting him out to that evil man."

It finally clicked with Ben who the man was. Ivan Shoop, eldest of the Shoop brothers. He hadn't been seen around Cactus Creek since Ben was in his teens. In fact, the last time he'd been in town, Ben's father had arrested him for robbing a stagecoach and sent him to Huntsville for a spell in the pen.

⁓

Carl wiped down the top of the display counter, eyeing Amanda and her friend. They'd slipped inside the bakery half an hour ago, and neither one had said a word. Of course, he was used to that where Amanda was concerned, but what puzzled him was how they both watched him and the older one kept writing on her tablet.

"Can I get you girls something? A biscuit maybe?" Why weren't they in school?

"Mr. Gustafson, why are you only selling biscuits?" the older girl asked,

Familiar chagrin prickled his skin. "'Cause that's all I know how to make."

She blinked and wrote something in her tablet. What was she up to?

Amanda tugged on the girl's sleeve and pulled her down to whisper in her ear. The bigger girl's eyebrows went up, and she cast a dubious glance his way.

"Are you sure?"

Amanda's curls bounced, and she whispered some more, guarding her lips with her little hand.

"Well, all right, if you're sure. Mr. Gustafson, my name is Mary Alice. Amanda and I would like to help you out. I'm very

136

good at mixing up cakes, and Amanda says she knows how to make cookies."

Carl smoothed his beard, unable to quell the burst of warmth in his chest when he looked down into Amanda's china-blue eyes. He hadn't been able to talk to her yet about her mother's unreasonableness about the mare and foal, and he'd thought for sure she'd think he had taken back his offer, but here she was, sweet as ever, and not only wanting to help him out in the bakery but bringing reinforcements, too.

"I suppose you can if you want to."

Before a half hour had passed, he was certain that if Mary Alice had been born a boy, she would have had a brilliant future as a general in the US Army. He had never been ordered around to such effect in all his thirty-two years.

"You have to whip those egg whites hard, until they're stiff, glossy peaks. If you don't, your cake won't have any loft to it. It will look and taste like a horseshoe."

He went back to slopping the whites in the bottom of a big copper bowl. Beside him, pinned into a pint-sized apron, Amanda cut circles out of cookie dough that she'd mixed and rolled out with an ease that made him squirm at his own lack of culinary skill.

Mary Alice spread butter into a cake tin with her fingers. "This needs to bake for about forty minutes, but you have to keep turning it in the oven or it won't brown evenly."

"Maybe you should write down all these instructions. I looked all over for a recipe book or box, but I couldn't find one."

"Mama doesn't use recipes. She says baking comes from the heart, not the mind." Amanda's high, childish voice snagged his attention. "Mama says she just knows when a dough or batter is ready. She learned when she was a little girl like me."

It was the first time the child had spoken above a whisper in his presence, and he tucked away the pleasure to mull over later.

"What else does your mama say?"

"She says giving men sweets is the best way to stay on their good side. Maybe if she gave my daddy more sweets, he wouldn't have been so mean."

Carl's eyes met Mary Alice's across the table. His curiosity roused and grabbed hold of his tongue, forbidding him from heading the little girl off, though he knew her mama wouldn't want her spilling secrets about the past.

For Amanda, it seemed once the floodgates had opened, there was no closing them. "My daddy was a mean man. He used to make my mama cry, he was so mean. I cried, too. He would say hurtful things, tell Mama she was weak and stupid and that she had shamed him because I was a girl and not a boy. Sometimes he would hit Mama. I wasn't a bit sorry when he keeled over and died. Does that make me bad?" Amanda finished putting the last round of cookie dough on the baking sheet. "I need some sugar now and some cinnamon to sprinkle on top." She said this in the same, matter-of-fact tone in which she'd just announced that her dead father had been a wife beater and child abuser.

"Mr. Gustafson?" Mary Alice asked.

Red mist formed at the corners of Carl's vision. He wished the sorry excuse for a man stood before him right now. He'd teach him a thing or two about violence. Beat him so bad he'd never raise his hand or his voice to a woman again.

"Mr. Gustafson?"

"What?" he barked the word harsher than he'd meant to.

"I think you can stop beating those eggs now." She rounded the table and peeked into the bowl. "In fact, I think you might've overdone it." Taking the whisk from his hand, she jabbed the mass. "They're starting to liquefy again. Maybe you'd better start over."

She expertly cracked and separated another half dozen eggs with an ease he knew he'd never acquire and handed him the whisk once more as he calmed his temper.

"Do you like my cookies? Mama says I make the best cinnamon-sugar cookies in all of Texas and Tennessee, too."

Amanda dusted each cookie with a precise dash of spice. "That's where we lived before. In Chattanooga. My daddy was a banker. We had a big house, and I had a nurse, and Mama had a maid. And there was a housekeeper and a cook and a valet, too. When Daddy died, Mama packed me up in the middle of the night, and we got on the train and didn't get off until the conductor said we were in Cactus Creek. Did you know conductors have brass buttons, and the ceilings on trains fold down to make beds?"

A banker? With a big house and servants? And running away in the middle of the night?

"I'm glad we came here. Mama is happy. She likes baking things and having a pretty shop. She hardly ever cries anymore, only sometimes at night when she thinks I'm sleeping."

Carl set the bowl aside until he could get himself better under control lest he ruin another batch of egg whites. He wanted to scoop Amanda up and assure her that nobody would ever hurt her again, The idea of Jenny crying herself to sleep at night made the muscles of his neck and shoulders knot. What kind of man would abuse a woman, especially one as small and delicate as Jenny Hart?

And why would a woman of privilege and status want to hide herself out here on the Texas prairie, having escaped from her old life in the dead of night?

⁓

Jenny finished walking and currying the sorrel and put him in the only empty loose box in the barn, opposite the pony mare and foal. None of his welts had broken open, but she bathed them with cool, clean water and applied salve anyway, apologizing the entire time for letting that horrible man rent him in the first place.

He seemed to accept her apology, nuzzling her as she trailed her hand down his face before she shut him into the stall. With a sigh, he lowered himself to his knees, then subsided into the straw, closing his eyes.

"You have yourself a nice old rest. I'll mix you up a warm mash before I leave tonight. And tomorrow we'll take a stroll and limber up those muscles of yours."

Now she needed to check on Copper and the baby. Every time she thought of the way she'd ungraciously shoved Carl's gift back into his face, shame licked at her with hot tongues of flame. Where did she draw the line between protecting Amanda and making a new and normal life for them here in this community?

The truth was, she could afford the horse. If she wanted to draw on the money in her husband's accounts in the First Bank of Chattanooga. But if she did that, she risked her father-in-law finding out where she was and possibly making good on his threat to take Amanda from her. Though he, too, had been disgusted when his grandchild had been born a female, he had let Jenny know at the funeral that he would be stepping in and taking over Amanda's upbringing. He'd brandished a will stating that Robert had named his father as the guardian of his child because Jenny was too weak and frail to undertake the task alone, and he'd bragged to her that he had a judge in his pocket who would sign the order within the week.

Which was all Jenny needed to bolt from the mansion in Chattanooga and vow never to return. Hart Sr. was every bit as evil and nasty as his son, and she'd die defending Amanda from him.

No, she couldn't risk trying to withdraw the money. Her father-in-law had probably emptied the accounts the minute he found out she'd fled with Amanda. As the owner of the bank, he'd have no trouble purloining the money that was rightfully hers and Amanda's and making it all look aboveboard. She still had a bit of the money she'd managed to take from Robert's desk the night they'd fled, but most of it had gone toward their travel and buying the bakery. With so little left in reserve, she couldn't spend it on the upkeep of a pony.

She entered the stall and closed the door behind her. In the shadows, the foal lay on its side, its ribcage rising and falling. For some reason, she'd been uneasy about the baby all day. Though she'd seen the filly attempt to suckle several times, she still had a pinched and hollow look to her.

Copper whickered and returned her nose to the hay in the manger, and Jenny knelt beside the baby. "Hey there, little one." The filly raised her head for a moment, then dropped it to the straw again. Something was definitely wrong.

Rising, she dusted her hands. Though it galled her to ask for help, her pride wasn't worth the life of this baby. She'd have to tell Carl. Quickly latching the gate behind her, she headed for the bakery.

She almost laughed at the urge she had to knock at her own back door rather than intrude on his immaculate kitchen. Grasping the handle on the screen door, she stepped inside. The most amazing smell greeted her. Warm cinnamon and a tang of lemon? Certainly not sourdough biscuits.

Carl turned from the oven, a sheet of cookies held in a dish towel-protected hand. She blinked. "You made cookies?"

He stopped, letting the hot pan come to rest on the tin-topped worktable. "And cake. You want some? I promise it has the right amount of vanilla in it this time." He pointed to where two sponge cakes sat, dripping with a golden glaze.

"Maybe later." The cakes looked quite appetizing. He appeared to be doing better at her job than she was at his, which made having to ask for his help even harder. "Actually, I came to ask you about the foal. She doesn't appear to be doing too well. It's strange, because I've seen her nurse several times, but she looks hungry to me. Now she's listless and lying in the straw."

He tugged at the strings holding the flour sack around his middle. Her lips twitched. He'd abandoned wearing her aprons at least.

"Maybe the mare's milk hasn't come in yet or she's not producing much. Do you have any cans of evaporated milk?"

She rummaged in a cupboard and produced three tins.

"Open them up and put them into a saucepan with about

three tablespoons of molasses and a can of water. We'll warm it up and see if we can get it into the little gal." He slid the cookies off the hot baking sheet onto the countertop to cool.

As she stirred the milk in the pan, she studied the cookies, each with a precise dash of cinnamon in the center.

"Was Amanda here today?"

He paused in the washing up. "Why do you ask?"

"Those look like her work. Some of the school kids were out and about this morning on an assignment from Ben, and I wondered if Amanda had come into the bakery."

Splashing resumed, and he kept his back to her at the washtub. "She and one of the older girls were in."

Baking cookies, and probably the cakes, too. She shook her head. Her own daughter working for the enemy. No, that wasn't right. Though Carl was her opponent in the Challenge, and a worthy adversary at that, he wasn't her enemy. There was something that appealed to her about him. Somewhere under all that beard and the muscles and the bluster beat a kind and generous heart. No, he wasn't an enemy. He was a friend. Just a friend.

She tested the milk. "I think it's ready. How are we going to get it into her?"

"Do you have any leather gloves? Like kid leather? And a clean glass bottle?"

Retrieving her church gloves from her bureau upstairs took only a minute.

He paused before taking them. "I'll get you a new pair."

"Don't worry about that." She opened a utensil drawer and took out a pair of shears and a roll of cotton twine. "We can empty out a bottle of vanilla. Oh, wait, we already have an empty one." She forced down a giggle as he harrumphed and snipped off one of the fingers of the glove.

Using a funnel, she poured the warm milk into the bottle, then held it while he tied the makeshift nipple on and poked a hole in it with her ice pick.

"There, one baby bottle. That should do for now. If the mare's milk doesn't come in soon, maybe I can order a real baby bottle from the catalog over at the mercantile." His hand dwarfed the vanilla bottle.

"I'll bring the rest of the milk. Just let me put the CLOSED sign in the front window and lock the door."

"Bring the funnel, too." He held the door for her, and they headed back to the livery.

The foal lay exactly as Jenny had left her, flat out and uncaring. Carl gently pushed the mare to the side of the stall, pinning her there with his hip as he bent to first look at and then palpate her udder.

"There's milk there, but she isn't letting it down." He frowned. "We'll deal with that in a bit. First, let's take a look at the little lady." Squatting, he ran his hand along the foal's side and picked her little head up off the straw to look at her eyes.

"I think you nailed it. She's hungry." When he held out his hand, Jenny was right there to give him the prepared bottle. "Come here, sweetheart. This will make you feel better."

Plopping down into the bedding and leaning back against the partition, he turned the foal to lie between his outstretched legs. Jenny helped arrange the foal's long legs and knobby knees while Carl held the bottle to the filly's lips, easing her mouth open and squeezing the improvised nipple to allow a few drops of milk to land on her tongue.

Her head jerked, and her ears flopped. Blinking, the baby's tongue moved convulsively. Her lips clamped around the teat, and she sucked. Her bottle-brush tail stirred the straw, and her eyes closed as she took long pulls. Carl kept his fingers tight around the neck of the bottle to keep her from swallowing the glove tip.

"That's a good girl. Nothing wrong with you that a square meal won't fix, eh?" Carl's enormous hand caressed the dark brown baby, and a smile softened his face.

Jenny sat back on her heels, wrapping her arms around her knees, watching how gentle he was with this animal that he had no real use for, that wouldn't earn her keep in a livery stable. Nothing like her former husband, who counted every decision, made every action based on how it would impact his power. Financial power, community power, domestic power. She couldn't imagine him wearing a flour-sack apron and washing dishes or sitting in the straw bottle-feeding a pony foal.

"You were right."

His voice jarred her from her thoughts. "What?"

"Amanda made those cookies. And the other girl made the cakes. I just watched and wrote down what they did and followed orders." He stroked the foal's neck, twining his fingers in the curly little stand-up mane. For an instant, Jenny wondered what it might feel like if he stroked her neck and curled his fingers into her hair. It had been so long since she'd been touched, and even longer since that touch was gentle or affectionate. An ache opened up in her chest.

"Since we're making confessions of getting help, I have something to tell you." She gripped her knees tighter, bracing herself. "I rented the sorrel gelding to a man, and he brought him back in terrible shape. Sweating and trembling and covered in welts." Forcing down the lump in her throat, she continued, "I didn't have the first clue what to do for the poor animal, but Ben Wilder was here, and he told me how to care for him."

Heat invaded Carl's eyes, and his fist tightened around the bottle. "Who was it?" The razor-edge in his voice sent a shiver up Jenny's spine.

"I didn't know him. You can be assured I won't rent him a horse ever again."

"What did he look like?"

"Not tall, dark hair, scruffy beard. Small eyes." Heat swirled into her cheeks. "He was impertinent."

"That's two strikes against him." He held up the bottle and peered at the scant few drops left. "She polished it off. We'll let her rest for a bit and allow that to settle before we give her more." He eased himself up after handing her the bottle. "Let's take a look at the gelding."

He still had that hard edge to his voice, as if he was barely maintaining a grip on his temper, and Jenny stood well back.

"Where is he?"

She pointed across the aisle to the other loose box. "Ben said to let him have plenty of room to lie down or move if he wanted to."

He opened the door. The gelding stood in the corner, his head down, one hind leg tucked under. As gentle as Carl had been with the foal, he was even gentler with the gelding.

"Easy there, boy." The horse raised his head and shoved his nose into Carl's chest, as if to say, "It was terrible. I'm so glad you're here now."

"What did Ben tell you to do for him?" Carl's voice rumbled low in his chest.

She quickly outlined the treatment and breathed a sigh when the livery man nodded, fondling the animal's ears.

"You did right. It's a fact of life that when you rent animals to strangers, you run the risk that they won't be treated well. Though I haven't had much trouble with that."

"Probably because anyone who rented one of your horses would think twice about returning it in poor condition. You're big enough to exact justice."

"Yet another reason this Challenge is a load of hooey. If I had been here, either the man would've thought twice about beating this horse, or he'd have paid in kind if he had. I knew this barn was no place for a woman, especially not a little thing like you." He edged out of the stall, and she noted his fisted hands.

Jenny edged a few steps away. "Will the horse be all right?"

"Probably. Don't rent him to anyone else for the month." He jammed his fingers through his hair. "This place is falling apart without me. The foal and the sorrel will need extra attention. Misery needs to be gentled if he's to be any use. Half the horses need a trip to the blacksmith, and the first hay crop is going to come in ahead of schedule and I won't be here to get it into the barn."

With every sentence, Jenny's confidence eroded, and she was transported back to her marriage where nothing she did was good enough, nothing she did pleased her husband.

Raising her chin, she looked him in the eye. What had made her think he would be any different, would treat her any better than Robert had?

"If you're through insulting me, I believe I'll head home now. It's almost closing time. Perhaps you can accomplish some of the many things that you feel are not meeting your high standards. Perhaps when I get to the bakery, I can do the same. Good day, Mr. Gustafson."

She turned on her heel and strode out, carrying her guilt and feeling smaller than that starving little foal in there. Men were all the same, and Carl Gustafson was. . .*samer*. . .than the rest.

CHAPTER 9

The sun was barely over the horizon when Cassie arrived at the jail. She glanced at the clock and the calendar. Almost halfway through the Challenge month, and she hadn't exactly been a rousing success as a sheriff. Certainly not enough so that Ben would be convinced that she was grown up and that their destiny lay on the same path together.

A rueful laugh clogged her throat. Her destiny. What a laugh. The man was thicker than two planks when it came to women. On the one hand, she supposed she should be grateful. After all, if he wasn't so dense, he probably would've married someone else while she was in Philadelphia. On the other hand, having him continue to view her as a child, and even to speculate about who might come courting her one day was galling.

"Mornin', Sheriff."

Speak of the devil and then he appears. Ben stuck his head through the jailhouse doorway.

"Good morning, Ben. I was hoping to see you today. Why is it that I've noticed my students running about town with tablets and pencils these last couple of days when they should be in school?" She crossed her arms.

"Your students? *My* students for the next couple of weeks. They're working on some projects. We might've gotten off to a rocky start, but I think we've hit our stride. You might see them around town again today. I haven't decided."

"They all melt away when I get close enough to ask them

what they're up to."

His smile cut two creases into his cheeks, distracting her for a moment. Her breath hitched, and she twiddled with her collar button. The man had no right to be so handsome.

"I told them to be inconspicuous. They aren't supposed to tell anyone what they're up to."

"That sounds. . .suspicious."

"Naw, just keeping our business our business, you know?"

A stab of jealousy seared her. The bond that Cassie had worked so hard to forge with her students was being obscured by Ben and his charm. What if, when she returned to her classroom, the children let it be known they preferred the sheriff's teaching to hers? Mary Alice hadn't been very forthcoming with her reports each afternoon, and she was getting far behind in her studies for her exams. Worst of all, she didn't seem to care, going on about how much fun they were having and how nice Mr. Wilder was. It sounded as if nobody missed Cassie at the schoolhouse.

A knock sounded and Ralph sauntered in. "Glad you're here early. Telegram came in for the sheriff of Cactus Creek." He started to hand the paper to Ben, but Cassie snatched it away.

"I'm the sheriff, remember?"

Ralph frowned. "This is serious, Cassie. Ben needs to know."

She shoved the telegram into her pocket. "You're legally bound not to reveal the contents of a telegram to anyone but the recipient, are you not?"

"Sure, but Ben's the sworn sheriff, and this isn't something to trifle about. When you read that, you'll agree that he and you will have to swap places back for a while."

"Not on your tintype, Ralph Campion. Not for eighteen more days."

The depot manager/telegrapher sighed, shook his head, and shot Ben a sympathy-seeking glance. "These Bucknell girls are hardheaded for sure. A man would think twice about courting them if they weren't so pretty."

"I'm going to tell Millie you said she was hardheaded." Cassie made a face at him.

"Well, when you do, be sure to tell her I also said she was pretty. You and Ben work this out between you. Show him that telegram, and you two decide together what to do about it. Otherwise, I'm going to tell him myself." He tipped his visor to her and left.

"C'mon, Cass, read it out. Is there a prisoner transport coming through and they need to use the jail? A bandit headed this way? What?"

She took the telegram from her pocket and scanned it. A dull pain hit her abdomen.

Ben crowded close and read it as she held it out.

"That tears it. This year's Challenge is over for you and me."

She put her hands on her hips. "Why?"

"What do you mean, 'why'? You read the message."

"I can handle this."

"You can't, and you'd be foolish to try. If word of this gets out—and you can bet your sweet little sunbonnet it will—every outlaw, thief, and bandit this side of the Pecos will be camped on the doorstep. You wouldn't stand a snowflake's chance in Houston of holding them off by yourself."

"Stop treating me like a child. It says a Wells Fargo guard comes with the shipment, and Jigger will be here, too."

"Did you read the paper on Monday morning? Dick Grabel splashed it all over the front page that we have a girl playing sheriff here for the next three weeks. The whole article gave me the cold sweats. It's practically an invitation to all the riffraff in Texas to come boiling in here for a good time. When they find out about a half a million dollars in gold bars sitting in one of our jail cells, they'll be tripping over each other to get at it."

"It's only for twenty-four to forty-eight hours. Just until the soldiers from Fort Benefactor get here. I don't see why you're so negative."

He flipped his hat onto the desk. "I'm not being negative; I'm being realistic."

"So am I. I'm a big girl. I can take care of the jail for two days while the gold is here, especially with a deputy and a guard to help."

"And how do you plan to do that?"

She folded the paper into a precise square. "I'm not sure yet. I'll confer with Jigger and come up with a plan."

"Did somebody say my name?" The deputy sauntered through the door in his usual cranky-morning humor, but instead of making his customary bow and hat tip, his boots hit the new rug she'd laid down the night before and skidded out from under him.

His arms windmilled, and he let out a little yelp as he slid toward the stove. Throwing himself to the side to avoid colliding with the cast-iron potbelly, he smacked into the wall, bracing himself with his palms to save his face from meeting the adobe. Something snapped with a dried-kindling sound and made Cassie's skin crawl.

Jigger howled and dropped to the floor holding his wrist.

Ben and Cassie sprinted to his side, pushing each other to get there first. Ben won.

"How bad is it?" Ben helped his deputy sit with his back against the wall.

"Busted." The word came out through clenched teeth. Sweat clotted on his brow. "Tripped on the rug."

Cassie touched the deputy's shoulder. "I'm so sorry. Here, let me see. Ben, you need to go get my father." She elbowed Ben out of the way to survey the damage.

Ben shot to his feet. "This is what you get for sissifying my jail. Rugs and pillows and cushions. They're a menace, and I want every last one of your so-called improvements out by tonight. Is that clear? Jigger, hold on. I'll go get the doc." He kicked the rug on his way out, sending it through the doorway ahead of him.

She took out her handkerchief and wiped Jigger's brow. "I'm

so sorry. This is my fault. I should've put something rough on the back of that rug to keep it from sliding. Does it hurt very badly?" The skin hadn't burst over the break, thankfully, but there was definitely an unnatural bend to his right forearm that said he had diagnosed himself correctly. "Can you get up and into a chair, or would you rather sit here on the floor?"

"Mebbe you could drag a chair over." He gave her a weak smile, then went back to clenching his jaw. "Don't fret. It was an accident. Don't let Ben get to you. He's always like this when somebody he cares about gets hurt. Takes things to heart, he does."

She pulled the desk chair over and helped Jigger onto the seat. His fingers below the break had begun to swell and discolor, and she prayed her father would arrive soon.

"What were you and Ben arguing about before I did my buffalo-on-ice routine?" Jigger shifted his injured wrist and sucked in a sharp breath.

"What makes you think we were arguing?" She tugged at her lower lip and paced, going to the door to see if they were coming yet.

"You were in the same room, weren't you? Seems all you two do these days is strike sparks off each other."

She paused, ashamed of herself. Just this past Sunday she'd vowed to behave better, to be nice to Ben and treat him as she wanted to be treated, to act like a grown-up. That resolve hadn't lasted through a full week.

"I'm trying, but Ben Wilder rubs me the wrong way."

"I might be a bachelor, but I have eyes in my head. If you two didn't care so much for each other, you wouldn't be scrapping all the time."

Panicked that he might've guessed her feelings for Ben, she sought to cut him off. "Maybe you shouldn't talk right now. The doctor should be here soon."

"Talking keeps my mind off the pain. Anyway, I'm happy for you two. Ben's a good man, better than he gives himself credit for. You two will do well once you figure out that you're meant to be together."

"Are you sure you didn't hit your head on the wall? Ben thinks of me as a child, a little sister. We argue all the time because he's impossible, not because we're fighting tender feelings for each other."

"Poppycock. Ben's busy right now trying to live up to his daddy's reputation, and that takes all his time, but if you'll be patient, he'll get around to noticing that you're all grown up and the perfect little bride for him."

As if she hadn't been patient for more than ten years already.

❧

Ben jogged up the street, fuming at her stubbornness. He'd like to turn her over his knee. Look where her girly ways had gotten his deputy. Laid up with a broken wrist. And now she was thinking to tackle protecting a gold shipment that would've had Ben telegraphing the Texas Rangers, his brothers, the Pinkertons, and swearing in a couple more deputies from right here in town to guard it while it sat in his jail.

Pounding on the Bucknells' fancy front door, he waited.

The doc himself opened the door, wiping his mouth with a napkin. Breakfasty smells hit Ben right in the nose. "Good morning, Ben. Care to come in for some eggs and bacon?"

"No, sir. Jigger's down at the jail with a broken wrist. It needs setting."

The amiable expression faded from Doc Bucknell's face, and he reached behind the door for his bag. "Mother, I'm headed out on a call," he shouted down the hallway.

As they hurried back toward the jail, Ben couldn't resist saying, "Sir, we're going to have to call off the Challenge this year as far as Cassie and I are concerned."

He frowned but didn't slacken his long-legged stride. "Over a broken wrist?"

"No, sir. Cassie can fill you in when you're done with Jigger, but something's come up that will mean I have to take my job back, at least for a few days."

The doctor frowned but mounted the single step to the jail porch and ducked inside. "We'll talk about it later." He went straight to Jigger.

Ben hovered in the doorway while Cassie leaned against his desk, her arms folded at her waist. A pair of furrows crinkled the normally smooth skin between her brows, and for some ridiculous reason—especially when he was so frustrated with her at the moment—he wanted to reach out and touch them, soothe them away and bring a sweet expression back to her face.

Of course, he was more likely to cause her to spit and scratch at him. She was so passionate about everything, never did anything by halves, and this sheriffing lark was no different. She'd jumped in, boots first, and now she was in over her head. The parents of the school children had told him she was the best teacher their kids had ever had, that she truly cared about them and taught them well. He wasn't a bit surprised. As a kid, she'd been a good student, a fearless adventurer along the creek bank, and a staunch defender of anyone she thought was getting a raw deal.

But he had to draw the line, for her own safety and that of the town, not to mention the army's gold.

The clock chimed, drawing his notice. He had a quarter of an hour before children would start showing up at the school. And today was a big day. The kids had begged him to teach them to track, and he had roped in his dad to help. Even now, his father was probably laying a trail from the school door to an unknown destination. And if Ben knew the old fox, it would be as full of twists and turns as a rattler winding through a patch of prickly pear. He'd want to test Ben as much as he would the kids. And Ben would have to call upon all his concentration to work out the trail. The last thing he needed was a distraction like Cassie or Jigger's broken wrist or a wagonload of gold sitting undefended in his jail.

"I'll be back after school to check on you, Jigger. Doc, take good care of him. And Cass, we're not done with our discussion."

He left before she could argue with him.

Odd how familiar the schoolhouse had become to him in just twelve days. He studied the ground in front of the steps, grinning when he spied his father's piebald paint's tracks in the dust. He hadn't forgotten. The trail wouldn't be long, because the kids would be on foot, but it should prove to be a good exercise.

He eased open the door, checked the water level in the crock, and walked into the schoolroom proper. He had a few minutes left before the kids would show up. Opening the top drawer of Cassie's desk, he scrounged for a tablet and pencil so he could jot a few notes about tracking to tell the kids.

Odd. He could've sworn he'd left the tablet in this drawer. *Hmm.* Must be in the next one. One after another he opened all the drawers, searching. No joy. He returned to the top drawer and pulled it out to its limit. A corner of paper caught his eye. Wedged into the slide. Careful to avoid tearing it, he worked it slowly back and forth until it came free.

A jolt went through him when he realized it was a letter addressed to him.

My dearest Benjamin,

How can I ever tell you what is in my heart? When I'm with you, I am awkward and tongue-tied. I say the most ridiculous things and all because I'm mesmerized by your beautiful brown eyes. Just seeing you walk down the street sets my heart aflutter, and when you take the time to speak to me, I treasure every word. I see you in my dreams and wake up longing to be with you. Why is it you don't even see me? Oh, you talk to me, and you are nice to me, and you help me in so many ways, but you never see the real me. What can I do to make you realize how much I love you? You treat me like a child when all I want is to be seen as the woman I am. Some days loving you lifts me to the skies with happiness, and some days it weighs me down to the point of despair. If only I thought there might be hope for us someday. How can I make you see I'm not the little girl you think I am, but a woman with all the longings, needs, hopes, and prayers that womanhood brings? My greatest fear is that you will fall in love with someone else before you realize I'm grown up and ready for love.

Though the letter was unsigned, he had no doubt who had put it in the desk. Tugging on his earlobe, he pressed his tongue against the backs of his teeth and scanned the page once more. From the outset of this little teaching jaunt, he'd known Mary Alice Watkins was nursing a crush on him, but this letter put it on another level. Leaving love notes. He hadn't had a love note left for him since he was in primer school and Ruthie May Grove pledged her eternal devotion with lots of hearts and flowers all over the scrap of butcher's paper she'd stuffed into his lunch box. That was right before she punched him in the eye on the playground and decided she liked Jimmy Richardson better.

Mary Alice had probably laid the paper neatly in the drawer, and all his scrabbling around for a tablet had wedged it into the drawer slide. Embarrassment prickled his chest. She thought he had beautiful brown eyes, and his walk set her aflutter? How was he even going to look her in the eye after this? And how did he divert her affection to someone more her own age?

"Good morning, Mr. Wilder."

He jerked and jumped to his feet, shoving the paper into his pocket. "G—good morning, Mary Alice."

"I thought I'd come in a few minutes early to fill the water crock and beat out the erasers for you."

Her dewy-fresh expression made Ben feel as if he were being pricked with a thousand red-hot sewing needles.

"Um. . .fine. . .yes. . .I. . .I'm going outside." He couldn't get to the door fast enough and made sure to make a wide arc around his enamored pupil. Outside, he took a deep breath. This was incredibly awkward and another reason this year's Challenge needed to be over now. Resettling his hat, he decided he'd just have to treat her the same as he treated the rest of the kids, perhaps with a little more distance, and hope she got over her crush quickly.

Several of the kids had arrived and, as usual, scampered here and there like mice. Though they didn't know it, they were obliterating the beginning of the trail his father had laid.

"Hey, c'mere, you wild children." He sat on the steps, willing to push the notion of Mary Alice and her love letter out of his mind for a while.

They clustered around, and he counted noses. "Where's Pierce?"

Chris shrugged. "He's got a drippy nose and a cough. He wanted to come, but his ma wouldn't let him. I had to promise to tell him everything that happened."

"All right. So we'll be eleven today." He was aware of Mary Alice coming out the door behind him. The back of his neck grew hot, and he forced himself to ignore it. "Now, we're going to learn about tracking today. Tracking is useful for all sorts of things. Finding game to eat, following a horse that gets loose, or, in my case, trailing a criminal."

Grateful for their attention, he squatted by the steps and pointed to the footprints and smudges in the powdery dirt. "Tracking isn't easy, but there are a few key things to watch for that will make it less difficult. First, when you come across a track, everything you need for finding the next one is right there. Never skip a track, and don't try to take shortcuts." He could hear his father's voice in his head.

"The more you know about your quarry, the easier tracking will be. You know a deer or buffalo is going to be heading toward grass and water and a herd if possible. But a man on a horse could be heading a lot of different places. He might be going toward a hideout or a railroad or a place where he can ambush you. If he knows you're chasing him, that affects his movements."

They hung on every word, eyes wide, a few with their mouths open in concentration.

"Now, there is a trail not ten feet from where you're all squatting, and we're going to follow it. A single horse with a rider. Let's see who can find the tracks first."

They fanned out like hens after bugs, all studying the earth, some even crawling on all fours. He smiled when they missed the obvious tracks. The only one not concentrating on the ground in front of the school was. . .Mary Alice. She stood beside him watching the kids and occasionally glancing up at him from under her lashes.

"Are you going to look for the tracks?" he asked.

"I thought I'd let the *children* look first." She smiled indulgently at the younger pupils as if she didn't count herself among them. "I actually know a little bit about following a trail. My dad taught me. We had a mountain lion causing some trouble last spring, killing calves on our ranch, and dad took me with him to track it down and shoot it."

He raised his eyebrows. "Did he get it?"

"I have a mountain-lion-skin rug beside my bed." She lifted her chin. "Maybe, if you come by our ranch, you can see it. My dad is very proud of it."

"I found one!" Bekah squealed and hopped up and down pointing at the ground.

Ben escaped Mary Alice and her awkward half invitation. "Be careful. When you find a track, back off a little bit to make sure you're not scuffing up others."

The kids formed a ring around the spot where Bekah pointed. There in the dust was a hoofprint.

"All right, what can you tell me about it?"

"It's a horse." Quincy snickered and elbowed Ulysses.

"It's wearing a horseshoe," Sarah offered.

Silence.

"That's it?" Ben looked from face to face.

"What else is there?"

"Check and see if there is any dew in the print. If there is, then you know the print was left before the dew showed up this morning."

They inched closer, bending to study the mark.

"Also, check to see how sharp the edges of the track are. The longer it has been there, the fuzzier the outline will be. I can tell from this track that it's fairly fresh, made within the last couple of hours, that the horse is being ridden, and that he's got a loose nail in his shoe. That mark will make it easy to follow this horse if we cross trails with another rider. Now, find the next one."

They followed the plain-as-day trail up the road first, heading west out of town and toward his parents' little spread. Ben, with the most experienced eye, noted where his father had ridden into town first, then doubled back to the school, the tracks going both ways over the bridge that spanned Cactus Creek. They passed the Wilder place, the marks evident in the dusty, brown dirt. His mother sat on the front porch, her sewing in her hands, and she waved as they walked by the front gate. Mary Alice stuck to his elbow like a sandbur every step of the way.

After another hundred yards or so, the tracks disappeared from the road.

"Where'd they go?" Thomas shoved his hands into his pockets. He had been in the lead most of the way, and the class clustered around him, staring up at Ben.

Shrugging, he tilted his head. "Is there any rule that says a rider has to stay on the road?"

They spread out in the grass, and he followed, stopping beside the first clear track. "Look here." He put his fingers into the slight depression, outlining the edges of the print. "When you're tracking over grass, you have to look for bent blades, small hollows in the earth, disturbed pebbles or leaves."

Once they knew what to look for, they found more hoofprints.

"Try to think about where your quarry might be going. Most

folks try to travel in a straight line to get where they're headed as soon as possible."

Ahead of them, a bend of Cactus Creek lay on the prairie, scrub trees and brush sticking up above the banks. Ben glanced over his shoulder. They'd covered about three-quarters of a mile, and so far, the only hitch in the trail had been getting off the road. He'd expected more from his father. Thomas took off along the hoofprints, quicker than the rest, already showing great promise as a tracker.

Without much trouble, he led the rest of the kids right to the creek bank.

"See where he stopped to let his horse drink?" Ben pointed to the deeper impressions in the damp earth.

"What did he do then? I don't see any more tracks." Thomas pinched the tip of his nose, his go-to gesture when he was thinking hard.

"What do you think happened? Work it out from what his options were." Ben spoke to the group, inviting input.

"He could turn back to town."

"He could, but did you see any tracks going that way?"

"No."

"What else could he do?"

"Ride along the creek."

"Yep, but you can see he didn't."

Amanda tugged at Mary Alice's sleeve and whispered into her ear when she bent down. "Amanda says he rode into the water."

"Good job, Amanda. That's exactly what he did. Boys, you shuck off your shoes and socks and roll up your pants. Wade over to the other side and divide into two groups. You don't know if he went up-or downstream. Follow along until you see where he left the water, then holler out. Girls, you'll divide on this side and look for tracks."

Of course he found himself in the group with Mary Alice and Amanda. Bekah and Sarah grabbed hands and headed upstream, running too fast to notice any tracks. Mary Alice batted her eyes, but he pretended not to notice.

Less than a hundred yards downstream in the direction of town, the twins shouted. "He got out here. There's tracks straight up the bank, but then he turned around and went back into the creek."

Ben turned around and put his fingers to his lips, letting out a piercing whistle to the teams upstream. The kids in that direction bolted toward him, the boys splashing through the water and wetting the legs of their jeans. Their shoes, tied together and hung around their necks, flopped and jounced with each bound, and he remembered his own childhood, the carefree days of skipping rocks and playing in creeks and chasing girls with frogs.

What wouldn't he give to go back to those days before he donned a badge, when he just *pretended* to be his dad, the greatest sheriff ever? Before the Challenge and gold shipments and students with puppy love and getting on Cassie Bucknell's bad side.

She would've liked today's lesson, since he remembered her tomboyish ways as a kid, climbing trees and racing the boys and flipping over rocks along the creek to see what creatures might be squirming around underneath.

And she was still trying to best the boys with her bravado and daring. But there was a big difference between being able to climb higher or whistle a grass stem better than anyone else and defending and protecting a town and a gold shipment. The boys she would be trying to best this time were bigger and stronger and more ruthless than she could ever be. The thought of her facing down thieves, standing in harm's way, turned his knees to water.

The twins found where the horse had exited the creek again. Ben was so preoccupied, he almost walked right over the trail.

"Where you goin', Mr. Wilder? The tracks lead this way." Mary Alice put her hand on his arm, and his mind jerked back to her letter and her crush and what he was going to do about it.

He snatched his arm away, then tried to cover it by pretending she'd startled him.

"Sorry, I was thinking about something. Go on ahead, Mary Alice. I'll follow in a minute." He sounded like a bumbling idiot. Maybe that was the way to turn her interest elsewhere. Act like a complete fool around her, and maybe she'd think she could do better and leave him alone.

Of course, the way things were going, he wouldn't have to act. If he polled the women in his life, most of them would probably say he had the fool role sewn up tight. Mary Alice ignored his suggestion that she go ahead and stayed by his side.

The trail soon rejoined the road, and by the time they reached his parents' gate once more, the kids could make out a horse and man across the bridge standing at the school's front porch. Most of them ran pell-mell, all elbows and knees and shouts of success. Amanda stayed with Mary Alice and Ben and arrived at the school a few minutes later.

"You found me." His father pushed himself up from the stairs. "And in pretty good time, too." He tousled the twins' curls and gave a light cuff on the shoulder to Thomas. "Good work. I thought I might give you the slip there at the creek."

Ben's chest puffed up. "Nope, between Amanda and the twins, they were hot on your trail pretty quickly. Not to mention Thomas, who has all the earmarks of a first-rate scout."

Thomas blushed and kicked a tuft of grass, hands shoved deep in his pockets. The twins hung from the stair railings, feet dangling on one side, heads on the other. "This is the best school day ever," Ulysses said. "When we have days outside with Miss Bucknell, she makes us write poems about trees and flowers." He screwed his face up, his tongue sticking out and his eyes crossing to an alarming degree. "I like tracking bandits better."

"Now, now, Miss Bucknell has her way of doing things, and I have mine, and both are important." Ben felt obliged to stand up for Cassie, especially since he'd undermined her curriculum and methods and turned everything upside down at the school this last week. "I wish y'all could vote in the Challenge though. Let's head inside. My dad has agreed to talk to us today about some of his favorite tracking techniques and tell you about how he faced down the Dickenson Gang right here on the streets of Cactus Creek and saved my life in the bargain."

As they swarmed up the stairs and inside, Ben held his father's arm. "We need to talk after school. Can you meet me at the sheriff's office and bring Doc Bucknell and Hobny with you?"

"Trouble?" His father's eyes brightened, and his focus sharpened on Ben's face. He reminded Ben of a hunting dog that had been retired but had just caught the scent of game.

"Plenty." And the biggest might be convincing Cassie to quit the Challenge at least as long as that gold was in town.

The minute school was out, Ben headed toward the jail. Surely by now Cassie had taken time to think of all the things that could go wrong while she was in charge of the gold shipment and realize that he should take over protecting it.

The council had arrived ahead of him. Hobny's Adam's apple bobbed precariously. He always looked like a wading bird who had eaten a fish too large for his gullet. Ben found himself swallowing hard and often whenever he was around Hobny Jones.

His father was in one of the jail cells examining the new pillows and straw ticks. His silvery moustache twitched when he caught Ben's eye, and he gave a quick wink and a glance toward where Cassie was busying herself tidying the already tidy desk. She rammed the edges of a stack of papers against the desktop and snapped them down into a pile. Her eyes shot bright jade arrows through him, and her pert little mouth looked ready to bite a nail in half. He almost smiled, she looked so worked up. Kinda cute, too. Not too difficult to see she wasn't pleased with his calling of an ad hoc council meeting.

Every chair in the jail had been called into service, and Ben was forced to stand, leaning against the wall near the window. Doc Bucknell, calm as ever, smoothed out the telegram on the desktop and read it silently.

A low grunt caught his attention. Poor Jigger sat on a chair in the corner, nursing his broken wrist. Ben went to his side.

"How's it feeling?"

"Hurts like sixty, Boss. Doc says the swelling should go down in a few days, but I can't even move my fingers right now." The skin was tight around the deputy's eyes, and his mouth bore signs of strain. "Who's going to look after Cassie now?"

Ben patted him lightly on the shoulder so as not to jar his injury. "Don't worry about it. You just do what Doc says and heal up. I'll take care of Cassie and the gold."

"No, you will not." Her voice cut through the air. She wasn't yelling or hysterical. No, her voice was dead calm and determined. "I'm capable of both looking after myself and the gold shipment, and I resent that you've called a council meeting without consulting me first."

Doc Bucknell rose, put his arm around her shoulders, and drew her back to her chair. "Cassie, we're going to sit down and talk about this rationally. Ben did the right thing alerting us to the issues. We're not saying you can't do the job, but it's a serious matter and it bears some discussion."

Though his tone was reasonable, it didn't seem to take Cassie's indignation down any pegs. She crossed her arms, plopped into the chair behind his desk, and set her jaw in a mutinous expression that reminded him not a little of one the twins wore every time he told them they couldn't do something.

"Did you get a chance to read the telegram?" Ben asked. They all nodded, Hobny's throat bouncing. "Good, then you understand how serious this is. I'm sure none of you want to risk the safety of any of the folks in town when word gets out that there's gold here practically undefended."

Cassie snorted, but Ben continued on. "Especially with Jigger now laid up. I propose that we cancel the Challenge and I take over my job again and Cassie takes over hers. Or, if you don't want to cancel it completely, then we take a break while the gold is in town and resume things after it has been picked up by the army and no longer poses a threat. We can even extend the Challenge for the days we'd miss."

"I object." Cassie put her palms flat on the desk. "What's the purpose of the Challenge at all if we can just bail out when things get difficult?"

Hobny cleared his throat. "You have to admit, these are some special circumstances. I've never even seen that much gold in one place. It would be a mighty big temptation, I would think. Especially considering that the newspaper this last week was full of articles about the Challenge and the participants. If I was ever inclined to larceny, I'd think that gold defended by a young lady would be a most promising target."

Ben nodded. "Exactly. Dad, what do you think?"

The moustache got smoothed a few times with his thumb and forefinger while he executed his "thousand-yard stare." Ben waited, knowing the signs, knowing he couldn't be rushed to judgment.

Eventually, Obadiah cleared his throat. "I'm thinking we should ask Miss Cassie what her plans for defending the gold are should there be trouble. I've always had a notion that Cassie was about one of the smartest people in this town, and I think we should give her a chance to prove it before we dismiss her out of hand."

Ben gaped. He'd counted on his father to be the voice of reason.

Cassie brightened, shooting a smile his father's way. "Thank you. I do have some ideas for securing the gold."

"Proceed." Her father waved his hand to give her the floor.

"First, the telegram says there will be a Wells Fargo guard accompanying the shipment. Earlier today, I wired this Colonel Briggenstern who sent the telegram to make certain the guard would be staying until the gold was picked up." She tugged open a desk drawer. "He wired me back just an hour ago. He's sending eight men plus the guard on the train, and he says he can leave one man behind with the guard if that would be of any help."

Ben tipped his hat back and considered this. Another man, a military man at that, would help, but it still left Cassie vulnerable, something that didn't sit well with him at all. Not to mention, he didn't know the Wells Fargo guard or this soldier. What was to say they might not decide to steal the gold once they saw the only thing standing between them and the money was one slip of a redheaded girl? No, it was still too risky. Surely his father and hers could see that.

The council put their heads together and talked for a moment before Doc Bucknell raised his head and asked, "What precautions do you plan to take in addition to the increased man power?"

"I'm glad you asked." She stood and paced the narrow area between the gun rack and his desk. "I know Jigger is wounded, so I thought it might be best if he stayed here at the jail. He can still shoot if necessary, and he can take his meals here for a few days and sleep in one of the cells. I've been assured that the two guards that will accompany the gold will not let it out of their sights, so they'll be bunking in here, too. If they take turns sleeping, there will be beds for everyone. My plan is to lock the gold into the first cell and take the keys down to Hobny's office and have him lock them in the safe. That way even if someone did storm the jail, they wouldn't find the keys here in the building, nor would they know where to get them. When the contingent from Fort Benefactor arrives, we can retrieve the keys and surrender the gold."

Ben had to admit the idea was rather clever. He might not have thought of it, instead trusting in his ability to hold off an attack.

"In addition, I don't intend to tell either the Wells Fargo guard or the soldier where to find the keys. Only the five of us in this room would know, and only Hobny knows the combination to his own safe, providing a further layer of protection." She stopped pacing. "I'm not without sense, gentlemen, and I have thought this through. I don't see how Ben could do a better job.

With three armed guards constantly in attendance, the gold locked up securely, and the keys kept in a safe up the street, security is as tight as can be. Minimizing the number of people who know about the gold even being here, as well as the number of people who go in and out of the jail over that time period will increase security."

Except that she was a girl, and she'd be in charge of grown men, and everyone who had read the paper knew the state of law enforcement in Cactus Creek for the next two and a half weeks. Her plan had some fine aspects, and when he got his badge back, he wasn't above utilizing them. He'd even give her credit at the Challenge Ball at the end of the month when the winners were declared. But the fact remained that she needed to step aside and let the men handle things.

Another huddle by the council, and Doc turned grave eyes on Cassie. "You've made a compelling case. I'm proud of you. You know what store I set by the Challenge and that I'm reluctant ever to allow a contestant to bow out."

"And," Ben's dad pitched in, "you've proven yourself more than capable up to this point."

"And you've obviously put quite a bit of thought into planning your security measures, what with wiring the colonel and getting more backup and all," Hobny added.

"Therefore," her father took over, "it is the decision of the council to continue with the Challenge in spite of this new wrinkle. However"—he held up one long, lean finger when Ben started to protest—"there are a few considerations to which you must agree."

Cassie's elation turned to caution. "Such as?"

"First, in order to protect your reputation, you will not stay at the jail past dark while the gold is here. With three grown men guarding the shipment through the night, your presence overnight is not necessary."

She nodded slowly while Ben considered this. Her reputation. Huh. He hadn't thought of her reputation needing protecting, but then again, he'd only just started to get used to the idea that she was almost twenty years old, not twelve. No way could she spend the night in a jailhouse full of men, no matter what the circumstances.

"Second, should any trouble arise around this jail, you will send for Ben with all haste. You will not be too stubborn or proud to get help. Understood?"

Her eyebrows darted toward one another, and a green storm brewed in her eyes.

"And third, if at any time while the gold is in your possession any member of the council determines that you or the gold are at risk, they are free to and encouraged to suspend the Challenge and remove you from the office of temporary sheriff." He leveled a paternal stare at his daughter. "If you cannot agree to this, then I'll be forced to shut the Challenge down right now."

She crossed her arms at her waist. The silence stretched as she considered his conditions, but finally, while Ben prayed she would refuse so they could call this whole thing off, she nodded.

"Very well. I accept the terms."

Ben stifled a groan. Of course she did. She was ten pounds of determination in a five-pound sack.

The council members filed out, and Jigger moved to follow.

"I think I'll go rest my arm for a while." He tugged on his wide-brimmed hat.

"I'm sorry about the rug." Cassie sent him a tentative smile. "Things are pretty quiet. You can knock off for the weekend. The gold isn't due until Monday. I can mind the jail until then."

"Thanks." He bobbed his head and avoided Ben's eyes.

The moment they were alone, Cassie jammed her hands on her hips and glared at Ben. "You have a lot of nerve, buster."

"Now, Cass, don't get in a lather. I'm just trying to look out for you."

"Really? How would you feel if I called a school board meeting this month without consulting you? To tell them I had no confidence in your ability to do the job. That I thought you weren't smart enough to teach or that the children were in danger if you kept to your part of the Challenge."

He blinked and stepped back, scratching his ear. "It's not at all the same."

She advanced on him and poked him in the chest. "It's exactly the same. It's like being tattled on, dragging my father and yours in here to complain."

Rubbing the spot she'd jabbed, he tried again. "It isn't my fault our dads are on the council. And it needed to be brought to their attention. If anything happens, Challenge or not, it's my responsibility and ultimately theirs as the council. I don't know what I'd do if something happened to you while you were doing my job." The words popped out with a ring of truth that surprised him and made her cute little mouth drop open. Time to backtrack. "I mean, I'd feel the same if it was Jigger who got hurt in my place."

Her mouth closed, and distance settled into her eyes. "Of course you would."

He jammed his hands into his pockets, and his fingers crushed the piece of paper he'd thrust there and tried to ignore all day. Just the thing to change the conversation and hopefully make her forget her peeve.

"Say, there is something happening at the school that I'd like your opinion on." He tugged the page out and unfolded it, much the worse for being wedged into the drawer slide and stuffed into his pocket. "I found this stuck in the top desk drawer at the school this morning, and I want to talk to you about it."

❧

The instant she caught sight of the pink scallop-edged paper, she wanted to slip through the cracks of the floor and die. How could she have been so stupid? Her heart thrummed in her chest, and a buzzing sound overtook her ears. She put her hand over her stomach, feeling the hollow, swooping sensation as it expanded outward, clear to her fingers and toes.

"I just don't know what to say. It caught me completely by surprise." He handed her the page.

"I . . . I . . ." she swallowed, trying to work a smidgen of moisture into her mouth. Hot tears of embarrassment pricked her eyes, and she drew a staggering breath.

"I mean, Mary Alice is a nice kid, and I don't want to set her back, but she can't be leaving notes like this for me. It isn't right." He shrugged, his troubled brown eyes meeting hers. "What do I do? It's clearly a case of puppy love. Do you think it will blow over if I just ignore it, or should I confront her? Though I don't have a spark of a notion what I'd say." Dull red dusted his cheeks, and he shrugged again.

She blinked. "What did you say?"

"Read the note."

Unfolding the paper, she scanned the lines, though she knew every word, every loop and whorl of her own handwriting. The page must've fallen out of her journal, the journal where she had poured out all her longing for Benjamin whenever she couldn't stand things any longer.

"Mary Alice has been acting strange since I started teaching." Ben set his hat, brim up, on the desk and tunneled his fingers through his dark hair. "She bats her eyes and tugs on her curls and is always offering to sweep up or clap the erasers or stay inside at recess and wipe down the blackboards. I put her off as gently as I can, but I bump into her every time I turn around. Should I have a few words with her? I don't want to hurt her feelings, but it's downright embarrassing."

Mary Alice. He thought Mary Alice had written the note and hidden it in the desk. She licked her lips and sought for words through the dust storm of relief blowing through her.

"If it would be any help to you, I could perhaps have a word or two with her."

He blew out a long breath. "You would? That would be great. I'd really appreciate you taking the reins on this one. Less embarrassing all the way around, I would think. I've never been in a situation like this. Maybe you should mention to her that in addition to me being miles too old for her, real men like to make the first advance, you know? It's mighty forward of a girl to declare her love for a fellow without him even having at least let his interest in her be known first."

A fresh dagger of mortification thrust through her heart. This was why he must never know how much she loved him until he first declared his feelings. If he found out first, he'd be appalled and run for the hills faster than a mustang with his tail on fire.

"I'll have a talk with her. It would be best if you didn't mention you'd found the page. No need to embarrass her further." And wouldn't it just, especially since Mary Alice would deny knowledge of the note, and Ben would put two and two together and it would come up Cassie.

The first chance she got, she'd go to the school and search the desk thoroughly to make sure no more journal pages had escaped.

CHAPTER 10

Cassie slipped from the house as the sun broke the horizon. In just a few strides, her skirt had wicked up the early morning dew, darkening her hemline. Unlocking the schoolhouse, she stepped inside and inhaled deeply, breathing in the aromas of paper, chalk, children, and lunches. She rounded the partition and entered the schoolroom proper, immediately noting the small changes that said someone other than herself had been in charge for the last two weeks.

Soft sunlight fell through the east windows onto the desks. Papers and books jutted from the small shelves under the desktops. Cassie always insisted the children spend the last five minutes of each day straightening their belongings before being dismissed from school. Though she'd clearly included this in the daily schedule she'd provided, Ben must be skipping that part. She walked up the aisle, letting the familiarity of the room embrace her. As much as she wanted to win the Challenge and enjoyed being the temporary sheriff, she missed her students, her classroom, her little kingdom.

The blackboard had been wiped clean—probably by the attentive Mary Alice—and the erasers lay neatly in the tray. As she approached the desk, she focused her attention on the top. Across a large sheet of store paper, the children had drawn and labeled pictures of Texas animals.

She tugged on her lower lip, mentally ticking through the curriculum. Wildlife study wasn't on any of the class lists for this quarter. She sat in her chair and examined the handwriting, identifying several of the children's work. A group project with every grade represented. *Hmm.* It was well done, she'd give them that.

The clock chimed, bringing her back to her errand. Beginning with the top right-hand drawer, she searched every nook and cranny, sifting through all the papers and books, taking everything out and putting it on top of the desk in order not to miss anything. When the drawers were empty and the desktop full, she sat back, relieved to have found nothing. Then a niggle of unease tugged at her mind. Had Ben found something more before she could remove it?

Her eyes fell on the grade book on top of a stack, and she couldn't resist opening it up to see how everyone was doing under Ben's tutelage.

She checked the first week, happy to see he'd kept careful records of attendance and assignments. Before she could turn to the next week, a sound drew her attention. She got to her feet.

Ben came around the partition, a stack of boards on his shoulder and a paint can dangling from one hand. He stopped short; then his face split in a smile.

"Good morning. I didn't expect anyone to be here." He glanced at the contents of the desk piled in plain sight. "What are you doing?"

What could she say that wouldn't be a lie? "I was looking for something."

He edged up the aisle, careful not to knock anything with the boards before leaning them against the wall. "What?"

"Um..."

Ben reached for the record book. "Are you checking up on me?"

"No, I really was looking for something." She knew she was blushing and mentally rued her fair complexion for betraying her. "I'll put it all back." *Oh, for the love of gingersnaps, why am I apologizing for looking through my own desk?* "What brings you here on your day off?" As she asked, she began restoring the contents of the drawers.

He shrugged and set the paint can on the floor. "I had a little project I wanted to do."

"Anything I can help with?" She stowed her writing paper and her favorite ink pen in the top drawer. Her ruler and extra boxes of chalk followed.

"If you like. I'm making a bookshelf. The kids said you're always saying you don't have enough storage."

Her hand froze on one of the drawer handles, touched that he would spend his Saturday doing something thoughtful for her. It was just like him to infuriate her to the point of madness one moment and sweep all those feelings away by being considerate the next.

"That's very kind of you."

He grinned and shoved his hat back. "I'm a nice guy." His brown eyes twinkled, and his smile made her feel as if she were melting into a warm puddle.

Time to get ahold of herself or she would surely betray her feelings and disgust him with her forwardness. "And humble, too. Are you conceding defeat?"

"What do you mean?"

"The extra bookshelves will come in handy when I win the Challenge. My cause is new books for the school." She gave him a saucy smile.

"I concede nothing. I think I'll take this wood back to the lumberyard." He growled and lifted one of the boards.

Smacking her hands on the lumber to pin it against the wall, she shook her head. "Oh no you don't. It's here, so you might as well finish what you started."

"I always finish what I start." He cocked a playful eyebrow at her.

"As do I." They looked at one another for a long moment before he broke the stare.

"I left something outside."

While he was gone, she shoved the last of the papers and supplies into the desk.

"I know what you were looking for in the desk." His toolbox clanked to the floor.

She went still. "You do?"

"Yep, I found them on Friday, and I put them in my vest pocket so I'd be sure to get them to you." He shook his head. "And then I forgot anyway." He opened his hand, and on his palm lay a pair of tortoise-shell combs.

"Oh, thank you." She took them, thrilling as her fingers touched his skin for an instant.

"Glad I could help. If you hold boards for me while I saw, this bookshelf won't take too long. I wanted to get an early start on it so I could get it painted today. If I get a coat on it this morning, I can come back and put another layer on this afternoon and it will be ready for Monday morning. It won't be fancy, but it should do."

She followed his directions, treasuring this time alone with him, trying desperately not to let it go to her head, but knowing she would always remember this morning.

"One more board to cut; then we'll put it together." He lifted the last long board into place, using two of the children's desks as sawhorses.

"Can I try?" she asked.

"You want to cut it?"

"Sure. How hard can it be?" She lifted her arm and flexed her muscle.

"Go ahead, ma'am. I'll hold the board for you." He handed her the saw with a laugh.

It was heavier than she'd anticipated, but she took it in both hands.

"There's the mark. Cut right across." He gripped the board, pressing it firmly onto the desks.

She eyed the pencil mark and set the saw teeth on the corner of the board as she'd seen Ben do. Dragging the saw toward her, it wobbled and stuck and bounced off the wood leaving a series of jagged marks that looked like mice had been busy nibbling the lumber.

Glancing up at Ben, she noted his innocent expression. She set her jaw and gripped the saw harder.

Same results. With a huff, she blew the hair off her forehead. "What am I doing wrong?"

"It's not as easy as it looks. You have to use some muscle, but you have to let the saw do the work." He moved behind her, and her breathing flat-out quit. "Here, let me show you."

His arms came around her, and every nerve came alive. He smelled of bay-rum soap and peppermint. His chest was a solid wall against her back, and his arms, all ropy muscle and sinew, blocked any escape. As if she wanted to escape. If she died right there, she'd die a happy girl.

Best yet, his hand engulfed hers on the saw, and he wrapped his fingers over hers. "This is a crosscut saw, so cutting action will happen on both the push and the pull stroke. Like a knife." He pushed then pulled, and with ridiculous ease, a quarter inch groove appeared. "Let the saw do the work. Right?"

She nodded, wanting to close her eyes and savor his nearness. Gradually, as she sawed, he let up the pressure on her hand, letting her take over more of the work—but he didn't let go altogether. Finally, the board parted, the cut end clattering to the floor.

"I did it." She let go of the saw and whirled, elated.

They stood bare inches apart. She smiled up at him expecting a grin in return, but he had the strangest expression on his face. He backed up a step, holding the saw in one hand and wiping the palm of his other on his leg.

"Yep, you did."

His voice sounded like he was strangling.

Puzzled, she asked, "What do we do next?"

"Um, hammer it together, I suppose."

"Are you feeling ill?" He looked flushed and pale at the same time. . .if that was possible.

"I'm fine." He dug into his toolbox and drew out a paper sack. "I'll hammer. You hand me the nails."

In a matter of ten minutes, they stood back and looked at a new waist-high bookshelf.

"All it needs is paint."

She glanced at the clock. Almost nine.

"I won't be able to help with that. I have to get down to the jail. I told Jigger I'd take the weekend so he could rest his arm."

"All right. I can handle it from here."

"Is something wrong?" He'd become so quiet, she couldn't help but wonder if she'd done something to offend him. And he hadn't said a word of complaint about the Challenge or the gold or anything.

"No. I just want to get this first coat on so it can start drying." He used a screwdriver to open the paint can.

Feeling as if she was being dismissed, she picked up her hair combs from the corner of the desk.

"I guess I'll see you this afternoon for the campaigning?"

"I'll be there."

He didn't have to sound so grim about it.

⁓

She couldn't leave fast enough for Ben. The minute her skirts disappeared and the schoolhouse door closed behind her, he sagged against the wall, trying to make sense of what had happened to him.

Whatever it was, it was wrong, sideways, and not going to happen again, that was for sure and for certain.

He scrubbed his fingers through his hair and dragged his palms down his cheeks. Though the smell of fresh paint drifted up from the open can, he couldn't get the scent of roses and female out of his mind.

Everything had been fine until he'd showed her how to use the saw. His eyes drifted closed, and she was back in his embrace, her shoulders brushing his chest, her hair teasing his temple, and her hand tucked into his like a bird in a nest.

And in a flash, his brain had turned to damp gunpowder refusing to fire, and the world had done a buck-and-wing beneath his boots.

Cassie Bucknell. Hoyden, minx, and all-around pest. That was what she had always been, and that was what she was going to stay. Forever fourteen. A sort of courtesy little sister. The baby of the Bucknell family.

Except she wasn't fourteen any longer, as she'd gone to great pains to tell him.

She'd sure felt all woman in his arms. And he'd come within a gnat's eyelash of kissing that sweet little mouth.

He swallowed hard, trying not to imagine what that might've been like. Guilt and thrill chased each other through his veins, along with relief that he hadn't done anything so stupid. She'd have smacked his face, and he would've deserved it, too. What on earth was wrong with him?

He squeezed his eyes shut for a moment, willing himself to forget this nonsense and get on with the job at hand. Digging through his toolbox, he found a flat piece of kindling and thrust it into the paint can, stirring the pigment.

Not for all the gold in the coming shipment would he ever tell a soul that he'd chosen the jade-green color at the mercantile simply because it matched Cassie Bucknell's eyes.

~ ❧ ~

Carl knocked on the back door of the bakery, peering through the screen mesh and inhaling yeasty, cinnamony, sugary scents. His mouth watered as he remembered he'd skipped breakfast to get a jump on the chores that had piled up during the week.

Jenny, be-aproned and with a flour smudge on her nose, stood on tiptoe, rocking the heels of her hands into a mass of dough on the worktable.

Her blue eyes widened when she looked up. "Come in."

Hinges squealed, and the spring groaned as he stepped inside. Pots and bowls filled the sink, pans and baking sheets covered the counter, and every crock and tub and container stood open around the room. Evidently she couldn't cook anything without using every implement in the place.

She dug her fingers into the flour crock and dusted her work surface before flipping the dough and kneading it again. "What can I do for you?"

Still frosty.

And he still hadn't a clue why. They'd been getting along quite well, taking care of the foal, seeing to the sorrel's comfort. But the minute he expressed any frustration with the Challenge, instead of commiserating with him and listing all the things he was doing wrong in the bakery, she'd gone chilly as an icehouse in January.

"I wondered if I could borrow Amanda for a little while." He glanced up and whisked his hat off. Where were his manners? He'd clean forgotten he was wearing a hat.

Her hands stilled. "Why?"

No mistaking the suspicion in her voice.

"The foal's nursing pretty well now, but she's got some catching up to do. I thought Amanda could give her a bottle."

She swiped at her hair with the back of her wrist, leaving a streak of flour along her temple, set her jaw, and pummeled the poor bread dough. Probably wished it was his head.

"Mr. Gustafson, I made it clear that we could not receive the gift of a pony. There's no point in letting Amanda get attached to either of those animals. It's just going to mean heartbreak later. She's already less than thrilled with me for refusing to let her have them."

He leaned across the table and covered her little hands with one of his to force her to stop torturing the dough and look at him. She stilled for an instant, then jerked away, wiping her fingers on her apron as if wanting to remove any sensation of his touch.

For his part, her hands, even dusted with flour had felt like satin. Womanly, small, and dainty.

"Why do you do that?" He looked for a place to set his hat, but there wasn't a spare inch of clean countertop. He wound up hooking it over the corner of the inside door, letting it hang by its stampede strap.

"Do what?"

"Wall yourself off? It's like you're afraid to let anyone get close, and it isn't just you. You keep Amanda from getting to know people, too."

Her arms crossed in a familiar stance, as if to ward off an attack. "I don't know what you mean."

"Sure you do." He gestured toward her posture. "You're doing it now. I watched you the other night at Doc Bucknell's. You talked with folks, but you never started the conversation, and you smiled every once in a while, but it was like you were all tensed up inside, like you were waiting for someone to drop a platter or something.

"And after church on Sunday, you kept Amanda glued to your side, even though the rest of the kids were running and playing. I asked Ben about it, and he said Amanda hasn't said a single word to him at the school, not in two whole weeks. She's always by herself when the other kids are playing, reading a book or drawing pictures. And when she's here, she barely speaks above a whisper, and she ducks in and out like a shadow."

The pink in her cheeks deepened, and the ice in her blue eyes hardened. "I can't see that my daughter's behavior is any of your concern, Mr. Gustafson. You know nothing of our past or what we've been through that might account for our behavior."

"Because you won't tell me. You won't tell anyone, unless it's maybe Cassie. She seems to be the only person in this town that you think is good enough to talk to."

She flinched, and regret stabbed him. He had a bit of a clue to her background, thanks to Amanda's prattling, but he wanted to hear it from Jenny, for Jenny to feel comfortable enough with him to trust him with her past.

"I didn't mean that. I'm just trying to help you and Amanda out."

"Why?" Her golden brows crinkled.

He shrugged. "Because it's the right thing to do. You don't have anyone to look after you. It's. . .neighborly." He tried to inject some levity into the discussion. "Besides, I owe Amanda a favor. If she hadn't made those cookies the other day, the town might've stormed the place and run me out of town. They're tired of biscuits."

A small smile tugged at her lips for a moment, and he thought he might've broken through her reserve for once, but it disappeared, and the distrust took over again. How had such a simple act of what he thought was kindness turned into such a chore?

She worried her lower lip, studying him in brief snatches, unable to hold his gaze. Finally, he shook his head and pushed himself away from the counter.

"It's all right. Don't strain yourself trying to find a polite way to say no. If you change your mind, I'll be at the stable all day. And if you aren't comfortable sending Amanda on her own, you are always welcome to come along."

He plucked his hat from the top of the door. "If you do come down, I'll send you home with something that might help you out around here."

"What is that?"

"Well, Mrs. Hart"—he trod heavily on her last name since she insisted on using his—"as much as you enjoy getting on your high horse, that doesn't help you when it comes to kneading bread. That table is about six inches too high for you to get good leverage. I'll knock together a sturdy box for you to stand on, and I'll even carry it over for you."

He let the screen door slap behind him, wondering if he'd done any good at all.

⁂

Three hours later, with twelve loaves of bread cooling on the counter and all the dishes washed and order restored, Jenny could no longer find an excuse to ignore Amanda's pleas. The little scamp had been sitting on the stairs out of sight and heard Carl's invitation. Since the moment he left, her daughter had given her no peace, first pleading verbally, then subjecting her mother to a series of imploring looks and soul-sucking sighs.

When Jenny had hung the last dish towel out on the porch rail, she let go of her final bit of resistance. Silly as it seemed, she actually missed the stable. Surely a couple of hours in Carl's presence wouldn't hurt anything. Returning to the kitchen, she plucked a basket from a shelf and bent a motherly stare on her daughter.

"Fine. We can go. Take this into the shop and fill it with some muffins and cookies." A peace offering to the livery owner probably wouldn't go amiss.

Amanda skipped and hopped at her side all the way there, her long golden curls bouncing. It did Jenny's heart good, and she couldn't help but wonder if what Carl had accused her of was true. Had she contributed to Amanda's guarded behavior? Was she holding her back from making friends?

But they both had reason to know that the world could be, and was quite frequently, a harsh and cruel place, and letting people get close meant being vulnerable to hurt. It meant becoming powerless, something Jenny had vowed would never happen to her again.

She paused, thinking back. Carl had been watching her, both at the dinner party and at church. She didn't know whether to be flattered or irritated, so she settled on uncomfortable—the way she felt about Carl most of the time anyway.

"Can I really give the baby a bottle? Do you think Mr. Carl will let me brush Copper? Maybe we can take them outside. Sunshine would be good for the baby, don't you think?" Amanda prattled on, not really expecting answers to her many questions and thus not pausing between them.

Carl closed the gate to the corral as they approached. He'd left his hat off, and his red-gold hair and beard gleamed in the sunshine. His suspenders bit deep into his broad shoulders, wrinkling the faded denim shirt he wore with the sleeves rolled up, baring his strong forearms.

"You came." He winked at Amanda, an action that got him a shy smile and an adoring glance.

Jenny tried to work some moisture into her mouth, and blushed at realizing she'd all but ogled the man. She couldn't think of what to say or where to look, so she raised the basket, holding it out to him.

"Tell me it isn't sourdough biscuits." He took the basket and raised the corner of the covering napkin, waggling his brows at Amanda, who giggled.

"No. Mama threw out all the biscuits from this last week. She said they were hard as doorknobs."

He paused, probably at hearing Amanda speak in something above a whisper, then sent a rueful glance at Jenny.

Heat rushed up her cheeks. "You picked a fine time to break your silence, Little Miss."

"Aw, she talks to me all the time, don't you, dolly? And your mama is right. Those things would sink like bricks if you tried to skip them in the stream." He sniffed the basket. "These muffins and cookies look a lot tastier than anything I could make. I can't wait to gobble them up. Speaking of gobbling stuff up, there's a bottle waiting on the bench in the equipment room, and a hungry, short-legged horse waiting for it."

Amanda broke into a run, gliding up the earthen ramp and over the threshold.

"Thank you for coming."

Jenny nodded, turning into the slight breeze and tugging a stray hair away from the corner of her mouth. "I'm sorry I was so hesitant earlier. It was churlish of me."

"I shouldn't have pushed you." He motioned toward the barn, and she went inside ahead of him.

Amanda knelt in the straw, giggling and stroking every part of the foal she could reach while the little filly butted the bottle she held against her side.

"Here, stand up, or she'll bowl you right over." Carl hung the basket on a peg and raised Amanda to her feet. "Hold the bottle with two hands. She might be little, but she's stronger than she looks." He glanced at Jenny, and she had a feeling that perhaps he wasn't just talking about the foal.

Copper came over to check Amanda out, sniffing her and blowing out, ruffling Amanda's curls. The foal clamped down on the bottle—a store-bought affair with a rubber teat that replaced the vanilla-and-glove stopgap—closed her eyes, and flicked her fuzzy tail.

Carl bent and whispered in Jenny's ear, his beard close enough to brush her skin, sending a shiver through her. "The foal doesn't really need a bottle. The mare's letting down her milk just fine now, but there's something awfully sweet about this picture, isn't there?"

Jenny had to agree. Amanda wore a grin wide enough to crease her cheeks, and her eyes shone with love.

Stepping a little away from the heat radiating from Carl's chest, she swallowed. "How did you manage that? The other night you said you'd take care of the mare, but I didn't hear what you were going to do."

He pursed his lips and stared at the ceiling for a moment. "You want the truth?"

"Of course."

"You might not like it."

Blinking, she couldn't imagine what he might do that would cause his cheeks to be ruddy and for him to be so hesitant to share it with her. Though she had no idea what he was skirting around, she knew without a doubt that he would never do anything harmful to one of the animals in his care. "It can't have been anything cruel, so just tell me."

Jamming his thumbs under his suspenders, he eased them

on his shoulders. "First, I went to the saloon and got a bucket of beer."

She made a conscious effort not to let her jaw drop open, but she couldn't stop the little intake of air that shot into her lungs. "Beer?"

"What, Mama?" Amanda looked up. Concern tightened her little face.

"Nothing, sweetie, just go ahead and finish feeding the baby."

Jenny marched to the doorway, her chest tight, in need of some air and distance.

Beer.

She should've known better than to abandon her instincts regarding men. The same thing had happened when she'd let go of her misgivings about Robert when he'd first started courting her. And he'd turned out to be a mean drunk. Now Carl was buying beer by the bucketful? And she'd almost entrusted Amanda to him alone this afternoon. What had she been thinking? She stared out at the horizon but saw only memories of Robert in a filthy, drunken rage, breaking all the china on the sideboard and slinging his empty wineglass at her portrait on the dining room wall.

Carl came up behind her. "I told you that you might not like it. I don't hold with drinking myself, but it's pretty near foolproof in getting a mare to relax enough to let her milk down."

"What did you say?" Her thoughts collided with her memories and created a cloud of noise in her head that his words barely pierced.

"I mixed up a mash for the mare using warm beer instead of water. Worked a treat." He studied her as if she had butterflies where her brains should be. Which she probably did.

"You didn't drink it?"

"Of course not." He frowned. "Alcohol for medicinal purposes only."

Once more, chagrin at her propensity for leaping to conclusions coursed through her.

He leaned against the doorjamb, crossing his arms. "Maybe one of these days you'll stop thinking the worst of me. I understand from the little Amanda has mentioned that your husband wasn't a very nice man, but when are you going to realize that I'm not him?"

Jenny couldn't meet his eyes. Carl wasn't like Robert. Perhaps if he was, it would be easier to steel her heart against him.

CHAPTER 11

Cassie stood in the depot waiting room and checked the clock for the tenth time that minute. The ten thirty was late. By at least three minutes.

"Relax, Cass, the morning train has been late so often this month, I'm thinking of changing the name to the 'sometime-around-noonish' train." Ralph erased the timetable chalkboard beside his ticket window and began updating the arrival times.

Jigger sat on one of the long, uncomfortable benches, his left arm in a sling and his right propping a shotgun upright on his thigh. "As much as I want this train to show up, the transportation I really want to see is the army detachment that will take this gold out of here in a couple of days. Trouble's coming. I can feel it." He scowled, his huge handlebar moustache drooping.

If Cassie was honest, she had the same misgivings. Once more she ran through her security measures, looking for any flaws, anything she could do—beyond abandoning her post as sheriff—that would increase the safety of the gold and minimize the risks.

Nothing came to mind. She glanced at the clock again.

Four minutes late.

"Stop biting your nails." Jigger shifted his weight on the bench, making the oak creak. "You've practically gnawed them off to your elbow already."

She couldn't take the lack of air in the depot anymore, though every window and door had been propped open. The platform would surely be better.

Shading her eyes from the morning sun, she followed the gleaming rails to where they disappeared on the eastern horizon. Miles and miles of open prairie lay around her, making her feel small, as if she stood at the center of a giant dome of pale, arcing sky. The wind tugged at her skirts and hair, and she turned into the breeze to keep stray hairs off her face. To the west, up the length of Main Street, she could see the schoolhouse. Must be morning recess, for she could make out the kids scampering around the building.

Mr. Svenson, sweeping the boardwalk in front of the mercantile, waved to her. She raised her hand in reply. Saturday afternoon's campaigning at his store had gone better than the first week. Everyone seemed to be hitting their strides in their jobs, and coins were accumulating nicely in both jars. Since things had been quiet all week, folks seemed to have more confidence in her abilities as the temporary sheriff. Next Saturday, when she could reveal that she'd successfully guarded a gold shipment that would more than purchase this town a couple of times over, she was sure folks would back her to win the Challenge. They'd fill out their ballots at the Challenge Ball and crown her the winner.

And to have the confidence of the people of Cactus Creek would surely get Ben's attention.

She still wasn't sure what was going on with him. Every time their eyes had met Saturday afternoon during the campaign period, he'd looked away. And when she'd caught him studying her a time or two, he had a puzzled expression on his face, almost like she'd done something wrong and he was trying to figure out what it was.

And men said women were the confusing gender.

She'd ducked into the school after church yesterday to see the new bookcase. Ben had painted it a pale green, and she knew she would think of him and his kindness every time she slid a book into place on one of its shelves. He'd avoided her after the church service, and though his family had come to dinner, he'd been absent. For the life of her, she couldn't think what she'd done wrong. . .unless he'd discovered that she was the author of the love letter. Anxiety tightened steel bands around her lungs and forced her heart high in her chest.

In front of the livery, Jenny tacked up a horse at the hitching rail, standing on a box to hoist the saddle over the animal's back. She turned her back to the horse and put the cinch over her shoulder, standing up to tighten the strap around the horse's girth. Cassie smiled. Jenny was so smart, tackling logistics and problems like a general. Petite, but tough as buffalo leather.

Turning back to the east, her heart accelerated. A dark smudge on the horizon grew larger, puffing smoke, clanging metal, roaring firebox. The ten thirty had arrived.

Jigger joined her on the platform, the shotgun lying on his shoulder. "'Bout time."

"Yes, let's let the passengers get off—if there are any—before we unload the gold." She checked to see that the baggage cart she'd wheeled out earlier still stood on the platform ready for its pricey cargo. The goal was to get the gold to the jail with no one being the wiser. Too bad it hadn't come in on a night train. That would've made things easier.

Only one passenger left the train, a drummer who juggled his heavy sample cases and tried to tip his hat to her at the same time. She nodded.

One car back, a ramp banged down onto the platform, raising dust and drawing attention.

Too much attention. Cassie felt someone at her elbow and looked down into Amanda Hart's little face.

"What are you doing here? You should be at the school."

She smiled, and before she could say a word, the twins piled through the doorway, landing in a heap on the boards and scrambling up. The entire school followed, with Ben on their heels.

"What's going on here?" Though she knew. Oh, she knew what he was up to.

His expression was so angelic, she wanted to roll her eyes. "We're on a field trip. We thought we'd explore the depot today and learn about trains."

"Oh really?" She yanked on his sleeve, drawing him away from the kids. "Is this your idea of keeping things quiet? A dozen witnesses who will go right home and tell their parents?"

"Quit squawking. The gold will be in a box, the kids will stay here at the depot with Ralph and learn about trains, and I'll be able to help with guarding the shipment between here and the jail without anyone being the wiser."

Ralph emerged, his green visor shading his eyes. "Cass, looks like someone over there wants to talk to you."

"You and these kids stay right here, Benjamin Wilder." She whirled on her heel and stalked over to where an army officer waited on the ramp. Ben *still* didn't trust her. He was checking up on her like she was in primer school. A fine red mist colored the edges of her vision, and her hands ached and shook from clenching them. She made a conscious effort to loosen the muscles in her jaw.

"Officer, I'm Cassie Bucknell, temporary sheriff of Cactus Creek." She offered her hand.

He scowled, touching her fingers briefly—without removing his gauntlet—and tugged on the corner of his long black moustache. "Captain Clancy. This is most irregular, ma'am. I know you've discussed the particulars with my commanding officer, but I have severe reservations about leaving this particular shipment in the hands of. . ." His Adam's apple lurched, and he pressed his lips together.

"In the hands of a woman. I understand your misgivings, but you have your orders and so do I." Great, another one who thought she had cotton batting for brains. "Where is the Wells Fargo guard?"

The group of young soldiers who bristled with guns and bravado parted, and a brawny, chiseled man stepped through. He carried a shotgun so large she wondered if it needed its own caisson to carry the ammunition.

The line of his jaw was so sharp, and the column of his neck so masculine, her breath hitched in her throat. If she wasn't already madly in love with Ben Wilder, she might've swooned.

His long, lean hand came up to tip his hat brim. "Ma'am. It's a pleasure to meet you. I understand you're the acting sheriff here?"

Oh my. His voice could melt chocolate.

Was her mouth hanging open?

"Uh-huh." *Oh, for pity's sake, pull yourself together, girl. It isn't as if you haven't seen a handsome man before.*

"I'm Randall Franks, with Wells Fargo. I would suggest we get the gold transported as quickly as possible. We're a might vulnerable out here in the open." He flicked a finger toward the soldiers, who stepped aside once more to reveal three strong-boxes chained to the floor of the car.

She gathered her considerably scattered wits and tried to appear professional. "I've got a baggage cart here and some canvas to cover the boxes. The jail is a block and a half west on the main street."

He tugged at the little tuft of hair just below his bottom lip, looking up the street toward their destination. "I suppose there's no help for it. We'll have to parade right down the main thoroughfare. I had hoped to arrive after dark and perhaps move the shipment without so many onlookers."

"What kind of gun is that?" Quincy appeared at her side. "Are you a lawman?"

"Have you kilt any robbers, mister?" Ulysses was quick to chime in. "What're you guarding? A prisoner?"

"Are you an army scout? You look like an army scout."

"Did you bring a horse? Are you tracking an outlaw?"

"Of course he brought a horse, you doorknob. How's he going to track an outlaw if he's afoot?"

"I ain't no doorknob. And you don't know if he's tracking an outlaw. He might *be* an outlaw."

Quincy's eyebrows rose, and he bounced on his toes. "Are you? Are you a real outlaw? Is the sheriff going to arrest you? What'd you do? Did you rob a train?"

Mr. Franks blinked at their rapid-fire questions, clearly unprepared for this Gatling-gun approach to interrogation.

Cassie put on her teacher voice. "Boys, get back into the depot this minute. In fact, get all the way back to the school."

Mr. Franks's brows lowered. "Who are these children, and what are they doing here?"

The temperature in her cheeks rose. "The local school appears to be having an outing today."

Ben strode over and stuck out his hand. "Sheriff Ben Wilder." He shook hands with the captain and with Mr. Franks. "At least I'm usually the sheriff, but as you can see, things aren't quite usual around here at the moment." He turned to the kids. "Mary Alice, please take the children back to the schoolhouse. You can have your lunch, and this afternoon we'll do something special."

"What? What will we do?" Quincy tugged on his arm.

"It's a surprise." He barely glanced down at the boy.

The twins crossed their arms and jutted out their lower lips in a stance that was all too familiar to Cassie.

"We know what that means." Ulysses nodded with all the wisdom of a nine-year-old boy. "That means you don't know what it is, and you are just trying to get rid of us. We don't want to go. We want to see the soldiers and talk to the man with the big gun. If we're going to be lawmen or bandits, we have to get as much information as we can. You told us that. How can we observe and learn anything if you keep us shut up in the schoolhouse?"

Cassie wanted to laugh at Ben's expression. He looked like he'd just bitten a wasp. "Ulysses. . ."

"Ma'am? If I might?" Mr. Franks squatted between the boys. "So, you think you might want to be lawmen or bandits?"

"Yep, we ain't decided which yet."

To his credit, he displayed no surprise. "It's a tough decision. Of course, I hope you'll come down on the side of law and order.

To answer your question, this is an eight-gauge shotgun." He stood the butt of the gun on the planks where it jutted a good foot over their heads. "It kicks like a Missouri mule, and it's got the bite of a grizzly. And without fail, it will make an outlaw pause and think before he does something stupid."

"Can we touch it?" Eyes round as cookies.

He gave them each a long, assessing look. "You can this once, but—and you listen to me carefully on this one—the only reason I'm letting you touch a gun is because I'm here holding it. You are never, never, *never* to touch a gun without an adult's permission. Understand?"

Their heads bobbed like ducks on a pond. Two small, grubby hands reached out and touched the blue-black barrels and the shiny wooden stock.

"Now, you boys scamper back to school. When you're grown-up lawmen, maybe you'll have eight-gauges of your own, and heaven help the bad guys then." He tousled their hair, earning him face-stretching grins, and watched as they followed the other students down the center of the street toward the white schoolhouse a quarter of a mile to the west.

"Thank you. That was nicely done."

Mr. Franks shrugged. "I have kids of my own."

Cassie readjusted her thinking to include a wife and family for Mr. Franks.

Ben's lips were set in a firm line, and his eyes flicked from Franks to Cassie and back. Her chin came up. If he thought he could take over her job, he had another thing coming.

"Captain, if your men would load the cart, we can get it covered and locked up."

The four soldiers with him set their rifles aside and latched onto the handles of two of the strongboxes. Their faces reddened and the muscles in their necks went rigid as they small-stepped with their load toward the baggage cart.

Ralph removed his visor and smoothed his hair. "You might want to make a couple of trips. Those boxes look awfully heavy, and that cart's seen better days."

"No, the fewer trips the better." Cassie tugged the canvas sheet over the boxes. "We're going to be conspicuous enough."

"Are you sure?" Ben shook his head. "That cart looks like it's about to collapse."

"It will be fine. Shouldn't you be at the school?" Why was everyone suddenly second-guessing her?

The captain tugged his gloves up higher. "Men, two of you pull, two of you push. Mr. Franks and I will walk ahead and behind. Put your rifles on the cart where you can get to them easily."

"And I'll be on guard, too." Cassie knifed her way into their conversation. What was it going to take to get a little respect around here?

The cart creaked alarmingly as they edged it down the ramp at the end of the platform and turned it toward town. Cassie forced herself not to look at the canvas lump on the flatbed but to keep sweeping the doorways and windows and sidewalks for any sign of trouble. Of course, Ben, at her side, was doing the same thing.

"Ben, I can handle this. You shouldn't be here. You're breaking the contest rules. And you promised to only interfere if there was a reason." She spoke out of the corner of her mouth, keeping her voice low.

"This *is* a reason. I'll go back to the school as soon as the gold is under cover."

At that instant, the cart, still a good thirty yards away from the jail, gave a loud groan, a ghostly shriek of metal, and a death rattle before subsiding in a heap of splinters and bent wheels. The strongboxes slid from under the canvas, tumbling in a heap on the ground.

Perhaps strongbox wasn't the best description, as the one that had been on the top of the pile crashed to the ground on one corner and sprang open, spilling gold bars into the dirt with dull thuds.

Everyone stood still as the dust settled. Sunshine gleamed off the gold, and the canvas flapped gently in the breeze.

The noise brought people outside.

"Look at that. Is that. . . ? Gold?" Footsteps and voices joined as it seemed every store and business along the street emptied. A circle formed around the junk pile that had once been a baggage cart as the soldiers dug their rifles out of the wreckage.

Carl Gustafson, wiping his hands on a flour sack apron, reached them with long strides. "You need some help here?"

"Everything's under control." Cassie faked a smile, though her chest felt caved in. What had she done insisting on making one trip?

Hobny and her father arrived, eyes wide, along with at least a dozen others. "Cassie?" her father asked. "What's going on here? I thought the idea was to *not* draw attention to what was going on." He kept his voice subdued, though why, she didn't know, since everyone could see the gold.

"Do you think I meant for this to happen? If I wanted this many people to know what was going on, I would've posted it in the newspaper."

"Cass, let us help you." Ben took her arm.

She jerked it away. "I can take care of this. I have it all planned out."

"Sure you do, but plans have a way of going off the rails from time to time."

"Don't patronize me."

"Fine." Fire blazed in his eyes. "You've got it all under control. You've got it all planned out. You don't need any help. But at the moment, the one secret you were in charge of keeping is sprawled all over Main Street."

Her eyes and throat burned, but she refused to give in. "If you don't have anything better to do than point out my flaws to every passerby, then you can just leave, thank you very much." She put up her hands and moved the encircling crowd back. "All of you go about your business. Move back." People politely backed away, though it appeared they were having a hard time pulling their eyes away from the riches on the street.

When she got to the Shoop brothers, they refused to budge. "Move along, boys."

"It's a free country, and this is a public street. I can stand here all day if I want to."

"There's nothing to see here." She held on to her temper as best she could.

"I think there *is* something mighty interesting to see around here. Lookit all that gold!" Melvin Shoop scratched his ribs and spat on the ground. "Where you taking it? And who's it for?"

Alvin elbowed him. "I could use me some of that there shiny metal, that's for sure. I ain't never seed nothing so pretty in all my born days. Maybe we should take some of it off yer hands." His eyes glowed as if he were in a trance, never wavering from the gold.

The captain barked orders to his men, who jumped to work, hefted the two undamaged boxes, and headed toward the jail.

"Guess we can help ya clean up the streets, *Miss Sheriff*, for a fee." Melvin spit again and took a step around Cassie, reaching for a gold bar. The smell of drink made her want to gag.

Her gun came out, and she cracked him across the wrist with the barrel. He howled, leaping back and holding his forearm.

"Did you see that? She hit me."

She stood her ground, though her insides quaked. "You're drunk again, Melvin. You and your brother get back like I told you, or you're going to get worse than a whack on the arm."

His eyes blazed, and he snarled. "No puny woman's going to tell me what to do. I aim to get me a look at that gold. I ain't never seed a real gold bar before, and I aim to heft one to see what it feels like."

"Melvin, I'm warning you one more time, get back. You're not laying a finger on that gold, now or ever. Understood?"

He swayed, breathing beery fumes into the morning air. Alvin, at his shoulder, glared at her, and they took a step forward.

An ominous click arrested the assemblage. "The lady said stand back."

She dared a glance over her shoulder. Randall Franks had moved to stand astride the glacier tongue of gold spilling from the broken box, the eight-gauge looking like a mountain howitzer in his grip. Beside him, Ben had his gun drawn, his face a mask of controlled anger.

The Shoop brothers froze. "We's just trying to help." Alvin's whine was like sandpaper on skin.

"That won't be necessary. Go about your business." His flat tone brooked no argument and left Cassie with the feeling that she might see the Missouri mule/grizzly bear action of the shotgun at any moment.

Two of the soldiers trotted toward them, returning from the jail. Lifting two bars each, they headed back the way they'd come. Ben studied the crowd as they backed up slowly.

Cassie eased to Randall's side to make sure she wasn't in the way of his aim. "I think you scared them off."

He jerked his chin, keeping his steely gray eyes on the Shoop brothers as they sauntered over to stand under the awning in front of the photographer's shop. Neither went inside, but they kept their distance.

When nothing lay in the street but broken baggage cart parts, Cassie swallowed hard. Carl stood with Jenny in the doorway of the livery, and he approached again, slowly, his hands in plain sight. "Cassie, I'll take care of the cart if you want. You and the. . .this gentleman will be wanting to get down to the jail, no doubt."

"Thank you, Carl."

When they reached the jail, there was hardly any room to stand. Soldiers and town councilmen crowded together. The only councilman not present was Ben's father, who as an ex-lawman might've been some help in the current situation. Instead, her father and Mr. Jones stood by the open cell door contemplating the gold and sending her uncertain looks, as if now that the treasure was here, they were having second thoughts as to her ability to protect it.

Mr. Franks took charge, giving Cassie a chance to gather herself. She carefully didn't look at Ben, knowing he would still be mad and that he had every right to be.

"Captain, the train's going to leave soon. You and your men should get back to the depot."

The officer agreed. "We're leaving Corporal Shipton here, as per orders. He's yours to command, but he got orders to be on the eastbound train forty-eight hours from now. Our squad is being transferred up to Fort Laramie at the end of the week."

Mr. Franks shook the captain's hand. "I plan to be on that train myself. The minute I turn this gold over, I'm headed back to Dallas."

"Sheriff." Cassie looked up, but the captain was shaking Ben's hand instead of hers. The knot in her stomach tightened.

Without even a glance her way, the military marched outside, leaving behind a ruddy-cheeked young man who held his rifle against his shoulder as if in formation.

Closing the door after a quick check outside, Mr. Franks raised his eyebrow at the corporal. "At ease, soldier."

Cassie tried to regroup. "Gentlemen, thank you for your assistance out there on the street, but I'm sure we have things well in hand now. Ben, you should be at the school. The children will be running wild by now. Dad, Mr. Jones, I'm sure you have plenty to do. I'll be down with the key after a while."

"Now, Cassie"—her father took her arm and led her a little away from the group—"you have to admit that what happened out there changes things. I think maybe it's time to set the Challenge aside, at least for a few days."

Pain lanced her heart. Her own father was considering withdrawing his support of her. He'd never raised a hand to her in her life, but she felt just as if he'd smacked her.

"Dad?"

"Hey, kiddo, you've done a good job." Ben stepped forward,

putting his hand on her shoulder. "Nobody would say you haven't. But this is serious business, especially since now the gold isn't a secret. Your father is right. It's time we called it quits and went back to our real jobs."

"No. It isn't. And don't call me 'kiddo.' I can do this, especially since Mr. Franks has proven himself to be so capable. Nobody would brace that gun, and with Jigger and the corporal, the gold is as safe as it can be. We'll lock it up, and Hobny will put the key in his safe. The plan will go forward, and forty-eight hours from now, a delegation will come and take the gold off our hands. I can't quit now. I *won't* quit now." She backed up against the desk, facing six men who all wanted to declare her a failure.

Randall Franks, cradling the shotgun, eased out of the line and sauntered over to stand beside her. "Gentlemen, I only know the barest of facts about this little Challenge you've cooked up here, but I think the lady deserves a chance. She certainly showed her mettle standing up to those two idiots out there. The gold is as safe as we can make it, and maybe she's right—that little show of force out on the street should give folks pause about coming through that door. It wasn't particularly reasonable to assume that nobody would get wind that the gold was here. Not with the telegrams and the soldiers and nosy folks being what they are."

Gratitude shot through her, and she straightened a little. "It will be all right, Dad."

Skeptical looks all around. "Daughter, this is the last time we rethink this. One more reason for concern, and it's over." They reluctantly filed out, Ben going last and shooting a "we're not done discussing this and you're so going to get it" look over his shoulder as he went.

When the door closed behind them, Cassie sagged against the desk and dragged her hands down her cheeks.

"Thank you for siding with me, Mr. Franks." She blew out a big breath.

"Call me Rand. I'm not sure I've done the wise thing, but you were pretty brave out there. I thought you deserved a chance to prove yourself. Anyway, we've got lots of firepower in here." He patted the shotgun. "Let's get the gold locked up."

Cassie picked up one of the gold bars on the desktop, surprised at the weight. "I guess I thought it would be coins. Currency not bricks."

"Not my decision, though bricks are harder to steal and harder to divide once they're stolen. Easier to see when one's missing, and heavier than lead to tote around. You can't fill up your pockets with gold bars and run away too fast. And a dozen of these in your saddlebags will slow you down, too." Rand lifted one in each hand and headed for the jail cell where the two remaining strongboxes sat.

As he passed her, she caught a whiff of shaving soap and leather. He wore a brown duster that swayed as he walked, exuding masculinity and capability.

"I'll see about getting another box, but for now, we can either stack them on the ones that are left or put them on the floor." She entered the cell behind him and waited until he put his bricks on the top box before setting hers next to them. "I'd planned to chain the boxes to the floor as well and had Jigger put these eyebolts in." She indicated the chains coiled on the bunk and the shiny, new eyebolts driven into the puncheon floor.

"Good thinking. You have the makings of a real lawman." He smiled, and she drew in a breath. The praise fell like rain on her parched soul, and she blossomed.

Once they got the gold moved, Rand surprised her. "There's no sense all four of us being cooped up inside. The corporal and I can stay here. You go see about a new strongbox, and your deputy here looks like he could use a little time with that arm propped up. Maybe he can sit down at the store or ease through the saloons and see if he can pick up on what folks are saying about the gold being here."

It was a sound plan, and Cassie knew it, but it was hard not to feel she should be here with the gold, at least in the daytime since she'd promised her father she wouldn't stay at night.

"Very well. I'll see about the box, deliver the cell key to the safe, and take a turn around the town; then I'll be back."

"Knock first. Anybody tries to come in without knocking, we'll start shooting."

Cassie swallowed and nodded, trying not to give in to the temptation to yank off her badge and run back to the schoolhouse to hide.

※

Ben knew he was acting like a bear with a badger-bitten behind, but he couldn't seem to stop. Why couldn't she see reason? And who was that guy Franks, anyway, siding with her when he didn't even know the situation?

The memory of her standing up to the Shoop brothers in the street made his knees wobble. Not that she hadn't given them something to think about, whacking Melvin's arm with her pistol, but what was she doing taking them on like that when there were plenty of men with guns around to do it? Why did she think she had to whip her weight in wildcats every day?

He yanked open the schoolhouse door, ready to corral the kids, only to find them sitting on the platform taking turns weaving strips of yucca into a basket, and though there were some gaps and bulges in the project that bespoke their novice attempts, they were using the technique he'd taught them last week and had made some real progress. Unfortunately, they hadn't drained the yucca too well after soaking it in the creek to make it pliable. A puddle had formed around the edges of the pile and looked to be advancing along the floor. He snagged the cloth they used to wash the blackboards off the nail by the back door and tossed it onto the encroaching dampness, mopping it up with his boot.

Mary Alice sat behind the teacher's desk sewing beads onto the parfleche the class had made out of a deer hide Ben had cured last winter, and Amanda stood at her side, handing her beads from a little box on the desk.

"Kids, did you have your lunch?"

Heads turned.

"Yep, what are we going to do next?" Pierce hopped up, scattering yucca leaves and willow staves.

Ben rubbed the back of his neck. Someone from the group asked that question at least ten times a day. As eager as they were to learn, he was constantly scrambling to come up with something to satisfy their curiosity and give them useful information they would need to succeed in life on the Texas plains.

"Grab your tablets and pencils. We're going on a walk. We learned last Friday about the different plants and grasses you find here on the prairie. Now you're going to pair off and go find at least fifteen different leaves or flowers or grasses, pick them, label them, and draw them. Find me something that is safe to eat and something that is poisonous to eat."

Ulysses screwed up his face. "Why do we have to draw them? Ain't it enough to know what they are and whether you can eat 'em or not?"

"No, it's not. You're creating a field journal like an explorer so that someone else can pick up your work and learn from it. Don't forget, draw the whole plant and bring back at least one leaf and flower if it's a flowering plant. Steer clear of picking anything with barbs or thorns unless you're wearing your gloves. Got it? Stay out of town, and don't cross the creek. There's plenty of stuff for you to look at between the school and the creek bank."

They abandoned the basketwork, leaving the pile of yucca in a damp heap on the schoolhouse floor. Mary Alice was more circumspect, gathering her sewing and the beads and laying them atop the new bookshelves. Tablets and pencils in hand, they all raced out into the sunshine.

He drew his fingers across the freshly painted surface of the bookshelves, and heat prickled his chest. As it had a dozen times, his mind went back to when he had his arms around Cassie, showing her how to use the saw and being distracted by the feel of her so close, the way her hair tickled his cheek, and how her eyes had sparkled when she'd finally sawn through the board. And as he did every time his mind went there, he yanked it back.

Time to get outside. He didn't think about her so much when he was outside concentrating on the kids.

Settling his hat on his head, he clattered down the steps. The children had fanned out, and most were sitting or squatting in the grass, heads bent, pencils working. He smiled at their enthusiasm. Once he'd abandoned the tedious, sissy, book stuff on Cassie's to-do list, the kids had really taken to school and could be counted on to be obedient. Well, mostly obedient. The terrible twins still gave him a run for his money.

Their golden heads bobbed as they ran in a beeline for the creek. Trust them to get as close to the boundaries as possible as quickly as possible. They'd probably try to uproot one of the scrub willows and drag it back for their nature study. Or fill their notebook with pictures of prickly pear or Spanish needle grass or sandburs.

Little Amanda stood in the sunshine fingering the end of her braid while Mary Alice drew a star thistle. He walked over, careful not to spook her. She didn't edge away as she would have when he first started this schoolteacher lark, but she didn't look directly at him either, casting glances up from under lashes and out the side of her eye.

"How're you coming along, ladies?"

Mary Alice blushed and added a few strokes to the page. "I wish I was a better artist. All my flowers look the same."

He compared a couple of her drawings and silently agreed with her, though he wouldn't say so. Not only did her flowers all look the same, but they also didn't look much like flowers. "Do the best you can; that's all you can do. Maybe you could give Amanda a shot at drawing one. There's some sunflowers starting to bloom over in the road ditch and some cattail reeds along the creek."

"Do you want to try to draw one, Amanda?" She held out the tablet.

Amanda shook her head.

"Go on, try it. Be brave. You might be good at it. Better than I am, that's for sure."

"I'm not brave." She whispered the words, but he heard them clearly.

Easing down on his knees, he leaned a little to her right until they locked eyes. He was so happy she'd finally broken her silence in his presence, he wanted to keep her talking. "Who said you weren't brave?"

"My daddy." She lowered her eyes and stared at the ground between them. "He said I was scared as a mouse and I didn't have any fort…fort…" Her blue eyes narrowed as she searched for the word. "Fortitude. What's that mean?"

"It means gumption or sand or grit, and your daddy was dead wrong."

She shook her head, her braids sliding up and down her shoulders, and her face sad. "I'm afraid all the time."

"Being brave doesn't mean you're not afraid. Being brave means stuffing your fear into your hat and then sitting on your hat. I sorta find folks are as brave as they have to be. Today you draw a flower, tomorrow you ride a horse or wrestle a bear or stop some train robbers." He chucked her under the chin, sad when she flinched. "You just have to decide you're going to do it and not let anything stop you."

She eyed him skeptically but took the pencil from Mary Alice and went with her to the road ditch to study the sunflowers. Small progress, but progress nonetheless.

He counted heads again, came up with a dozen, and let his attention wander toward town. A couple of wagons and teams stood along Main Street, and Mr. Svenson swept his boardwalk again. He was obsessive about keeping the floors and boardwalk of his store clean and must go through a broom a month.

The bakery door stood open. Carl seemed to be doing better at making cookies and cakes, but Ben had a feeling that Jenny was restocking things on the weekends.

The bricklayers were almost finished with the bank. Their

scaffolding encased the building like the bars of a cell. If the workers would have been faster, maybe the bank would be finished and that gold would be the banker, Mr. Carruthers's, responsibility. It could have gone in his safe instead of the jail.

Movement caught his eye, and his chest tightened.

Cassie closed the sheriff's office door behind her and sashayed up the street as if she hadn't a care in the world. Sunshine gleamed on her copper-bright hair. She mounted the steps in front of the mercantile, spoke to Mr. Svenson, and they both went inside.

He envisioned them walking through the store to the back where Hobny Jones kept the office where he did his "lawyering," and Hobny removing the leather-bound law books to reveal his small safe set into the thick adobe wall. Dial in the combination, swing open the door, and lay the key inside with whatever papers and treasures he kept in there, shut the door, give the dial a spin, and replace the books—Ben went through the steps in his head.

When enough time had passed for all that to be accomplished, he rocked on his heels, glancing over his shoulder to check on the kids from time to time, waiting to see Cassie reappear. But she didn't. What was she doing in there? Had Hobny forgotten the combination? Had someone intercepted her? Nothing else moved in the street save a swirl of grit stirred up by a passing gust of wind.

He had just made up his mind to go see what was going on when she emerged from the store. He exhaled and shook his head. What was wrong with him? He had Cassie on the brain, and it was affecting his work.

She waved to him and started toward the school. He didn't know if he was glad or annoyed. The last thing he wanted was to have her spouting off about how she had everything under control, that standing guard over a fortune in gold wasn't that big of a deal, and how he didn't need to worry. He was worried, and that was that, and it worried him that she wasn't more worried.

"You look mad." Her voice carried across the open space.

He glanced down at his arms folded across his chest and his boots braced apart and forced himself to relax. She drew up in front of him, flashing him the jade sparkles that made his heart whump against his breastbone. The breeze teased the hair at her temples, and for some outlandish reason, his fingertips itched to touch the tendrils and smooth them back into the braid she wore coiled on the back of her head. Or loosen the braid altogether and let the bright hair tumble around her shoulders. *Whoa, son, where did that come from?*

"What are the children doing now?" She leaned to look around him. "Are the twins climbing trees?"

He tore his eyes away from her face and looked toward the creek where two lithe bodies appeared and disappeared among the foliage of a wind-twisted hackberry. "Yep. They're doing a nature study of the vegetation of the plains."

"They seem to be having a good time, but aren't you concerned about them getting behind in their lessons with all these outings and nature studies? Are they keeping up on their arithmetic and spelling and grammar?"

Ben waved his finger in her face. "Ah, ah, ah, no butting in, remember? They're learning, and that's what matters. Did you get the key delivered?"

"Yes. And Rand and the corporal are sitting with the gold."

"Rand?"

She nodded. "Mr. Franks."

"First names already, huh? What are you supposed to do if they're watching the gold?"

"Patrol the town. Jigger is going to poke around and see if he can pick up any gossip. Rand and Corporal Shipton will stay with the gold."

"What about when they need to eat or…go outside?" He jammed his hands into his pockets and locked his elbows at his sides.

"I'm taking them food, and they'll. . .spell each other when one needs a break." She ran the tip of her tongue along her bottom lip and watched the kids zigzagging through the grass.

Had her features always been so delicate? The top two buttons of her blouse were open, and the wind pushed back one side, revealing the outline of her collarbone and the hollow of her throat. He swallowed hard and raised his eyes to stare at the horizon.

"Well?" Her hands went to her hips.

"Huh?"

Her green eyes rolled. "I asked if there was anything else you could think of to keep the gold safe, but I guess not. You're wool-gathering, so either you think my preparations and precautions are sufficient, or you think they're so woeful that they don't even bear listening to."

"Stop trying to do my thinking for me." The words came out gruffer than he had intended because he didn't want her to guess what his mind had really been on. "If you're supposed to be sheriffing, then you'd best get back to it." *Before I do something stupid like forget you're supposed to be like a sister to me.*

Her chin came up. "Fine then. I don't know what's come over you, Benjamin Wilder, but I liked you a lot better before we switched places."

"That goes double for me, Cassiopeia Bucknell." She hated her given name with a white-hot passion, and he only used it when he really wanted to goad her or get her out of his hair when she was being a pest.

She had just turned on her heel to march back toward town—the very picture of high dudgeon—when a holler went up from behind them.

Several of the children stood beneath the tree the twins were in, looking up and pointing. Pierce ran toward Ben, arms and legs pumping. He skidded to a halt, planting his hands on his knees and gasping.

"Quincy's hanging upside down by his britches and can't get loose!"

Ben broke into a run, pounding across the fifty or so yards of prairie between the school and the creek bank. The knot of kids opened to let him in, all of them looking up into the leaves.

"Quincy?" He ducked under a low branch, trying to spot the kid.

"Help, I'm stuck!"

He sounded more mad than hurt, a good sign. "Where are you?"

"Up here."

Ben took a quarter turn around the trunk and glimpsed a pair of skinny legs sticking out of a pair of overalls. Boots dangled a good thirty feet above the ground.

"Where's Ulysses?"

"I'm up here, too, but I ain't stuck. I tried to get him loose, but I can't lift him high enough. He could always just unhook his overall strap, but then he'd prolly hit about a thousand branches on his way to the ground." He sounded cheerful and unconcerned.

Cold-blooded little monster.

"Ulysses, can you get down?" Ben jumped and grabbed the lowest branch, hauling himself up by his arms until his belt buckle lay across the limb.

"Yeah, but if I do, I won't have as good a seat for the action."

Ben picked his way up another tier of limbs, squirming through the grasping twigs. The boys were a lot smaller than he was, and this tree was a bramble of crossed limbs. His slick-soled boots slipped, and he clutched at a branch to steady himself. "Any kid I find in this tree that *doesn't* need rescuing when I get up there is going to have to stay after school and write spelling words on the blackboard until his fingers fall right off."

"What tree?" Ulysses appeared through the leaves on his way down, fast and sure as a squirrel.

"That's what I thought. And be careful getting down. I don't want to have to explain this to your mother."

He shot Ben a cocky grin and disappeared toward the ground.

"Mary Alice?" Ben shouted.

"Yes, sir?"

"Get the kids back. I don't want anything"—*or anyone*—"to fall on them."

"Ben, be careful."

Cassie. Of course she'd stayed.

He raised himself up, testing the last few branches that were too small for his comfort. About halfway out on the limb above, Quincy dangled like a worm on a fishhook, his overall strap caught on a branch.

"Don't move, kiddo."

"I can't." He looked more aggrieved than scared, but his position was precarious. If the limb or the strap gave way. . .

"I have to work my way above you. I don't want both of our weights on that branch." Ben climbed around the limb the boy hung from and lay full-length on the branch above him, praying it would hold and that he wouldn't tip off.

"Easy." He inched along, reaching down with one hand while wrapping his other arm around the limb he lay on. The wood gave a suspicious pop, and he froze. Slowly, he wiped his forehead on his shoulder. "I'm almost there."

"Hurry," Quincy whispered. "These pants are cutting into my. . .manly bits."

A chuckle worked its way up Ben's throat. Trust the kid to say something so outlandish and probably truthful at such a moment. He worked his fingers under one overall strap and pulled.

The limb he lay on trembled, and his arm shook at the dead weight hanging from his grasp. "Slowly." He forced the word through his clenched teeth.

Inch by inch, he raised Quincy until he was free of the spar he hung on. Then, as quickly as he could without falling, he swung the boy toward the tree trunk. "Grab hold of something."

"I got it." The weight lifted from Ben's grasp as Quincy found purchase on a solid limb.

"Now sit still and let me get below you. You can follow me down." That way if the boy fell, maybe Ben could grab him or cushion his fall or something.

"Wouldn't it be better if I got out of your way?"

"No. Do as you're told." The kid sounded like they'd just been for an easy stroll down Main Street while Ben felt as winded as a stampeded horse. Heights were definitely not his thing. He worked his way down, limb to limb, until he was beneath the boy. "Now, easy does it until we're down." After which time he might throttle the kid for scaring him this way.

Ten feet from the ground, Ben's slick boots slipped off a branch, and he knew he was going to fall. "Look out!"

Whump, wham, smack, thump! He hit the ground flat on his back, all the air whooshing out of him like a stomped-on bellows. Unfortunately, it didn't come rushing back in. Ben forced his eyes open, telling himself not to panic...the air would come back...it always did...When was it going to come back?...*My lungs are broken... I need air now... I'm going to die!* A dozen young faces clustered around him, eyes wide, mouths open. Some even gulped precious air as if to help him breathe.

White-faced, with wide eyes, Cassie loomed into his narrowing vision. She raised her fist, and before he could protest, she punched him in the gut.

Thwack!

Her fist hit him just below the breastbone, and he gasped, warm spring Texas air rushing into his starved lungs. He lay still, just breathing, but all the things he wanted to say collided in his head. She'd hit him. When he was down. What a bully.

Overhead, Quincy shinnied down the tree, squatted beside him, and let out a low whistle.

"I think you hit every branch on the way down."

Hard to tell if the kid was pitying him or admiring him.

Ben eased up onto his elbows to assess the damage. Every muscle protested. "I think you're right. Next time you get stuck in a tree, I'm going to leave you hanging there. You can build a nest and grow some feathers for all I care."

Quincy snickered and stood. The kids backed up, and another face cut off Ben's view of the tree. This one was pale as milk and had long-lashed green eyes full of concern. "Are you all right?"

Time for at least a little show of manliness. He sat up, nearly bumping noses with her. "I'm fine. Just testing out gravity. It still works, if you're wondering." He rubbed his shoulder and tried not to grimace.

She swatted his arm, which hurt. "Stop being silly. I need to know whether I should run for my dad. Are your ribs all right? Any broken bones?"

He got to his feet, wincing, checking himself over. "All the parts that are supposed to bend do, and none of the parts that aren't supposed to, so I'm good." He found his hat and eased it onto his head. Gingerly he explored a tender spot over his right ear. "Good thing all those branches broke my fall. Though I gotta say, slugging me was uncalled for."

"I was trying to get your diaphragm working again." She scowled at him.

Rubbing his middle gingerly, he shook his head. "A likely story. You seemed to enjoy it way too much."

"You'd best be grateful, or I'm liable to do it again." She fisted her little hand and shook it up at him, a kitten playing tiger. He engulfed her clenched hand in his and lowered it.

"Let's smoke the peace pipe, shall we?" He slowly released his grip on her smooth, pale skin. "I think we've bickered enough for one day."

The kids had fanned out again once they saw him on his feet, and they ran among the trees shouting, even Quincy. "Is it healthy or heartless that they think I'm indestructible?"

She touched his jaw, turning his head, and his skin tingled where she touched. "It's probably healthy. You're going to have a nice bruise here."

"And a few other places, I imagine." Dusting himself, he ran his tongue over his teeth to make sure they were all there. "Puts me in mind of another time I rescued a kid stuck up a tree. Though that time it wasn't overalls that got caught. If I remember correctly. . ." He grinned.

"Ben, you promised never to tell anyone about that." She folded her arms and glared at him.

"Caught by your bloomers up a tree not too far from this very one. Good thing I happened along when I did, and that I am so good at rescuing damsels in distress." He grinned at her, enjoying the roses blooming in her cheeks and the sparks flying in her eyes.

"I was eight and trying to keep up with the boys."

"You're still trying to keep up with the boys." For some reason, his voice dipped an octave or so and rumbled around in his chest. "You know that I'm standing by to rescue you if you ever need it?"

She nodded, trailing her fingers down his arm and patting his hand. "You always have been. Thanks for not saying '*when* you need it.'"

"No problem. I'd better gather the kids up. I'm thinking my next lesson might need to be about treating wounds and injuries." He tried to keep it light and not focus on the smell of roses coming from her hair or the zip along his arm where her fingers touched him.

Cassie started back toward town, and he tried not to watch the gentle sway of her hips or the way her hand brushed the gun belt she'd slung around her slender waist as she walked. Working some moisture into his mouth, he put his fingers to his lips and let out a piercing whistle.

He waved the kids toward him, and as they clustered around, he herded them toward the school. Once more he counted noses, only this time he came up one short.

Amanda.

～◎

Ben's whistle rent the air as he called the kids together. Cassie resisted the urge to turn around and take one more look. Hard as it was, she was trying to come to terms with the notion that he might never see her as a woman, that she might have to give up on her dream of being Mrs. Benjamin Wilder.

Her mind knew it, but her heart wasn't having any part of it. When he'd fallen out of that tree and lay there gasping like a fish, her knees had turned to water, and her heart had flipped right over. When he'd finally stood up and brushed himself off, she was so relieved he wasn't dead or maimed, she'd come within a small cat's whisker of throwing herself into his arms and sobbing like a hysterical little girl. At least his teasing banter had saved her from making a fool of herself.

"Amanda!" Ben's shout stopped her.

"Amanda! Amanda!" The kids' voices joined in.

She turned back toward the creek. Pierce and Thomas pounded up to her.

"What's wrong?"

"We can't find Amanda. The sheriff told us to fan out and look for her."

Forcing herself to remain calm, she put one hand on each of their shoulders. "Pierce, you go look inside the school. Thomas, check the privy."

"Yes, ma'am." They scampered away.

Cassie headed for the creek. The sluggish water was one of her greatest concerns for her students. Though Cactus Creek wasn't fast-moving or deep, quicksand formed and disappeared with every rain. What had once been a solid bank could become deadly overnight.

"Amanda!" His shout rang under the brushy trees.

She skidded down the sandy bank and emerged into the sunshine. Ben stood at the edge of the water scanning up and down the creek.

"Any sign of her?"

"She can't have gotten far." He whistled again, the sound echoing off the water and the far bank.

"Two of the boys are checking the school and the privy."

Nine children clustered around him. "Mary Alice, you take the kids back up out of the creek bed and fan out. You couldn't hide an egg on the prairie up there, but make sure. Search be-tween here and the school, and if you don't find her, I want y'all to stay in the schoolhouse." He stared hard at the twins. "I don't want any of the rest of you to go missing. Understood? Work on the baskets or the beading or something, but don't stir a step until we get back. Got it?"

Heads nodded, and they fought their way up the bank and out of sight.

"Where would she go?"

Cassie shook her head. "She doesn't go anywhere by herself really." She snapped her fingers—a gesture that usually got her a disapproving frown when she did it in front of her mother. "The bridge. She likes to drop a stick on the upstream side and wait for it to emerge under the bridge on the downstream side."

"I told her she might want to draw some of the cattails there, too."

They started back up the bank, since it would be quicker to go through the prairie grass than fight their way through the brush and trees that bordered the creek. The bridge was only about a hundred yards from where they stood.

Ben's long legs ate up the ground, and Cassie had to trot to keep up. Her sidearm banged against her leg, and she clamped her hand on the gun to keep it still.

The log-and-plank bridge lay in the April sunshine, spanning the muddy creek on the stage line road to Amarillo. Her heart sank when she couldn't see a little blond in a plaid dress at the rail.

Ben stopped, pushing back his hat and sweeping the area with his hawkish brown eyes. "This is ridiculous. Maybe she's back at the schoolhouse."

"Or she went by on the road. Maybe your folks saw her?" The Wilder place was just up the road past the bridge. Perhaps she'd gone there? But why would she?

She looked back toward town. "Maybe she went home? Or to the livery? Jenny said there's a new foal at the livery that

Amanda's in love with. I'll go check there."

"Wait. I think I see something." Ben started toward the bridge, Cassie on his heels. "There she is."

Weak joy bathed Cassie, and she started forward. The little girl stood near the water's edge, looking down at something. "Amanda Hart, you scared us to death. Why didn't you come when Mr. Wilder whistled? Come on up here. It's time to go back to school."

Amanda didn't move, nor did she look up.

Ben held out his hand to stop Cassie when she started down the slope toward her. "Wait."

He squatted. "Amanda, is there a reason you didn't come when I called?"

Her head barely moved when she nodded.

Ben slipped his gun from his holster.

"Benjamin Wilder, what are you doing? I don't like you wearing your gun around the students. You'll scare Amanda to death."

"For once in your life, don't argue with me."

"What is it?"

"I have an idea, but I'm going to go see. Wait here." He eased down the bank toward Amanda. "Hey, sweetheart. You're doing great. Just stand really still, all right?"

A dry buzz cut through the air and sapped all the strength from Cassie's limbs. A rattlesnake. Her mouth turned to ashes, and her hands went clammy.

Ben worked his way around Amanda, looking down. The snake must be just to Amanda's right, down the slope from her.

"Amanda, darlin', I'm going to have to shoot this snake. The gun's going to be loud, but don't jump. And don't you worry. I'm a good shot, and at this distance, I can't miss."

Oh, Lord, guide his aim. Don't let that precious child get bitten.

He slowly raised his arm, the gun coming up. How could he be so steady and calm? Cassie stopped breathing as he thumbed the hammer back.

Though she was braced for it, the shot still caught her by

surprise. She jerked, and in the same instant, Ben grabbed Amanda around the waist and hauled her backward, putting his body between her and the snake.

Cassie ran down the slope, skidding to a stop and snatching Amanda from his arms. She stood the girl up, checking her all over for any damage. Tears blurred her vision, and her heart felt weak. "Oh, baby girl, are you all right? You didn't get bitten?" She alternately hugged the child and held her away to check that she wasn't harmed.

Ben walked over to the scattered rocks along the bank and reached down. He pulled and pulled and pulled. "Got to be close to four feet long. Or at least it would be if it still had a head."

Amanda threw her arms around Cassie's neck and clung tight. Cassie brushed back her hair and murmured to her. "I'm sorry I yelled at you for not coming when called. You did exactly the right thing by staying still."

"Yep," Ben chimed in. "I knew you were brave, and not just brave, but smart to boot."

"I was scared." Her whisper brushed the base of Cassie's throat.

"Anybody would've been. Being scared when there's something to be scared about is the smart thing to do. And you know what we do with our fear?" He still held the snake away from his body.

Her head came up. "We stuff our fear in our hat and then sit on our hat." She gave him one of her rare smiles.

"You realize when we get back to school the twins are going to give us no peace at all. They're going to be mad that they missed all the excitement."

Cassie forced a weak laugh. "That's because the twins are barely human. And don't bring that nasty thing any closer. Throw it in the creek."

"Not a chance. I'm going to skin it out. Anyway, Amanda gets the rattles."

"Yuck. Why on earth would she want them?" Cassie grimaced.

"You don't want them, do you?"

The little girl looked uncertainly at Ben.

"Sure she does. They're a badge of honor, a sign of how brave she was. She'll be the envy of the entire school. She might even get her name in the paper."

At this, Amanda brightened, and Cassie stifled a groan. What sort of wild outlaws were her students becoming? Two weeks under Ben's tutelage and even her most ladylike and circumspect student was almost unrecognizable.

Cassie sighed and checked the angle of the sun. It was leaning toward time for school to be out, and she'd been away from the jail much longer than she'd planned. The day had been way too eventful thus far. Surely the night would be incident-free.

CHAPTER 12

"What do you mean you're leaving?" Cassie almost dropped the basket of food she'd brought for the guards' breakfast. Her nerves had been stretched thin since the gold's arrival yesterday, and lack of sleep last night had left her jumpy and unsettled. When she did sleep, she dreamed of snakes and clattering tree branches and shotguns.

Rand Franks held the telegram out to her. "I have to go. My daughter has been injured, and my wife needs me at home."

Cassie set the basket on the desk and scanned the half-sheet of paper.

FELICITY INJURED IN FIRE. RETURN HOME WITH ALL SPEED. PHOEBE NEEDS YOU.

It was signed by a Doctor Phillips.

Cassie looked up into his handsome face. "Felicity?"

"She's four." He stuffed his jacket into his duffel. "Phoebe is my wife, and she's due to deliver our second child in less than a month. Doc Phillips is our family doctor in Dallas."

Uneasiness trickled down Cassie's spine. "Have you confirmed this?"

"Confirmed it?"

"Might this be a ruse to get you out of town and leave the gold exposed?"

He stopped his fussing and frowned at her. "It's signed by my doctor. Who else would know who our physician was?"

"I don't know, but if I was a robber, I'd be looking pretty hard for a way to get my biggest obstacle out of the way before I tried to seize the treasure."

Rand removed his hat and jammed his fingers through his hair, tugging on it as he thought. "What time does the eastbound train arrive?"

She glanced at the clock. "Twenty minutes."

"Then there is no time for me to telegraph Dallas to confirm. It would take them more than twenty minutes to get to my house or the doctor's office and get a reply back to us. I have to go. If I miss this train, there isn't another one until tomorrow. What if Felicity is so badly hurt she dies? I can't risk it." He picked up his shotgun and pack. "Keep the door locked, keep your wits sharp, and keep your guns close. The detachment from Fort Benefactor will be here in another day or so."

Jigger's brows lowered, and he hitched up his pants with his one good hand. "Cassie, just in case, maybe you'd better send a telegram to Dallas anyway. If it is a ruse, we could use that information."

Rand nodded, his hand on the doorknob. "Good idea."

Cassie tugged on her lower lip. She was afraid, but Ben's words on fear came back to her. *"Stuff the fear into your hat and sit on your hat."* That's what she would do. She could be no less brave than Amanda had been with that snake.

"Perhaps it would be best if you didn't advertise that you were leaving. I'll go ahead of you to the train station and get your ticket and send the wire asking for confirmation. They'll hold the train for you. When you hear the first whistle, hotfoot it to the station and get right on board."

"Hey, I have an idea." Jigger stood up and plucked a disreputable striped garment from a peg behind the door. "If you pull your hat down low and wear my old serape, folks might mistake you for me. Everybody in town knows this serape. They might not think twice seeing a man walking down the street in it."

"That's good. You can hide the shotgun under it, too." Cassie took the gun from Rand while he poked his head through the ragged hole in the middle of the garment. "Jigger's had that thing since I was a kid. You're just lucky I got it away from him long enough to scrub it a couple of times."

The Wells Fargo guard replaced his hat on his brown hair, ducked his head, and slouched a bit, a good imitation of the deputy. "I can't imagine what it looked like. . .or smelled like before," he mumbled.

"That's perfect." Cassie gave him the shotgun. "I'll go to the station now. You follow when you hear the whistle."

Though she scanned the street as she closed the door, she saw nothing out of the ordinary, no strangers skulking about, casing the jail. Mrs. Pym ambled along the boardwalk near the bakery, a basket on her arm and her little dog on a leash, trotting proudly ahead of her.

Forcing herself to walk calmly instead of hiking her skirts and running to the depot, Cassie's mind tumbled through the possibilities.

Lord, if little Felicity is truly injured, I pray You would comfort her, that Your healing hand would be on her. And I pray for her parents. I know how I feel when one of my students is hurt or in danger. It must be even worse when it is your own child. Give them strength, and protect that little unborn baby.

And if this is some sort of trick to get Rand out of town, I pray that You would help me to discern it and to protect the gold. Keep my mind sharp, and please, if at all possible, keep anybody from getting hurt.

She continued to pray as she strolled past the saddle shop and the photographer's studio. Jenny carried a bucket, heavy from the way she tilted away from the weight, and waved a gloved hand as Cassie went by.

The depot sat quiet on the east end of town, a bookend to the school on the other side of Main Street. As she reached the rectangular red building and mounted the steep steps up to the platform, she spied the eastbound train in the distance, a black smudge of smoke announcing its imminent arrival.

Ralph's eyebrows rose as she entered. "Hey there, Cass, I didn't expect you today. You meeting the train?"

"I need to purchase a ticket to Dallas right away for Mr. Franks."

He nodded, slipping the bit of pasteboard from his pocket. "I figured he'd be leaving when I got the telegram. Made this up for him as soon as I got back from delivering it."

"Thanks, Ralph. Don't tell anyone he's gone. We wouldn't want word to get out. He'll be here in a few minutes. We thought it would be best if he boarded at the last minute."

"Good thinking. I won't tell a soul what was in a telegram, but you'd be wise to let Ben know Franks is leaving." He stood a little straighter, his pale moustache bristling. Though Ralph wasn't her particular cup of tea when it came to men, her sister had chosen well. He was steady and dependable, and he doted on Millie and would make her a good husband in just about two weeks.

She checked the clock. "I saw the eastbound on my way over. Have you heard any talk about the gold?"

He hefted the mail sack from behind the counter, ready to put it on the train. "Sure. The whole town is talking about it. It was the main topic of conversation at your parents' house last night. Your father wasn't pleased that you didn't join us, by the way."

"I know, but I had work to do." He had forbidden her from spending the night at the jail, but that didn't mean she would leave off patrolling the town in the evenings. Although her patrol last night had netted her one public scolding when a cowhand had tried to ride his horse into one of the saloons, it hadn't turned up any potential thieves. The bartender had assisted in shooing the horse and rider back out onto the street, and then proceeded to yank the rider off his horse and toss him into the dirt. The horse had taken off, back to the ranch, no doubt, and left the chagrinned and chastened cowhand afoot, which under the circumstances, Cassie deemed punishment enough.

The only other incident of the night was when a cowhand had mistaken her for a sporting woman and tried to proposition her. She'd shaken off his hand on her arm, showed him the badge at her waistband, and asked if he wanted to spend the night in the pokey. He'd blinked his unfocused and more than slightly intoxicated eyes, shaken his head, and whistled. "A girl sheriff? I think I need to lay off the rotgut. I'm starting to see things." He'd reeled away, passing through the flopping saloon doors, evidently not heeding his own advice.

The train hissed and chugged to a slow halt, sidling up to the loading platform, clicking and wheezing in the morning sunshine. Two passengers got off, the Gullivers who had been visiting their daughter in Denver. Cassie smiled and nodded as they met in the depot doorway.

"Why, Cassie, what are you doing here? Is there no school today?" Mrs. Gulliver sniffed and tugged at her gloves. "Is that a gun?"

"There is school today, but it's Challenge month, remember? This year the council included women for the first time. I'm the acting sheriff, and Mr. Wilder is teaching school. That's why I'm wearing the gun."

Mr. Gulliver chuckled. "Well, if that isn't an interesting turn of events." His cheeks jiggled, and his round belly bounced.

Cassie couldn't help but laugh, remembering how once at a church social Mr. Gulliver had been laughing, and Ben had bent down to whisper in her ear, "That has to be jelly, because jam doesn't shake like that."

Cassie had nearly choked, stifling laughter. She missed the easy way she and Ben had gotten along before the Challenge had come between them. Would they be able to go back to that when May rolled around? Not that she wanted to go back to that, exactly, but anything had to be better than the way they were bickering now.

"Really? What were those men thinking?" Mrs. Gulliver

sucked her thin cheeks in and pursed her lips. "We're gone for a month and the town falls apart."

Biting her tongue lest she say what she was thinking, Cassie stepped aside to allow them on their way into the depot. "Nice to have you folks back."

From the corner of her eye she spied movement and turned toward it, tense and ready to pounce, but when she saw the Shoop brothers leaning on one another and careening unsteadily toward their horses tied in front of the saloon, she relaxed. Those two were so drunk they couldn't hit the ground with a hammer, and at this hour of the morning, too. But at least they weren't brawling in the street.

Rand Franks wisely skirted around the depot and approached from the far end of the platform just as the departing whistle sounded. Cassie handed him his ticket.

"Good-bye, and thank you for all your help. We'll be praying for your family."

He clasped her hand, worry bright in his eyes. "Thank you. I'll wire when I arrive. Take every precaution with the gold. I'd stay if I could."

"I know. We'll be fine." She said this with more confidence than she felt. He released her hand, swung aboard the stage as it began to pull out, and took with him a great deal of the assurance with which she'd been protecting herself.

❦

Jenny leaned on the corral fence, resting her chin on her crossed arms. Misery stood on the far side of the enclosure, swishing his tail and eyeing her. They'd declared an uneasy truce since the biting incident, mostly because she pitch-forked hay over the fence and slid a fresh bucket of water under the bottom rail of the corral twice a day and left him mostly to his own devices.

And felt a failure as a result.

For some reason that horse had become a symbol of all she had not done right in her marriage, how she'd let someone dominate and bully her, make her walk in fear every day, refused to even try to change things after a while.

Today her behavior changed.

She knew her decision had much to do with the inner turmoil currently writhing in her middle, her constant companion since hearing of Amanda's near miss with a rattlesnake yesterday. The child had told the story with excitement and glee, relating how Ben had praised her bravery, and she hadn't understood why her mother had hugged her repeatedly last evening, or why Jenny had wanted to sit beside her bed as she fell asleep.

Misery stomped his hoof and blasted a whinny, shaking his mane and baring his teeth. All along the edges of the corral, he'd worn a groove in the dirt. A part of her felt sorry for the big fellow, fenced in for the first time in his life, though he ate better and was safer here than running wild.

Jenny fished into her skirt pocket for the selection of edibles she'd brought. An apple, some sugar in a little twist of paper, a sourdough biscuit, and half a stick of peppermint candy. When she'd asked Ben what kind of treats a horse might like, he'd rattled off half a dozen ideas.

She'd try the apple first. Entering the barn, she dipped a scoop into the feed bin and dumped the contents into a metal bucket. Approaching his stall, she let the handle clank against the bucket's side and rattled the grain. As she'd hoped, the stallion stuck his head through the door into his stall, nostrils quivering, eyes bright.

"Hey, big fellow. Are you hungry?" Speaking with much more ease than she felt, she reminded herself that horses had the ability to sense fear.

Much like her husband had.

Setting the bucket on the ground at her feet, she withdrew a pocketknife and cut the apple in half so he could smell the fragrant juice. "If you come here and be nice, you can have some of this."

His big feet rustled in the straw, and he blew through his

nose, obviously unhappy that she hadn't just dumped the food and backed off as always.

She remained still, half the apple on her palm, stretched over the half door. He glared at her, his nostrils wide as he inhaled.

Impasse. Her arm began to tremble.

Her mind drifted to a bit of Amanda's prattle. Something about Carl singing to horses to calm them.

Though she always suspected she couldn't carry a tune in a crate with a lid on it, she cleared her throat and began to sing—a hymn, since those were the only songs to which she knew all the words.

> *"Abide with me; fast falls the eventide;*
> *The darkness deepens; Lord, with me abide.*
> *When other helpers fail and comforts flee,*
> *Help of the helpless, O abide with me.*
>
> *Swift to its close ebbs out life's little day;*
> *Earth's joys grow dim; its glories pass away;*
> *Change and decay in all around I see;*
> *O Thou who changest not, abide with me."*

Misery stopped pawing the dirt. Slowly his ears went from being pinned back against his head to forward and upright.

> *"I need Thy presence every passing hour;*
> *What but Thy grace can foil the tempter's power?*
> *Who, like Thyself, my guide and stay can be?*
> *Through cloud and sunshine, Lord, abide with me."*

Holding completely still, she waited, humming under her breath as the giant took a hesitant step forward, then another. When he was just a foot away, he stopped, snorting and bobbing his head. An inch, two, and his breath blew hot on her hand. Forcing herself not to remember the viper-like quickness he'd displayed when he'd bitten her arm, she remained still. So softly she wondered if he could even hear it, she sang:

> *"I fear no foe, with Thee at hand to bless;*
> *Ills have no weight, and tears no bitterness;*
> *Where is death's sting? Where, grave, thy victory?*
> *I triumph still, if Thou abide with me."*

With a whoosh, the apple disappeared, and Misery backed away. She smothered a smile and placed the second half of the apple on top of the gate while finishing the hymn.

> *"Hold Thou Thy cross before my closing eyes;*
> *Shine through the gloom and point me to the skies;*
> *Heaven's morning breaks, and earth's vain shadows flee;*
> *In life, in death, O Lord, abide with me."*

Backing away from the door, she turned to pick up the bucket at her feet.

"Mama, Mama, Mama, look what I got." Amanda's little button-up boots pounded the hard-packed dirt of the barn floor.

"What is it?" Jenny grinned at her daughter's disheveled hair and glowing skin. It was as if, over the past few weeks—since this Challenge began, in fact—that a chrysalis had broken from around Amanda and a butterfly had emerged, beautiful and ready to fly. Was it Ben's rather unorthodox lessons, or Carl's patient gentleness, or the pony and foal, or was it just the natural consequence of finally being free of her father's tyranny? Perhaps all of it had played a part in the changes in her little girl.

"Mr. Wilder made it for me." She held up a small buckskin pouch. "And listen." She shook it, and the wicked buzz of a rattlesnake sounded.

All around them, horses stirred, and Misery trumpeted. Jenny's hand came down on the rattle, stilling it. A cold shiver went up her spine at this reminder of how close Amanda had come to real harm. But the little girl was so pleased, had told her mama several times how brave she had been, that Jenny couldn't let her revulsion show.

"That's great. But we can't rattle it in here because it upsets the horses. Horses don't like rattlesnakes, and they don't know that it's just the tail you have there and not the whole snake."

"I don't want to scare them." She tucked her treasure into her pinafore pocket. "I showed it to Mr. Carl."

"You stopped there first?"

She nodded. "To drop off my schoolbooks. I don't know why I have to carry them to school every day. We don't use them at all. Can I go visit Copper? Are they outside?"

"Yes, they're in the corral in the back. Why don't you take them an armful of hay?" She dug in her pocket. "And you can give Copper this." She handed her the broken peppermint stick. "Don't eat it yourself. It's been on the floor and in my pocket, and it's nasty."

As she dropped the candy into Amanda's hand, Misery thrust his nose over the stall door and whinnied. Jenny jumped and screamed, throwing herself to the side away from the large black muzzle.

The stallion snorted and bared his teeth before turning and racing out of his stall into his pen. Jenny rubbed her elbow where she'd barked it on a stall divider, trying to calm her racing heart.

"That animal is going to be the death of me. I think I just undid all the progress we made today."

Amanda curled the end of her braid around her finger and tilted her head. "I think he's ornery because he knows you're scared of him. Mr. Carl says animals can tell if you're scared. Then they get naughty or they get scared, too. Misery might get both."

Jenny had been treated to a healthy dose of "Mr. Carl says" over the past few days. As if it wasn't enough that the man invaded her own thoughts more than was comfortable, Amanda seemed to bring him up with every other breath.

Without waiting for a response to her secondhand wisdom, her daughter scampered toward the corral.

Jenny tugged on her gloves and studied her next task. Several burlap sacks of corn had been stowed in the loft at some point, and now mice had gnawed through the bags and gotten at the corn. She'd managed to shovel what remained into two new sacks, but it needed to be brought down and put into one of the grain bins.

Hiking her skirt, she mounted the ladder to the loft. Once there, she wrapped her arm around a support pillar and leaned way too far out to grab the rope that hung from the pulley system fastened to the peak far above. She dragged the rope to the bags and wrapped it around them, tying a secure knot.

"There." She nudged the bags with her toe. "Now all I have to do is lower you down to the floor."

Navigating the ladder once more, wishing she could do the scandalous thing and wear pants in the barn instead of tripping over her skirts all the time, she got herself to the ground. The rope was thick and hard for her to handle, probably the perfect girth for Carl's immense paws, but unwieldy for Jenny.

She reached high and tugged.

And nothing happened. The bags didn't budge.

Frowning, she gripped the rope harder, leaning back.

The bags moved a little closer to the edge of the loft but didn't lift. Jenny let go of the rope and studied her options. What she needed was a little leverage. An idea sparked, and she wrapped the rope around her waist and tied a knot. She slid the loop down until it was below her hips. Bracing her foot against one of the support beams, she leaned back and sat into the loop, pulling with all her might. The bags slid across the loft floor to the edge, and with another tug, they dropped.

And Jenny flew into the air like she'd been shot out of a cannon. The rope around her bottom bit hard and hauled her up into the air. The bags hit with a thump, and she jerked to a stop, halfway between the floor and the peak, more than fifteen feet off the ground.

"Oh dear." She wriggled and the rope shifted upward. Squeaking, she froze. "Oh dear."

Her hands shook on the thick rope. The rough hemp bit into her backside. Her heart pounded in her ears, and her breath came in hard little gasps. She turned her head, looking for anything she might grab onto and pull herself to safety, but she was in the center of the barn, too far from either loft, too far from the pulley overhead, and certainly too far from the floor. Well and truly stuck.

How humiliating. And she'd been doing so well, too. If word of this got out. . .heat bloomed in her cheeks. She'd just have to find a way to get down without anyone knowing, that's what.

She kicked her feet, pumping like a little girl on a swing, shifting her weight. Perhaps she could swing far enough to get a toehold on something. . .the bags on the floor below moved a couple of inches and sucked all her momentum away. She dangled like a worm on a hook.

Jenny pressed her cheek against the raspy rope as her legs tingled and went numb.

One of the horses in the corral whinnied, and a giggle followed.

Amanda. . .in the corral with Copper and the foal. Hope blossomed.

If she could get Amanda's attention, perhaps she could run for Cassie, who would help and wouldn't tell a soul about this little predicament. Jenny opened her mouth to call for her daughter.

"Hi, Mr. Carl. Mama's inside." Amanda's piping voice drifted up from outside.

Oh no. No. No. No. Anybody but him.

Boots thudded in the dirt, and as she dangled in a slow circle, she looked over her shoulder and down at the doorway.

"Jenny?" Carl called. "Are you here?"

Maybe she could just stay silent and he'd go away.

Please, go away. Please.

So of course he walked right in.

"What in the world?"

Her heart sank. But he wasn't speaking to her. He was looking at the grain bags, and he bent and reached for the knot.

"Don't!"

His hand jerked back, and he whirled to stare up. "What are you doing up there?"

"I'm enjoying the view. What does it look like I'm doing?" Her embarrassment made her tart.

"It looks like you're stuck, that's what it looks like." His big hands went to his hips, and his mouth split into a broad grin. "This might take some thinking over. I might need to call some folks in for their opinions. . ."

She closed her eyes, but the gentle sway of the rope unnerved her, and they popped open again. "Very funny. Just get me down from here. It's most uncomfortable."

Chuckling, he loosened the knot on the bags, taking the tension and lowering her slowly. When she was a few feet from the ground, he reached up and grasped her around the waist with one arm, then let the rope go. She slid slowly down his broad chest until they were eye to eye, nose to nose. . .lip to lip.

Her hands rested on his shoulders, and his hair brushed her fingers. He held her as if she weighed next to nothing, his arms like steel bands, stronger and yet gentler than the rope. All humor went out of his robin's-egg-blue eyes as they stared hard into hers.

Could he hear the pounding of her heart?

He had thick golden lashes and a small scar at the edge of his left eyebrow. And chiseled lips. Was his beard rough or soft? Would it tickle when he kissed her?

Was she about to find out?

"Mama?"

Carl dropped her like a hot rock, and she stumbled a bit, jarring back to earth in more than one way. Jenny smoothed her skirts and patted her hair and didn't look at Carl.

"Yes, sweetie?" Her voice sounded like she'd swallowed a cracker wrong. She cleared her throat and tried again. "Yes?"

"Do you have any more treats for Copper? She liked the peppermint. Then can I go with Mr. Carl and make a pie?"

"Of course. Let's see if Copper likes sugar." Jenny hurried over to the door, praying Carl wouldn't follow so she could have some time to assess what had just happened and gather her scattered wits.

When she looked back over her shoulder, Carl was striding through the barn toward Main Street as if he couldn't get away from her fast enough either.

≈≈

Carl rolled the piecrust, leaning on the rolling pin.

"Mama says you shouldn't work piecrust too much or it will get tough." Amanda plucked raisins from their stems and dropped them into a bowl. "Mr. Wilder is teaching us to braid grass into rope. Do you think I could make a halter for Copper?"

He grunted, turning the pie dough, not caring if it turned into beef jerky. What had happened back there in the barn? He'd come within a flea's whisker of kissing the Widow Hart, that's what.

"Then I could lead her around and maybe take her for a walk, and she could eat grass. I need to think of a good name for the baby, but I can't find just the right one."

Amanda finished plucking raisins. "There, now you can put them in the pot to cook with the sour cream. I don't like sour cream and raisin pie, but Mr. Lawyer Jones sure does. Have you noticed that he looks like a hound dog? He has such a long face and such sad eyes. Almost like he might stick his nose in the air and howl any minute."

The child swapped directions faster than a grasshopper in a hot skillet. And she was dead-on about Hobny's long face. He stuffed down a chortle. "Amanda, why don't you get those dish towels off the line while I put this piecrust in the oven?" The clock was racing on toward five, when Jenny usually came home from the livery.

What would he say to her? What could he say? He'd taken total advantage of her situation in the barn, trapping her in his arms and not letting her go. What would have happened if Amanda hadn't come in just then?

He stifled a groan, slid the piecrust in the oven, and slammed the door. *What were you thinking?* She's barely six months a widow. . .though in an admittedly unhappy marriage. But still. She wasn't a woman to trifle with, and he had no intentions of marrying again, so he'd best mind his business and remember that.

Amanda returned, her arms full of dish towels. Jenny came in right behind her, holding the screen door so it wouldn't slap closed. She kept her attention on Amanda, who babbled about something.

Carl wiped his hands on his flour-sack apron and tugged at the knot. "There's a piecrust in the oven, and Amanda's been working on a filling for it. She says it's going to be sour cream and raisin?"

"Yep, and then we'll have some for Mr. Jones when he comes in." Amanda dumped the dish towels on the worktable.

Jenny went to the washtub and dunked her hands into the water, scrubbing hard. "That's fine. I can finish it up." She spoke with her head down, her voice clipped. "I finished greasing all the axles on the wagons. And all the horses are fed and watered."

He reached for one of the clean towels and folded it into a precise square. Amanda sent a puzzled look between them, no doubt picking up on the tension, and took one of the towels from the pile, spreading it out on her front and folding it over unevenly.

"You're going to take your skin off." Carl laid a clean towel on Jenny's shoulder, then bent to check his piecrust. He'd learned over the past couple of weeks that the oven was an unpredictable animal and could burn a baked good quicker than Misery could kick a bucket.

"Mama?"

"Yes, Amanda."

"Can we invite Mr. Carl over for supper?"

Jenny turned from the wash basin, her hands buried in the tea towel, and her eyes collided with his. The prettiest rose-red color rode her cheekbones.

"You said that meals are always better when you share them with someone, and Mr. Carl doesn't have anyone to share with." Amanda plopped her folded towel onto the little stack. "And meals with friends are the best meals of all. You and Mr. Carl are friends, aren't you?"

"Yes, but..." Jenny's hands went slack. She sent Carl a pointed look. Clearly she wanted him out of her kitchen, but she didn't know how to say so without being rude in front of her daughter.

Carl shrugged, trying to ignore his disappointment. "Don't worry." He squatted beside Amanda. "Thank you for the invitation, little one, but I can't stay tonight. Maybe some other time."

Or maybe not. He nodded to Jenny and slipped outside, taking a deep breath. *Get ahold of yourself and remember, you're not looking for entanglements.*

Which was all well and good telling himself that, if only he could forget how she'd felt in his arms.

CHAPTER 13

"Where is that contingent from Fort Benefactor? They said forty-eight hours, seventy-two at the most. It's been a full week. I feel like we're sitting on a keg of black powder and striking matches just to watch them burn." A headache began a faint thrumming behind Cassie's eyes. Every day since Mr. Franks and the corporal had departed, the tension had risen. The council and Ben were rumbling about the situation, but so far, they'd left her in charge.

Jigger tipped his chair against the far wall and massaged his splinted wrist. "I don't like it. We're whittled down to just you and me now. I felt bad for Corporal Shipton. He stayed as long as he could, and you could tell he felt awful about leaving."

She walked to the cell door to peer in at the chained-down strongboxes. The blacksmith had finished another box to replace the one that had shattered on the street. This one had iron strapping and a pair of hefty locks that made the other two containers look as sturdy as hatboxes. He'd offered to make a couple more for her, but she prayed there wasn't time before the army showed up.

"Folks at the saloons are still buzzing about the gold," Jigger said. "Lotsa talk about how it's just sitting here for the taking. Lots of talk about what folks would buy if they had it." She'd sent him out to make a quick tour of the saloons last night, just to get a sense of which way the wind was blowing.

"Anything serious or just pie-in-the-sky stuff?"

"Hard to say. When the likker's flowing, men gabble like prairie chickens. Don't know that anybody will come busting in here to get it, but there are more than a few that would take it if the opportunity arose."

"With just you on nights and two of us here in the daytime, that opportunity may look more appealing." She tugged on the cell door, testing the latch.

"We're not exactly alone. Might as well come clean, I guess. Ben's been sleeping here at the jail at night, helping me stand guard. And he spends more time standing in the schoolhouse doorway every day than he does teaching school. Maybe it's time to get Ben back in here full-time. Or hire another deputy. Nothing says you can't hire some temporary help, is there?"

Cassie didn't know whether to be infuriated or relieved. Ben had been helping her and watching the jail on the sly. If she let on that she knew, or if she asked for his help, it was tantamount to admitting failure. Surely there was someone else she could hire on as a temporary deputy without compromising the Challenge, but who? Nobody had any law enforcement experience except for...

"What about Ben's dad? Having Obadiah Wilder standing guard might discourage would-be thieves."

"There's an idea." Jigger slapped his leg. "And I bet he'd be glad to get back in the saddle again."

Cassie paused. How would such a move affect Ben? She knew he felt overshadowed by his famous father as it was. Would calling him in be a slap to Ben? As if she thought Mr. Wilder was better able to help her? And yet she must protect the gold above all else. When she had several armed men to help, it hadn't seemed that difficult, but now the responsibility and danger sat squarely on her shoulders, and every day they delayed the gold transfer just made it worse.

"Maybe I'll head over there and discuss things with Mr. Wilder, see what he recommends. Can you handle things here?"

"Sure. Nobody's liable to hit the place in broad daylight."

Jigger let the legs of his chair thump down to the floor and drew his pistol, laying it across his lap. "When you come back, bring some food, will you? That corporal might've been built like a lamppost, but he ate like a starving buffalo. We're cleaned out of provisions."

"I will. Bar the door behind me." She let herself out, scanning the street in the afternoon sunshine. Not much moved on this Monday. Only a week to go for the Challenge now. The gold had been sitting in her jail for seven full days. Agent Franks had been gone for six of those days, telegraphing back of his safe arrival in Dallas and his daughter's recovery. Though she was sorry for the little girl, Cassie had been relieved that the emergency had been legitimate rather than a ruse to get the guard away from the gold.

She hurried along Main Street, headed west out of town. Passing the schoolhouse, she heard laughter and chatter. Her heart constricted. She missed her students, the exploration of ideas new to them, the sense of accomplishment when one of them mastered a new skill or demonstrated a new ability. Ben had firmly told her to keep out of his business while he was the schoolteacher, and she couldn't help but wonder if the kids missed her at all. He had them running all over the countryside studying things she'd never thought of as useful. She'd be fortunate if she could get any of them to sit still and learn after this month was over.

The Wilder spread lay just over the bridge past the schoolhouse, a small adobe home surrounded by young trees and corral fences. Obadiah Wilder, famous Texas lawman, had retired here to raise horses after raising three strapping sons and fighting outlaws and renegades for years. She'd always liked Ben's parents. Mrs. Wilder seemed unfazed by anything her husband or sons did, the calm anchor that kept the family grounded. And Mr. Wilder maintained a single-minded focus, no matter what trouble he was facing down.

She turned in the gate, hurrying up the path, uneasy about leaving Jigger alone at the jail. Dust rose from one of the corrals, and she headed that direction. Mr. Wilder stood along the rail looking at a trio of young horses kicking up their heels and trotting around the perimeter of the pen.

"Hello, Cassie, what brings you out here today?" He spoke without turning around.

"How did you know it was me?"

"Old Indian trick." His eyes crinkled at the corners just like Ben's. "Actually, I saw you coming up the path. Did you need something? Is Ben giving you trouble?"

"No more than usual." She brushed a breeze-tossed strand of hair off her cheek. "Actually, I wanted to talk to you about Ben and the gold. Get some advice if I could."

"Fire away." He turned away from the horses and leaned his shoulders against the top rail, crossing his arms. One thing she always appreciated about Obadiah. When he listened, he did it with the same intensity that he did everything. He wouldn't miss a word she said, and he'd catch most of the ones she didn't.

"I came to see if you would be interested in being a deputy for a few days, but now I don't know." She drummed her fingers on the fence rail.

His eyebrows rose. "You don't think I'm up to the job?" Humor lurked in his expression, and he tilted his head, again reminiscent of his youngest son.

"No, that's not it at all."

"You're afraid it would be a smack in the face to Ben if you asked me instead of him?"

It was her turn to be surprised.

"I'm not as ignorant about my son as some folks might think. I know Ben's struggling to prove himself as a lawman, and having me as a father means, in the eyes of the town, he's got some big boots to fill." He sighed. "I wish he'd realize he's a better lawman that I ever was; he just hasn't had a big-time, newsworthy case to prove it. If I hadn't captured the Dickenson Gang, nobody would've ever known my name outside Cutler County, Texas, and Ben wouldn't think he had to take on the world to prove he's a good sheriff."

"It's just that he admires you so much. And his brothers. They're off chasing bad guys, and I guess, in his mind, covering themselves in glory and parental approval, and he might be afraid that he's never going to measure up in your eyes to either your own exploits or theirs."

He patted her shoulder. "You're a good girl, Cassie, very perceptive. I wish Ben was as perceptive."

She frowned. "What do you mean? Ben's got great insight. He forestalls trouble before it has a chance to even get started most times."

His chuckle rumbled in his chest. "You're right, when it comes to protecting his town, Ben's instincts are the best. But I was referring to his blindness in another quarter. His mother and I are waiting for him to wake up to the notion that there's a perfectly beautiful and sweet girl right under his nose who has been in love with him for a long time."

Heat swirled up her cheeks and into her ears, and she swallowed, unable to look him in the eye. He knew? And Mrs. Wilder, too? Who else knew her secret?

"Don't worry. I don't think it's common knowledge. I could have a word with Ben if you'd like."

"Oh no, don't do that." She clutched his arm. "It has to come from him, be his idea. . ." She'd just die if his parents shoved her at him. What pure torture to wonder if he ever really cared about her or just courted her to please his folks.

"All right, I won't say anything, but when it comes to women, my sons are singularly dense."

One of the horses whinnied, kicking up its heels. "About the gold. You need to talk to Ben, but as a councilman, I think I'll have to advocate for you and my son swapping back your jobs until the gold is picked up."

Cassie sighed. "That's what I thought you'd say. And I know that's what my father will say, too."

"It isn't a failure, Cassie. It's only practical. You've done a splendid job thus far, and your precautions when it came to protecting the gold were top-notch. The council will see that the voting public is aware of the circumstances when it comes to choosing a winner at the Challenge Ball."

Nodding, she tried to shove aside her disappointment. The month was almost up, and not only was she going to have to admit defeat when it came to being a sheriff, but it looked increasingly as if she was going to have to admit defeat when it came to winning Ben's affection.

"I'll talk to Ben after school is out for the day."

Pierce and the twins helped Ben move the teacher's desk to the side of the platform to clear a space. The Monday afternoon sun slanted through the open schoolhouse windows, and a sweet spring breeze, freshened by a morning rain shower, passed through the room, bringing the scent of nourished grass.

"Pair up with somebody around your own size, boys with boys and girls with girls."

The kids snapped to obey him, eager for this lesson that he'd been promising them all week. Easy and relaxed, he was confident that this was one subject on which he could be considered an authority. As the youngest of three boys, he'd had plenty of experience.

"Self-defense is something you should all know so you can take care of yourselves. Particularly you girls. A little information and practice could make all the difference if you're ever confronted with trouble. What I'm going to teach you today has nothing to do with playing fair or fighting honorably. It's about protecting yourself and playing dirty if necessary. You need to use every advantage you can, be crafty and wily, and bide your time, waiting for the perfect opening."

Eager faces nodded.

"Come here, Thomas." He motioned to one of the older boys. "I'll demonstrate with you, and then you can practice, slowly." Ben gave a warning glare. "We're not going to go full speed, because somebody is sure to get hurt if we do. Anyway, there isn't enough room in here for real scrapping, and we don't want to break anything." He took Thomas by the right wrist. "Now, suppose someone grabs you by the wrist. What are you going to do?"

Thomas wrenched his arm back and forth, but Ben held him easily.

"Are you stuck?"

"Yes."

"Anybody have any ideas?"

Pierce nodded. "Grab his thumb or one of his fingers and yank it back."

"Excellent. All you need is a little opening to escape, and if you can wrench his finger, he'll loosen his grasp. But there is something else you can do that is almost guaranteed to get you free."

"Twist around so his arm is behind his back?"

"That might work if you're fast enough and strong enough. But there's something else you can do."

"I know!" Quincy fisted his skinny hands and mimicked a roundhouse followed by a jab kick. "Punch him or kick him in the goolies."

"Well," Ben laughed, "I was going to say kick him on the inside of his knee, but that would work, too."

"Excuse me?" an outraged voice cut through the room.

Heads swiveled to the door where a bald little man with wire-rimmed glasses stood. He wore a checked suit that said 'city fellow' and held a sheaf of papers to his chest.

Mary Alice let out a squeak, and every child bolted for their desks, leaving Ben on the platform alone. The students sat ramrod straight, feet together, eyes forward, hands in their laps. Mary Alice sent Ben a stricken look.

"Excuse me, but did you just instruct these children to kick a man in the. . .er. . .oh my. . ." He wiped his forehead with a handkerchief. "What sort of chaos is this? Who are you, and where is Miss Bucknell?"

Ben propped his hip on the corner of the desk and crossed his arms. "Who are you and why do you want to know?" He sized the fellow up, seeing nothing to be afraid of and not caring for his fussy, indignant manner.

The short man drew himself up to his full height, his narrow moustache twitching. "I, sir, am Mr. Stoltzfus, the superintendent of schools for this district and Miss Bucknell's boss. I repeat my question: Where is Miss Bucknell?"

"Well, I reckon she's down at the jail where she's supposed to be this time of day." He deliberately swung his leg, letting his boot heel clunk against the desk.

"She's in jail?" His eyes rounded like half dollars behind his spectacles. "Whatever for?" The handkerchief took another tour of his pate.

"I said she's down *at* the jail. This is Cactus Creek's Challenge month. I'm Sheriff Ben Wilder, and for one more week, I'm the schoolteacher and Miss Bucknell is the acting sheriff."

He scowled, as if shocked anything had ever happened on earth without his prior knowledge and permission. "This is most irregular. Are you an experienced and licensed teacher, sir?"

The twins snickered, but a look from Ben quelled them. "Not what you'd call licensed exactly, but I'm getting experience every day. And I'm more than competent to teach these kids what we've been learning."

Mr. Stotlzfus stepped farther into the classroom, his piercing eyes sweeping over the half-finished yucca baskets, and the stuffed and mounted coyote on the teacher's desk, and finally coming to rest on the snakeskin tacked out and drying on a slab of wood hanging over the blackboard.

"What sort of teaching are you doing? When I arrived, it seemed as if you were instructing the children in hand-to-hand combat. No one was in their desk, and chaos seemed to be the modus operandi."

Ben shrugged. "I'm teaching them things they need to know if they're going to live out here on the prairie. Self-defense is part of that. It might look a little chaotic to you, but I had things under control."

"And how do you fit in these self-defense lessons with the curriculum prescribed by the school district? Or do you bother? I don't see a single grammar or arithmetic book in sight."

"Oh, we don't need to know that stuff." Ulysses turned in his seat and rubbed his nose with his thumb. "All that poetry and nonsense is for women and weak sisters. Mr. Wilder said so."

Mr. Stoltzfus's mouth dropped open, and for a moment he reminded Ben of a catfish thrown on a riverbank. "Did you say such a thing?"

Ben scratched his ear, his chest prickling, feeling like a little kid caught playing hooky. Had he really said that? "It's not that they don't need to know how to read and write and figure and the like, but I might've said something about the poetry and the deportment and stuff that won't help them a lick when it comes to surviving on the high plains. Miss Bucknell can teach them the ciphering and spelling, and I'll teach them other things."

Cactus spines broke out all over Mr. Stotlzfus's attitude. "This is most irregular. Miss Bucknell had no authority to turn her school over to the likes of a Luddite such as yourself."

"What's a Luddite?" Quincy asked.

Ben wondered the same thing but refused to show his ignorance by asking. "I decided to bring in a little extra to the curriculum—survival skills, plant and animal study, and the like."

Ulysses popped up out of his desk, nodding. "He taught us how to track and how to do surveillance and how to clean and load a gun. Next week we're going to go hunting and fishing and cook a whole meal over a campfire, and maybe we'll even do some target shooting or make bows and arrows." His blue eyes gleamed, and he talked with his hands, pantomiming shooting an arrow. "He learned us some Comanche words and how to skin a snake and how to make baskets and bags like the Indians do.

It's been the most fun school ever, cuz we shoved all our books in our desks and haven't had a smidgen of homework since Mr. Wilder took over."

With each new revelation, the superintendent grew paler and tighter strung. "This is disastrous. Wasting the county's money and time, not to mention these children's education. Miss Bucknell will certainly hear from me, and she'll be lucky if she keeps her position. I don't know what she was thinking. Look at this mess. No discipline, no structure, and no one in charge. From what I can see here, you encourage the children to speak without permission, to roam the classroom freely, and to ignore the basic building blocks of their education."

"Hey, now"—Ben held up his hands—"what we're working on here isn't any of Miss Bucknell's doing. I'm the one who changed the curriculum, and I can do it because it's the Cactus Creek Challenge." When Cassie found out about this, she was going to kill him and bury his body out on the Staked Plains where he'd never be found.

The short man's twenty-after-eight moustache twitched, and red suffused his cheeks. "I have no knowledge of this so-called Challenge, but I do have authority over this school and Miss Bucknell's employment. She's been most derelict in her duties as these children's teacher, and she shall be brought to answer for it."

Getting dressed down when he didn't feel he'd done anything wrong didn't sit well with Ben, especially if that dressing down was taking place in front of twelve pairs of inquisitive little eyes. He straightened and motioned toward the door. "Mr. Stoltzfus, maybe we should discuss this in private."

"There is nothing to discuss. You will clear all this. . .wilderness refuse. . .out of this classroom, and you will teach the subjects the school district has directed—and *only* those subjects. These children will be taught in a disciplined and orderly manner, and Miss Bucknell will answer for leaving her charges in the care of an uneducated ruffian with no more notion about education than he has about propriety." He took a deep breath as if taking a firm hold on his temper. "I will return to this school in one week, and I will expect not only order to have been restored, but an exhibition of the children's progress in the way of a formal program of recitation and demonstration. If they have not satisfied my requirements, Miss Bucknell will be asked to leave the school." He straightened his tie, swept the room with a supercilious glare, and turned on his heel, slamming the door behind himself.

Nobody moved, but the kids slid sidelong glances at one another and at Ben. The breeze ruffled the yucca leaves, skittering them across the floor, and Ben took a good look at the classroom, comparing it to how it looked his first day. It was a *little* untidy, but it certainly didn't deserve the ticking off he'd received.

Mary Alice's hand went up. "Mr. Wilder, what are we going to do?"

Good question. He rubbed his palm on the back of his neck. He couldn't let Cassie get fired over something he did.

"I guess we're going to prepare a program to satisfy Mr. Stoltzfus that you're all smart as little foxes." Though he had no idea how to go about such a thing. Recitation and demonstration? Recite what? Demonstrate what? "Any of you ever done a school exhibition before?"

Mary Alice nodded. "We do them at the end of every school year, but this one will be a month or so early if he's coming next week."

"So, you think we can pull one together?"

Their uncertain looks at one another did little to bolster his confidence.

No doubt about it, Cassie was going to kill him dead as a poleaxed steer.

CHAPTER 14

He said what?" Cassie dropped into the desk chair and put her head into her hands.

"Basically that he didn't approve of my teaching methods and that you'd be lucky to keep your job if the kids didn't put on a show for him next week." Ben smacked his hat against his thigh before pitching it toward the hooks on the jailhouse wall. It bounced off and hit the floor. "That about sums up my day."

"It's about to get even better." The empty feeling in Cassie's stomach stretched and grew. Fired from her teaching job on top of everything else?

"How so?" He glanced toward the cells. "And is there any word from Fort Benefactor?"

"There's still no sign of the envoy from the fort to pick up this stupid gold. Jigger and I have been alone for almost a week now, ever since the corporal left to rejoin his unit. I talked to your father, and he says it's time to call off the Challenge, at least as far as you and I are concerned." Failure tugged her shoulders down, and she had to force herself to look him in the eye, dreading any sign of gloating on his part.

Rather than gloat, Ben plopped down on the corner of the desk and ran his fingers through his hair. He looked so worried she wanted to round the desk and put her arms around him.

"Where's Jigger now?"

"He's doing a little reconnoitering around town. In the evenings, he's been hanging around the saloons and listening, keeping an ear out for trouble. He decided to go out a little early today since he'll be cooped up here in the jail all night."

"And he left you alone?"

"Who else was there?" She spread her hands. "Anyway, I figured you'd stop by as soon as school was out." He'd done so every day of the Challenge, checking up on her even before the gold had arrived. At first it had been an irritation, then an annoyance, and yet she'd longed to see him all the same and had taken to watching the clock every afternoon. For the past week, his afternoon appearance had come with a healthy dose of relief.

"My dad really said we should swap back? And you're all right with this?"

If Cassie was honest with herself, the notion of tossing the whole problem into Ben's lap had a certain appeal. She'd toted the burden the best she could for the past three weeks, but she'd fought feelings of being overwhelmed every step of the way. Having someone else to help her, to come alongside. . .just like a partner. . .like a husband would, would be a welcome easing of her burden. "I wish it didn't have to be like this, but I don't see any other choice that won't end badly. And with Mr. Stoltzfus showing up at the school and laying down the law, I can't jeopardize my real job any more than we can jeopardize the gold."

"I'm real sorry about Stoltzfus. He wouldn't listen to my explanations at all. The kids were pretty shook up, but I think they'll be all right. They were studying their books so hard after he left, I thought they might do themselves an injury, especially the twins, since they aren't used to it."

A tug of homesickness for her students swept over her. She really did belong in the schoolroom, not the jail.

"I imagine the strain on the twins to behave has been extraordinary. Mr. Stoltzfus will be back next Monday? And he expects a full exhibition?"

"That's what he said. What are you going to do? I feel like I'm dumping you in the creek laying all this on you."

"You? What about me? Letting things get into such a snarl

here at the jail then dropping it all in your lap?"

He laughed, easing the tension between Cassie's shoulders. "Aren't we a pair?" His smile jolted her heart, and for the first time, she felt things could turn out all right. Working together might be the best solution.

"I'll tell my father that we're swapping back. Hopefully the gold will get picked up soon so you don't have to worry about it anymore."

The doorknob rattled, and persistent pounding started on the other side of the door. Ben slipped off the desk, his hand going to his sidearm. "Who's there?"

"Sheriff Wilder!" Harder pounding. "It's us, Sheriff. Let us in."

"Sounds like the twins."

Cassie eased aside one of the shutters to peek out. "It is. Are you going to let them in?"

Ben slid the bar aside and the kids tumbled into the room atop one another like puppies. "Hey, what are you two doing here? You can't be hanging around the jail right now, you know that." He took a quick peek at the street as he closed the door and let the slab of wood drop back into place to bar it shut.

"Sheriff, he took her." Quincy gasped and pushed himself up from the floor. Ulysses disengaged himself from the tangle of legs and arms, nodding, his narrow chest heaving. "She's gone."

"Hold up there, boys. Who are you talking about? Who's gone?" Ben put his hands on their shoulders and lined them up before him.

Ulysses rubbed the heel of his hand up his nose, his round, blue eyes flicking from Ben to Cassie and back again. "Amanda."

꧁⊷꧂

Ben squatted and stared the boys hard in the eyes. "Tell me what you saw." Steel bands tightened around his chest when they said Amanda's name, but the twins were such tricksters, he had to make sure they weren't joshing.

"Me 'n Quince was up a tree, the one he got stuck in the other day. We wanted to see if this time we could climb higher than the branch where he got hung up."

"Of course you did, but what about Amanda?" He wanted to shake the story out of them, but he held back.

"She was playing on the creek bank. Floating sticks in the water and sort of humming to herself. We could see her real well from where we had climbed to. Anyways, this man jumps up out of the brush and grabs her. She was kicking and squirming, but he put his hand over her mouth and dragged her up the bank."

"We climbed down lickety-split, but by the time we got to the ground, he was on his horse with her up in front of him racing away."

Ben straightened, his mind zipping faster than a summer wind through the prairie grass. Who would kidnap Amanda? And why? What could they hope to gain? Money? Jenny had purchased the bakery outright, and she wore fine clothes. Everybody in town surmised she'd come from money somewhere, but did she have enough for a ransom?

Jenny.

He'd have to tell her. Dread swelled in his gut.

Cassie grabbed the twins by the chins, raising their faces and looking deeply into their eyes. "You're sure? Cross your heart? A man took Amanda?"

Quincy jerked his chin from her grasp, his hands going to his narrow hips. "We told you, didn't we? We wouldn't lie about something like this."

Ben touched her arm. "That's all right, Cass. Quincy, I want you to go to the bakery and fetch Mr. Gustafson. Just tell him I need him over here at the jail, and then you go to the doc's office and tell him the same thing. Ulysses, you run to the livery and ask Mrs. Hart to come here, too. Don't tell her about Amanda yet, just that Cassie needs her. Then saddle my horse and one for Mr. Gustafson. Both of you go quiet and try not to draw attention, all right?"

He let them out the door, then turned to the gun rack behind his desk, digging the key from his pocket and unlocking the chain that ran through the trigger guards.

"What are you going to do?" Cassie twisted her fingers together under her chin.

"Go after her." He yanked his favorite rifle out of the rack and took a box of shells from the shelf to load the gun. "Watch the door. Carl will be here soon."

He picked his hat up from the floor, settling it on his head and taking his duster off one of the pegs on the wall. Extra shells went into the pocket, and he shrugged into the well-worn garment.

Boots sounded on the boardwalk, and after a quick check, Cassie opened the door. Carl strode inside.

"What do you need? I can't be away from the bakery. I have muffins ready to put in the oven."

Ben jerked his thumb toward the gun rack. "I need your help, but I need you to stay level-headed, all right? Pick out a weapon." Carl had a temper, and he'd become quite fond of Amanda over the past few weeks. Ben needed his friend's help, but not if he was going to go into a rage.

"What's going on?" Carl's beefy arms crossed, and he planted his boots as if bracing for trouble.

"Amanda's been taken by someone, a man, down by the creek. I want you to go with me to fetch her back."

A quiver went through the big man, and his eyes turned to hardened steel. "When?"

"We just learned about it." Ben cradled the rifle in the crook of his elbow and unholstered his sidearm to check its load. "Fill some saddlebags with provisions and meet me at the stable. Someone's saddling our horses now."

Without a word, Carl snatched a shotgun and a box of shells from the rack, turned on his heel, wrenched the bar from the door, threw it to the ground, and slammed the door behind him.

"What do you want me to do?" Cassie lifted the lid on a

basket on the desk and began taking out bundles. "I brought some food for Jigger for overnight, but you'd better take it with you instead."

Ben tossed her a pair of saddlebags. "Put the food in those. I want you and Jigger to sit on the gold. When he gets back here, neither of you stir from this building until I get back or the army picks up the shipment. I'll stop by my folks' place and send my dad in to help you."

"What about you? Shouldn't your dad go with you?"

He shook his head. "We'll travel faster and lighter just the two of us. Dad's leg has been bothering him, and he wouldn't be able to ride for very long. He'll be better off in here sitting behind a shotgun."

"Sheriff?" Jenny's voice sounded from the boardwalk.

Cassie flew to the door and let her in. At the sight of Ben armed to the teeth, Jenny paused. "Is something wrong?"

"Jenny, you'd best sit down." Ben motioned to the chair Jigger usually sat in. She frowned and eased onto the seat. He squatted before her, taking her hands.

"First you need to know we're going to get her back, all right? Carl and I will get her back." He squeezed her hands as fear invaded her eyes.

"Amanda?" Her voice came out a tortured whisper.

He nodded. "Somebody snatched her while she was playing by the creek. Do you have any idea who would take her, or why?"

The blood drained from her face, and her eyes took on a shocked, faraway look. "She's just a little girl."

Shaking her hands, squeezing them hard, he tried to draw her back. "Jenny, do you know who might've taken her?"

She blinked, focusing on his face. "Maybe her grandfather, if he found us. He threatened to take her from me. That's why we ran away from Tennessee. To get away from him. But how could he have found us? I was so careful."

Ben glanced up at Cassie, raising his eyebrows. Did she know about this?

She shook her head, biting her lower lip.

Jigger sauntered through the door. "Hey, why isn't this door locked? Oh, hi, Boss. I been watching from up the street, and the jail's getting busier than the Amarillo railroad station, folks coming and going."

"I'm glad you're here. You stay with Mrs. Hart and the gold until Cassie gets back. Cass, you come with me over to the livery so we can go over a few things. Jigger, Cassie will fill you in on what she knows when she gets back." Ben felt as if he had too many irons in the fire, too much to do, and way too little information to go on, but in the back of his head, a clock was ticking, a fuse was burning. He had to get to Amanda quickly. The longer they waited, the less chance they had of finding her safe.

Crossing the street, he kept an eye out for trouble. Cassie trotted at his side. He angled toward the livery where Carl was tightening cinches and strapping on saddlebags. He tossed his own over and gathered the twins to him, squatting in the stable doorway.

"You boys did great. Now I need you to do a couple more things for me."

They nodded, and Quincy bounced on the balls of his feet as if ready to jackrabbit off at the first word.

"I need you to scoot on out to my folks' place, find my pa, and tell him he's needed to stand guard at the jail. Cassie will fill him in on what she knows, but tell him it's urgent. After you do that, I need you to get on home. You can tell your folks what happened, but ask them not to repeat it. The fewer folks who know about this the better, right?"

Their curly forelocks bounced, and they shot out the door, but Ulysses skidded to a halt a dozen or so yards away and turned back.

"Sheriff, I remembered something when I was saddling your horse."

"What?"

"The man who took Amanda. I've seen him before."

Ben's attention focused on the boy, and his voice sharpened. "Where?"

"The day we was practicing our surveillance." He pointed to the hay loft. "The man who took Amanda was the same one who brought the horse in all whipped up that day. Remember? Miss Bucknell and Miz Hart was facing him down, and you was hanging out of the loft with your gun out?"

He glanced at Cassie, mindful that he hadn't mentioned that he'd even been in the barn that day. She tilted her head at him, and her eyes said they'd talk about it later.

"You're saying Ivan Shoop snatched Amanda?"

"I don't know his name, but it's the same man."

"Thanks, pard. That's helpful information. You get out to my dad's place now, and hustle. Time's wasting."

Ben took Cassie's elbow and drew her farther into the barn. She looked up at him with her enormous green eyes, her skin so pale the freckles stood out like red pepper flakes. "When you get back to the jail, you can tell Jenny it wasn't her father-in-law. It's local boys. You're going to have be extra careful. If Ivan Shoop took Amanda, it's a surefire sign he and his brothers are up to something. Either they want to ransom the child for the gold or the kidnapping is a ploy to get us out of town and leave you and the shipment vulnerable." Were Melvin and Alvin with their rotten oldest brother, or were they skulking around town somewhere? "Have Jigger scout around town as quiet as he can, see if he can detect which way the wind is blowing."

She nodded, her bottom lip disappearing between her teeth. "I will."

She looked so vulnerable, his hands came up to cup her shoulders. "I hate leaving you like this. I wouldn't go if I didn't have to."

"Amanda's so little, and so afraid of strange men. I can't imagine what she's going through right now. I'm counting on you to get her back." Moisture glistened on her lower lashes, tearing a hole in his gut.

"And I'm counting on you to hold that gold." It was too much to ask of her, too much to throw on her slim shoulders. Her womanly scent, roses and soap and female, filled his senses, and his heart felt like a sandbag with a hole in the bottom.

"Ben, you coming?" Carl's shout cut through the barn.

His hold on her arms tightened. "I have to go."

She nodded and stared at the front of his shirt. He raised her chin to look into her eyes once more, this girl-turned-woman who had somehow become ridiculously dear to him. Without stopping to wonder if he was making a mistake, only knowing he couldn't leave without doing it, he lowered his mouth to hers.

Her lips were warm and so sweet, his head spun, the barn floor lurched under his boots, and his heart thundered in his ears. After a moment of shock where she stood stiff as a fence post, her mouth went soft and pressed against his, her fingers gripping his shirtfront as if she, too, felt the ground shift. His arms came around her as natural as breathing.

This was Cassie Bucknell, the scamp, pest, and all-around pain who had plagued him for years—and yet this was Cassie Bucknell, the woman he cared about, worried about, laughed with, argued with, thought about, and wanted to provide for and protect the rest of his life.

Slowly, he eased back and her eyelids fluttered open. Bewildered, confused, stunned green eyes met his, echoing his own emotions at this turn of events. As much as he longed to stay with her, to thrash everything out and badger her to consider his suit, he had to go.

"Come on, Ben, or I'll go without you!" Carl slammed his shotgun into his scabbard and swung aboard his big-boned paint gelding.

He closed his eyes for a moment and then set Cassie away from him. "I'll be back. You take care."

She pressed something cold and heavy into his hand. Glancing down, he set his jaw, nodding. "Thanks." He pinned his badge onto his vest, grabbed her up close, pressed a quick, hard kiss to her lips, and turned away.

Without looking back, he strode outside and stepped into the saddle. He'd work through what was going on between him and Cassie later. Right now he had a snake to find.

~≈◎

Cassie raced to the stable door, hanging onto the doorjamb to steady herself, and stared after him as he rode out of town toward the creek where Amanda had been taken. She vacillated between elation at what had just occurred between them and fear for his safety as he rode into unknown danger. His kiss had turned her insides to warm honey, and her wits had flown right out the door. She touched her fingers to her lips, her hand trembling.

Ben Wilder had kissed her—not some brotherly, annoying peck on the cheek, but the kind of kiss a man gave a woman. What did it mean? Was it simply a result of an overcharged moment, or did he truly have feelings for her? When he came home—*please, Lord, let him come home safe with Amanda*—what would change? In the span of a single kiss, she'd dreamed more dreams about him than in all the previous ten years, her girlish crush had matured into a woman's love, and she knew she'd never be the same again.

Ben had kissed her.

And he'd entrusted her with keeping the gold safe. He could've turned everything over to Jigger or his father, but he'd left her in charge. Her hand went to the gun strapped to her hip.

As she made her way back to the jail, she surveyed the street, her eyes lingering on each business, each alleyway, each stack of crates on the boardwalk, and each wagon and saddle horse. She'd do as Ben said, send Jigger out to reconnoiter, and she'd stay with the gold.

The dress shop door opened, and Mary Alice slipped outside holding a paper-wrapped bundle.

"Hello, Miss Bucknell. I was just on my way to the jail to bring you my report. The most dreadful thing happened today. Mr. Stoltzfus showed up and he was mad about what Sheriff

Wilder was teaching us. He said the school was a mess, and we were learning all the wrong stuff, and that he was coming back and we'd better put on a good exhibition of having learned our studies properly or he was going to make you leave the school. He said self-defense and tracking and surveillance weren't part of our curriculum, and Mr. Wilder looked like he wanted to shove Mr. Stoltzfus right out the door." The words tumbled out without giving Cassie a chance to interrupt. But while she babbled, an idea struck Cassie.

She grabbed Mary Alice's shoulder and gave her a shake. "Stop. I need you to listen to me. Gather as many of the students as you can and have them report to me. . ." She glanced around. She couldn't draw them to the jail. That would be a dead give-away. ". . .at the bakery. Quick as you can. I have an assignment for you."

Mary Alice's eyes rounded, she gave one quick nod and scurried away without asking questions. "Good girl."

In ten minutes she had six students crowding around her.

"This was all I could find, Miss Bucknell. I looked for the twins and for Amanda, but I couldn't find them." Mary Alice tried to smooth her hair where it fuzzed out of her coronet of braids, color flying in her cheeks from her exertions.

The twins were still on their errand to get Obadiah Wilder, and some of the kids lived too far out of town, but it warmed Cassie's heart that so many of the children had come. She laced her fingers, tucking them under her chin, and looked into their eager faces.

"I can't tell you how much I've missed seeing you all, and I wish we could just sit and talk and you could fill me in on everything that's been going on, but I have a big job to do, and I need your help."

Pierce and Thomas stood a little straighter and nodded, and Bekah and Sarah clasped hands.

"What can we do, Miss Bucknell?" Mary Alice asked.

"Sheriff Wilder taught you the basics of surveillance, right?"

Nods all around.

"I need you to be my eyes here in town. I'm sure you've all heard about the gold over at the jail?"

"We did, but Sheriff Wilder told us not to talk about it." Thomas tucked his hands into his pockets and locked his elbows. "Said a robber might be listening, and that it might put you in a bind."

Warmth flooded her. Ben had been doing his best to take care of her all along. "He was right. Now, I have to be at the jail to guard the gold, which means I can't be out and about looking and listening for trouble. And if I was, folks would be suspicious. But nobody would suspect you kids if you're hanging around the stable or the stores or the depot."

Wide grins split their faces.

"Go in pairs, remember everything Sheriff Wilder taught you, and bring any of your suspicions to Mary Alice. In particular, I want to know if Melvin or Alvin Shoop are in town, and if so, where they are."

Pierce snickered. "If they're in town, they're at one of the saloons."

"Don't go in there. Hang out across the street at the blacksmith's shop or the feed store. Watch who goes in and out. Mary Alice, if somebody brings you information, you bring it to me at the jail. Got it?"

"We understand. But where is Sheriff Wilder?" Elizabeth put her hand on Cassie's arm.

She put her arms around Elizabeth and Pierce, bending a bit at the waist. "He had to leave town for a little while to chase down a bad man who did a bad thing. He's counting on me—on us—to keep the town safe until he gets back. Can you help me?"

"Yes, Miss Bucknell," they said, in chorus.

"Good. Be discreet and be smart. But above all, be careful."

Chapter 15

Carl let Ben take the lead, trying to get a grip on his emotions. When the Harrison kid had told him someone took Amanda, his heart turned to stone and his blood ran cold. But his temper was white-hot. He wanted to get his hands on the man—the worm—who had the gall to kidnap his sweet Amanda. He'd make the kidnapper wish he had never been born.

They swung toward the creek past the schoolhouse and down the bank. His chest tightened at the sight of a little pile of sand with twigs poking out of it surrounded by little footprints, mute evidence of where Amanda had been innocently playing—building sand castles and floating sticks on the sluggish, sun-dappled water. His vision narrowed, and he realized he was holding his breath, his chest muscles tight. She should've been safe here. She should've been able to go about the business of being a little girl without worrying about danger slithering out of the bushes.

Ben pulled his mount up and swung out of the saddle to study the water's edge. Carl stayed mounted, scanning the far bank. The sheriff led his horse east along the water's edge, head bent, studying the tracks.

"Here's where he grabbed her." Ben pointed to a couple of narrow gouges in the sand, imprints of little heels. "Yanked her off her feet and dragged her through the high weeds here." Several stalks were bent and broken. After studying the area briefly, Ben remounted and pointed to a mesquite thicket.

"He had his horse tied up over here. There's cropped grass and some hair from a mane caught on this branch. He must've been here for a couple of hours, waiting. Maybe he was waiting for school to be out. Impossible to tell if he was waiting for Amanda specifically or just any kid he could get his hands on. If the goal is to get me out of town and leave the gold exposed, any kid would do." He raised his head to study the angle of the afternoon sun.

"Easier if the kid is small. And if they were thinking ahead, they would know that if they took Amanda, I'd be hot on her trail with you. That would leave fewer men in town who can handle a gun to guard the gold." Carl nudged his horse alongside Ben. "Where would he take her?"

The tracks were plain, courtesy of the overnight rain softening the dirt. A single horse. "He's staying close to the creek, smart since he'd be below the level of the prairie and out of sight of the town. He's headed east, which means he isn't going to the Shoop place."

"Palo Duro Canyon?" Lead settled into Carl's gut. One hundred twenty miles long, tens of thousands of acres of winding, wild wilderness in which to hide, steep walls, mesquite and juniper thickets, and rugged nothingness. The Grand Canyon of Texas. An outlaw's paradise.

Ben nodded. "That's where I'd go if I wanted to shake a posse. We'd best brace ourselves for a hard ride. He's got about an hour's head start. If we ride fast, maybe we can catch him before he slips into the canyon." He tugged his hat down and booted his horse into a canter, leaning over the animal's neck to keep an eye on the kidnapper's trail.

Carl's big paint jumped to follow, feeling fresh from not being ridden in a couple of weeks. He'd chosen the mount with care, swapping his saddle from the mare the twins had originally saddled. The paint had bags of stamina, was stubborn as a goat, and would go until he dropped. He was also big-boned and strong enough to carry a man of Carl's stature and not show any strain.

They passed north of town, going under the railroad trestle bridge that crossed Cactus Creek, and continuing east. He couldn't stop thinking about Amanda. Was she tied up? Gagged? Scared out of her wits? Strangers made her leery. To have a man jump out of the bushes and grab her must've terrified her. His hands tightened on the reins until the braided leather cut into his palms. In the space of three weeks or so, that little girl had climbed right into his heart, slipped past every defense he'd thrown up. He had to get her back.

His thoughts jumped from Amanda to Jenny. She and Amanda were so close—the daughter a miniature of her mother. Jenny must be going out of her mind with nothing to do but wait and worry. At least he had a purpose, something to focus on, somewhere to put his rage.

All Jenny and Amanda had in the world was each other.

Though the resolve he had to change that had somehow come into focus in the past hour.

I wish I could've seen her before I left, talked to her, told her something. . .anything. . .to make her feel better. Promised to bring Amanda back safe. Jenny needs someone to lean on, to shield her from the winds of life, to ease her way. I never thought I'd marry again, but as soon as I get Amanda back, I'm going to do it. I'm going to lay all my cards on the table and ask Jenny if she'll have me.

But before then, he had to stay steady, think clearly, and focus.

"When we find him, he's mine," he hollered ahead at Ben's back.

The sheriff had sense enough not to argue with him.

⁂

Jenny's mind was numb, her heart one big ache in her chest. She could feel the hard seat of the ladder-back chair, her toes pressing her boots primly together on the plank-and-peg floor of the sheriff's office, her fingers laced together, gripped tight in her lap, but she couldn't seem to marshal her thoughts beyond the fact that someone had taken her sweet Amanda. She could hear and feel and see, but she couldn't think.

The door opened and she half rose, praying it was all a mistake, that Amanda had been found safe and sound.

Cassie entered, alone, her face a mask of worry, and Jenny slumped back into her chair, regripping her hands to keep them from trembling. Her friend knelt before her, taking her elbows and squeezing them.

"Ben and Carl have gone after her. They'll bring her back." She took Jenny's hands in hers. "You're ice cold." Chafing Jenny's fingers between her palms, she looked over her shoulder at Jigger. "Stoke up a fire and get some coffee on." The deputy, who had been hovering anxiously, went to work as if grateful to be told what to do.

"I can't believe this is happening," Jenny whispered. "I was so careful. How did he find me?" She had no doubt her father-in-law was behind this. He wouldn't come himself, but he wasn't above hiring someone to do his dirty work.

Cassie rose, peeking through the gun loop in one of the shutters, checking the street. "The twins recognized the kidnapper, and it's someone local."

"What?" Jigger rattled the dipper against the coffeepot. "Who?"

"Ivan Shoop." She turned to Jenny. "You've met him. So have I. He's the man who returned the horse to the livery all covered in welts and sweat. Ben says he's the oldest of the Shoop brothers, and he's been in the state penitentiary in Huntsville for the past few years."

Ivan Shoop. The name meant nothing to her. She remembered the obnoxious, hateful man from the stable, but that was a couple of weeks ago, and she'd seen no trace of him since.

"Why would he want to take Amanda?" Her heart clawed up into her throat. That such a cruel, hard man would put his hands on her daughter—hot tears burned her eyes.

Jigger clanked the coffeepot onto the stove and hitched up his belt with his good hand. "Obadiah Wilder sent Ivan Shoop to jail. The whole lot of them are thieves and layabouts."

Picking at a thread on her cuff, Jenny shook her head. "Is he angry with me about the horse? Is that why he took Amanda?"

Cassie leaned against the desk. "Ben thinks he took her in order to get Ben and possibly Carl out of town, leaving the gold more vulnerable, possibly for his brothers to go after. Anybody watching the jail over the past few days might've seen Mr. Franks and Corporal Shipton leaving. They'd know Jigger broke his wrist. Thanks to my stubbornness, I let the gold be spilled on the street so every busybody in the county knows it's here." She pounded her fist against her thigh. "If only I hadn't been so stubborn and single-minded."

"Now, Cass"—Jigger shuffled over and patted her shoulder in tender awkwardness—"this ain't your fault. The wind has been blowing hard in your face this whole month. Why, me and Ben can go a month or six weeks and never have to even raise our voices to protect the law around here, and you've had one crisis after another, it seems."

Hasty footfalls echoed off the boardwalk, and someone hammered at the door. Jenny's heart hammered right along with it. "Teacher. Miss Bucknell!"

Cassie opened the door to allow Quincy Harrison inside. He panted and sweat darkened the curls at his temples.

"Where is Mr. Wilder? Is he coming behind you?"

He shook his head, still gulping for air. "He ain't coming."

Cassie paled, her eyes widening. "Isn't coming?"

"No, ma'am." Quincy swallowed hard. "He got throwed from a horse he was breaking and busted a couple of ribs. Your pa is out there right now doctoring him. Mr. Wilder said he'd come anyway, but Mrs. Wilder said she'd snub him to the bedpost like a green-broke mule if he didn't stay in bed until he could breathe without feeling like he was sucking in knife blades."

Jenny bit her lip, staring from Cassie to the gold and back again. Yes, the gold was important, but not more important than getting Amanda back. She should've gone with Carl. Her heart was already out there with him anyway.

No, that wasn't right. She stopped listening to Cassie and the boy. Her heart wasn't out there with Carl; it was with Amanda.

True. With all of her mother's heart, she ached for her daughter, feared for her safety, prayed for her return.

But her woman's heart, if she was honest with herself, was also with Carl, praying he, too, would come back safely. How she'd come to rely on him the past few weeks. He'd made her laugh again, made her feel alive again, feel worth something, someone who had some other purpose than to be a punching bag for a drunken, cheating, no-good husband.

He'd made her feel like a woman again.

Time to worry later about what those feelings meant. For now, she'd put them away, concentrate on Amanda, and pray harder than she'd ever prayed before.

~✺~

Cassie sent Quincy out to join the students in their surveillance and barred the door behind him. She closed her eyes for a moment, leaning her head back against the jamb, feeling as if every ounce of that gold was sitting squarely on her shoulders, pressing her into the ground until she disappeared under the weight of it.

Another knock on the door. Cassie drew her gun and approached. "Who is it?"

"Cass, it's me, Millie."

She unlocked the door and drew her sister inside. "Millie, I don't have time for a visit right now."

"And I'm not visiting. Mama sent me to fetch you. Louise has started her laboring. Mama wants you to come and help out. Dad had to go patch up Mr. Wilder, but he'll be back at the house soon."

Mama had gotten her way, and Louise and Donald had moved into the Bucknell house for Louise's confinement about ten days ago. Since then, Mama had been watching her eldest daughter like she might explode at any moment.

"Tell Mama I can't come. She doesn't need me there anyway. Give Louise my love, but I have to stay here."

"She's not going to like it."

"Dad will explain it to her. Now go." Cassie gave Millie a nudge out the door and dropped the crossbar into place again.

Jigger cleared his throat. "That tears it right down the middle, don't it? Obadiah laid up, Ben gone, me with a busted hand, and all your help trickling away like sawdust out of a rag doll. What're you going to do?"

With her eyes closed, she was back in the stable with Ben, his hands on her shoulders, his eyes staring down into hers, regretful at leaving her behind with such responsibility, and yet putting his faith in her to see it through, to do her best. She raised her chin and straightened away from the door. "I'm going to protect that gold. Jenny, you should go. No point in you being in harm's way."

The petite baker stood and put her hands on her hips. "What a ridiculous thing to say. I'm in this now. It's my daughter who has been taken, and I'm not going to let her suffering be for nothing, which it would be if the kidnappers' plan succeeds and they get their hands on the gold. I'm staying, and that's that."

They shared a long look, and Cassie drew comfort from the stubborn light gleaming in Jenny's eyes. She held out her hand and Jenny clasped it, squeezing her fingers.

"Very well. It's going to be nightfall in a couple of hours, and I imagine if trouble's going to start here at the jail, it will come then. Jenny, whoever might be watching won't suspect you've thrown in with us or are in any way a danger, so it might be best if you were the one who went out and got us some provisions. I gave what I brought to Ben and Carl for their journey. We've got water and coffee, but some food wouldn't go amiss. I have a feeling it's going to be a long night."

Scratching his ear, Jigger scowled. "Are you sure you shouldn't at least try to get some other menfolk from town in here to help?"

"Suppose I did? Who would come? Hobny? Ralph? None of

them are any good with a gun. They might end up getting hurt, and I couldn't live with that. Donald isn't an option either. His place is with Louise right now. And anyway, if something happened to him, I'd never forgive myself. I think it's best if it's just us three. Any more than that is asking for trouble of a different kind." Cassie opened a shutter a crack and watched the street. Mary Alice looked out the bakery door, and up the street two of Cassie's students played mumblety-peg in front of the mercantile, watching every person who went in or out.

"When you get the food, check with Mary Alice. She's manning the bakery and collecting whatever news the kids can bring her."

Jenny nodded and slipped outside.

Now they just had to rely on their scouts and pray for Amanda's safe return.

Chapter 16

Ben kept up a stiff pace for close to an hour, pushing his horse at a canter across the open ground, following the churned-up trail Ivan Shoop hadn't even tried to hide. His gelding began to flag, tossing his head, throwing flecks of foamy sweat, so Ben eased him into a trot, then a walk to give him a breather. After three weeks of doing pretty much nothing but eating his head off and loafing around, his mount was both fresh and a bit soft. Getting there quickly was important, but getting there at all even more so. He angled down toward the creek and pulled to a stop to let his horse drink.

Carl drew up alongside, reaching for his canteen and yanking out the stopper with his teeth. "He's making a straight shot for the canyon rim, isn't he?"

"From what I can tell." Ben accepted the canteen, took a swig, and handed it back. The water was lukewarm, but it was wet and tasted good. "I don't know that we're gaining on him, but we're not losing him either. And at the rate he's going, his horse is going to be played out before ours."

With a grunt, Carl looped the canteen strap around his saddle horn. "He's not one to care about his horse's comfort. He'll ride him into the ground if it will get him what he wants. You saw that sorrel he brought back to the livery. He's lucky I wasn't there then. I'd have broken him like kindling. I wish I had been there. I might've stopped all this foolishness before it started." His big fist covered his saddle horn and squeezed as if he wished it was Shoop's neck.

"I did have one thought about what he might be up to."

"What's that?"

"If the Shoops just wanted to get us out of town, Ivan might've snatched Amanda, ridden off with her out onto the prairie, and dropped her off. Then he might swing around and head back a different way to help his brothers with the heist."

Carl's eyes burned like the blue part of a candle flame. "So she could be wandering around alone out here."

"More likely, she's either sitting down waiting for us to come get her, or she's using what I taught her and tracking her way back to town."

He ruminated on that, stroking his beard. "If he turned her loose, I'd put my money on her heading home. She's a smart little thing, like her mama."

"I noticed you two seem to be striking sparks off each other lately. You got the look of a man who's thinking hard thoughts about becoming a husband."

A grunt and a sideways glance. "You should talk. Did I or did I not see you and Cassie in a clinch in the center aisle of my barn? I wasn't aware of just when you changed your mind about her."

Warmth flooded his chest, and the memory of her in his arms invaded his head like a drug. "Actually, I think that *was* the moment when I changed my mind about her. She's quite a woman."

"'Bout time you figured that out. I thought that little gal was going to have to club you over the head and drag you to the preacher before you put it together that she's been in love with you for as long as I've known you both."

"She's what?" He shoved his hat back, grabbing hold of that slippery notion. "That's ridiculous."

"You think so? You may be a good lawman, but you aren't very bright when it comes to women. I've seen the way she watches you, like you were the last peppermint stick in the candy jar. And just let anyone say a crossways word about you, and she turns into a wildcat defending your honor. Not to mention what Amanda told me."

The blows kept on coming. "Amanda?"

"She's a right observant little thing, and she said she thinks 'Teacher' is sweet on you, because she and that big girl who looks out for her at school—Mary Alice?—found a love letter a couple of weeks ago that Cassie wrote to you. I guess you'd sent the two of them inside to get something out of the desk, and they came across the note. Amanda said they put it back, way inside the drawer, but she hoped you'd figure things out and love Miss Bucknell back as much as she loves you."

Ben couldn't stop the grin that split his face. Cassie, the little scamp. That had to be the note he'd found and taken to her at the jail, and she'd let him believe it was Mary Alice's work. He was going to give her some guff about that. Right after he kissed her breathless, that is.

Once they got Amanda back, got the gold safely to the army, and finished out this taking-forever Challenge month.

"You think Cassie's all right guarding the gold? I sure hated leaving her like that."

"Sure she's all right, especially with your dad coming to help her. I'd put my money on Cassie and Obadiah together to be able to turn back a stampede of rattlesnakes if they put their mind to it."

Ben took comfort from the notion of his experienced, steady, and fearless father backing Cassie's play. He owed him a lot, from the lessons he'd taught to the example he'd been all Ben's life. Fathers didn't come any better than Obadiah Wilder, and it chagrinned Ben that he'd never told him that. Something else to rectify when he got back to Cactus Creek.

Glancing behind him at the angle of the sun, Ben tugged his hat down and shook up the reins. "Daylight's burning." They moved out at a steady lope once more following the trail.

After another hour or so, Ben scowled and pulled back on the reins. A couple hundred yards away, near where the ground started breaking up and sloping toward the Palo Duro Canyon rim, something dark moved. He unstrapped his field glasses and put them to his eyes.

"What is it?" Carl's horse sidled into Ben's.

Readjusting his grip on the glasses, he drew focus in the waning afternoon light. "It's a horse." He swept the area to either side but saw no one. "No saddle, but he was ridden recently. He looks stove in."

Slipping the glasses back into their pouch lashed to his saddle horn, he lifted the reins. "Let's go careful. I don't see any cover for an ambush, but we'll be on the lookout anyway."

The only sound was the creak of leather, the clop of hooves, and the sighing of the wind in the grasses. The horse, when they drew near, stood, head down, sides crusted with sweat, and nostrils wide as he blew like a bellows. Ben slid from the saddle and studied the ground while Carl dismounted and coaxed the spent animal to let him lay a hand on him.

"Looks like he had a fresh horse picketed here." Ben pointed to the hole in the ground where the peg had been driven and the area of close-cropped grass. Judging from a couple of piles of horse dung that weren't exactly fresh, the horse had been here for some time, at least half a day. Disgust laced his voice. "No sign of a bucket. Shoop left him here with no water."

"This one, too." Carl dug in his pack and produced a collapsible canvas bucket and dumped the contents of his canteen into it. The exhausted horse sucked in the water, slobbering and shoving his nose into Carl's shirt before lowering his head once more. "Sorry, fella, that's all you can have right now. Any more and you'll get sick."

"We'll have to leave him here. Maybe we can pick him up on the way back to town." Ben glanced toward the west where the sun was falling ever closer to the horizon. "It's going to be dark pretty soon. You can see where he took Amanda out of the saddle." He squatted in a sandy patch of dirt. "See her little shoe prints?"

"Think he turned her loose somewhere around here?"

The hope in Carl's voice pinched Ben's chest. "No. He swapped his saddle and hauled her up with him. There are no other tracks that belong to Amanda. He's still got her, and he's headed down into the canyon."

"Then we'd better go." Carl stuck his boot in the stirrup and swung aboard, his face set like flint and aimed east.

Ben took the lead once more, and in less than half an hour, as the sun slipped below the edge of the world, they reached the rim of the Palo Duro.

A tiny tap on one of the windows stopped Cassie from pacing the small area between the desk and the cells. Jigger's head came up and the front legs of his chair came down, and Jenny sat up from the cot in the back cell where she'd been attempting to rest—though Cassie knew she wasn't really sleeping, not with Amanda in the hands of a kidnapper. Cassie put her eye to the gun loop in the shutter and peered out into the dusk.

"Miss Bucknell, it's me, Mary Alice. I got something to tell you."

She hurried to the door to let her student in. The girl's eyes were round, and her breath came in gasps. "I came as quick as I could. Those boys, they took a terrible risk."

A cold finger of fear slid down Cassie's spine. Without asking, she knew Mary Alice was talking about the twins. "What did they do?"

"Ulysses went into the saloon and asked the bartender if he could carry out the empty bottles and sweep the floor. Said he wanted some pocket money. And Quincy found the Shoops' wagon and climbed right into it and under a dirty canvas." She gripped Cassie's forearm. "Pierce came and told me about both of them, but there wasn't anything I could do without causing a scene."

"Is Ulysses still in the saloon?" *His mother is going to kill me, then kill Ulysses, then me again.*

"He came to find me a few minutes ago with the word that the Shoop brothers were in there, but they weren't drinking much, just a couple of beers, and they were nursing those pretty careful. And they weren't gambling either. The taller one kept checking his watch, like they were waiting for something."

Cassie glanced at Jigger, who nodded, his face a sober mask. Just as Ben had thought. The snatching of Amanda must've been a diversion to get Ben out of town.

"There's more." Mary Alice twisted her apron in her fists. "Quincy finally came out of the wagon and reported in. He says there's a box under that canvas, and it's full of these." She slipped something from her pocket and laid it on the desk.

The pair of small, paper-wrapped tubes made Cassie's blood flow in frozen chunks. Jigger let out a low whistle, and Jenny braced her palms on the desktop.

"Is that what I think it is?" Cassie pressed her fingers to her lips. The notion of Quincy and Mary Alice toting it around like it was a beeswax candle made her stomach lurch.

"That's the real thing." Jigger picked one up and flipped it in the air, making Cassie and Jenny draw in twin gasps.

"Be careful!" Cassie stepped back, barking her hip on the edge of the desk.

He chuckled. "Don't worry. I could throw this thing against the wall or step on it or bang it on the desk and it wouldn't blow up. You need a blasting cap or a fuse. TNT is very stable. Almost a shame. If those idiot Shoop brothers were using liquid nitro, they'd blow themselves up long before they got near this jail and save us a lot of trouble." He tucked the explosives into his shirt pocket like they were cigars. "We'll have to assume that they do have blasting caps or a fuse and that their plan is to blow a hole through the wall to get to the gold.

Jenny sank into the desk chair and put her head in her hands. Cassie went to her and put her hand on Jenny's shoulder, squeezing.

Jigger hitched up his pants at his hip. "I don't fancy sitting in here waiting to get blown sky-high."

Cassie agreed. "All right, how do we stop them?" She left Jenny and went to the door. "Mary Alice, you've done well. Thank you. I want you to gather up every child, those terrible twins included, and send them home. Tell them no arguing and no excuses or I'll be very angry with them. Get home and don't alarm your parents. Tell the children to start studying up for this program we have to put on for Mr. Stoltzfus next week."

Not that the school program was high on her priority list at the moment. Time enough to cross that bridge. . .if it didn't get blown up first.

She let Mary Alice out the door, her mind whirling. "Here's what I think. Jigger is right. If we stay in here, we're like sheep in a pen. This place won't withstand a dynamite explosion, even a small one. And we can't just march into the saloon and arrest the Shoops. They haven't done anything we can prove yet."

Jigger scratched his jaw, his fingernails on his stubbly beard sounding like sandpaper. "I agree. The thing is, we have to catch them with their hands in the cookie jar, so to speak."

"To do that, we have to be outside." Her mind spun. "But we have to make them think we're still inside."

"How do we do that?" Jigger asked.

"Go get the straw ticks off the bunks, and bring the blankets, too." She retrieved Jigger's ladder-back chair and set it in front of the window to the right of the door. "What we need are some decoys."

In short order, using straw stuffing, the despised curtain material, her sunbonnet, and her apron, she'd created a scarecrow-like apparition. It had no legs, which didn't matter since legs wouldn't be visible from outside anyway.

Jigger, with Jenny's help, had another decoy, wearing Jigger's hat seated behind the desk. "I reckon if we leave one lamp burning but turned down low and the shutter just cracked a bit, it might work. Anybody with a lick of sense would see through it in a hurry, but nobody ever accused the Shoops of having any sense."

"The trick is going to be slipping outside when they aren't looking."

"That's where I can help." Jenny adjusted Jigger's hat on the straw-filled bag that made up the decoy's head. "I can find out if they're still in the saloon, then come back and give you a signal."

"If they're not in the saloon," Jigger added dryly, "you'd better give us a signal, too."

Jenny nodded before easing through the doorway.

The wait was interminable. Cassie bit her thumbnail while Jigger rubbed his broken wrist over and over.

Ben, where are you right now? Have you found Amanda? Are you on your way home yet? I don't want to let you down. I'm scared.

Two soft taps on the door alerted her. The Shoops were still in the saloon. They could slip out without notice.

Jigger gathered up his scattergun while Cassie turned down the lamp until the small flame illuminated only a small area on the corner of the desk. Leaving the window shutter open a couple of inches, she followed Jigger through the door.

"We'll go around the back." His whisper barely reached her. Jigger amazed her with the light-footed way he moved in spite of his bulk and the heavy gun. His bald spot reflected the moon-light. She kept on his heels as they entered the alley between the jail and the harness shop.

Jenny was waiting for them. "They're still in the saloon, but they were paying the bartender when I peeked in. I think they might be getting ready to go."

Cassie surveyed the area. "I want to be able to see the jail from all sides, so Jigger, you find a place to hide back here where you can see down the alley and along the back. Jenny, how about you and I set up over at the bakery. If we keep the place dark, we can watch out the windows and see the front and the other side of the jail. That way they can't sneak up on the place."

"If you see them, don't move too soon. We want to catch

them in the act of setting up the explosives." Jigger broke open the shotgun, checked his loads, and snapped the gun shut. "And don't forget, it's more than just Melvin and Alvin. Ivan might be out there somewhere, too. There's always a chance he left the little girl somewhere out on the prairie and doubled back."

Jenny bit back a sob, pressing the back of her hand to her lips.

"Sorry, ma'am, but it might be the way the wind is blowing, and we have to be prepared." Jigger faded into the shadows.

Cassie peeked out onto the main street, holding Jenny's hand as they ran across the open space and into the bakery. Once inside, she studied the front of the jail. Faint light shone around the shutter edges, and she could see the brim of Jigger's hat.

A rider went by, his horse's hooves clopping on the hard-packed dirt. Cassie observed him, trying to see if she recognized either the man or the mount. Jenny touched her arm. "That's Hawk, a foreman at one of the local ranches. He and his men helped me move some feed my first day down at the stable."

"The Shoops might not come until very late. If it was me, I would want to wait until most everybody was asleep."

"Do you think Amanda is out there on the prairie all alone?"

Cassie chewed on her lower lip for a moment. "I don't know. He couldn't have known the twins were in that tree or that they would recognize him. If he'd taken her to that hovel the Shoops call a ranch, Ben and Carl would've found her and been back by now."

Please, God, let them find her safe and sound. And help us to stop all the Shoops before anyone gets hurt.

Jenny squeezed her hand, her eyes closed and her lips moving. Cassie squeezed back, knowing their prayers were intertwined.

The already-quiet town settled even further into nighttime somnolence. Lamps went out, window shades were pulled, music from the saloon quit at midnight as per the town ordinance. Cassie stretched and paced every so often to stay alert.

Just past one in the morning, she peered over the café rod and frilly lace curtain, blinking to focus her tired eyes. Something moved in the shadows in front of the harness shop.

"Jenny, look."

Her friend shot out of her chair and came to the window. "Is it Carl with Amanda?"

Her plea sent a shaft of pain slicing through Cassie. "No, I think there's someone hiding in the doorway of the harness shop."

Jenny peered hard but shook her head. "I can't see anyone. It's too dark."

Cassie grasped her elbow. "Look, coming from the other direction." This time the shifting shadow was easier to see, man-shaped and sinister as it slunk along the shop fronts on the east end of town. She made out the squarish shape of a box in his arms. Her breath stopped up in her throat, and she found herself gripping the butt of the gun Ben had given her. "That has to be them."

Chapter 17

Ben pointed his horse along the narrow trail that meandered down the ever-rising walls of the canyon, grateful for the moon coating every surface in silver. At least he didn't have to worry about losing the trail. There was nowhere to turn off, nowhere to hide, and only one direction to go. He only had to worry about his horse stepping out into nothing, missing his footing, and sending them plunging down the rock face.

He leaned back in the saddle to help balance his weight, keeping a tight grip on the reins. Maybe they should've gone down on foot, leading the horses? But would that be any safer if one of the animals stumbled and knocked them off the ledge? This ancient trail had been carved out over the ages by deer, antelope, buffalo, Indians, and outlaws.

His horse stumbled, and Ben's heart shot into his throat. Recovering quickly, the animal stopped, gathered himself, and continued on. Ben patted his neck, his entire body tensed like a brand-new barbed-wire fence.

Carl followed, and when the trail finally widened and emerged on the level ground, he heaved a sigh that carried to Ben. "I'm not a fan of heights under the best of circumstances. Dropping down into the Palo Duro in the dark is *not* the best of circumstances." He wiped his forehead with his sleeve and resettled his hat.

"I was of two minds on whether to try it at all in the dark." Ben used his kerchief to wipe the sweatband of his hat and try to relax the knot between his shoulder blades. He wouldn't be a bit surprised to wake up tomorrow morning to find his hair had turned snow white after that descent.

"We can't afford to wait. It was worth the risk, and anyway I'd have gone without you if you'd decided to wait." Carl dismounted and loosened his cinch, holding the saddle and blanket up a few inches to allow some air to circulate. Ben swung down and did the same, chastising his legs for being so wobbly.

When they'd rested the horses, they cinched up again. "How 'bout we walk for a bit?" Ben asked.

"Fine."

They set out, leading their mounts. Every so often, when he found a good place where the flame wouldn't be seen too far off, Ben would kneel behind a rock or clump of mesquite, strike a match, and scout for tracks.

Ivan Shoop had definitely followed the game trail, which led in a winding path to the closest water, the Prairie Dog Town Fork of the Red River. As Ben and Carl reached the water's edge, they let the horses drink, squatting themselves on the upriver side to fill their canteens and drink deeply.

Studying the riverbank, mindful of how sound carried on water, Ben whispered, "He stopped here for a bit, then turned south."

"Think he'll ride all night?"

"Guess we'll see."

Ben had barely swung back up into the saddle, his back and rear end protesting after the tense hours of riding, before he dropped back to the ground, startling both his horse and Carl.

"What is it?"

"I saw a campfire." He tethered his horse to a juniper, motioning for Carl to do the same. "He must've been banking on nobody being able to follow him down the canyon trail in the dark."

"Nobody ever said he was smart." Carl jerked the reins into a knot around the bole of a tree. "He's going to find out it isn't so healthy for a man to snatch a little girl and carry her off." He yanked his shotgun from his scabbard.

Ben paused, his hand on Carl's shoulder. "I need you to be calm. We'll sneak up on him, make sure that fire isn't a trap, and see if we can lay eyes on Amanda. Once we see how things are, we'll move in on him. You wait for me and follow my lead. I'm going to swing around and get on the other side of the fire. You hang back in the shadows and don't make a move until I do. I'm pretty sure it's him and not some other cowpoke riding the grub line, because there aren't any other tracks but Shoop's, but it would be best to make sure. I'd hate to plug some tinker or whiskey trader or wrangler by mistake."

"It's him." The grim tone in Carl's voice sent a quiver through Ben's gut. "Shoop is mine, don't forget that."

"Shoop is whoever can get him without Amanda getting hurt. Don't forget that. It'll take me awhile to work my way around quiet-like, so don't go rushing in. Wait for me before you move unless Amanda's in immediate danger. Got it?" Ben unholstered his sidearm, checked the load, and slipped into the brush.

Calm resolve settled over Ben, and he was surprised at how nerveless he felt now that the moment was upon him. His quarry was within his grasp, and if he played this right, Amanda would soon be safe.

Careful where he put his feet, easing around rabbit brush, mesquite, juniper, and soapberry, Ben made a wide arc around where he'd seen the campfire. He caught the tang of smoke and burning cedar on the faint evening breeze, and through the foliage, he caught glimpses of flames.

The camp was backed up to the riverbank in a clear spot surrounded by salt cedars. Ben squatted beside a wind-tortured hackberry, trying to keep his eyes away from the campfire and preserve his night vision.

There she was, huddled a few feet from the fire, her arms wrapped around her knees, her face hidden. Her hair had come out of its braids and hung around her thin shoulders like a pale shawl, and in the flickering firelight, he glimpsed bare skin where her sleeve had been ripped away from her dress. A sob escaped, wracking her little body.

Ben tamped down the fury that flared along his veins. Now wasn't the time for anger. He only hoped Carl didn't see Amanda crying until Shoop was safely in custody. His best friend set high store by that little girl, and if Ben was angry, Carl was probably ready to erupt like that Krakatoa volcano Ben had read about in the papers a few years ago.

Shoop squatted close to Amanda and the fire, throwing sticks into the blaze, apparently unconcerned about anyone watching. In keeping with what Ben knew about Ivan Shoop, he'd tied his horse to a dead tree without so much as a mouthful of grass or leaves within his scope of movement.

"No cold camp for me. I want me some coffee. You kin have some, too." This was met with another sob and a raising of a wan little face, enormous eyes reflecting the firelight and tear tracks cutting through the grime on her cheeks. She shook her head and buried her face again.

"Ungrateful brat. I should've cut your throat and left you out there on the prairie. If those idiot brothers of mine don't get that gold after all the trouble I've gone to, I'm going to gut 'em and feed their lights and livers to the coyotes." He spit into the snapping, sparking fire. "And quit your sniveling, or I'll belt you again. Never seed such a crybaby before in all my born days. If you was my kid, I'd drown you in the river like an unwanted pup."

He was close to Amanda, too close. But there was little cover left between Ben and the camp. If he bided his time, perhaps Shoop would move away and he could get the drop on him. As it was, Ivan was so close to the little girl, he could snatch her up and use her as a shield before Ben could cross half the distance.

"I said quit yer crying. I told you I'd let you go in a couple of days when my brothers meet me here with the gold. All they gotta do is blow a hole in the jail and get past one puny girl and a busted-up deputy. I figure the explosion will kill the girl or the deputy. Mebbe both. Then it's grab the gold and go. And if those bonehead brothers of mine botch the robbery, well, I'll still have you to ransom. I can't imagine the townsfolk wouldn't trade the gold for you. It ain't even their gold."

Blow a hole in the jail? Ben's guts knotted and his hands shook. Cassie. . .what did I do leaving you there? *Please, God, protect her. Give my dad an inkling as to what's going on, and please, don't let them be injured. The gold isn't worth their lives.*

Amanda inched away from Ivan when he dropped onto his haunches and dug in his pack. He drew out a bag of Arbuckle's and dumped some of the ground coffee into a battered spatterware coffeepot. He dragged out a burlap bundle and flicked a strip of jerky expertly at her. It landed in her skirts where she ignored it, staring at him with those heartrending eyes.

"Eat it. It's all you're gonna get."

With a regal lift to her chin, she picked up the jerky, skewered him with a glare, and flicked the dried meat into the fire. "My mama told me never to take food from strangers."

Atta girl. Ben's chest swelled. She might be scared, but she was hanging in there and even giving him some sass-back.

Ivan's face darkened, and before Amanda could move, he backhanded her across the face. She shrieked and tumbled to the side into the sand, and Ben leaped upright, his gun forward.

A roar split the night, and Carl, shotgun aimed at Ivan Shoop, erupted into the camp. Thankfully, he didn't fire, since the blast would've caught Amanda as well.

Canny when it came to self-preservation, Shoop grabbed the little girl and held her before him, shielding himself from his attacker, his gun held to her jaw.

"Stop right there or I'll shoot her, so help me." He faced Carl who halted in his tracks. "How'd you get here? No way I figured you'd try that trail in the dark."

"Let her go, Shoop, or I'll make a sieve out of your hide." Carl's fists engulfed the shotgun, holding it at his waist.

"No chance. She's my only hope of getting out of this pickle alive." He angled away from Carl toward the river, putting him in profile to Ben. Amanda squirmed and Shoop shoved the gun harder into her cheek. "Hold still, you little. . ."

Ben cocked his handgun, stepping out of the shadows. "Put her down. There's no way out of this."

Shoop jerked his head around over the top of Amanda's. White ringed his eyes, and spittle appeared at the corner of his mouth. "Don't you come no closer. I'll kill her. I will." He edged toward the water, half-circling the fire to put it between him and them.

"You do and you'll die of lead poisoning. I can guarantee it." Carl snarled at him but moved no closer.

"Steady. Let's all just be calm." Ben couldn't risk spooking Ivan completely. Shoop's finger was on the trigger, and a mere twitch would send Amanda right into the hereafter.

"Never figured you boys would try that trail in the dark. You must be powerful attached to this kid. If that's the case, then you'll let me ride out of here alive." He kept his head on a swivel, trying to see both Ben and Carl at the same time. "Don't know why you'd care about her though. She ain't done nothin' but cry and cower the whole time. Ain't hardly worth the bullet it would take to get rid of her."

"Amanda, don't you listen to him. We're going to get you out of this, darling. Hang on." Ben kept his tone calm. His brain ran at a gallop, calculating a way to make his words come true.

"I'm going to beat you into a powder if you don't turn her loose right now, Shoop." Carl advanced a step, his eyes skewering the kidnapper.

"Stay back." Both Ben and Ivan spoke at the same time.

He stopped, his chest heaving as if he was within a breath of launching himself at Shoop and burying him in the mud with one punch.

"Amanda, darlin', do you remember when we were down by the bridge and you showed me how brave you were?" Ben eased to his left to get more in front of her and Ivan. Her little shoes dangled off the ground, and Ivan's forearm pinned her to him around her waist.

She nodded. Her little hands bit into her captor's forearm, but she was no match for a grown man.

"You remember the gift I made for you?"

He saw the moment she started following the trail he was laying.

"I remember."

"You're a brave girl."

Her hands relaxed, and she slumped against Ivan. Ben edged a little more to his left, trying not to give away the whole show. Her fist went into her apron pocket, and she withdrew it, clutching something, her eyes never leaving Ben's.

With the barest of nods, he told her it was time.

She shook her hand, and the sound guaranteed to make any man's blood run cold buzzed through the night.

Shoop reacted as if he'd been scalded. His gun jerked, he all but threw Amanda from him, and he whirled, firing at the ground. The instant the little girl was clear and he had a clean shot, Ben took it, planting a bullet between Ivan Shoop's eyes at the same instant the outlaw whirled to shoot at Amanda. Carl's shot followed hot on Ben's, jerking Shoop's body up and back.

He fell into the river with a splash, and Ben drew a shaky breath, holstering his smoking weapon. Amanda covered the distance between herself and Carl in an instant, launching herself into his open arms with a cry.

Ben went to drag Ivan's corpse from the Prairie Dog Town Fork of the Red River before it floated away, and when he turned back, he smiled. Amanda had her little arms around Carl's neck, and the big livery-stable man was stroking her hair and whispering to her. Ben wasn't sad that the child had run to Carl instead of him. It was as it should be.

She pulled away a bit, and Carl perched her on his forearm. Ben put his hands on his hips and grinned at her over the fire.

"Amanda Hart, you're, without a doubt, one of the bravest females I know."

"Of course she is. And smart, too. I couldn't think what you two were up to, but she caught on like a prairie fire." Carl hugged her, grinning, his relief pouring off him in waves.

"Carl, I have to head back to town. You heard what he said. His brothers are going to blow up the jail." He had to get back to Cassie.

His friend nodded. "You go ahead. Amanda and I will follow, and we'll bring him, too." He jerked his thumb at Ivan. "No sense in us slowing you down. Be careful on that trail though. We probably won't risk it until daylight, but I see why you can't wait. When you hit town, after you take care of the rest of this so-called outlaw gang, be sure to tell Jenny that Amanda's all right and I'm bringing her home."

Ben winked at Amanda, nodded to Carl, and headed upstream to get his horse, his only thought now on getting to Cassie before it was too late. *Please, God, don't let me be too late.*

Cassie's hand trembled as she twisted the doorknob and slipped out of the bakery door and into the closest shadows. The man with the box had disappeared around the corner toward where Jigger was waiting. Her job was to swing around to the east, cross the street near the depot, and come up on them from the other direction.

But—Jigger's warning rang in her ears—not too quickly, because they had to catch them in the act of robbing the jail if they wanted the charges to stick.

Jenny had been tasked with going out the back, heading west along the backs of the buildings, and trying to locate the wagon the Shoop brothers were using. It had to be somewhere nearby to carry the gold, but not too close, or they risked the horses bolting at the explosion.

She shook her head as she darted toward the livery stable.

Surely the robbers didn't think this plan would work. An explosion would bring every person in town running. And even if they blew through the wall, the strongboxes were still chained to the floor.

As Jigger said, nobody ever accused the Shoop brothers of having an excess of brains.

Now well down the block and almost to the depot on the edge of town, she judged it safe to cross the street. Bright moonlight washed over her as the nearly full moon did its duty in the midnight sky, and she hustled across the open space faster than a tumbleweed in a high wind. Skirting around the back of the newspaper and print shop, she headed west toward the jail.

Two buildings away, she could see them, crouched along the adobe wall. Easing closer, she tried to quiet the sound of her heartbeat in her ears so she could make out what they were saying. Perhaps they would incriminate themselves further or give her some word or notion about Amanda's whereabouts and their plans for her.

"Good thing you spotted that old codger in the brush back there. I thought he was in the jail with the girl and the gold."

Cassie froze. Jigger.

"Yeah, saw the moonlight on his bandage. That's what took me so long getting here; I had to sneak up on him from behind and crack him on the head. Hurry up and get that hole dug. This whole plan is giving me the fidgets. Ivan must've been outta his mind to dream this up."

"I'm digging as fast as I can. This dirt's like granite. Anyway, we gotta be quiet or that gal inside will hear us. Where'd you put the wagon?"

"Down by the mercantile. Tied to the fence out back. Soon as you light that fuse, I'll run down there and be ready to move. Shove over. A granny with a teaspoon could dig faster than you."

Cassie ran through her rapidly dwindling options. Jigger was either knocked out or dead—the latter option didn't bear thinking about. He would not only be no help to her right now, but was potentially in danger of being blown up where he lay, depending on the size of the charge they were using.

"How many sticks of dy-ne-mite did Ivan say to use?"

"I don't know that he said, exactly. He don't got no more experience with this stuff than we do. Better to use too many than not enough, I reckon. We won't get more'n one crack at this."

"S'pose you're right. Better put them all in then. How many are there?"

"Six, seven maybe. I didn't count 'em."

Less the two that the twins had stolen from the wagon. The dynamite Jigger had stuck into his pocket. A germ of an idea began to form in the back of her mind.

A low, dull clattering sound rose as they scrabbled for the sticks of explosive and stuffed them into the shallow crater they'd dug along the back wall of the jail. Cassie took the chance and eased a few steps closer.

"Get the fuse, will ya? I've got the blasting cap."

"Where'd you put it?"

"It's in the box." Melvin—she could make out his weedy beard—wiped his forehead. "I sure could use a drink."

"We get our hands on that gold and we can buy a whole blessed saloon." Alvin scrabbled in the crate and withdrew a spool of dark-colored fuse. "How far are you going to string it out?"

"Ivan said it would burn about two feet a minute. I figure six feet of fuse will give us plenty of time to get out of the way."

Six feet. Three minutes. Cassie began working her way around the robbers toward where Jigger had taken up his post.

"You gotta put fuses on all of them?" Alvin unwound a piece of fuse about as long as he was tall and cut it with a pocketknife.

"Naw, just the one. Blow this one up and the others will follow."

"Be careful with that blasting cap. Ivan said if you mishandle it, you'll have to pick your nose with your elbow for the rest of your life."

"Ivan's gonna get an earful from me, leaving us here to do the dirty work. I told him I could snatch that girl as easy as he could. He's probably sitting by some river, throwing sticks on the campfire and thinking about how he's going to spend his share of the gold. And here we are risking blowing ourselves up or getting nabbed if that gal inside ever wised up as to what was going on right outside her own jail."

"Ivan's the one who set all this in motion when he intercepted the dispatch to Fort Benefactor out of Fort Worth and changed the date for when the gold was supposed to be picked up. If he hadn't done that, the army'd a picked up the gold long ago, and we wouldn't even have had the chance to think up how best to get it out of the jail."

Cassie tightened her fingers around the handgrip on her gun. So that was why the army hadn't come to get the gold yet. Ivan Shoop had somehow altered the army orders.

"Stroke of luck them doing the Challenge this month and the schoolteacher being named the sheriff. Snatching the little girl was Ivan's idea, too. No way he wanted to try stealing the gold with Ben Wilder around. With just the schoolmarm, it's a stroll down Main Street."

Arrogant fools. She'd show them.

"There. It's ready. You got a match?"

"You idjet. You brought dynamite and fuses and the like, but no matches?"

Cassie rolled her eyes. She reached the back corner of the building where Jigger lay slumped over. *Thank You, Jesus.* He had a pulse. She rolled him onto his back and plunged her fingers into his shirt pocket, finding the paper-wrapped tubes. Grabbing them up, she turned back toward the jail in time to see the flare of a match strike. It lit up the Shoop brothers' faces like ghouls, and Melvin touched the flame to the end of the fuse which sparked to life like an angry snake. They dropped the fuse and took off running around the front of the jail, probably toward the mercantile and their wagon.

Cassie prayed Jenny would be smart and safe.

As soon as they were out of sight, Cassie ran to the fuse, but though she stomped on it, it refused to go out. She finally yanked it from the pile of dynamite and held it away from her body.

"What are you planning on doing with that?"

She almost expired right there. "Ben Wilder, what do you mean sneaking up on me that way?" She was so vexed, she forgot her predicament for a moment. "Oh, Ben, did you find Amanda?"

"She's safe. Carl's bringing her in." He swung from the saddle. "But I'll ask again. What are you doing with a lit fuse?"

"Get back into the shadows. They might be watching us." She grabbed his arm and pulled him toward the back of the harness shop. "It's the Shoop brothers. They're trying to blow up the jail and get the gold."

"And you thought you'd help them?"

"No, of course not." She held up the two sticks of dynamite and the fuse, which still sputtered and sparked. "I thought I might cause a diversion."

"Where'd you get an idea like that?" He took out his knife and opened the blade, nipping off the burning end of the fuse.

"Actually, from the twins and their outhouse explosion." She filled him in on her plans in whispers while she jammed the un-spent fuse into one of the sticks of dynamite.

"You're pretty smart, you know that?"

"Thanks. Maybe you'd better get the dynamite out of that hole, just in case. They'll be coming back soon to see what happened."

He returned with half a dozen sticks. "Where's Jigger?"

"They knocked him out. He's on the back porch next door. And Jenny went in search of the Shoop's wagon."

"I think I hear it now. You get back."

"I will not. This was my idea, Benjamin Wilder."

He thrust the dynamite at her, took the one stick with the fuse, and gave her a quick shake. "For once in your life, Cassie Bucknell, let somebody take care of you."

"And for once in your life, Ben, let somebody help you. You

set off the dynamite, but I'm coming with you." She piled the extra explosives in a little stack beside the harness shop back door and followed him out a ways onto the prairie behind the jail, crouching and waiting in the darkness.

Alvin and Melvin jogged along the backs of the buildings, coming from the mercantile.

"It's weird, that's what. Where'd those horses go?"

"How should I know? I was with you the whole time. Somebody stole them, that's what."

Jenny must've found the wagon and taken the horses. Smart.

"What happened with the dynamite? It shoulda blown by now." Alvin's whisper came across the grass toward them.

"You musta did it wrong."

"I did not. Maybe we got duds."

"Maybe you're a dud. Go check." Melvin shoved Alvin toward the back of the jail.

"You go check. I ain't gonna get my head blowed off."

"Neither am I."

"Let's go together." They inched forward, but well back from the jail.

Ben put his lips to Cassie's ear. "They're so dumb, they'd kick their gramma upstairs."

"I almost feel bad for them, but then I remember they kidnapped Amanda and tried to blow me up in my office."

"*My* office." Ben's teeth flashed in the moonlight, and he flicked a match with his thumb. "Cover your ears and lie flat."

She couldn't resist looking. The sparks from the fuse described a neat arc in the air and landed a dozen feet from the Shoop brothers. Ben fell flat beside her and put his arm over her head, pushing her into the grass.

For a long second, nothing happened, then. . .

BOOM!

The earth shook, and Cassie's lungs quaked. Bits of grass and dirt rained down on them. Ben pushed himself up and headed toward the blast area, and Cassie was hot on his heels. Smoke filled the air, and a small crater smoldered, casting eerie light in a circle on the churned up grass.

At the edge of the circle, four boots lay sprawled and unmoving. Ben said something, but Cassie's ears were ringing so loudly, she couldn't hear him. He shrugged and cuffed Melvin's left wrist to Alvin's right, then pointed to the building next door.

Cassie got the hint and went to check on Jigger. Men were running and shouting, coming out of the darkness to investigate the blast. She grabbed Hobny Jones and Mr. Svenson and got them to help her carry the groggy deputy into the jail.

"I'm all right," Jigger groused, pushing their hands away.

His voice sounded far away, but at least her hearing was coming back. "Of course you are. Now sit still. I need to go help Ben."

Cassie returned to the melee outside, pushing her way through the circle of townsfolk all clustered about. Ben had the Shoop brothers on their feet. "Just waiting for you, Sheriff." He grinned and motioned for her to take them into custody.

She moved behind them, and grabbing one by the collar, pushed toward Main Street. A wall of people followed, questions coming like popping corn. With great satisfaction she shoved the Shoop brothers into the empty jail cell and slammed the door.

A cheer went up from the folks who had crowded inside the jail. Ben winked at Cassie.

"Amanda?" Jenny wormed her way through the crowd, the shotgun all but dragging the floor. "Ben, what happened to Amanda?"

"She's fine. Carl's bringing her back. That's one brave little gal you have there, Mrs. Hart. Smart, too."

"What about Ivan?" Melvin croaked out.

Ben sobered. "He's coming back, too, but he's lying across his saddle. You boys picked the wrong girl to kidnap and the wrong town to try to pull off a robbery."

"You're sure Amanda is all right?" Jenny sagged against Cassie.

"She's fit as a fighting fiddle. Carl will have her back here tomorrow around midmorning. He didn't want to risk the canyon trail in the dark with her."

"Ben, the cell keys aren't here," Cassie reminded him.

"Good thing I have cuffs then." He released the prisoners from their bracelets and fastened the door closed with the handcuffs. "That will hold them." He slung the cuff keys onto the desk.

"Folks, the excitement's over. Why don't y'all head back home?" Ben began ushering people outside, assuring them that everything was under control and they'd all know more in the morning.

Jigger sat with his chin on his chest, breathing deeply. Cassie knelt in front of him. "Hey, how are you doing?"

"My head feels like it got stomped on." He touched the nape of his neck and groaned.

The door opened, and everyone jerked, hands going for guns.

"Whoa there." Cassie's father held up his hands. "What's been going on here?"

Cassie sagged, tensions bleeding from her. "I'm glad you're here. Jigger's been hurt."

"Again? Seems like working for you, Cassie, is a hazardous experience. What was the explosion I heard?"

While he examined the deputy, Cassie filled him in on the night's doings. Finally, Dad snapped his bag shut. "I'll take Jigger to his rooming house, and Cassie, you take Mrs. Hart home. I think it would be best if you made her a cup of tea and tucked her into bed. You should stay the night with her. Ben, I trust you can man the jail for what remains of the night?" His white eyebrows rose.

"Yes, sir, after I tend to my horse."

"By the way, Cassie, you're an aunt. Louise had a healthy baby girl tonight."

Her father left with Jigger, and Jenny headed for the door. "Cassie, you wait here while Ben takes care of his horse. I'll leave the back door unlocked for you." She sent a knowing look between Ben and Cassie. "Don't hurry on my account."

"Mrs. Hart"—Ben put his hand on her shoulder—"tomorrow, when Carl gets back with Amanda, he'll tell you everything. She's safe with him, you know?"

Jenny nodded, her movements lethargic, as if she were tired down to her very bones, which Cassie could sympathize with. Jenny wouldn't be totally at ease until Amanda was wrapped in her arms, but until then, she must be drawing great comfort to know that Carl was watching out for her little girl.

When Cassie was alone in the jail, she shoved the straw man onto the floor and sank into the chair behind the desk. She laid her head on her arms, wanting to cry in gratitude and relief that Ben was home, Carl and Amanda were safe, and the gold remained under lock and key. And to top it all off, Louise and her baby were fine. What a night for Cactus Creek.

Ben returned, and Cassie wished with all her heart that the cells were empty. She had so much she wanted to say, so much she needed to know, but with their felonious audience, speech was impossible.

"I'll see you tomorrow?" She unbuckled the gun belt and laid it on the desk.

Ben's hand came up and cupped her cheek. She wanted to melt into the warm caress, and tears came to her eyes.

"Tomorrow, kiddo." He dropped a chaste kiss on her forehead, the kind that used to drive her crazy because it was done in such a brotherly, patronizing manner. But not this time. This time his kiss comforted and promised.

CHAPTER 18

Jenny was up with the birds, too churned up and eager to sleep, and it was all she could do to let Cassie persuade her not to ride out to find Carl and Amanda herself.

"They'll be here." Cassie stretched and slid from Amanda's bed where she'd spent the rest of the night. "Ben promised."

Jenny observed her friend, dressed in just her shift, reaching for the crumpled dress she'd worn the day before. "What else did Ben say?"

Cassie turned innocent wide green eyes her way. "Whatever do you mean?"

"I saw the way you were looking at each other last night. Something happened between you two or something is about to."

Her blush was delightful, filling Jenny's parched and knotted heart with warmth. "I knew it."

"Nothing's settled yet." Cassie tugged the sprigged red calico over her head and began trying to make some sense out of her tousled red curls.

"Of course not. There's been no time, what with the she-nanigans the Shoop brothers have been trying. Just you wait. When things settle down, Ben Wilder will be knocking on your door."

At that moment, a knock sounded on Jenny's door, and she flew down the stairs, leaving Cassie laughing behind.

Flinging open the door, her heart soared. Carl Gustafson

filled the doorway, and perched on his arm, beaming at her, was her darling daughter.

"Mama!" Amanda launched herself into Jenny's waiting arms, and they sank to the floor together. Jenny held her daughter tight, trying to meld them together so they would never be separated. Tears flowed as she kissed her hair, held her away to check her over, then clasped her close again.

"Oh, baby, I was so worried. Are you all right? You didn't get hurt, did you?" Jenny took in the torn dress, the dirty face, the disheveled hair.

"I'm not hurt, Mama, except you're squeezing me so tight." The aggrieved tone in Amanda's voice did more to ease Jenny's worries than anything. She loosened her hold a fraction, laughing and wiping tears.

She became conscious of Carl still standing there and scrambled to her feet, keeping her arm around Amanda. "How can I thank you?"

"No thanks necessary, ma'am." For some reason, he seemed distant, gruff, even shy. Gruff she was used to, but shy? Carl Gustafson? And he'd called her ma'am.

"Can I get you some coffee? Please, come in and sit down."

"No, thanks. I need to tend to the horses, and there's some other things I have to do." He jerked his thumb toward the open door, and she spied the body of Ivan Shoop draped across his saddle.

"Of course." She looked away and into Carl's eyes, trying to read there what had changed. He revealed nothing, just squatted to speak to Amanda. To Jenny's astonishment, Amanda wrapped her arms around his burly shoulders, whispering into his ear. His eyes finally twinkled, and he shrugged and nodded.

Jenny stared at his retreating back, unable to believe he'd left so abruptly. *You were hoping for more, weren't you, girl? Much more. What did you think he would do? Sweep you into his arms and swear his everlasting devotion?*

Of course not, she argued with herself, even as her cheeks grew hot.

Liar.

"You must be hungry, darling. We'll feed you and get you a hot bath and fresh clothes. Miss Bucknell is upstairs getting dressed. She spent the night here so I wouldn't be lonely until you got back." She held her hand out to Amanda. "By the way, what did you say to Mr. Gustafson?"

Amanda looked up at her reproachfully. "Mama, if I told you, it wouldn't be a secret."

Carl led his mount and that of the unfortunate Mr. Shoop toward the stable, kicking himself for being the biggest fool in Christendom. The sight of Amanda and Jenny together had nearly undone him. He'd come awful close to scooping them both up and holding them pretty near forever. The way she'd whispered into Amanda's hair, the tears she hadn't tried to stem, the look of peace that invaded Jenny's face, a maternal look he would never understand but always be in awe of, made her so beautiful, he had barely resisted dropping to his knees and pouring out his love for her right there.

He glanced down at his trail-stained self. Dirty, tired, with a beard only a mountain man would envy. No prize from any civilized quarter. Certainly not in any shape to go courting. Anyway, Jenny deserved time with Amanda without him barging in. He could wait.

Probably.

He entered his livery stable and breathed deeply, inhaling the scents of hay and grain, dust and horse, his life. He heard voices, young voices from the far end near Misery's stall.

"Who's in here?" His voice vibrated the rafters.

Two blond, curly mops stuck their heads out into the aisle. "Hey, Mr. Gustafson. You bring Amanda back?" The Harrison twins tumbled out of a stall like bobcat kits. "We figured with you out chasing bandits and Mrs. Hart all worried about Amanda, there might not be anyone to look after the horses. We come to help."

He grinned and engulfed the boys' heads with his palms, giving them a shake. "Thanks, troops. I appreciate it. Amanda's home safe, and the bandit is done for."

Their eyes grew round as they peered around him at the horses, one with his grim burden.

"Did you kill him?"

"My shot was a bit too late. Sheriff Wilder killed Ivan Shoop when he tried to hurt Amanda."

They beamed. "I knew it. I knew he'd get the bad guy, just like his dad. Cactus Creek has the best sheriffs in Texas." They hunched their shoulders, ramming their hands in their pockets.

"That decides it for me. I'm going to be sheriff when I grow up," the one on the left said.

"You can't. *I'm* going to be the sheriff," the one on the right countered. "You can be my deputy."

"Forget that nonsense. I ain't going to be your deputy. You can be *my* deputy."

Sensing a never-ending argument cresting, Carl leaned forward, put his hands on his knees, and stared them into silence. "How about you both be my deputies for the day and help me tend to the horses." He poked the left one in the shoulder. "You go tell the minister to call his grave diggers so we can plant Ivan. He isn't going to keep forever."

The boy scampered away, full of life and energy. His brother stood his ground. "What do you want me to do?"

"Help me unsaddle these horses, curry 'em, feed 'em, and turn 'em out."

They fell to work, and he had to admire the little fellow. There was no quit to him, even when he got nearly buried by the large stock saddle as he pulled it from Carl's horse.

Once they had all but Ivan's horse cared for, Carl stretched his back. "Hey, buddy, think you can handle things from here? I'm going to cart the body over to the jail; then I need to get cleaned up a bit."

"Sure enough. Quincy will be back soon."

"Just stay away from the stallion down at the end. I'll feed and water him before I go."

"You don't have to. We already did. We been watching Mrs. Hart, and if you sing to him, he's nice as molasses cookies. She's got him right gentled now. She sure knows how to tame down wild things, don't she?"

Don't she indeed?

Carl left the stable, willingly counting himself one of her victims.

~~~

It seemed no matter how hard she tried, Cassie could not get Ben alone. She raced home from Jenny's place to change her clothes—after a brief, happy hug fest with Amanda—and paid a quick visit to Louise's room to cuddle her new niece, who was perfect in every way, from her button nose to the dusting of fiery red hair on her sweet head. Donald stuck his chest out and beamed, rocking on his toes, and Louise, pale and tired, rested on a mountain of pillows.

Cassie tripped down the stairs to head back to the jail only to find her mother in complete disarray. The arrival of the new baby had pushed everything else from her mind until the dressmaker arrived with her sewing kit and lethal pins to remind Mama that Millie's wedding was less than five days away. Cassie, who had somehow forgotten all month to get her bridesmaid dress fitted, was corralled and forced to stand on a footstool in the parlor with her arms out like a scarecrow while Miss Rosenblatt poked, prodded, and pricked her way through an hour of dressmaking. Cassie's only saving grace was that she loved the soft, green gown and couldn't wait for Ben to see her in it.

When she would've made her escape, Cassie was all but frog-marched by her mother into the dining room to sort silk flowers and create the hair accessories and bouquets and boutonnieres for the wedding party. Millie's eyes sparkled, and she giggled her way through the day thinking of nothing but her upcoming nuptials. Cassie watched the clock, praying she could get away. Ben would think. . .well, she didn't know what Ben would think, but if she didn't get to see him soon, she was going to lose what little she had left of her mind.

Her father tapped on the pocket door. "May I enter?" He'd taken to asking that question to every closed door in the house after once inadvertently walking in on a wedding dress fitting and being promptly shooed out.

"Come in, Papa," Millie sang out. She hopped up from her chair as he entered, and held a silk flower boutonniere up to his lapel. "What do you think?"

Without looking, he said, "It's beautiful, just like you."

She scrunched up her face and stood on tiptoe to kiss his cheek. "Thank you, even if you are a silly goose."

"Actually, I came to talk to Cassie if you can possibly turn her loose for a moment or two."

Millie sighed and plopped back into her chair. "You might as well take her. She's mooning around here like a lovesick calf as it is. I'm not getting any work out of her."

Cassie straightened. "I am not mooning."

Father's eyebrow rose. "Well, if you're not, a certain sheriff, who is waiting on the front porch certainly is. We've had us quite a talk, and I told him I'd be most glad to have you taken off my hands if he was brave enough to offer for you. Should I shoo him away?"

She barely heard the last part as she raced through the house scattering flowers and ribbon and pins behind her. Hitting the door at a near run, she all but fell onto the porch.

There he was, unshaven, trail-worn, and the most handsome man she'd ever seen. An attack of sudden shyness, now that she stood on the precipice of all she'd dreamed and hoped for, engulfed her, and gaucheness clogged her brain. Though perishing to speak with him all day, now she couldn't think of a thing to say.

He didn't speak either, just opened his arms, a smile splitting his face. With a grin and a glad little hop, she rushed into them.

Laughter bubbled up, sheer joy at being where she'd longed to be for so long, not just in his arms but in his heart.

Ben hugged her tight, rocking her a little as they both laughed. When his embrace eased, she leaned back on his arm to study his face.

He brushed back a lock of her hair. "Say, I was looking for the schoolteacher, a grown-up lady, and here I find you, a giggling girl." With a tilt of his head, he regarded her. "Seen the grown-up anywhere?"

"She comes out sometimes." Cassie flattened her palms on his chest, delighting in the thudding thrum of his heart. "In fact, she's about to make an appearance right now." Her hands came up to cup his whisker-roughened cheeks.

"Good. I like her." His voice deepened, sending ripples vibrating through her. "You do know I love you to distraction, don't you?" His lips came down, brushing hers, teasing, meshing and withdrawing in brief encounters that drove her mad. She tunneled her fingers into his hair, tugging, dislodging his hat. Finally, with a sigh, he stopped playing and took possession, angling his head and deepening the kiss.

Somewhere, she knew she heard angels singing, but it might've been in her head. She was flying, floating, her heart soaring to join with his as she returned his kiss. Stars exploded behind her eyelids, and her hands slipped to his lapels, seeking an anchor.

He withdrew slowly, by increments, nipping and pecking, scattering kisses across her cheekbones and along her brow. She sighed, melting against him.

"Promise me you'll kiss me like that every time I come back from a manhunt."

She chuckled, pressing her lips together. "Promise me you'll kiss me like that every time I arrest thieves for trying to rob the jail." She stiffened, drawing back to look into his eyes. "Speaking of which, why aren't you at the jail?"

He tweaked her nose, stooped to snatch up his hat, and drew her around the house to the back porch where the cushioned wicker swing swayed in the breeze. He tugged her down to sit beside him. "This is better. I prefer to do my courting out of sight of any passerby who might amble along." He studied their arrangement and frowned. "Hmm, this won't do. You're too far away. C'mere." Spanning her waist, he lifted her to sit on his lap, tossing his hat to the seat beside him. "That's better." The swing swayed gently, and she looped her arms around his neck, hardly believing Ben was holding her as if she was his most precious treasure.

"A detachment of soldiers arrived this morning from Fort Benefactor, three officers and twenty enlisted men, all bristling with guns and officialdom, and whisked the gold out of the jail. On their heels, the federal marshal arrived on his regular route, and he took custody of the unfortunate Shoop brothers and all the evidence, including the box of dynamite. Those boys'll stand trial up in Amarillo next month. You might be called on to testify, by the way. So the jail's empty, and I was feeling a little lonely and neglected. I figured you'd be dropping in first thing today. You do have a job to do as the sheriff of Cactus Creek for six more days, you know." His eyes reproached her, his mouth twitching to hide his teasing grin.

She smoothed his hair where she'd ruffled it earlier and drew her hand down his cheek, delighting in the rasp of whiskers, reveling in the thought that he hadn't even taken the time to clean up before coming to see her. "In my defense, I was taken prisoner by the matrimony madness taking place in the house. Not to mention my niece decided to put in her appearance last night, and Mama is run ragged fussing over the baby and overseeing the wedding preparations. Dad is looking for a place to hide until it's all over. Millie just smiles and giggles and sails blithely on, content that in a few days she'll be Mrs. Ralph Campion." She rested her cheek on his shoulder. "And anyway, aren't you supposed to be teaching school today?"

"I declared a holiday. The kids all came to the jail when nobody showed up at the school. They were bursting to tell me all about how they helped scout the town for you and kept an eye on the bad guys. I'm so proud of them, I'm busting my buttons."

"They were fantastic. I'm so glad for all the things you taught them. If it wasn't for those lessons. . ."

"So maybe I haven't been such a bad teacher?" He grinned, squeezing her waist. "I might just win this Challenge after all."

His velvety brown eyes twinkled, and for an interval, speech was impossible.

When she caught her breath, she snuggled her head on his shoulder. "What about Jigger? I feel terrible. He's had a hard month."

"I checked on him on the way over. He's beginning to wonder if you aren't a Jonah. A deputy for almost twenty years and barely a scratch, then you breeze in, and in less than thirty days he's got a broken wrist and a crack on the brainpan." She jerked upright, ready to dispute that claim, but he tucked her head back under his chin. "He's got a headache and a goose egg knot on his noggin, but he says he's fine, and he was just teasing about you being a Jonah. He's tickled to death with the job you've done, says you're by far the cleverest sheriff he's ever worked for." Ben chuckled, and the sound rumbled under her ear. "I'm thinking he's earned a few days off. If only I could find a deputy to take his place for a couple of days. . . Maybe I'll have to scout around for a pretty girl to help me out."

She straightened this time and sent him a suspicious glare, her heart as light as it had ever been. "You had better be talking about me, because if you're not, Cactus Creek will be looking for a new sheriff in the near future. You know, it's hard to concentrate with you kissing my ear."

"Do you want me to stop?" His breath tickled her neck.

"Not especially." Laughter bubbled up again. She couldn't imagine being happier. "But we have so much to talk about."

With a sigh, he shrugged and shoved his hat aside to set her back on the swing beside him. "You're right. I never would've suspected *you'd* turn out to be the mature one in the relationship."

That earned him a swat on the leg.

She wagged her finger at him. "I've *always* been the mature one. It took you half of forever to realize it. I think I've been waiting all this time for *you* to grow up, not me."

"I suppose, since I've spent the last little while kissing you senseless, I should do the grown-up thing and ask you to marry me." He slipped from the swing to one knee, taking both her hands in his. "I don't even have a ring, that's how unprepared I was for you to bull-rush your way into my heart. I just know that I don't want to live another day without you. Cassiopeia Bucknell, will you do me the honor of becoming my wife at your earliest convenience?"

The reality was so much better than her dreams, she burst into tears, then into laughter at the panic that invaded his eyes.

He tilted his head. "I'm sorry, darlin', but I have no idea what that means. Is that a yes?"

She nodded, mopping the happy tears with the backs of her wrists. "Provided you never call me Cassiopeia again. The name is Cassie."

"Agreed if you will do something for me, too."

"What?" Suspicion laced her words, especially since his eyes were sparkling.

"Put me out of my misery and tell me you love me." He clasped his hands to his breast and implored her, batting his eyes.

"You nut." She framed his face, leaning close, her lips a breath away from his. "Benjamin Wilder, I love you with all my heart. I have for a long time, and I always will."

She slid from the swing into his arms, feeling as if she was coming home.

CHAPTER 19

They kept their engagement a secret from everyone but their parents so as not to steal any of the attention from Millie and Ralph's big day, but it was hard, especially when Ben caught sight of Cassie walking down the aisle in her bridesmaid finery.

She was so beautiful, his chest constricted and he got dizzy. The best man really shouldn't sag onto the steps at the front of the church and put his head between his knees. He willed his noggin to clear and his knees to stiffen, knowing he'd never live it down if he keeled over.

Her green eyes, just the shade of her dress, glowed, and her glorious red hair escaped in little tendrils to lie on her temples and neck, just begging him to touch them, to kiss her luminous skin. *It really isn't fair that she should eclipse the bride like this.* She never took her eyes off him as she made her way to the front of the church.

When the ceremony was finally over, she threaded her arm through his to walk out of the church, and his heart about burst with pride that she was his. If he allowed himself to think of how he almost let her slip through his grasp through sheer ignorance, he broke into a cold sweat.

She leaned in to whisper. "Is that Carl? I hardly recognize him."

Ben pulled his gaze away from her to glance at the burly man in the back row. He blinked and stopped, staring at his friend.

Resplendent in a black suit and a boiled shirt, he would've

commanded attention in any crowd. But Carl had gone so far as to trim his beard—he must've taken eight inches off—and cut his hair. He held a genuine bowler hat and looked anything but comfortable.

Across the aisle, Jenny and Amanda Hart sat close together. Amanda waved enthusiastically to her teacher and at him. He winked at her and let Cassie pull him toward the door.

"Something's going to happen there and soon, or I miss my guess. Nothing short of falling in love would make Carl cut his beard." He helped her up into the buggy waiting to take the wedding party back to the Bucknell house for the reception. Millie and Ralph, in the seat in front of them, had eyes only for each other, which suited Ben just fine. He refrained from putting his arm around Cassie, but he wasn't above searching for her hand at her side, clasping her fingers under the edge of her skirt and giving them a squeeze.

"I told Jenny weeks ago that I thought Carl would be a wonderful husband and father. She said that was nonsense, but I think she's changed her mind since. And he certainly has a champion in Amanda. She talks of no one else, and I don't think it's just the pony and foal at the livery that she loves." Cassie tucked a stray curl behind her ear and leaned her shoulder into his.

Arriving at the house, Ben found himself positioned for way too many photographs. At least he was next to Cassie for most of them, but the blinding flashes of powder left him seeing spots. Wedding guests arrived and milled around, and all he wanted to do was grab Cassie up and head for the creek where they could be alone.

Louise and Donald held court on the porch, Louise in the swing, cradling her newborn daughter. Ben, when invited by Donald to admire his firstborn, found himself struggling for something complimentary to say. After all, she was red and scrunched and squirming. No teeth, wrinkles, and carrot-red hair.

Louise kissed her head. "You know, I think she might grow up to look like Cassie. Her eyes are such a hazy blue green. They might turn jade just like Cass's."

The infant suddenly got a lot cuter to Ben, especially when he realized that once he married Cassie, this baby would be his niece. "Lots to be proud of there, Don. Congratulations."

Donald puffed up like a turkey, grinning as if he'd invented daughters. "All right, you've done your duty. Go find Cassie and ask her to dance."

"Am I that transparent?"

"Only to another man in love."

Ben figured his soon-to-be-brother-in-law was a smart man and went to do as he said.

⁓⊚

Carl's collar bit into his neck like a too-tight halter. The suit, still bearing creases from the box, had set him back a pretty penny, but he couldn't exactly come to a wedding in his stable overalls, could he?

Something bumped his leg, and he looked down. "Hey, sweetie, you sure look pretty."

Amanda hunched her shoulders, and her smile reached her eyes and his heart. "Mama does, too."

"That she does." Carl's eyes found her. She stood behind one of the tables serving the beautiful wedding cake she'd concocted and iced. At least she'd taken that burden from him. He shuddered to think what would've happened if he'd served up that over-vanillaed disaster of a cake he'd made a couple of weeks ago.

"Are you going to ask her to dance?" Amanda took his hand and swung it while she watched the dancers whirling on the flagstone floor Doc Bucknell had installed in his backyard.

"You think I should?"

Her curls bounced on her shoulder as she nodded.

"She looks awful busy right now. How 'bout if you dance with me instead?" He lifted her onto his arm and whirled her around a few times, laughing when she leaned back, letting her hair fly out, trusting him completely to keep her safe. She'd sure come out of her shell in the past few weeks. Not much of the withdrawn, serious, timid child remained.

They stopped when he got dizzy, and she threw her arms around his neck, giggling. He looked up from her straight into her mother's eyes. Warmth spread through his chest, and he tried to read her expression, but for the life of him, he couldn't. He let Amanda slide to the ground and patted her head. She scampered off in the direction of some of the school kids congregating beneath a cottonwood tree.

He didn't know how he crossed the distance between them; he only knew he was standing in front of Jenny, unable to say a word, unable to look away. His hand went out, and he inclined his head toward the dance floor.

She set aside the cake server, put her dainty little fingers into his paw, and let him lead her onto the floor. He held her as if she was spun sugar icing, feeling every inch of his six foot three and two left feet.

Then she smiled up at him and he could breathe again.

"I like your haircut. You look so nice."

"Figured it was about time. Hadn't trimmed my beard since... for three years."

"It's all right, Carl. You can say it. You haven't trimmed your beard since your wife died?"

"Agatha didn't like my beard at all, but she'd tolerate it if I kept it short." Carl twirled her as if they'd been dancing together for years while the fiddle player sawed away, and he concentrated on not stomping on her tiny feet with his clodhoppers.

Jenny glanced up, as shy and rosy-cheeked as a girl. "I like beards, I think. My husband was clean shaven, but I've always wondered. . ." She broke off in delightful confusion that made him want to hug her tight and gave him hope.

"How long does this shindig last, anyway?"

"Hours more, I'd imagine. There'll be more dancing and the toasts and the gift opening. It will be well after dark before they wrap things up."

"Sure are a lot of people. Think anyone would notice if you and me went for a walk down by the creek? There's something I need to say to you."

They stopped dancing, and she lowered her eyes as if searching for something inside herself. Then she nodded with a sweet smile. "Just let me get someone to keep an eye on Amanda."

⁂

Jenny left her daughter in the care of Mary Alice and found Carl. She put her hand in the crook of his elbow, and they strolled down the gentle slope away from the house and toward the bend of Cactus Creek. Her heart felt like it was crowding high in her chest, as if it might fly right out.

The late spring breeze rustled the leaves of the cottonwoods and hackberry trees, and sunlight glinted and twinkled in a dazzling dance across the creek water that lapped the bank.

Carl steered her to the shade of a tree. One thick branch, low to the ground, bent over the water into a handy seat, and he shrugged out of his jacket and laid it there for her in a gallant gesture that touched her heart. Her late husband never would've thought to do something so simple yet so selfless.

No, she didn't want to think about him now. She was done with all that. The old Jenny Hart no longer existed, the woman who had cowered and feared and walked small. She was a capable business owner who had successfully made a place for herself in this community. She'd run a stable, gentled a stallion, helped arrest a pair of thieves, had her daughter stolen and restored to her, and bless her, she'd fallen in love.

"Amanda seems fine after her ordeal." Carl stood looking out over the water. He reached up and snagged a branch, tearing leaves off, dropping them in the water.

"I think the fact that she played a role in her own rescue has gone a long way to staving off nightmares or fears. I hated that snake rattle when she first brought it home, but it saved her life."

"She's a smart little thing. I was afraid for her right after the rescue, when Ben took off for town. She didn't say anything, just hugged me tight and cried for a while, then fell asleep." He sent a few more leaves into the slow-moving current. "But the next morning she popped up from her bedroll and started chattering, and I don't think she's stopped since."

"It might interest you to know that you are the primary topic in her conversation. I hear all day long about 'Mr. Carl.'"

"That's too bad. You must be sick of it."

"I didn't say that. I. . .quite like it." *Oh, go ahead and say it. You'll regret it forever if you don't.* "I've missed seeing you the past few days."

"You have?" The branch splashed into the water, and he covered the distance between them in two strides.

She nodded. "I kept expecting you to walk through the stable door. I'd find myself listening for your footsteps."

He took her hands. "Funny, I had the same trouble down at the bakery. Every time Amanda came home from school, I'd quiz her for news of you. With all that's been going on, and you staying up late to make the wedding cake, and all, there never seemed to be time for us to talk. Then the doc asked me to help lay the last of the flagstones for that patio so the wedding guests would have a place to dance. But all I did was think about you. The truth is. . ." His throat lurched as he swallowed. "Jenny Hart, I love you. I want to marry you and be your husband and be Amanda's father. I promise I'll spend my whole life taking care of you two."

She sucked in a breath, and he gripped her hands hard, as if his whole life depended on her answer.

"Carl, my first marriage wasn't a good one, and I swore I would never marry again and put myself in a position to be dominated by a cruel man."

The light faded from his eyes, and his hands eased on hers.

"But all that changed. . . . I don't know when it happened. Maybe it was the way you kept your tack room so neat, or how you knew just what to do for that foal, or the concern you showed

when I was hurt, or maybe it was all those ridiculous biscuits. . . ."
She laughed, squeezing his hands. "Whenever it was, however it
came about, somewhere along the way, I fell in love with a man,
a man who is nothing like my first husband. You couldn't be cruel
if you tried. You've always treated me with respect, even when
we were having a disagreement. I know you weren't doubting
my intelligence, only my muscle power and experience running
a stable. And the way you care for Amanda makes me want to
cry with thankfulness." She took a shaky breath and reached out
to touch his face and said the words she'd never thought to ut-
ter. "In answer to your question, yes. I will marry you and count
myself the most blessed of women."

His hug nearly broke her ribs.

And she learned kissing a man with a beard was very, very
nice.

EPILOGUE

Cassie stood at the back of the schoolroom, a covey of quail fluttering in her middle. She'd had no time to prepare the children for this. Ben had insisted she let him take care of the school program for Mr. Stoltzfus, and she should tend the jail and help with wedding preparations all week. Now that the final day of the Challenge was upon them, she'd spent the hours alternately twiddling her thumbs and biting her fingernails. Her teaching job rested on tonight's performance. All her life she'd dreamed of only two things: being a teacher and being Mrs. Ben Wilder. The latter was now within reach, but the former seemed to be slipping away.

Her father stepped onto the platform and rapped his knuckles on her desk. "If you'll all come to order, we'll get this evening started. Thank you for coming, and the council thanks you for being willing to postpone the Challenge ball in favor of the children's program tonight. We'll hold the Ball this coming Saturday, though we plan to announce the winner of the Challenge tonight when the kids are through with their part and everybody has a chance to cast their final votes." He tucked his fingertips into his vest pockets. "We'd like to welcome Superintendent Stoltzfus, and now we'll turn things over to the children and their teacher."

Cassie crossed her arms at her waist, pressing her palms into her sides to try to quell her butterflies as two men pushed the desk to the side and the children filed in two lines onto the platform. From Mary Alice down to Amanda, they were all dressed in their Sunday best, and even the irrepressible twins had suffered the indignity of having their hair slicked down with pomade.

Ben stood just to their side and addressed the crowd. "Evening, folks. The kids have worked real hard, and they're anxious to show you what they've learned.

"First, Ulysses and Quincy will demonstrate their arithmetic skills." The students parted, and the twins went to the blackboard.

"If a bank gets robbed at three p.m.," Quincy drew a square on the board and then two stick horses racing away from it. "And the bank robbers are traveling at twelve miles per hour. . ."

Ulysses grabbed the chalk and drew another square. "And the posse leaves town at three thirty, traveling thirteen miles per hour. . ."

Cassie didn't know whether to laugh or melt into the floor.

The students moved on to observation skills, botany, zoology, and a wild version of campfire domestic science that had the audience rapt. The spelling portion had Cassie biting her lip as they spelled words like *surveillance* and *penitentiary* and *incarceration*. And for a coup de grâce, they finished with a dramatic rendition of *The Legend of Obadiah Wilder*—taken straight from the pages of the dime novel by the same name—which afforded the twins the opportunity to die glorious and prolonged deaths, flopping on the stage and groaning like Shakespearean specters.

Cassie dared a glance at Mr. Stoltzfus, who sat as if in a bell jar, completely still and wide-eyed.

She wasn't sure where it started, but someone began clapping and others joined in. Soon everyone was applauding, some were stomping their boots, and a few even let loose some ear-splitting whistles. Chairs scraped as people got to their feet.

The children beamed, some clapped, and Amanda hopped, her braids bouncing. The twins scraped themselves up off the floor and bowed like theater veterans. Cassie found herself threading through the crowd to get to them. When they saw her, they clustered around, faces lifted for her reaction.

"Oh, I'm so proud of you all. What a wonderful program.

You covered every subject, spelling, arithmetic, science, history, drama, and so much more." She hugged them. What did she care that Mr. Stoltzfus might give her a dressing down? The children had demonstrated that they had more than mastered the material put before them. They had learned and they had applied it to real-life situations. Wasn't that what education was all about?

Her father mounted the platform and called for order. The children went to their parents, and Cassie joined Ben along the side of the room. He took her hand, lacing their fingers out of sight of onlookers.

"That was. . .amazing."

"It was the kids' idea."

"Do you think I'll keep my job?"

He didn't answer, just squeezed her hand. "I'll see to it that you don't starve if old Stoltzfus gives you the boot."

"Ladies and gentlemen, it might seem quite an anticlimax after such a wonderful showing, but we do have the little matter of the Cactus Creek Challenge to wrap up tonight. If you'll take the ballots out that you were given at the door, we'll hear from our contestants one last time. Shall we start with Mr. Gustafson?"

Carl's boots sounded loud on the floorboards as he made his way to the front. He shoved his hands into his pockets, rocked on his heels, and said, "'Bout the best thing I can think of in my favor is that nobody died from my baking."

Laughter filled the air.

"Truth be told, I don't think I'm the one who deserves the prize this year. Any of the other three did a better job, I think. Jenny came to my rescue this weekend and turned out as pretty a wedding cake as I've ever seen. . . . I'm hoping she'll bake one like it for our wedding." He grinned down at her in the second row, and she blushed and nodded. A smattering of applause rippled through the crowd. "Whether you vote for me or not, I'm coming out of this month a winner." He took his seat next to Jenny, engulfing her hand in his.

Ben left Cassie's side and took the stage. "When we first started this venture—seems like half of forever ago—I was dead set against trading places with a woman. My Pa said something that I didn't appreciate at the time, but I've come to recognize as wise words. He said the Challenge wasn't meant to make things easy on the contestants. It was for stretching folks, making you carry someone else's burden for a while. He also said we might be surprised about what we learned, not just about the other person, but about ourselves. He sure was right. I think, if you asked all the contestants, they'd tell you the same thing. We've all accomplished more than we thought we ever could, and our. . .I guess you could say. . .opponents sure did more than we ever imagined they were capable of doing. We've learned about each other, and we've learned about ourselves."

He held out his hand to Cassie, who joined him on the stage, and he motioned for Carl and Jenny.

"I don't know if the council intended for matrimony to be the result of the Challenge this year, though I wouldn't put it past any of them." Ben raised his eyebrows at the three men lining the wall to his right. Doc put up his hands to protest their innocence, and his father's white moustache twitched as he put his hands in his pockets. "I suspect you'll have bachelors applying in droves for next year's Challenge."

Laughter once more. Cassie's heart swelled at the easy way he commanded the room and expressed himself.

"Tell you what, folks. We all four needed help with some part of the jobs we took on, and I'm happy to say, we found that help in each other and in you, our neighbors. Whether it was moving a load of feed or baking a wedding cake or tracking down a kidnapper or guarding a fortune in gold, we all got help in our jobs. We all had some rough adjustments, from outhouses blowing up"—he had to pause until the laughter stopped—"to a couple of students teaching a stable hand to make something other than biscuits, or even a few of our most observant kids practicing their surveillance skills and helping us catch a kidnapper and some robbers. Nothing seems to have gone as planned for us this month, but I don't know that there's much I would change."

Folks nodded. Ben squeezed Cassie's hand, and his eyes twinkled down into hers.

But he wasn't finished. "There is one thing you might not know, though. Doc Bucknell introduced Mr. Stoltzfus, the superintendent of schools, before the program got started. He's Cassie's boss, and when he heard that she'd traded places with the sheriff for a month, he wasn't best pleased. He's the one who called for this school program tonight, and if he determines that the kids haven't been taught up to scratch, Cassie might just lose her job. If you approve of the way Cassie has taught your kids for the last year, and if you think the kids did a great job here tonight, be sure to take the time to mention it to Mr. Stoltzfus. Seems to me the parents and community might have some pull when it comes to who they want to teach their kids." A murmur rose as people digested this bit of news. Cassie's cheeks grew warm, and she forced herself to remain calm and composed.

"Anyway, I just wanted you folks to know that the Challenge was a success for all four of us this year in ways we never expected, so however you vote, like Carl said, we're all coming out of it winners. We sure appreciate your patience with us as we figured out how to bake and teach and saddle horses and run a jail. Mrs. Pym, where's that punch bowl? I'm ready to cast my vote."

Ben walked Cassie home under a beautiful three-quarter moon.

"You won. And your job is safe. How does it feel?" Ben stopped her under a willow tree alongside the creek, lacing his fingers behind her back and drawing her close.

"I still can't believe it. And I don't think you can say that any of us really lost. There was enough money donated for both of the causes, a record amount according to my father. And Carl and Jenny fell in love. Not to mention us." She laid her head on his shoulder. "It's hard to believe the Challenge is over. It's been quite a month."

He brushed his lips against her temple, wrapping his arms tighter around her and leaning against the willow trunk. "We'll be married in a couple of weeks. I have a feeling our real Challenge is just beginning."

"And much like tonight, I think we'll both come out winners in the end."

ABOUT THE AUTHOR

Erica Vetsch is a transplanted Kansan now residing in Minnesota. She loves books and history and is blessed to be able to combine the two by writing historical romances. Whenever she's not following flights of fancy in her fictional world, she's the company bookkeeper for the family lumber business, an avid museum patron, mother of two, and wife to a man who is her total opposite and soul mate. Erica loves to hear from her readers. You can find her on the web at www.ericavetsch.com or email her at ericavetsch@gmail.com.